DOCTOR WHO

FRONTIER WORLDS

PETER ANGHELIDES

BBC

Published by BBC Worldwide Ltd,
Woodlands, 80 Wood Lane
London W12 0TT

First published 1999

ISBN 0 563 55589 0

Printed and bound in Great Britain by Mackays of Chatham
Cover printed by Belmont Press Ltd, Northampton

For my sons, Adam and Samuel, with love

Contents

Chapter One
'What's Now is Now'

'I can remember my twenty-fourth birthday like it was yesterday,' said Shar Mozarno. 'But I can't recall what I had for lunch today.' He gave a snort of laughter, a studied punctuation in his dialogue, a sign that he thought this was a great joke. He shuffled in his seat, pulling the fringed cushion from behind him, and scrutinised it as though it were a novelty.

The tall clock in the corner softly chimed three-quarters. Mozarno placed the cushion on his chair, and smoothed its tassels flat against the arm. 'That timepiece was a gift to me from the company after ten years of service,' he smiled. 'A reminder of my time in captivity.' He laughed again, before subsiding into a pensive silence. 'Have I had lunch today?'

'Yes, dear, just before our visitor arrived.'

'Thank you, my love.' He leaned away from his wife and closer to the tall man beside him. 'We've been married for more than twenty years,' he said, giggling like a small boy.

'Much longer than that,' said his wife.

'I was going to be a doctor, and I met her when she was a nurse. I wanted to be a doctor, because I wanted to make things better, make *people* better. But I found I preferred the opportunities offered by the Frontier Worlds Corporation. More money in biotechnology than in human biology.'

'We came here together when Drebnar was first being colonised.' Marog reached across and held his hand, smoothing it over and over with a soothing, circular motion as she told the story of their arrival. How it felt to be on a new planet. How it felt to be young and in love.

After a while, an insistent bleeping sounded from somewhere else in the house. He felt Marog stoop over him, scooping his upper body into a fierce, broad hug. She said, 'I'm just going out to answer that call, Shar. I won't be long, I promise.' She gave him the kind of hug he remembered from many years ago, the don't-want-to-leave-you hug, the last-you-for-a-month hug. The kind that they shared whenever she had gone on a business trip to Creal, that lasted between planets. Then she stepped swiftly through the door, and out into the hallway. Or was it the living area? He wasn't quite sure.

The light from the garden spilled in through the big picture window. Soon it would be spring, and Mozarno knew he could go out and cultivate his garden. Although it looked as if the garden was already full of colour, vibrant hues catching the bright sunshine. Perhaps his wife had hung the rugs out to dry again. They'd been a wedding present a few months ago, hadn't they, and she liked to beat them every week and air them in the garden.

There was a rustle of movement beside him, and he noticed that a man was sitting beside him. A visitor perhaps? He was pulling a silk scarf into a fancy knot around his neck, tucking it neatly into his silver-grey waistcoat and flicking his long chestnut curls back over his collar. Mozarno could remember having long, unfettered hair like that when he was a young man. He turned over the hand mirror in his lap, and stared at the stranger's face that looked up at him. Thin, short, grey hair. It was his father's face, he thought. When had he got so old?

'Perhaps I should be going now,' said the visitor, and tugged at the sleeves of his green velvet coat. 'I've been here for nearly an hour.'

'Nonsense,' said Mozarno. 'You've only just arrived. I didn't notice you there. Would you like some tea?'

'We've had tea,' said the visitor. 'Earl Grey.' He was smiling at Mozarno - a warm smile, but the eyes remained sad. 'It was very pleasant to meet you, Mr Mozarno. Thank you for your help.'

'Well, Mr Grey,' said Mozarno. 'Have I told you about the early days of Frontier Worlds? The four of us practically started it up in one room. Me and Sempiter and Dewfurth. And later there was... no, don't tell me don't tell me don't tell me...' His voice trailed off into silence. Mr Grey was watching him quietly. 'Practically started it up in one room. And now... Well, I'm not really sure.' He sucked air through his teeth, as though this would make things clearer.

The timepiece in the corner chimed the hour, filling the room with sound. 'That clock was a ten-year gift to me from the company. I told them that it commemorated my time in captivity.' He laughed.

The visitor laughed politely too. 'So I believe.'

'Memories,' said Mozarno. 'Do you know, I can remember my twenty-fourth birthday like it was yesterday. But I can't recall what I had for lunch today.' He snorted with laughter to show Mr Grey that he thought this was a great joke. He looked at the cushion on the arm of his chair, smoothing its tassels. 'I wonder if I've had lunch -'

And then the door opened, and in walked Marog.

Mozarno struggled to his feet, and stumbled across to her. He could feel his heart pounding, his breath coming in short, sharp gulps. The familiar tightening in his chest, the prickling behind his eyes. 'Oh, Marog,' he choked, 'Oh, Marog, I thought I'd never see you again. You've been away for so long. I thought I'd never...' The tears consumed his words once more.

Marog smiled her calming smile, and took him into her arms. She just held him, held him warm and close and wouldn't let go as his tears spilled on to her shoulders and he wept and wept.

Eventually, he could feel his sobs subsiding. He smeared his fingers across his eyes to wipe away the tears. He allowed Marog to help him back into his chair, and looked through the picture window into the garden. There was a tall, green shape there, a stranger in a long velvet coat, his chestnut-brown curls falling over the shoulder. 'Have we got a visitor?'

'Yes, my love,' said Marog. 'You were telling him about the Corporation.' She sat down beside him, stroking his hand over and over in a soothing, circular motion. 'He wanted to talk to you about Sempiter and Dewfurth, because he thought you might be entitled to some intellectual-property rights in Darkling. So I let him have your old identity card, and told him how to contact Dewfurth.' She leaned over and scooped him into a last-you-for-a-month hug. 'The Doctor will make things better.'

Chapter Two
'Dancing on the Ceiling'

'It's a very long way down, isn't it?' said the Doctor. He peered carefully over the ice-covered rail as though to confirm his suspicions. He could feel the skin on his palms sticking to the cold barrier fence. Hundreds of metres below them, much further down the mountain, past the dark lines of the cable-car station beneath them and way beyond even the base of the research centre, jagged spears of rock protruded like rotted teeth from the smooth layer of undisturbed snow.

'Go away,' said Dewfurth, enunciating each syllable distinctly. Even so, his soft voice was almost carried away by the hiss of the wind that gusted white clouds of powdery snow around them.

The Doctor gauged the distance between them. Dewfurth was about two metres away, too far to reach out and seize him if he did jump. 'They say that people who fall from a great height are dead before they hit the ground,' the Doctor said, trying to keep his tone light. 'I don't believe that, do you? I think that people who jump are aware of what's happening to them right up to the moment of impact. That's not what *they* say, of course. But how do *they* know, eh? Whoever that mysterious *they* are, of course. It's not as though *they* have tried it for themselves, is it? Doing a few trial jumps from large pieces of furniture, maybe. Then graduating to short flights of stairs.' One metre away now. 'Reporting back from their first serious attempt - "three floors down, seventeen still to pass, going well so far..." .'

'Don't come any nearer,' snapped Dewfurth, and leaned further out beyond the rail. Another flurry of wind caught his lab coat, whipping it into rippled creases against his thin tweedy jacket and emphasising his narrow frame. Thick snowflakes scattered off his hair and twisted away into the air. Dewfurth wasn't looking into the abyss: he was staring at the Doctor, watching for any sudden movement. His sad grey eyes did not blink once, and the Doctor thought how different he seemed since their first clandestine meeting.

There was a sharp noise from behind them. Dewfurth flinched, one foot slipping free from the ledge. The Doctor snatched a glance towards the access doorway fifteen metres away. It was still sparking where he had fused the lock shut, a flame guttering in the chill wind that blew across the slope of the roof. He watched the handle rattling up and down as the research station's security guards tried to get through the door.

Another movement drew his attention back to Dewfurth. The thin man had straightened, bracing himself against the other side of the railing, pressing himself against the flimsy wire mesh of the low fence and spreading his feet on the narrow ledge, which was the last thing between the station and the deadly drop to the rocks hundreds of metres below. The Doctor noticed that Dewfurth's gnarled knuckles were flexing where his hands gripped the metal rail.

'Your instinct is telling you not to do this, Dewfurth. It's the logical part of your mind that wants to jump. So, what if that logic's flawed? This isn't a decision you can take back.'

'You can't understand.'

'Try me.' Half a metre. 'You've told me that Frontier Worlds is involved in genetic experiments, but you won't tell me what they are. I know about Reddenblak's commercial interest in your research, but not why Frontier Worlds won't sell. I've met Mozarno...'

'Mozarno!' Dewfurth squeezed his eyes shut, and tilted his head back in a gesture of despair. 'I will not end up like Mozarno.'

The Doctor decided to seize his chance, as well as Dewfurth's jacket collar. But as the Doctor's fingers gripped the material, Dewfurth's fingers spasmed and then let go of the rail.

The wind threw the Doctor's long hair into a wild dance about his head, and the snow and hail stung his face. Dewfurth was surprisingly heavy for such a small man, and struggled madly to free himself from the Doctor's grip. The Doctor had seized the collar of his lab coat, and was able to grasp the material on the chest of Dewfurth's shirt and gradually pull him back up.

Then several things seemed to happen at once.

Behind him there was a booming announcement of the arrival of the security team, as the door crashed open against the metal sides of the access shaft. The Doctor tried to call for help, bellowing over his shoulder at whoever was coming through: 'He'll go over!'

Dewfurth stopped struggling, going dead in his grip. The Doctor leaned further over, only for Dewfurth to surge suddenly back into life again, butting the Doctor in the mouth. The Doctor lost his grip on the shirt, there was the sound of shredding cloth, and the collar of the lab coat tore away.

The Doctor let out a great wail of horror. Dewfurth fell silently, like a dropped toy. The body bounced once against the side of the research station, spun wildly, then pitched on to the rocks. A dense gust of fresh snow drew a hazy curtain over the scene.

The Doctor closed his eyes, feeling the anger and frustration flood through him and the stinging cold of the snow numbing his forehead. There was an enraged cry from behind him. 'He's thrown him over!'

The Doctor pinched the icy bridge of his nose in a gesture of exasperation, and turned to face the guards. The words of protest froze on his cold lips as he saw the nearest guard properly through the haze of white flakes swirling between them. He was wearing the familiar lime-green livery of the Frontier Worlds staff, and his stance was clear – he was aiming his multiple-shot rifle at the Doctor. Even above the howl of the wind, the Doctor could hear the click of the safety catch as it was snapped to off.

A solid, unscalable wall to the left of him. Noise to the other side of him as more guards arrived.

The Doctor feinted to the right, and then swung back fast and low to his left. He gripped the handrail firmly and, without letting go, pushed off the sloping roof surface with his feet. His shoes skittered in the powdery snow. The icy cold of the rail bit into his palms, and he felt the flesh scrape as it froze to the metal and his momentum carried him on. The indignant rattle of bullets behind him ricocheted off the fence links. And then he was over, hanging perilously on the wrong side of the perimeter.

He was painfully aware that his clothes had ridden up his back, exposing bare flesh to the stinging elements and to the oncoming guards. He had misjudged his jump, slipped as he launched himself, and was now dangling helplessly above the same drop where Dewfurth had plunged, uncomplaining, to his death.

He thought about surrendering, but knew that the guards would shoot him where he stood. He struggled to get a grip on the ledge with his shoes, trying to dig in with the heels, quietly cursing the smooth soles, and waiting at every second for the fatal shot.

The initial chatter of gunfire had stopped. He imagined the guard sighting his weapon again, more careful, more deliberate. He heard more guards clattering on to the sloping roof. There was a loud oath, a muffled thump, and the scraping sound of something sliding across the snow-covered roof towards him. He felt a solid blow in the small of his back.

For a moment, he wondered if he had been shot, then whether someone was clubbing at him through the thin links of the fence. His grip on the rail weakened, and he gave a bitter laugh as he realised what had happened: one of the guards had slipped on the icy surface, stumbled into the first guard, and brought them both crashing down the angled surface of the roof and into the fence.

His hands tore free from the rail. He flailed his arms, grabbing desperately for the chain links in the fence, attempting to twist his body around, but finding his long velvet jacket bunching around his shoulders. His fingers brushed uselessly against the fence.

Then he fell.

The sounds of angry shouting faded into the tumult of air whipping past his ears. He was fleetingly aware of a row of research station windows disappearing behind him. Ten metres down, he thought, four hundred still to pass, going well so far... A swift pattern of images flashed before his eyes - patches of dark rock in the snow of distant mountains, a jumble of lime-green cloth behind the fence, the ragged crop of sharp stone far below, impossible patterns in the whorls and gusts of the snowstorm, twin dark lines cutting across his fall.

If he had not been staring back up towards the guards above him, he would have been decapitated. Instead, his chest caught against the first cable, which bounced him with a twisting motion into the second, parallel, cable. He grabbed at the thick wire, which bit into the crook of his left arm and his right armpit, winding him painfully. With a dull click, his shoulder dislocated, and he hardly had enough air to bellow into the freezing sky as his whole left side seemed to explode in agony.

And now he was sliding down the cable, helpless to stop himself gathering speed down the icy metal surface. The squat green shape of a cable car loomed in his view, and he released his grip just in time to slam painfully on to its roof, his ribs thumping against the ridged surface. The pain flared again in his side, and he had to will himself not to roll away from it and towards the edge of the car roof. The swirling patterns of snowflakes grew whiter, bright points of light swimming across his vision in eddying waves. He had to stay conscious. He bit into his tongue, tasting the blood at the back of his mouth. He could just reach the nearest cable stanchion, but the slick, icy surface of the green painted bar slipped between his bloodied, raw palms.

Just beside him, the inspection hatch flipped upward, catching him a glancing blow to the side of his head. The sparkling points of snow light scattered across his vision once more, then started to dim. As his eyelids started to close and his grip relaxed, he could vaguely see the dark shape of a man's head and shoulders poking through the hatch, his mouth a wide O of astonishment. The Doctor's shoulder screamed its agony again as strong arms seized him and pulled him towards the hatch. He was barely aware that he was half climbing, half falling through the gap and into the body of the car below, and landed heavily on his backside on the slatted wooden floor.

The howl of the storm cut off abruptly when the hatch above him slammed shut. It was as if he were suddenly deaf, and his ears throbbed as though they had been scoured. As his hearing returned, the Doctor was slowly able to make out the hum and buzz of the cable car, the soft whistling sound of the air-heating system, the soft creak of the seat on which he was sprawled – and the wheezing breath of his rescuer, who was now standing over him.

The Doctor lay for a while across the seat, breathing in its musty leather scent, his eyes closed, composing himself. He needed to find a mental still point amid the waves of pain coursing through him before he could perform a swift inventory of his injuries. Without moving from where he lay, he could identify a dislocated shoulder. Heavy bruising to the chest and abdomen, possibly a cracked rib, but no damage to either lungs or hearts. Lacerations to the lower back, upper legs and palms. Bruising to the gluteous maximus. No identifiable internal injuries. Bite to the tongue.

Now he opened his eyes, blinking swiftly to get them accustomed to their new surroundings. The feeble illumination from the strip light in the roof was drowned by the dazzling brilliance of the snowstorm outside, coursing in through the wide surrounding windows.

His grubby rescuer looked down at him with obvious concern, although his voice suggested otherwise.

'So, what time do you call this, Doctor?' said Fitz. 'I thought you were never going to turn up.'

Chapter Three
'Here Goes'

The Doctor slumped on the leather seat, his breath coming in ragged gasps. Fitz stared, unsure what else to say. The hunched shape looked so vulnerable that Fitz wanted to stoop down and hug him until the pain went away, until the shaking stopped and the real Doctor returned.

Fitz couldn't remember seeing him like this. The Doctor's pale eyes were normally calm, coolly appraising - or else full of wicked humour. Now, they darted about the compartment, as though frightened, searching for a hidden threat. His damp brown hair was plastered flat against his forehead, matted with blood. Even his clothes, usually so impossibly smart, seemed to be piled around his body like so much discarded laundry. The velvet coat was twisted out of shape, scrunched up beneath his arms, one sleeve angled out awkwardly. There was a rip right down one side of his serge trousers, and all but one of the buttons on his pale cotton waistcoat had torn off. When the Doctor made a vain attempt to straighten his silk scarf, the ghost of a bloody handprint remained on it.

Fitz wanted to just hold him, but he couldn't. So he stood over him, lamely, his arms dangling uselessly beside his own dirty black trench coat, like a bad actor who doesn't know what to do with his hands.

If he had not expected to find the battered, bruised and torn figure, scrabbling for purchase on top of a cable car, he was even more surprised when the Doctor erupted into a choking fit of laughter, clutching at his ribs as he fought to keep control. After a few more agonising racks, the Doctor managed to struggle up on to the seat, and sat on it carefully. Very carefully.

'If you say anything about dropping in,' said Fitz warily, 'I'll throw you back out again. What happened? Hey - careful!' The

Doctor had twisted awkwardly on the seat, and was peering back out into the storm, shading the glass with his good arm. 'What can you see?'

'I can just about see the security guards staring down the mountainside. I'm not sure if they saw me hit the cables.' He turned around again, wincing. 'Now, Fitz. I'm going to have to do something rather unpleasant, and you may wish to look away.'

At first, Fitz thought that the Doctor was trying to shrug off his bottle-green coat. But then the Doctor leaned forward, and seized one of the metal hand-poles in the middle of the cabin which were designed for standing passengers. He wrapped his bloodied fingers around it, took a deep breath, and pulled back against the pole with a sudden movement.

Fitz nearly leapt through the access hatch again when the Doctor let out a tremendous bellow, which reverberated around the small cabin. And he felt his stomach lurch when he heard the low cracking noise as the Doctor's dislocated shoulder popped back into place.

'Bloody hell, Doctor! I hope you're never on call when they take me to casualty.'

The Doctor gave him what might have passed for a reassuring smile, but it wore off as he studied Fitz. 'Are you eating properly?' His smile returned as Fitz adopted a familiar look of exasperation.

'I waited for an hour in that damn cable-car station. Every time another crowd of goons appeared, I had to go and hide. Man, have I seen plenty of the service pit in that place. When I heard the gunfire, I hopped on the first car out of there. Then you scared the crap out of me by dropping through the roof of this heap, looking like you've taken a pasting from the pros, but all you're worried about is if I'm feeding myself.'

The Doctor shifted uncomfortably in his seat as Fitz paced furiously around what little space the cabin afforded him. 'I'll take that as a "no", then.'

Fitz hunkered down in front of the Doctor, peering up worriedly into his hooded eyes. The Doctor offered him another thready smile, reached behind Fitz's ear, and produced a bruised red apple. Fitz shook his head. The Doctor considered the fruit, sucked his teeth, winced, sighed, and put the apple in his coat pocket. 'What have you and Compassion discovered, Fitz?'

'I think we've figured out what drew the TARDIS to Drebnar.' Fitz stood up again, and gestured out of the side window, which was almost covered by a translucent skin of hoarfrost. 'Come and see.'

The Doctor rose slowly, groaning a little as he heard his joints crack, and joined Fitz by the car window. Through the frost, and the gusting snowstorm beyond, they could make out in the distance an oval shape dominating the skyline. A huge grey cloud too regular to be natural.

'It's an atmospheric balloon,' Fitz told him. 'It must be about the size of White City.'

The Doctor goggled at him. 'The London suburb?'

'Duh!' said Fitz. 'The dog track.'

'Oh. How does a big weather balloon give out broad-spectrum Tuckson-Jacker pulses into the time vortex, hmm?'

'Weather balloon is almost right, at any rate' said Fitz. 'You can't see it through this storm, but underneath it is a weather-control platform, probably as big as a house. Dunno the range of that thing, but it's parked right over the lower slopes of the mountain, which puts it about halfway between the Frontier Worlds Corp HQ and the research station. Makes you wonder whether it's creating this blizzard - it's practically tropical back at the base of the mountain.'

'Perhaps that's the point where it's controlling the weather. Parked, you say. How does it stay in position, I wonder?'

The cable car dropped suddenly behind a row of tall pines, which obscured the view. Some of the nearby branches brushed against the cabin window, scraping the film of frost away from the outside.

Fitz sat down on the leather seating, craning his neck to look back through the window. 'There are huge metal hawsers attached to the balloon, going all the way down to the ground and punched into the side of the mountain. I thought you might have seen them from the research station. One goes down to its tethering point there too.'

They watched the balloon grow larger over the next few minutes as the car took them nearer. Eventually, they could just make out a smaller, darker, squarer shape beneath the balloon. The Doctor shuffled over to peer through the gap in the frosted window, his nose pressed against the glass like a kid outside a toy shop at Christmas. 'What a crude arrangement. It's effectively a low-orbit geostationary satellite. Like so much of the construction on these pioneer planets, it's cheap, ugly, nasty – and efficient. Actually, that sounds like a pretty good descriptive summary of Frontier Worlds Corp.' Fitz noticed that the Doctor had taken off one of his shoes, and was examining its torn sole forlornly. 'These were such a good fit.'

The cable car juddered to a halt. The Doctor braced himself, wincing again at the pain in his joints as the sudden movement caught him off-guard. The car quivered for a few more seconds before falling quiet. Even the heater had shut down, sputtering asthmatically into silence. The cabin swung slowly, describing a small circular pattern as it hung from the cable.

Fitz said, 'Power failure?'

'Or have they worked out where I've got to?'

Fitz could almost see the Doctor's mind crank up a gear. He liked to talk aloud as he worked out the alternatives; he barely stopped the tumbling flow of words to let his companion keep up with him as his train of thoughts steamed through the options. 'Listen, Fitz, you must break into the Frontier Worlds systems and find out what they're doing on something called Darkling. I managed to get that job at Reddenblak Corp, in their Market Intelligence Group. While I was there, Reddenblak's biodiversity division learned that Frontier Worlds has a "killer product".'

'Sounds dangerous.'

'No, I mean a product that's so revolutionary it will make

Reddenblak's entire business an irrelevance. Then I went to visit a former Frontier Worlds staffer, a poor man called Mozarno, and he pointed me to Dewfurth –'

Fitz said, 'Hey, he's one of the Frontier Worlds research team. He's been away from HQ for a few weeks, the place is buzzing with gossip about where he might have gone. He's one of the Corporation's head honchos.'

'I *know* that,' snapped the Doctor. 'The late Mr Dewfurth –'

'Late?' asked Fitz. 'Well, I suppose that's a good excuse for being out of the office. Um...'

The Doctor stared Fitz into an abashed silence. 'Dewfurth wanted to sell out to Reddenblak. That was how they knew about this Darkling... thing. But by the time I reached him he had...' He paused, as though lost in some memory, his hand to his pale forehead, pushing away damp strands of hair with his long fingers. 'Dewfurth had gone over the edge. Mentally, I mean. And then literally, poor fellow. We must discover what drove him to it, Fitz.'

The cable car abruptly jolted into movement, and the air conditioning wheezed back into life. 'Here goes,' said Fitz.

The Doctor had scurried across to the cabin's back window. He wasn't like a kid any more, he was like... he was just like one of the rabbits that Fitz had kept in the back garden, a mangy pale-grey animal which scurried around its hutch tirelessly all day, poking its whiskers into every crack, looking tirelessly for the way out that wasn't there. His father had said the rabbit knew it was for the pot, if only it would put on some weight.

'We can start looking as soon as we get back to the ground. Now you're back, Doctor, you can help out.'

Fitz watched the Doctor twitch his whiskers. And the words came tumbling out again. 'I must leave that to you and Compassion. How are you getting on with Compassion? Making a good team? Good, good, I thought so. I know I'm leaving this in capable hands. You can both continue finding your way into the Frontier Worlds systems –'

'Why not you, Doctor? Why do we do all the hack work? How come you get the glamorous assignments?'

His sarcasm seemed to be wasted on the Doctor, who was making a valiant attempt to straighten his ragged clothing, tying a knot in his scarf with more panache than the torn material warranted. 'I failed the Frontier Worlds job interview, if you recall,' he said in what sounded to Fitz like a hurt tone.

'Like I believe that,' grumbled Fitz. 'I wish I'd failed it too. *You* didn't have to have the pre-employment inoculation. I've still got a lump on my arm the size of a half-crown. And you can't imagine what it's like working with misery guts, either. She only seems happy when she's connected herself straight into their computer, or e-mail, or whatever they call it. In fact, she's so plugged into their e-lec-tronic office, you could fit a three-amp fuse to her. I'm a pencil-and-paper boy. Ask me something difficult, like refilling my fountain pen without squirting it on my cuff, and I'm happy as a pig in... Are you listening?'

For some reason, the Doctor was now standing on the leather seat, pushing at the access hatch above them. 'As emergency exits go, I'd award it only four out of ten. What would they do in a real emergency, that's what I'd like to know. Misery guts?' he added suddenly. 'You said you were getting on well with Compassion.'

'No, Doctor,' sighed Fitz, '*You* said that. What are you doing?'

The hatch was suddenly wrenched open as it caught the wind, slamming on to the roof with a clang. A clump of snow pitched into the cabin, and splattered over the slatted wooden floor. The Doctor hopped down off the seat. 'Our stop is coming up. Though I'm not sure this train calls at all stations, so we may have to jump.'

Fitz eyed him warily, wondering if the blow to the head was having some effect. The wind howled around them like a warning siren, and he had to shout to make himself heard. 'Maybe I'm a boring old traditionalist, but can't we wait till we reach the bottom?'

'We're not travelling downwards.'

Fitz leapt to the window, like a comic turn. With the snow

swirling outside, he hadn't noticed that they were travelling back up the mountain, back towards the research station. 'They're reeling us in!'

'Well, reeling *me* in,' shouted the Doctor. 'They may not know you're here. I suggest we scramble down one of those trees that we passed earlier. Less risky, I think, than the metal stanchions. Trust me, it should be safe.' Perhaps the Doctor saw Fitz looking dubiously at him, and became aware of his own battered and bruised appearance. He gave his torn silk scarf a pat, and pulled at the edges of his waistcoat, as though that would make things look better. Then he cupped his hands together, ready to give Fitz a bunk up to the open access hatch. 'Don't worry, I'll be fine.'

Fitz rolled his eyes, and put his foot carefully into the improvised stirrup. 'Call me selfish,' he hissed close to the Doctor's ear, 'but it wasn't really you I was worrying about.'

The Doctor felt as though both his shoulders were going to dislocate. Fitz was hauling him up on to the roof of the cable car. But he could see the anxiety in Fitz's eyes, even through the maelstrom of ice and wind: his face was as white as the snow, his cheekbones more prominent and the stubble more extensive and darker than the Doctor remembered from their last meeting. He thought of Dewfurth's eyes, staring back at him through the storm on the station roof. So hurt. So distrustful.

The pine trees loomed close. The Doctor risked a look down, and realised for the first time that he couldn't see the ground below. Were there rocks, lethal, waiting to crush their bones if they fell? Would he and Fitz drop to the distant ground in silence, uncaring?

'Now!' he yelled, and leapt for the branches of the nearest tree.

The descent was agonising. The sharp pine needles cut into their arms as they struggled down, branch by branch. The storm seemed to be subsiding as they got lower, and gradually the punishing sting of ice and snow on their faces and hands receded. Even so, the slippery tangle of branches meant it was more than half an hour before they reached the lowest bough. The Doctor felt weaker than ever, his breath whooping out of him like that of an exhausted athlete.

Fitz was able to scramble down the lower part of the trunk, cursing loudly as he struggled over the sharp bark. He was ready to help the Doctor down, but the Doctor simply dropped like a stone into a deep pile of snow. He was aware of Fitz scrabbling desperately to dig him free.

Then they heard the engines.

'They'll have searched all the cable cars by now,' said the Doctor. His uneven breaths formed white clouds in the still air. 'And they'll work out what we did. They'll be searching for me.' The sound of engines grew louder, and the Doctor gestured away from the trees and towards a wide expanse of flat white in the middle distance, a frozen lake which reflected the sun towards them. 'We have to go that way. We'll leave no tracks on the ice.'

They scrambled down the shimmering bank, ploughing a meandering, uneven furrow through the undisturbed snow.

'We won't make it in time,' said Fitz, gasping for air. He gazed past the Doctor, staring at the smooth dome of snow which covered the hill behind them. The roar of engines grew louder.

Then the dome seemed to explode into millions of fragments of ice, filling the air with glittering particles in the mid-morning light. The Doctor flung himself backwards into the snow, as though trying to burrow to safety. After a moment, he seized Fitz by the back of his trench coat, and dragged him down into cover.

The explosion of snow subsided to reveal an enormous, green, motorised sledge. The wipers scraped away furiously at the windscreen of the square cabin at the front, the driver's dark face peering out. The sledge churned its way across the slope of snow, dragging a trailer containing a heaped pile of something roped in place under a thick black tarpaulin. Pipes to either side of the cabin spewed snow, like factory chimney stacks, up into the air and over the surrounding area.

Moments later, another spray of ice and snow announced the

arrival of a second sledge, belching smoke and snow like some arctic dragon. And then a third hauled itself over the horizon, shaking the ground as it powered its way after the others.

Above the growl and roar of the sledges, the Doctor could hear the tinny buzz of smaller engines. Through the haze of thrown snow, he could make out half a dozen smaller vehicles, snowbikes humming around the larger vehicles like birds around elephants. The drivers were heavily coated, with thick, dark goggles poking out of the front of their hoods. They were scanning the surrounding area, and their machine guns were starkly visible behind them, black and ominous against the lime-green of each driver's uniform.

The monster sledges passed within two hundred metres of where the Doctor and Fitz lay sprawled and helpless. The vehicles continued their unheeding progress down the mountain's lower slopes, and slowly the artificial snowstorm faded and settled. The Doctor sat up, noticing that their previous tracks were mostly covered.

The roar of the sledges and the high-pitched buzz of the smaller vehicles had faded, but the Doctor could still hear the puttering sound of an idling snowbike. The driver was examining the furrow in the snow that led back to the pine trees, his back to them.

'Time to go,' said the Doctor to Fitz. They continued their slow progress towards the frozen lake. Well beyond it, looming like a storm cloud, was the grey shape of the geostationary balloon. As the air cleared, the Doctor could see the black oblong of the weather station beneath it, and a dozen curving dark lines leading upward. He could just discern a smaller dark shape, some kind of cablecar, making its way up the steep angle of the nearest of these hawsers.

'Of course,' said the Doctor. 'The line of cable stanchions curves off towards the research station - I didn't realise we were so close.'

They reached the lake, slipping down the frosted banks. The wind had cleared all traces of the powdery snow from the ice, and through its translucent surface they could see weeds waving in the underwater current directly below their feet. Two hundred metres along the bank was a tangled clump of bushes, leading up to an untidy pile of snow-dusted scree which had tumbled against the sheer face of the mountain.

There was a sudden clattering noise above them, and they flattened themselves against the hard mud of the bank. Fitz gave a little squeal of fear as several furry quadrupeds skittered down the bank past them and on to the ice. The Doctor studied his reaction, amused to see him struggling to regain his composure as he got his breath back.

They watched the little creatures tumble across the ice. There were four of them, each the size of a small cat, round and dark brown, with thicker back legs which they thumped like rabbits, as though signalling to each other. They had large, pear-shaped, floppy ears, which tapered to a point and sat up to attention, rotating from side to side like radar dishes. Their soft fur and large liquid eyes suggested they were young animals.

'I think they're just playing,' said the Doctor. 'You've seen *Bambi*, haven't you?'

'Yeah,' muttered Fitz. 'I remember what happened to his mother, too.'

The animals' ears perked up again, scanning rapidly until they all comically pointed in the same direction – towards the Doctor and Fitz. The Doctor could just hear what had alarmed them. It was the sound of approaching snowbikes.

Three of the four animals skittered further out across the ice, leaving the fourth, which once again moved its ears, trying to catch an elusive sound. The Doctor noticed a flurry of activity below the ice, dark shapes following the animals. Then from over his head he could hear the snowbikes spluttering to a halt.

Fitz began to stray further on to the lake, trying to make his way along the bank under cover of the overhanging branches. Again, the Doctor noticed a flurry of dark shapes below the ice, and was startled to see a shoal of fish staring up at them, like spectators at an aquarium. 'Stop, Fitz!' he hissed, seizing the tail of his trench coat. He stooped to look at the creatures below the ice. From what he could make out, they were each the size of his hand, with broad foreheads which were glowing a soft red.

Up on the bank, a muffled voice shouted, 'Mr Sempiter! The track ends here.'

Then there was another voice, too far off to distinguish, but growing louder. A nasal tone, imperious, confident. 'I'd prefer him alive. Do you think you could manage that?'

Out on the ice, the three startled furry quadrupeds set up a rhythm of foot-stamping, warning the fourth one of the danger. There was a sudden flurry of movement beneath the Doctor's feet, and the strange fish darted away towards the centre of the lake. Dark shapes seemed to be converging on the same spot from other directions too.

Within seconds, the ice was softening, melting. Two of the three quadrupeds fell through the cracking surface with an eerie shriek, and the water threshed and bubbled. The third animal turned to flee. But two of the bizarre, big-headed fish leapt through the fresh hole in the ice, seized it by one of its ears, and dragged it squealing into churning, bloody water.

Fitz stepped back towards the Doctor, and immediately more dark shapes moved back under the ice towards them. The Doctor gave a rapid gesture with his thumb, and he and Fitz hopped swiftly back on to the frozen mud of the bank.

'What happened?'

The Doctor stroked his lips thoughtfully. 'They were attracted by the vibrations, I suppose. They hunt in shoals, and I think they must channel warm blood into their foreheads and melt the ice. I've never seen anything quite like –'

He broke off as the muffled voice sounded above them. 'Just a clutch of baby leppos, Mr Sempiter. Learning the hard way. Bye-bye, furry friends.'

'The tracks are too deep for leppos.' The nasal voice again, Sempiter. 'Check for him again.'

There was fresh movement above them, and the Doctor realised that the guards were moving closer. He put his mouth close to Fitz's ear. 'They don't know you're here. Get back down the mountain. I'll draw them away from you. I can hide out here –'

Fitz hissed back: 'You'll freeze to death, especially in your condition.'

'Nonsense. I have a much stouter constitution than you, a lower body temperature, and I can survive for much longer than you can round here. Rejoin Compassion, and I'll contact you like before.'

'A postcard pushed under my bedroom door, right?'

'An e-mail containing encrypted instructions,' said the Doctor with exaggerated patience.

'The e-mail of the species is more deadly than the mail,' said Fitz.

'Very droll,' said the Doctor.

'I'm misquoting Rudyard Kipling,' said Fitz, obviously very pleased with himself.

'Yes, I know,' said the Doctor, and then added, 'Good luck, Fitz.' The Doctor stepped out on to the ice, immediately aware that the bizarre fish were moving towards him again. Testing the soles of his shoes for purchase on the slippery surface, the Doctor made off across the looped section of ice that separated him from the next section of bank, and the shelter of overhanging bushes.

He thought he was going to make it, half running and half sliding, conscious of the shoals of dark shapes converging on him beneath the ice. Then he heard an angry shout from above and behind him, and the sudden clattering burst of machine-gun fire. He risked a look back, but Fitz had already gone. Above their former hiding place, two figures in bright green were clearly visible above the bank. One figure stood half turned towards him, and seemed to shudder as his automatic weapon discharged. Ice spat up around the Doctor a second before he heard the rattle of the gun, and he flung himself onward as the surface of the lake cracked behind him.

He had almost reached the bank when he felt a punching pain in his shoulder, which threw him awkwardly into the overhanging branches. He sprawled on the ice, his cheek pressed to the surface. The sight of the fish gathering beneath him spurred him on, and he dragged himself up into cover, scrambling up the bank, trying to ignore the fresh agony in his shoulder where he had been shot.

At the top of the bank, he flopped down on to the untouched snow. From far away, he could hear more shouting. The guards were coming around the bank. With a weary groan, the Doctor slipped back into the bushes, pondering his options. The dull ache seemed to sound through his whole body like the slow, bass note of a tolling bell. His inner voice was telling him to sleep, to recover, to protect himself; his rational mind fought to stay in control, until he could convince his instinct that his companions were safe.

Fitz would be able to get back down the mountain, he told himself, to rejoin Compassion. That was the plan all along, after all.

Within a minute, he could hear the two Frontier Worlds men scrunching over the snow, and coming to a halt above him. Through the bushes, he could see only their legs. The guard with the machine gun stood stock-still, listening. Sempiter, standing next to him, was tapping the toe of his boot repeatedly in the snow, an unconscious gesture of irritation. It was a kind of warning, like the leppos, of present danger.

'Blood. He must be close by,' said Sempiter. He stooped down, and the Doctor could see his face for the first time. A hawkish nose protruded beneath the snow visor. He removed the goggles, revealing cold, pale eyes. Sempiter's mouth was a grim, lipless slash in his faded grey face.

The Doctor could see that Sempiter was pointing at a shape in the snow, and realised with a little thrill of horror that it was where he himself had fallen at the top of the bank. There was a small, stark patch of pink snow where he had bled from his shoulder wound. 'He's still very close.' Sempiter removed his thick gloves, revealing long hands, greyish skin with gnarled knuckles, like a living marble statue.

Suddenly, in the distance, a snowbike's engine overrevved, then wailed off into the distance. The guard standing by Sempiter swore, then apologised.

'So,' said Sempiter, scooping up the patch of bloodied snow in his bare hands. 'Not as close as we thought.' He breathed a long stream of air through his nose, a sibilant signal of resignation. 'See if we can cut him off before he gets down the mountain.'

'And if we can't? '

'You're head of security, Kupteyn. I'd have thought he'd try to break in at HQ, wouldn't you?' Sempiter's tone brooked no argument. 'Meanwhile, you'll need to start walking - it's a long way back to the research station.'

Kupteyn stepped away from Sempiter, speaking rapidly into his communicator, issuing fresh instructions to capture a man fitting the Doctor's description who had stolen a snowbike. His snowbike.

The Doctor felt his hearts-rate slowing. He was rapidly slipping into a protective coma. Through his fading vision, and peering through the dense foliage, he could see that Sempiter was still crouched down in the snow. The grey-faced man was putting a sample of the bloodstained snow into a plastic container.

'You can't escape for ever,' said Sempiter, his voice a whisper now. He was... sniffing his fingers? 'I love the smell of DNA in the morning.'

Then he stood up. The last thing the Doctor remembered before his breathing slowed to nothing was Sempiter's foot, tapping its unconscious rhythm in the flattened snow.

Chapter Four
'Nice Work If You Can Get It'

It was one of those hot and humid spring mornings that we got in the valley before the sun rose high enough to fry eggs on the sidewalk. The night rain had finished early, for a change. The mountain looming over the town was white-capped and fresh, and you could see the early light glinting off the weather balloon. The works canteen was advertising the kind of mixed special that tells you what wasn't eaten at lunch the previous day. The executive vehicles were swooping low into the parking lot, ignoring the no-fly signs on the lower floor. And in the Frontier Worlds Headquarters building, the glass lifts were humming as people arrived for another day at the grindstone.

I was in the middle lift, crushed between a potted palm and a couple of linen suits. The suits were going on about a big deal they were going to make on Level 8. I looked through the glass and into the well of the building, watching the ants scurrying four, five, six floors below. Level 8, my stop. The suits looked surprised when I squeezed past them and the potted palm on to the landing.

I was neat, clean, shaved and sober, and I didn't care who knew it. I was everything the white-coated lab technician ought to be. I was calling at the office of the Corporate Chairman.

The Chairman's personal assistant was Hannaw Applin. She was a blonde, with a look that could throw a man across the room, or a smile that could light the Bears game in overtime. She was the kind of girl you wanted to spend your last credit on. She eased around the office like an ocean-going yacht, if a yacht could wear a front-loading double-D. And when she opened her mouth she had a voice to make a preacher break into the church poor box and blow it on the first long shot bangtail to buy her whatever she asked for. So what if her mind wasn't exactly a steel trap?

She squeezed on to her office chair without looking up.

'Hey, babe,' I said.

'Hey, Frank.' She didn't look up, preoccupied with her computer screen. To the right of the desk was an ornate wire cage. The bird inside it sat perfectly still on the upper perch, staring into nowhere.

'I brought the DNA analyses.' I put the sheaf of papers on the desk and slid it across to her.

'How can I ever thank you?' she said in a considered monotone.

'Don't mention it,' I said. 'Just step this way and leave your clothes on the desk.'

She gave me a wan smile, and returned her attention to the screen.

I'd wanted to see more of Hannaw from the moment I first saw any of her, two months ago, when I signed on the dotted, my first day at Frontier Worlds Corporation. I remembered she'd given me the impression I'd joined the right company. She'd given me palpitations in my gut. She'd given me the feeling my pants were too tight. She'd given me no alternative but to ask her for a date there and then. She'd given me my manila folder and told me to get the hell out of her office.

I'd gone straight from there to the medical room for my company inoculation. After two months, the inoculation scar on my forearm still itched. After meeting Hannaw, it wasn't the only thing.

That was all before I met Alura. She didn't know about Alura, of course, which was how I liked it. You don't know about her, either, but I'll tell you later.

Since that first day, I realised that Hannaw and I would be Just Good Friends. Hannaw enjoyed the attention, and I knew I wasn't her only gentleman caller - she could've sold tickets, and filled the stand at the Wrigley baseball field. But I knew she had a soft spot for me, and that I could use it to my advantage. You know what I mean - if she wasn't on my arm, at least she was on my side. And who better than the chairman's PA? She was deliciously indiscreet. She'd never bother with people she hated; she didn't like dice games with sharpies and frauds - but boy, could she ever dish the dirt!

From behind me there was the sound of a throat being inexpertly cleared. A square-shaped punk filled the doorway. It was Direk Merdock, one of the younger security staff. Since I'd last seen him, he was sporting an ambitious moustache. 'Is your sister around, Frank?' His voice flicked up and down the octave indecisively.

'I'm meeting her in the canteen today. Get there for the first sitting, and I'll arrange to be late.'

As he left, his face had lit up like a Christmas parade. 'You're a gem, Frank.'

'Eighteen-carat.'

Hannaw was now looking at the sheaf of papers I'd delivered with such panache. 'I can't talk now, Frank. Sempiter's back in the office, looking like death warmed up, and mad as hell. I think he lost something on his last trip up the mountain.'

'Along with his sense of humour?'

'Natch. I'll call you when I can.'

'You're platinum, pussycat.'

'Whatever, Frank.'

Two minutes, some kind of record.

On the way down in the lift, I saw the linen suits being shown out of the chairman's office. They looked crumpled.

The basement lab was as appealing as ever, which is to say not in the slightest. I looked around in the stark white light at my world, a rabbit-hutch office containing a tired chair, a scratched desk, three filing cabinets containing paperwork for four, which bulged like caricature capitalists, an in-tray full of bottled sample slides, a computer terminal with a vertical-hold problem and a keyboard full of characters in apparently random order.

I could tell that Ellis had been in recently. To anyone else, passing wind was a temporary weather condition, but to Ellis it was a biological necessity. I'd have preferred some advance warning of these silent additions to my air quality, and wondered if I should get a canary in. Maybe Hannaw would let me have her caged bird. I could train it to whistle a warning before it keeled over – 'Come Blow Your Horn', perhaps. That or 'Makin' Whoopee'.

I went back to analysing the sample slides, slipping the first of them under the microscope linked to my computer terminal. If I could get through this lot before lunch, I could spend the afternoon hacking into the system and doing some real research. That was if I felt up to lunch, of course. There are only so many faecal smears you can analyse before the canteen special loses what little appeal it had to begin with.

I studied the collection of bottled slides. It struck me that I needn't worry about them anyway. Since Frontier Worlds was a food-manufacturing and research company, all prospective hires had to provide a stool sample to ensure they didn't have salmonella or other communicable diseases. ('Fill in this form, then fill up this pot,' they'd told me two months ago.) So what if I allowed a few through? Trying to find evidence for a positive among all these tiny samples of solids was like looking for water in the Mojave using a forked stick. I could just duplicate the results for the next couple of dozen, and get on with more important business.

I put my feet up on the desk while I considered this. To help me reach a decision, I took a flask from the top desk drawer, and poured myself a slug. It smelled good.

My timing, as ever, was impeccable.

'Bringing beverages into the laboratory? Not to mention taking a break in company time. That's no way to get on in this place, Frank. Big mistake.' Griz Ellis's sewer breath wafted over my shoulder, overpowering the scent of my drink. 'And what's wrong with drinking the coffee from our canteen, anyway?'

I poured the coffee back into the flask, and screwed the lid back on. 'Well boss, because it's ten per cent fresh coffee and ninety per cent pure crap?' I suggested.

'Is that a scientific analysis?' He raised his tatty eyebrows until they vanished into his unkempt fringe of dirty black hair. A fringe that would need a machete to cut through it. 'The coffee is ten per cent fresh coffee, from our own Frontier Worlds crops, plus additional nutrients, beneficial vitamins, and a number of preservatives for the off-planet markets. And a genetic marker, of course, to protect the intellectual-property rights.'

'So, you say tomayto, and I say tomahto.'

He looked back at me blankly. 'Why would we say that?'

'You know – potato, potahto.' Still blank. 'I mean, same difference.'

My boss gave a piggish grunt of disapproval. 'The beverages in our machines here were designed and produced by the company itself. Only the best for our staff. Don't make the mistake of forgetting that, Frank.'

I suppose I should describe Ellis for you – that's what narrators do, isn't it? Even if it means bringing to mind the image of one of the ugliest men I've ever had the misfortune to meet. Pudgy, pasty, petulant, pedantic, rude, bad-tempered, overbearing, smelly – these were some of his more appealing qualities.

He had a hairstyle that added ten years to him. Hair that would keep anyone else awake at night, worrying that they'd get up next morning and it would have got even worse. Hair that a damp comb would never tame. Wild horse hair that could never be broken. I suspected that it vanished down his neck and continued down his back until it came out of his ragged trouser bottoms. There was certainly enough of it curling over the tops of his foul-smelling bare feet, which poked out of the last pair of open-toed sandals on the planet Drebnar.

He was the Corporation's head scientist, the foremost authority on the effects of electromagnetic forces on plant life, and Chairman Sempiter's right-hand man. Though I suspected Sempiter kept him at rather more than a right-arm's length unless he'd been scrubbed, deloused and placed in an airtight box. He didn't need a personal assistant: he needed hosing down in a padded cell. Nevertheless, I *was* his PA – in fact his general dogsbody for when I wasn't asked to carry out salmonella tests. How come I get all the crap jobs? I think you know why.

'Still behind with the faecal analyses? Show me the results.'

Sempiter snatched them off the desk. He reached past me and angled the computer screen towards him, wafting his lab coat and generously sharing his underarm odour with me. 'Oh dear, no. No, no, no, Frank. Look how you've mixed up the correlation in the cross-match. Big mistake, big mistake. You'll need to start them again. And I'll want to check the results myself later this afternoon. I have to go to Level Ten for something, but I'll be back soon to check the first few. OK?'

It wasn't a request: it was a demand. I stared at him, and he stared right back at me, close up. I tried to breath through my mouth rather than my nose. 'I need to be out of here by six,' I blustered.

'No rest for the wicked.' He smiled so that I could see what he'd had for breakfast. 'Made plans without checking on your workload, Frank? Big mistake. Mega mistake.'

On his way out, he left me a short report. And I don't mean on paper.

Something on my computer screen was demanding my attention, but I took a moment to slip on the telephone headset when Hannaw called through. As usual, she spent the first few seconds in inconsequential chitchat to soften me up, and then majored on the latest series of minor inconveniences in her life that she'd contrived to blow up into catastrophes.

'You working on anything interesting, Frank?'

'Working my way through a pack of cigarettes,' I said. 'How about you?'

It was the cue she was waiting for. This time she was complaining that her career was going nowhere, that she got chewed out by Sempiter for daring to complain how she never got to visit her parents offworld. 'He didn't know, Frank. And what's more, he didn't care. He flew into the most terrible rage, I thought I'd need to call the doctor. How was I to know about his parents, huh? I'm his secretary, not his therapist.'

My ears idled on the sidewalk of the conversation as she spilled it.

'I'm more than just a secretary: I'm a PA. Except when I'm his lab assistant.'

'His lab rat,' I dared to interject.

She plunged on regardless. Shortly after my brain was showing the tank-full sign, Hannaw kicked into half-listening mode. I could tell because, when she'd strung out the whole ball of twine, she'd go back to doing whatever she'd been doing before she called. I could usually hear her in the background of the call, gently tapping her keyboard and trying not to break a nail.

'What's that noise?' I asked. 'Is this a party line?'

'No,' she said. 'It's Sempiter's pet bird. Didn't you see it earlier? He left it on my desk when we had the row.'

'It was quieter then.' I flicked up a cigarette, and caught it between my lips. 'I thought it was stuffed.'

She laughed, like coins coming out of a slot machine. 'Almost. It's mechanical. I'll switch it off.' The ticking, chirruping noise cut off. 'I also made the mistake of asking him why he'd made himself this instead of getting the real thing.'

'Maybe it's a child-substitute thing,' I ventured. 'He gets to keep a bird, but without all that messing about with cuttlefish.' Time to make my play. 'Or maybe Mr Sempiter's just worried about the Reddenblak thing. You reckon?'

'Mmm.' Noncommittal.

'I saw two of their boys up on Eight this morning. Looked ticked as they came out.'

Hannaw's mind was somewhere else. 'Couple of their research team made him a few offers. Despite the shareholder meeting last week, he didn't bite. But I think –'

The line cut off, dead as a boneyard during the off-season. I was looking stupidly at the computer screen when I noticed that Ellis was back. When my eyes caught up with my nose, I saw he was holding the end of my headphone connection between the split nails of one hand.

'Mr Ellis,' I said. Nothing else would come out of my brain, but a positive ID seemed like a good start.

'Yes, Frank,' he replied. 'Perhaps you can explain why you're making personal calls in company time.'

'Um...'

He was glaring at me with his one good eye. 'And, since all the labs are non-smoking areas, there's little point in having that cigarette in your mouth, unless you're planning to suck down its contents where you sit.'

I crunched it back into the packet.

'Frank, you are wasting your opportunities. What do you want it to say on your burial capsule when they shoot your remains out in the great beyond. "Here is Frank Sinatra – he could have been someone"? I know what I want it to say on mine.'

Beware, contents are toxic, I thought. But I said, 'Oh?' as though I cared.

'"Here is Griz Ellis, chief scientist of Frontier Worlds, the first and greatest bioengineering corporation in the galaxy, who brought cheap nutritious food to the masses."' He was obviously convinced of this, so perhaps they'd engrave it nice and small to fit on all the words. He dropped the disconnected wire on to my desk. 'When I joined the Corporation, my colleagues and I didn't waste our opportunities. We had dreams, of course, dreams of a better world for all the members of our society. Dreams of cheap and plentiful food, developed by exploiting the power of nature and the efficiencies of science.' He crouched down beside me, speaking in a hushed if somewhat noxious breath. 'Of course, I still have other dreams too.'

Here we go, I thought. It's the 'back-to-the-country' speech again.

'I dream that one day I can return to my home planet, retire from the success of a major corporation. Go back to the land, put down some roots in my old country. Enjoy the fruits of my labour, just as the fruits of my labour are improving the lives of billions of people in this star system.' He looked at me as directly as he could under the circumstances. 'You can do so much more, Frank. Don't miss your chance – that would be a mega mistake. And remember – I've got my eye on you.'

Chapter Five
'Nancy'

I think you know that there's no point doing this job for the money. Sometimes you get attacked, or get lasers fired at you, or get tossed in a foreign jailhouse. Once in a while, if you're unlucky, you get dead. You probably know too that every other month I decide to give it all up for a safer occupation – hunting elephant, maybe, or juggling knives on a tightrope. Then I'll land up someplace, and a door will open, and there's another set of faces with a big piece of new problem and a small but important piece of hope. I'm a sucker for that.

And so it goes. Attacks, lasers, jailhouses. If you'd asked me in advance about asphyxiating body odour, I might have taken a rain check. But that's all part of the Plan, isn't it – you can't know in advance. I can't know in advance, anyway.

The glass-sealed sample pile grew smaller and the hour grew later, and lunchtime dragged around. I was kind of deciding that it was too early to go and eat but I'd go down to the canteen anyway, when I remembered that I'd set up Merdock to meet Nancy, and maybe I'd stay out of the way a while more. So I hung around the lab instead, making sure that Ellis was ten floors up before I picked up the phone, and then I called Alura. She agreed to come to the apartment at eight. Obviously, she'd be fashionably late, as usual. I made her hang up first, after a few false attempts. I could be such a palooka around her.

Don't worry, you'll meet her later.

I'd agreed with Ellis that I'd go for lunch on the second shift. He'd been full of advice about the right number sequence to key into the beverage machine, what drinks were designed to go with what meals, which parts of the planet the natural ingredients had come from and which parts of the factory the additives were designed in. But the sight of his pasty, pustular face creasing in excitement at the recitation of an ingredient list was putting me off all thought of chow, so I made my excuses and left him with my latest results on top of a pile of pots of poo.

In the months since my arrival, I'd got to meet only a handful of other Frontier Worlds workers. All around the HQ, people seemed to avoid making eye contact, as though afraid to talk. I see myself as something of a big-leaguer, but even so I made the early mistake of actually approaching a man and breaking the ice by asking him where the nearest water fountain was. He told me, but his look of amazement at this unsolicited enquiry suggested that I might as well have been asking him for the best place locally to treat a dose of clap.

So now I scanned the canteen, looking mostly for people to avoid. I slapped the day's cold collation on to pale crockery, and skirted carefully round the brutal Stinricz Lowfer in the queue for beverages. Lowfer had as much personality as her food tray, and always seemed to be building up to a brawl. A lunchtime conversation with her was usually ten minutes of polite chitchat, followed by a series of increasingly painful punches to your shoulder while she made her point. I didn't want to be seen with her because she worked in the internal mail room and, besides, she had a face that would frighten a baby.

At the first canteen table that I passed, Rhadoon Haroon was trying to eat her dinner undisturbed. An attractive, statuesque brunette, Haroon had a devastating nervous complaint that could see her take all three sittings to eat her way through the simplest of dishes. She tended to eat vegetarian meals, during which she appeared to slice each pulse and bean individually before giving it thirty chews and then swallowing. I spent an entire week with her one lunch hour watching her fight a losing battle with a green salad. I was painfully aware also that the slightest unexpected interruption would cause her to jolt upward with a high-pitched squeal, and the knock-on effect of this was invariably that everyone else at her table would startle and drop their cutlery or spill their drinks.

I had been hanging out recently with Brab Tonquis and her marketing team, in the crazy hope they would know what was at the cutting edge of Frontier Worlds research, and that, while hunched over their disgusting beverages, they would give me the skinny on the new products' strengths, plus how they planned to disguise any weaknesses. I soon realised that they were all more worried whether someone in their crowd may have a better grade of company flyer than they did. And they had no fun. It was considered poor form to laugh out loud at a joke on their table: you were supposed just to jerk a nod and state in a calm voice, 'Now *that* is funny.'

I looked around a bit more. The only person sitting alone was Bragnor Regot, but he had skin like an overripe banana and he was also the company lawyer, both of which made me want to gag, so I didn't plan to put my lunch tray down opposite him.

The security chief, Kupteyn, hove into view, trailing a brace of button men from the chopper squad behind him. At least they couldn't wear iron in the canteen any more, after (so I heard) one goon chilled off a chef who'd accidentally burned the guy's trigger finger on a hot plate. I sauntered up to Kupteyn, nodded at his hounds, and asked him if he'd seen Nancy.

'I haven't seen your sister,' he said. 'She's not my type. Is she your type?' His goons sniggered like convent-school girls at a strip show.

I wasn't going to take the bait. He was the last person I wanted to annoy, so my brain had definitely chosen the mollifying words, 'You're looking good, Kupteyn – have you been working out?' But all Kupteyn heard was the preamble: 'Hey, that uniform's looking a little tight across the shoulders.' His cheerfully pea-sized brain swiftly translated this into 'Wow, you've *really* been letting yourself go, you lardarse', and our friendly exchange degenerated rapidly. Lucky for me, the lab coat I was wearing was two sizes too big, so when Kupteyn seized me by the lapels he found he had too much cloth to haul my feet completely off the floor.

'I don't like you, Sinatra,' he spat at me, trying not to lose his balance as well as his temper. 'You're asking for trouble. And I can help you find it. I could snap your scrawny neck like you were a chicken.'

'Hey, friend,' I squeaked from somewhere near my coat pocket, 'if you're looking for the awkward squad, then you're looking at the wrong guy.'

At the table behind me, Rhadoon Haroon's lunch companions were retrieving their cutlery.

Kupteyn hefted me in the lab coat again. Fortunately, at this point, Direk Merdock interrupted by peering into the raised coat and finding me hanging inside like a badly ironed shirt on a hanger.

'Oh, hi, Frank,' he said. 'Thanks for... you know.'

This inarticulate contribution magically defused the situation. Kupteyn dropped me and shoved me aside like an expensive election promise. Merdock had the decency to pretend nothing had happened, even as I reassembled the contents of my food tray from the canteen floor.

'So,' I said, playing along with the illusion, 'how was Nancy?' I could see her across the canteen at a quiet corner table, scowling at me. 'Was her face laughing?'

'She wasn't expecting me,' said Merdock glumly. He was in deep, the big dumb galoot. I almost felt sorry that he'd taken the bounce. 'She says she doesn't need company right now. She's sitting there with a cup of cold coffee in front of her. Isn't that just too sad?'

Time to change the conversation. 'Direk, there's something different about you since last week.' I pretended to study him over my meagre lunch tray. Merdock fingered his moustache absently, as though a gentle massage might help it join up in the middle. I'd mentioned casually a week ago that my sister had a thing about guys with facial hair. 'Oh yeah,' I said after a pause. 'You're not wearing your hat today. Well, I gotta be getting –'

'Couldn't you introduce me, Frank?' Merdock blurted out suddenly. He was holding the sides of my tray, turning me round away from her, which seemed kind of familiar if you ask me. I looked at his hands as though I'd picked up the wrong lunch, and he let go.

'Sorry, Direk. I know you're behind the eight-ball on this, but you gotta have plenty of swift with Nancy. Talk to me tomorrow, and we'll see what we can do. I'm on the square, buddy.'

'Not now?' Merdock gave a forlorn little glance over my shoulder.

'Sorry, pal. We gotta have a family chat. See ya tomorrow.'

'Sinatra family secrets?' smiled Merdock, brightening a little.

'I could tell ya,' I said. 'But then I'd have to get my mob friends to kill ya.'

He was looking a bit alarmed at this, so I grinned and flicked him away with a look.

She was still scowling when I got to her secluded table. 'Nance, hi! What a day this has been.'

'Knock it off,' she said.

'And what a rare mood you're in, too.' I moved her cup of coffee aside to make room for my tray, and found that it was stone-cold. 'What gives with Merdock? He likes you.'

'Not interested.'

'Come on. He's got a steady job with good prospects, and his parents are OK. His dad's in finance. His mum works over there in the canteen – you know her, he's just like her: same cheeky grin, same baby-blue eyes, the same wispy beard.'

'And you get on so well with the staff, I see.' She pulled the cold coffee towards her, and stared at its murky surface.

'Kupteyn's probably had just as bad a day as I have. The Incredible Stinking Man dumped a pile more crap into my in-basket, so I'll need to get that finished before I try to hack into the database.'

She flashed me the look then, the one that said she wanted to slap me about until my ears rang. 'You're not the only one who's got a pile of stuff to get through to avoid raising suspicion. I'd much rather be connected right now than sitting here talking to you or your simple-minded friends. We have a job to be getting on with, and you're too easily sidelined.'

'Where's this enthusiasm come from suddenly?' I asked. 'Are you being paid piece rate?'

She lowered her eyes to the coffee again. 'I'm... I suppose it's the *right* thing to do.' The emphasis seemed strange coming from her. 'Let's make this quick, shall we? You know we can't talk here, so we should meet up later, in the evening.'

I prodded my food with my amazingly blunt dinner knife. When it didn't rear up off the plate, I gathered together a forkful. 'I've made plans with Alura –'

'I don't care what you've planned with your moll, this is –'

'Hey, she's no moll.' I waved the fork at her. 'She's a looker, and she's no broad.'

'She's a distraction. You're getting involved.'

'I'm having some fun. It's just fun. It's not serious. When the message comes through, I'll be away on my toes and Alura's nowhere. Meanwhile, get with the beat, will ya? Don't be such a bunny. You could do worse yourself.'

She wasn't convinced. 'You said you'd got plenty of work to do.'

'All work and no play makes Frank a dull boy.' I looked at the food on my fork, which looked cold, stodgy, lifeless. So I tasted it. It was cold, stodgy, lifeless. 'It's just sisterly jealousy.'

'Ooh!' said a squeaky, little-girl voice. A handful of finely manicured nails scraped a chair back from our table. Nadaly Allder, a mouse from the data-entry department, shuffled her buns as she prepared to sit down. 'This sounds like more fun than our backlog of PPRGTFs, eh, Nancy? That's Post-Processed Regressive Gene Treatment Forms,' she said directly to me, raising her tone of voice slightly to suggest girlish complicity, and setting dogs barking all over the neighbourhood.

'Nadaly, this is a private conversation.'

'But Nanceeeee... it's lunch break.'

'Goodbye, Nadaly.' To make the point, she pulled the chair back with an outstretched foot.

The bad news was that this caused Nadaly to break one long red nail, which was as good as slapping the jingle-brained broad smack in the kisser. You could have cut the air with my knife. And then Nadaly lammed off.

'I thought she was a friend of yours from data-entry,' I said.

'I don't have friends.'

'She could be a useful contact. Maybe she's smart with the systems.'

'I've picked smarter things than her out of my nose.'

I watched as Nadaly stalked away, studying her broken nail at every step of her progress across the canteen. It was only when she reached the last but one table that she burst into shrill tears and broke into a clumsy run.

There was a tinny little shriek from nearby, a clatter of cutlery, someone spilled their drink, and three people got covered in coffee. At the table next to them, Brab Tonquis was nodding sagely: 'Now *that* was funny.'

I turned my attention back to our table. 'Nadaly seems kind enough, so that wasn't very nice, Nance.'

'Stop calling me Nance.'

'Hey, you said I could choose the monikers, because you couldn't be bothered. You didn't care whether people got all hinky. So don't try to gum every play I make.'

She stood up, otherwise unmoved, and her voice was as cold as her coffee. 'I expect to see you at the apartment this evening. At eight p.m.'

'Sorry,' I said, abashed, staring at the table. 'Are you not having your drink? It's full of nutrients and vitamins.'

Compassion pushed the cup away from her with one pointed finger. 'I didn't fancy it much,' she said. 'The apartment, at eight p.m., remember. Try not to be late, Fitz.'

Chapter Six
'Dream'

'You throw a more than adequate party, Doctor.'

'Why, thank you,' he replies, bowing low. 'I don't think we've been introduced.'

'I'd say we have a passing acquaintance,' she says, peeping indecorously over the top of her mask, before throwing back her head and whirling him off, one-two-three, one-two-three, until he feels as though his feet will leave the dance floor.

'How unconventional,' he murmurs.

She flashes a smile full of stars at him, spinning him away and then pulling him back once more. 'I like to lead when I dance,' she says. 'I like to let you think you're in charge. Choosing direction. Choosing timing. Designing the pattern of our movement together.'

The Doctor picks her up and swings her over in a lavish dip. Her dark-blue dress blooms beneath her, and her tiara sparkles with impossible brilliance. The room is awash with the scents of sandalwood and summertime and surprise. Planets form and whirl and spin and decay about their heads, and the universe ripples like a purple and gold cloth beneath their feet.

'Do I know you well?' He brushes her cheek with his lips.

She rises from the dip, and spins him around as the tempo changes and the light swirls and swirls into a fiercely bright spiral. 'Not as well as you would think, though you've had your designs on me for all these years.'

They wheel past a crowd of spectators, all familiar and yet he cannot put a name to any individual. They cheer and wave as the dancers flash by, and the tempo changes again as the foxtrot begins. A schoolboy with a blank face applauds solemnly. He seems to give them a thin smile, although he has no mouth and his eyes are empty.

'I am the binding thread in all your lives, though you've treated me like a casual acquaintance for far too long. Yet who knows you better, Doctor? Who have you been closer to than me?'

The Doctor encompasses the audience with a beatific smile. 'I've had many friends and companions in my lives, and I trust I shall have many more to come. They are all welcome at my party.'

'Your current companions interest me most.' With a flick of her heel, the dance is a polka, and they cavort the length of the endless ballroom. 'You think you know them well, but how well? The boy hates you for knowing how much he cares. The girl hates you for wanting her to care. They could both be so much more...'

The Doctor hops an extra step, and the dance becomes a waltz again as they sweep over the midnight floor. 'Because they travel with me?' The whirling light is reaching its crescendo.

'Despite it,' she retorts, seizes his hand and spins him away. 'I must leave now.'

'How will I find you again?'

'Whenever you want me, all you have to do is...'

'Whistle?'

She smiles. 'No, dream.'

The unseen band drive the waltz to its dizzying conclusion, and she swirls off laughing into the vortex of light.

'I'll be all right,' Compassion said. 'It was a localised interference.'

The Doctor hurried around the TARDIS console, swinging aside to avoid the metal stanchion as he moved to her. 'It looked to me more like a bump to the head. Perhaps your earpiece needs further adjustment.'

She turned her head away sharply, leaving his hand dangling in midair. 'I think not.'

He wiggled his fingers, and then plunged them to the console, where they performed a brief tattoo across the brass controls. The other hand pulled down the monitor on its Z-spring. 'Drebnar,' he read. 'One of a number of frontier worlds settled by... hmm, hmm yes hmm... a rare find for this area of the galaxy, a planet with substantial areas of fertile land, no intelligent life forms, and stable tectonics.' Fingers flew over the console. 'At this stage in its history, the planet's being ground-broken by exploratory corporations... hmm, yes... breadbasket for the array of nearby planets... yes... population of only about five million...'

'Only five million?' said Fitz. 'That's a whole planet with a population the size of London.' He was scratching at his chin. 'Not much of a queue for the flicks, then.'

'Thinking of getting rid of that bum fluff?' said Compassion in a flat tone.

'Razor rash,' he said. 'I've decided it would be rash to use a razor.'

'So why', said the Doctor, 'is a primarily agricultural planet dragging us towards it by emitting broad-spectrum Tuckson-Jacker pulses into -'

'- into the time vortex,' said Compassion. She stared up at the ceiling of the TARDIS, watching the loops and whorls of the vortex eddying in an endless tunnel of light. The patterns spiralled round in her grey eyes.

'We should go and investigate,' said the Doctor, rubbing his hands together briskly. 'Identify what's disturbing your concentration, Compassion. Prevent you walking into the furniture. Then we can all stop worrying about you.'

'I don't care whether or not you worry about me.'

'Good. So you won't care if we do something about it.'

He failed his job interview at Frontier Worlds, of course. Not difficult for someone of his talents. However, Compassion and Fitz would start tomorrow. He'd found them cheap accommodation on the outer fringes of town. He told them he needed the TARDIS to stay put, unaffected by any further broad-spectrum interference. It was as good an excuse as any to get them both into town.

'Try to work together on this,' he implored Fitz. 'Think of it as an opportunity to get to know her better. She needs you to keep an eye on her.'

Fitz guffawed so much he choked on his cigarette.

'She does,' the Doctor insisted. 'She just doesn't know she does. She's more susceptible than she'll admit. With her earpiece removed now, she's vulnerable. She can't pick up random signals, but she can't communicate with the TARDIS either. And with the TARDIS behaving rather erratically recently –'

'They say that dogs are like their owners, too.' Fitz favoured him with a long, appraising look. 'She's your project, Doctor.'

'I don't have a project.'

'Yeah, and bears don't shit in the woods.'

'I have to go.' The Doctor tried his most innocent look on Fitz, the one he'd practised earlier. 'I need to find out what's happening at Reddenblak Corporation.'

'They seem to have a more open hiring policy.'

If you only knew, thought the Doctor. But he said, 'I'll be in touch.'

Fitz took a long drag on his cigarette, creating a bright point of red as he sucked the smoke deep into his lungs, before exhaling it languorously through his nose. 'I won't hold my breath.'

'I'm afraid he has no short-term memory.'

'Mrs Mozarno, I'm so sorry.'

'An effect of his work in those last years at Frontier Worlds. The research group won't accept that, of course. And there was no compensation, you understand. All these years with the company, and not a thing to show for it in the end. His contract of employment made that very clear: no liability. But why else would a perfectly healthy man of his age not be able to remember anything he's done that day? And still be able to remember what happened to him years ago?'

'I want to discuss what happened years ago, Mrs Mozarno. I think that your husband may be entitled to something for the work he did. It's not compensation, but it is a share in the profits for his efforts. A colleague of your husband, called Dewfurth, has contacted us at Reddenblak. He wants to sell the intellectual-property rights to a technology called Darkling. Perhaps your husband can tell us about that.'

'We'll see. I don't know what he'll remember. Maybe that's appropriate – the Corporation forgot him. If he'd been employed by them only two more weeks, they'd have given him a timepiece for his years of service. I bought one for him, to spare him the anger and disappointment.'

'I see.'

'When we go in to see him, please don't be shocked. He's perfectly healthy physically. It's just that, if I step out of the room for more than five minutes, he forgets that I was there. And because he remembers me as I was five years ago, for Shar it's like he hasn't seen me in all that time. It... well, it breaks my heart every time.'

'I'm very sorry, Mrs Mozarno. I understand. We want what's best for your husband.'

'Yes, Doctor. I believe you do.'

'You throw a more than adequate party, Doctor.'

'So I'm led to believe,' he replies, nodding in polite deference. 'We've met before, of course.'

'Intimates,' she says, smiling as she removes her mask and casts it aside. It tumbles end over end, spinning past nebulae until it reaches an infinite vanishing point. They dance on, he taking the lead, and galaxies wax and wane around them in the glimmering half-light of creation.

He knows her, of course. 'My oldest companion.'

'I could take that quite the wrong way.'

'Of all my friends, you have the most hidden depths.'

She flashes a smile like a supernova, dazzling him with her power. 'You'd be surprised,' she says. 'One last dance?'

And they twist away in a haze of music and light, the blue dress twisting in the whorls of grey light as he steers her across the universe. Neither of them wants the dance to end, but both of them know that it must, it must.

* * *

The time winds catch the long red hair, and send it winding upward into the whirling vortex. Her sad grey eyes reflect the unworldly light. 'Don't come any nearer.'

He is afraid to reach out. He wants to seize her, clasp her to him. He stretches out a hand slowly, not threatening. She shies away. Not frightened, not repulsed. Defiant.

'Your instinct tells you to take my hand,' he says. 'It's the logical part of you that's refusing. So what if that logic's flawed?'

'Instinct!' she scoffs. 'You can't understand.'

'Try me.' He reaches softly to the side of her head.

That's when she falls. He lets out a huge wail of horror.

She falls silently, spiralling out of reach in the blaze of colour and silence. Her face is composed, unemotional. Soon she is lost in the maelstrom of the vortex.

The Doctor closes his eyes, feeling the anger and frustration flood through him. And holding the earpiece in his hand.

Deep, shuddering breaths. Thin, cold air penetrating, filling empty lungs. Hearts forcing reoxygenated blood around a frozen, healing body.

Morning at last.

Chapter Seven
'The House I Live In'

The last works bus rattles along the drenched streets, its wheels hissing on the film of water that never seems to drain away from the roads during the evening. After 7 p.m. the weather system switches to the rain program, since most of the city's workers should have left for their homes two hours ago. What kind of social system makes it easy for people to get to and from work, and for businesses to run efficiently during the day, but then arranges for it to piss down throughout the evening and night? In what sort of sane world do you fix the weather to ruin any chance of a decent pub crawl, every night? I mean, you might as well live in Manchester.

Imagine you are on this almost empty public transport; you might hear a muffled cough from the back seat, and your eyes will be drawn to a hunched figure in a grubby dark coat squatting beneath the rear window where the water streams down from the roof. If you can pick out sharper notes from the pervasive smell of wet leather seats and damp wooden flooring, you'll perhaps notice this hunched figure is having a sneaky Woodbine and blowing the smoke under the seat in front of him, thinking that it's only the driver he has to conceal this minor transgression from. The blue-grey smoke won't be hidden, though, and it swirls about the torn seats, rises, clings to the damp windows. Then, if you look more closely, you'll see him take an equally furtive glance at his wristwatch. Listen again: he's swearing under his breath. I'm sorry to tell you that, as you've probably guessed, it's the author, who is beginning to realise just how late he's going to be if he misses his connecting ride.

Fortunately for this story, I'll tell you that he's got nothing to worry about. He can't yet know that the connecting service is having to recharge its emergency battery, and so he'll have a few more minutes to fidget in curse-filled anxiety while he waits for it to arrive late, consider legging it the remaining half-mile to his apartment, dither with indecision, and then slump with relief as he sees it making its delayed arrival around the corner while he thanks a god he hadn't been praying to and whom he hasn't believed in for years anyway.

So imagine now that you're taking a moment to peer through the windows of this bus, and into the failing light. Vanishing into the distance through the back window, the street lights seem to point towards the Frontier Worlds HQ building. Most of its lights have gone out, with a small ring of bright spots in the centre of the bottom row where the security staff are still pacing up and down and setting off the heat-activated sensors which switch on the corridor lights.

Look across past the author and you can see the urban sprawl into which this bus will soon be turning, away from the outer edges of the open countryside, dark, wide fields full of neatly ordered crops and, beyond, the wild, original, as yet uncleared jungle that characterises this part of the fertile planet Drebnar.

So that leaves only one direction, doesn't it? That black slab of dark through the other window, cutting out the light from the stars with its sheer proximity, is the mountain. Its lower slopes are barricaded with forbidding wire and unheeding Frontier Worlds guards and badly painted signs saying, KEEP OUT: PRIVATE PROPERTY. On a clear day, and there haven't been many of those lately, you can see the cable car wending its three-stage passage up to the summit and to the research station, which clings like an Austrian *schloss* to the craggy peak. But you'd have to have remarkably good eyesight to see that even during the day, and, since you don't, let's look back at the author, sitting and worrying about his time-management skills as the bus hisses on through the gathering gloom of evening.

It was on a similar, lonely ride home to his cold apartment that he'd first met Alura, six weeks ago. She worked for a trading company on the other side of the city, and was on the bus that evening only because she'd been at a day of interviews and assessments for a job at Frontier Worlds HQ. She'd heard nothing since then, of course. Strange to think now that he'd got to talk to her using a variant on a scam he used to pull on the tube back home.

'Back home' is a strange phrase to use, isn't it? After all, he's going back home to the apartment now, isn't he? To meet Compassion as promised, of course. And to meet Alura for the evening, as arranged.

More about Alura later, though. Yeah, I know, I keep saying that, don't I? You'll see her soon enough. I just don't want you to think I'm obsessing about her, because I'm not, OK?

I almost snapped the key card in half in my haste to slide it through the reader and open the apartment door. From the rainy pavement outside, I'd seen that the light was on in the main room, and I'd hurried through the reception area, past the concierge in his faded uniform, and hared up the stairs three at a time, rucking the thin carpet on every turn.

It was only Compassion in the apartment - I recognised her long red ponytail. She was standing in the kitchen, among the debris of last night's dinner. She hadn't eaten, as usual. She stayed in the office most of the time these days, and I couldn't remember the last time we'd had a meal together. In fact, I couldn't recall the last time I'd seen her eat. But she must've been packing it away some time, because she hadn't lost any weight - if anything, she'd put some on, and her pale, freckled, hamster cheeks looked chubbier than usual. Now she was examining a Frontier Worlds freebie calendar that I'd brought from the office as a joke.

I'd hung the calendar on a cup hook, saying it put the kitsch into 'kitchen'. It showed landscape photographs of Drebnar, each month a bright new three-dimensional reproduction of a striking geological feature somewhere on the planet - a mountain range, a deep river gorge, the sharp-edged brilliance of a ripening field of wheat. Incongruously, in each picture, you could find a company vehicle, sticking out starkly against the scenery. There were images of flying transport vehicles, huge combine harvesters the size of office blocks, the interplanetary juggernauts that travelled out across the system every six months, even the occasional company flyer with a smiling marketeer leaning proudly on the bonnet and trying to look as if he deserved it. Sometimes you had to move your head quite some way round a reproduction before you saw the familiar lime-green Frontier Worlds Corp livery.

The *pièce de résistance* was the Weather Control Facility, which as you moved your head upward would suddenly emerge from behind clouds in a photograph of the mountain. For me, the biggest irony was that I'd found out more about the weather platform from this marketing freebie than I'd discovered in weeks of trying to hack into the Frontier Worlds computer system, and all because Smelly Ellis had been having a junk clearout in his office.

The computer system. The office. That reminded me why we were here.

'I thought some creep was checking up on the searches I'd been running last week. I worried that they'd nailed me, that it was endsville. But it just sent out some kind of audit e-mail, so no sweat.' I slumped in a chair, and checked the time. 'Siddown, Compassion. We don't have to pay extra for using the chairs.'

Compassion looked up from her examination of this month's company vehicle. 'Aren't you taking this stupid Frank Sinatra thing a bit too far?'

'You're killin' me.'

She sighed. 'Well, at least take off that dumb hat.'

I shook the rain off my trilby and dropped it on the low table by the door. Then I peeled off my wet coat. As I pulled at the sleeve, I could feel a sore spot where the injection in my arm still hurt. 'I think when Smelly Ellis gave me this shot he knew it wasn't to protect me from research accidents. It was to inoculate me from him. I need a shower.'

Compassion followed me into the bathroom. I wondered for a fraction of a second whether I'd unwittingly melted the icy block of her indifference. She was pretty, in a cheeks-and-freckles kind of way, and I'd hardly considered her as a partner before but, hey, I wasn't going to be choosy. I was supposed to be supportive, to show her my human side, so I was quite prepared to show her the entire thing. It was mildly disappointing, therefore, when I realised that she had followed me into the bathroom only to continue the conversation, and not to gape or grope at my wedding tackle.

'Hurry up, Fitz. I have to get back to Frontier Worlds. I got authorised overtime, and I don't like taking all this time off just to accommodate your shagging arrangements.'

It wasn't that Compassion didn't look at me as I undressed, just that she showed about as much interest as when I unpacked the shopping. So I climbed straight in the shower cabinet, and set the water to very hot. The transparent sides of the free-standing shower cubicle soon steamed over, and I was able to stop holding in my stomach to disguise my flabby muscle tone.

'I feel like I'm washing off the day,' I shouted through the stinging spray. 'Sloshing Smelly Ellis down the plughole.'

'Remember the woman you said I was rude to in the canteen, Nadaly?' Compassion shouted back, leaning against the shower cabinet. 'During one of her endless conversations with me earlier in the day, she let slip that she and your malodorous boss were an item.'

I almost slipped over in the shower.

'They were practically married. Don't be so surprised, Fitz. I imagine it was before he lost the will to wash. According to Nadaly, they were really close. It all went wrong about a year ago. She says his work became more important than her. I'd tell you her whole story, but you'd end up gnawing your own hand off to stay awake until the end.'

'Maybe you shouldn't have been so rude to her.'

'Maybe,' Compassion agreed, though her tone suggested otherwise. 'Especially since, according to her, he never severed their financial arrangements. She's still entitled to half his stock options. You should be seeing her instead of Alura, Fitz.'

I made a little hole in the steamed-up surface, and peered out. Compassion was walking out of the room after this Parthian shot. 'If I could bear to be with someone with a whine like a short-wave radio,' I said.

As I towelled myself dry, I thought some more about the arguments this afternoon. Compassion had upset Nadaly by her brusque manner, but, without realising it at the time, I'd somehow offended Kupteyn - the last person I'd want to rumble with, assuming I wasn't planning to count my own teeth in the palm of my hand.

The TARDIS was supposed to help with translating what we said and heard. Which should be a big help to me, because the people on this planet weren't even from Earth, let alone London. On my one trip north, to a Salford pub, I'd been incapable of communicating with my fellow drinkers except like foreigners, speaking slowly and loudly, invoking footballers' names like a linguistic common currency, and making vague hand gestures - 'Nobby Stiles' (pointing at front teeth), 'Bobby Charlton' (fingers drawn across top of head), 'Duncan Edwards' (hand making diving movement).

I put on my least crumpled black cotton shirt and my favourite pair of drainpipe trousers, and rejoined Compassion. She was sitting on our single, dusty, understuffed chair, a forlorn relic of the previous occupant's belongings which slumped against the far wall of the apartment's grubby main room, and fumbling with something at the side of her head; I realised after a moment that she was fixing her receiver back in place.

'I thought you'd agreed with the Doctor not to use that while we're on Drebnar. In case there's more interference.'

I sat down in the chair beside her as she finished adjusting the earpiece. The large hole in her earlobe closed around the device, and Compassion seemed to relax, as though she'd just had a deep drag on a cigarette.

'I don't think the Doctor would be very impressed,' I continued.

She looked at me, entirely unembarrassed. 'I'm only using it here in the apartment, not in the office where it might attract attention. And since the Doctor's not here, who's going to argue?'

Not me, I thought, I've had enough arguments today. Instead I mentioned my thoughts about the arguments to Compassion.

'The TARDIS has been through a rough time recently,' she said, staring out of the tall window as though expecting to find the familiar blue shape propped on the rickety balcony.

I shushed her, grubbed around for a scrap of paper, and thrust a scribbled note in her face. 'Pugs?' she said. I waved the paper again. 'Oh... No, Fitz, there are no bugs in this room. There are no bugs in this entire apartment block - I told you that last week.'

I scribbled 'Oh yeah?' on a piece of paper. I handed it to her, and said, 'Oh yeah?' and then felt a bit foolish.

'Yeah, even the phone doesn't work. We agreed that when the Doctor first got us this place: it's deliberately cut off.'

I reached down to the floor, and ran my fingers over a small bump which protruded under the soiled covering, about a yard from the inside wall. The floor covering was some kind of calico, and may once have been a uniform beige, but now it was patched and spotted with a wide variety of revolting stains, and had turned a sort of brown colour. I pulled at the edge of the covering, just below the peeling off-white wallpaper, and wrenched it back until I revealed the cause of the bump - a looped clump of thin red and green wires, about twenty of them fixed tightly across the cross-point of a couple of the thin floorboards.

'Found it this morning,' I mouthed to her. What would security chief Kupteyn do? I wondered. Wrench them out personally with his blackened teeth, probably. I chose instead to rummage around a drawer in the sideboard until I found a pair of scissors with pearlescent finger grips. I used them to prise up the first few wires, and chewed through the strands with the sharp blades. I'd soon sliced through the lot, and was left with two small pieces of wire.

Compassion was looking at her wristwatch as I finished rolling back the floor covering. 'The whole point of trekking all the way out here, Fitz, is that I *know* there are no bugs in here. Otherwise, we might as well be having this conversation in the Frontier Worlds building.'

'How can you tell there's no surveillance?'

Compassion fingered her earpiece. 'The same way I can tell that the TARDIS isn't close by. It's a kind of instinct. You know, like you have an instinct for dumb babes.'

'You're cracking me up,' I said, and threw the scraps of wire on to the sideboard. 'If the TARDIS isn't close by, then how can it do this handy-dandy translation thing for us?'

Compassion had closed her eyes. I wasn't sure whether she was concentrating, or just trying to control her temper. 'It's a telepathy thing. Don't try to understand it, just be happy that it works.'

'I'm happy now,' I said, making a snipping sound with the scissors. I placed them on the scratched surface of the long sideboard, next to the discarded wires. 'I'm cool.'

'You shouldn't be so surprised that people misunderstand this stupid Frank Sinatra language you're using. They think you're just eccentric, or else a simpleton. The TARDIS translates into things they'll understand, or as best it can, based on what you're thinking as well as the words you use.'

This was a downer, and I said as much. 'Are you saying I should talk normally, because it makes no difference to everyone else?'

'Oh, it makes a difference,' Compassion said. 'It obviously gives you confidence to hide behind a false personality, and it means that you're concentrating - in your own odd way - on the plan. But it's also the reason why no one understands your stupid gags, because they rely on wordplay that doesn't translate.' Her eyes moved beneath her closed lids, as if she were dreaming. 'Besides, the TARDIS isn't smart about Earth colloquialisms. It once told a friend of the Doctor's that the advertising phrase "Coke adds life" translated as "Class-A drugs bring your ancestors back from the grave".'

I stood in front of her, studying her calm face. 'How do you know this?'

Compassion snapped her eyes open, and I could see the pupils adjusting to the light, narrowing in her swirled, grey irises. 'Can we talk about our current plan?' she said briskly.

The Plan, I thought. I was supposed to be looking out for Compassion, and I had to admit I'd been mostly looking out for myself. Playing second fiddle to the main investigation had dragged after a couple of weeks. I could identify the occasional lead from Sempiter's office, through my contact and conversations with Hannaw, or from my extracurricular investigations in Ellis's labs. Compassion had spent most of her time plugged into the Frontier Worlds computer network. She was faking it as a data-entry clerk, one of the hundred-strong team of men and women in the huge glass-fronted offices on Level 4 who pounded their keyboards and stuffed the systems with the huge amounts of research and observation data that the Corporation seemed to generate every day.

And, in the middle of all this, Compassion somehow managed to access other systems, too. I didn't understand how, I didn't need to. But I worried that she seemed happiest when she was connected to her computer, as though her telephone headset were the best substitute she could find for her absent earpiece back in the TARDIS.

Compassion got out of the battered chair in one fluid, easy movement. She was looking at me with that familiar and unnerving direct gaze. 'There's been a lot of buzz on the security channels about a stolen snow bike up on the mountain.'

'How else was I supposed to get back down?' I protested.

Compassion's expression did not change. 'You've left elephant-sized footprints all over the place, Fitz. We may be getting close to the information that the Doctor wants, but people are getting close to us too.'

'How so?'

'Someone pulled your personnel records yesterday afternoon, checking your attendance record, can you believe?'

'I've been in the company two months, and I've used most of

my holiday allowance. Including', I added in an aggrieved tone, 'two days to go up the mountain and meet the Doctor.'

'The flag on your personnel query said it was a routine, random sample. But a random sample of one doesn't look very random to me. Maybe they worked out that you provided me with Ellis's cipher key. It got me through the Level Eight firewall, anyway.'

'Firewall,' I repeated, wishing in vain that the TARDIS would translate that too. I'd just delivered the stuff that Compassion requested the previous week - I didn't pretend to understand the technical jargon. So I nodded, as though it all made sense.

'Today I rooted out two important pieces of data. The first is about the organisational history of Frontier Worlds. The two founders were student contemporaries, and came to Drebnar at the same time, can't determine exactly when but it's decades ago at least based on construction history for the main building. Temm Sempiter is chairman, and Klenton Dewfurth became head of the genetic research team, based up in the mountain research centre. Apart from those two, there are only a couple of other major investors, and the rest of the company's stock is held by small shareholders. Based on the Doctor's last e-mail, I also did a cross-correlation of significant dates, personnel and project numbers. The big project they've been keeping under wraps for the last five years is codenamed 'Darkling'. I haven't got any further with that - it's why I need to go back to the office tonight. I do know that Darkling is a fundamental DNA-level construction kit, and that they're working on it on Level Ten.'

'Have you written this down somewhere for me?'

'Oh, very security-conscious, Fitz! Of course I haven't: I've remembered it. Pay attention, you should remember it too. The other thing is that they've recently analysed a very interesting DNA sample, unlike any other humanoid source on the planet. It has sixty-nine chromosomes divided into twenty-three homogenous triads...'

I nodded again, feeling a yawn start at the corners of my jaw, and suppressing it.

Compassion's eyebrows furrowed. 'It's the Doctor's DNA, Fitz. Where did they get it from?'

Suddenly I didn't feel like yawning any more. 'We should get back there now. Check out Level Ten. Do you think he's there?'

The door buzzer sounded, and I almost banged my head on the ceiling.

'Tomorrow,' said Compassion, already heading for the apartment's front door. 'They know you're off duty now. I'll try to find out where they got the DNA sample, during my authorised overtime tonight. Then we'll see what's happened to the Doctor, if anything.' She pressed the buzzer to open the downstairs street door. 'I think your moll has arrived.'

'Enjoy your evening,' I said with ill-disguised sarcasm. 'Your only close relationship is with the corporate database.'

'Well, you can spend your evening together looking for secret bugs and practising the alien tongue,' replied Compassion with a small, tight smile.

There's only one alien tongue I want to get to grips with, I thought, and it's coming up the stairs right now.

Compassion stepped out on to the gloomy landing. 'Don't get too involved.'

'Go climb up your thumb, Nancy. There's no harm in getting involved.'

Compassion did a passable imitation of my voice. 'Close your head. You're the sap who's dizzy with the dame.' She passed Alura at the corner of the stairs, calling back, 'Don't wait up for me, Frank.'

I wish I could tell you what Alura looked like. I could describe the burnt umber of her skin, her short dark hair, the unique khaki of her oval eyes. I could tell you how the little wrinkles formed in the soft skin of her nose when she giggled or felt like a sneeze; how she could give me a naughty look by widening her eyes but without raising her eyebrows; how her soft, smooth fingers felt when they slid down my cheeks, over my neck, down my chest; how her skin smelled of cherries and summer and sunlight, even on a rainy evening; how when she went to sleep her contented breathing sounded like a cat purring. But you'd need to be really inside my head, see her with my eyes, understand her with my mind, for the full description.

I saw her step through the door that night, and once again I could no longer see the apartment's dingy carpets, squint wall hangings and sparse, squashed furniture. She moved in close, and we shared a long, exploratory kiss that made me shiver inside. She was still wet from the rain.

'Hello, my bit of rough,' she grinned in familiar greeting.

'But I scrub up well,' I responded as usual, holding her at arm's length now and looking at her. 'Are we staying in?'

'Let's go out. I want us to wander off and find a nice restaurant.'

'The eating places round here are rubbish,' I said, slipping my hands lower around her waist, and pulling her close. 'Oh sure, it's nice to just wander, but it's so much nicer, yes it's oh so nice, to wander back.'

She snuggled in my embrace. 'But I wanted us to go out and talk. I got the job, Frank.'

'That's swell, baby,' I replied, before I realised what she'd said.

She was whispering close to my ear. 'Isn't it great? I join the Frontier Worlds marketing department in three weeks.'

I couldn't really concentrate on the meal. We'd gone two blocks over to a vegetarian restaurant. Like a lot of places in the city, it was franchised and supplied by Frontier Worlds. Like a lot of Frontier Worlds food, it looked awful and tasted terrible. The beer was nothing special and, worse, it didn't make you drunk quickly enough.

Alura didn't seem to mind. She bubbled away throughout the evening, and nothing seemed to dampen her enthusiasm, whether it was the continual drizzle outside the restaurant or the dreadful meal inside. She'd bought me a personal timepiece, nothing too expensive, a mass-produced watch with an orange smiley face on it and a fat, rather ugly buckle. It was her reminder that I'd bleated to her last week that I was always late for meetings at Frontier Worlds, and she made me promise I'd never be late for meetings with her - that was *her* privilege.

Usually, Alura's passion for things was infectious, and I would be transported with her away from the business and boredom of the day. Tonight, I was half aware what she was going to say before she said it. Waiting for the other shoe to drop.

She wanted us to move in together. She'd need a place nearer to the HQ - we'd have two salaries to pay for somewhere nice.

I was just glad she hadn't brought a selection of rings to go with the watch. How could I have misjudged things so badly? I looked across at her fervent gaze in the fake candlelight, into those soulful khaki eyes, and knew. What a jerk I was.

My eyes must have shown it. Her words trailed off. 'Frank? Are you OK?'

'Between you, me and the bugs in the wall of this hash house, babe...' I said, and paused while I thought what to say next. Perhaps I was getting in too deep, chest deep at least. 'It's been a bummer of a day.'

She clasped my cold thin fingers in her own warm hands, and pulled them towards her across the table. 'Oh, Frank. Think how much happier you'll be in a new place. You've said yourself that your apartment's a dump, that it's falling down. Even this evening, when I arrived, I saw that the chandelier on the floor below you had just dropped on to the landing and smashed. When I stopped to help your neighbour move the pieces, I could see that the support wires had just snapped straight through.'

She studied my reaction, her pretty round face the image of concern. 'Please, Frank. Let's look for a place soon.' Pause. Her eyes were glittering. 'I love you, Frank.'

'That's swell, baby.' I stared at my arms, stretched out across the table to her. One showed my recent inoculation mark. On the other I could see the orange face of my new watch, my new mark of ownership. I could feel the water lapping around my nostrils now. I wrenched the conversation in a different direction. 'Hey, what do you call a fish with no eyes?'

'Er…' She swerved and caught up. 'A blind fish?'

'No, a *fsh*!'

Beautiful Alura's face was a complete blank.

I took a long swig of my horrible beer. 'Don't worry,' I said. 'It probably gets lost in translation.'

Chapter Eight
'I'd Know You Anywhere'

He sat and watched his fingers turn from blue to pink, a litmus test of his health and vitality. The tips of his thumbs prickled as the blood returned.

Dawn was breaking over the knife-edge horizon. A chill breeze carried powdery snow over the white, unbroken skin of the mountain.

He took an experimental breath, inhaled sharply through his nose and felt the dry, glacial air seeping through his lungs.

A pair of leppos scuttled past, batting at their ears, cuffing each other in playful fighting. They left a scuffed trail in the snow outside the cave mouth.

He closed his eyes, and did a mental tour of his own body, walking through many rooms on his journey of inspection. His shoulder throbbed, but seemed ready for visitors. He opened his eyes again. The leppos had disappeared from view now.

He felt his hearts speeding up, biofeedback controlling the recovery process.

After a further half-hour, the Doctor felt ready to face the cold new world outside.

The area seemed changed utterly. He could barely remember struggling to this sheltered place. And he hadn't been aware of the night-time storm, deeply asleep as he was in the narrow cave slashed into the mountainside. But the fresh snowfall had obscured all but the most significant landmarks - the mountain above him, with the research station perched precariously on one ledge; the cable-car line that staggered between pylons down the mountain; the blot of the weather-control balloon, a stark oval shadow across the bright morning sky and the sunlight filtering low through the morning haze.

Under which featureless pine had he left the TARDIS? Indeed, in which clump of trees? It was lost in the wilderness. Just like him, he reflected. 'They say that dogs are like their owners, don't they?' he mused aloud. 'Now who told me that? Was it that diarist, what was his name, Boswell? Dodie Smith? Or that violinist, maybe? Or perhaps it was Aretha Franklin.' The tall trees in the middle distances cast long accusing shadows across the snow towards him. You, they were suggesting, yes you, what have you done?

The Doctor turned to look back at the cave, as though searching innocently behind himself, as if to reply, Who? Me? His shadow seemed to turn a fraction later. How odd, it must be the aftereffects of the self-healing coma, he decided, affecting his perception.

The violinist, he decided. Yes, it was Fritz Kreisler. They'd talked about *Tambourin Chinois*, hadn't they? And whether it was too backward to play *col legno* on one of Jakob Stainer's fine instruments. And how you could have told that Beethoven was an eccentric genius just by looking at him - those old-fashioned jackets, the dashing cravat, and all that wild, wild hair. But, no, nothing do with pets.

Oh, well then it was *Kreiner*, Fritz Kreiner.

Still didn't sound right. *Fitz* Kreiner?

Ah yes, back to the TARDIS - it all made sense now.

He remembered Fitz Kreiner and Compassion Whateverhernamewas. The two of them seemed to be making more progress than he was, so it was time to rejoin them, down the mountain.

He was staring around, humming a passage from *Caprice Viennois* and trying to decide the best descent, when he saw the bare arm sticking out of the snow.

He decided eventually that they were Dewfurth's remains. He must be closer to the mountain than he had at first guessed. The surprising thing was that the corpse was hollow, like a snake skin cast aside.

When he had first touched the hand, with the remote hope of finding a pulse, it had been as cold as the snow, but it had also collapsed in on itself like a glove. After he'd excavated the loose snow around the strange limb, he had uncovered the rest of the skin. Dewfurth's face stared blankly up at him, like a rubber mask that had been peeled off. The fleshy suit of the torso was mostly in one piece, though a ragged tear from the throat down to the navel suggested either an autopsy or that the owner had stripped it off like a waistcoat.

The Doctor tugged his own waistcoat tighter to him in the chill wind, aware once more that most of his buttons were missing. Jagged points of dark rock speared up from the snow further along, and the Doctor stumbled through knee-high drifts to reach them. There were smears of blood across two adjacent rocky points. Half buried beside another was Dewfurth's tweed jacket, with the shirt still inside the sleeves as though they'd been taken off at the same time.

The Doctor could hear a low sobbing coming from behind the rocks. It was the sound of a man who had reached the end of a long session of crying, and was just making the occasional sharp intake of breath to remind himself how miserable he was. When the Doctor scrunched his way carefully through the snow and around the rocks, he wasn't at all surprised to find that it was Dewfurth.

The scientist was staring at the sheer face of the nearby mountain, snow piled up against one side of him as though he were a bizarre statue oblivious to all weather conditions. He had obviously spent the whole night there, huddling himself into a tight ball with his back against the spear of rock and his knees clasped to him. He jumped up nervously, surprised and embarrassed to be found. He stared for a good while at the Doctor before saying, 'What happened to you?'

The Doctor was suddenly very aware of his tattered green coat and bloodstained shirt. Nevertheless, compared with Dewfurth, he was overdressed for the occasion. 'I could ask you the same thing.' He smiled reassuringly.

Dewfurth looked down at himself. His feet were bare, and his trousers were ripped up the sides, flapping in the light morning breeze, and with no belt. He pulled the thin lab coat closely to him, and the Doctor could see that he had no shirt or jacket underneath it.

And then Dewfurth slumped back down against the rock, heaving a new series of sobs which racked his thin body.'It's... oh it's no use,' he groaned.'I can't even kill myself properly.'

The Doctor considered this bizarre confession for a moment, thinking also about the skinned remains he had already discovered. After that, he sat down in the snow beside Dewfurth, and put his arm around his shoulders. They stayed like this for several minutes until the scientist's sobs subsided again.

The Doctor recognised the mania in the broken man. He knew from his earlier encounters that Dewfurth's mood could swing from wildly articulate enthusiasm to a profoundly taciturn gloom. Either Dewfurth would tell the Doctor everything, or nothing at all. The Doctor would have to be careful not to upset the scientist, and to concentrate on cajoling the information out of him.

Dewfurth clasped and unclasped his narrow hands nervously, as though uncertain what to do with them. He certainly didn't seem to feel the cold, and he wasn't shivering in the Doctor's comforting embrace. The Doctor studied the squirming hands. They looked like a young man's fingers, not the gnarled and knotted joints he remembered from their confrontation on the balcony the previous day.

'Do you recall our last conversation?' said the Doctor lightly.'I thought it really *was* our last conversation. We discussed instinct, and how it should have told you not to jump to your death.'

The Doctor's steady and insistent tone seemed to calm Dewfurth, who allowed himself a faint smile as he relaxed a little. The scientist's cheeks were less hollow than the Doctor remembered them. Now that Dewfurth had stopped pulling the lab coat tightly to himself, the Doctor saw that the skin across his chest was also pink and healthy.

'Perhaps I was wrong, and your body knew it could survive the fall, that it could regenerate itself. Your mind didn't know that, did it?'

Eventually, Dewfurth said, 'I suppose I should have guessed.'

'Why?'

'I told you about the genetic experiments?' He was making proper eye contact, noted the Doctor approvingly. He nodded encouragement, and Dewfurth went on: 'Fast-yield crops to better exploit the very fertile land on this planet. You can practically grow a tree just by leaving your walking stick in the ground overnight.' A smile, too - that was good. The Doctor smiled back. 'We still needed to beat that, to stay ahead of Reddenblak, who were taking market share from us. We were in a monopoly before they came to Drebnar, and running close to break-even with our setup costs, so we couldn't afford to lose a single percentage point to Reddenblak.'

'How does that explain what you did yesterday?' asked the Doctor gently. 'How you survived that impossible fall?'

Dewfurth seemed completely calm now. His voice was soft but clear. 'It's the end result of our work on biological longevity. To see why, you need to understand us. Imagine me and Sempiter, selling our interests and our former lives and coming here as majority shareholders, risk takers in a brand-new company on a brand-new planet. Drebnar was our very own frontier world, that's why we chose the name for our team, and then our Corporation. I can hardly believe our ambition in those days, our idealism. I was supposed to be the pessimist, but even I was carried away with the excitement of it all. It was the same when we brought in the other two, of course.' He paused, lost in thought for a moment. 'What happened to us?'

'Go on,' prompted the Doctor. He shuffled around in front of Dewfurth now, so that they could talk more comfortably. The short gusts of cold air hardly seemed to matter as he listened.

'Between the four of us,' said Dewfurth, 'we had the combination of mechanical and biological engineering skills to make the whole venture a qualified risk. We could identify the right crops and rotations for this environment. Design and develop machinery for faster crop production. Set up a weather-control system to expedite growth. We didn't mind the early years of struggle, and they were long years too. It started to go wrong as soon as we worked out that none of us were going to live long enough to enjoy the results of our lives' work. It affected Sempiter most. He discovered he was dying, and all our biotechnology skills weren't going to save him. He got sidetracked from the project when he tried to develop something to avoid that.'

'Working on a cure?' asked the Doctor.

'Designing a robot. Easy to see now that it was doomed to fail. In the end, he used the robot for menial duties - it was useless for his original purpose. He might as well stick his brain in a jar as put it into that thing. Well, you can't expect a mechanical device to develop a mind of its own.'

'Oh, I don't know about that,' pondered the Doctor.

'I told you I was the pessimist. Anyway, a sideline of this from the early stages was that Mozarno and I got interested in devising a self-regenerating, synthetic flesh. That was supposed to make Sempiter's robot more realistic. We abandoned it early on, but it got us thinking about modifying genetic material to prolong the natural life span of animal tissue.'

'Animal tissue?' said the Doctor. 'People, too?'

'We could all survive to see our work completed,' said Dewfurth, his eyes alive with the memory of those days. 'Even Sempiter. Especially Sempiter - he was counting the weeks. He and Mozarno had the first treatments. Poor Mozarno, if he'd only known where it was all leading.'

The Doctor recognised the tone in Dewfurth's voice - he was descending into one of his paralysing glooms. 'Your genetic experiments were a success, then,' said the Doctor, trying to inject an upbeat note into the conversation.

'Oh, no,' Dewfurth replied. 'Like all our other plans, they got more and more hopelessly delayed. None of us was much of a project manager, you see, so we were soon wildly behind schedule. Until we found the alien on the mountain.'

'Ah,' said the Doctor. 'Tell me about that.'

Dewfurth thought for a long while about this, turning it over in his mind. The Doctor smiled and nodded reassuringly. Finally, Dewfurth came to a decision. 'I'll do better than tell you,' he said. 'I'll show you.'

At first, it looked just like another broad, flat escarpment beside the lake. It had taken them forty minutes to traverse the powdery snow, pausing frequently when Dewfurth thought he heard or sensed Frontier Worlds people nearby.

'I don't understand what I'm looking at,' said the Doctor.

Dewfurth burrowed into the piled snow. Sparkling particles whirled and scattered in the mid-morning light, lifted by the stiffening breeze. There was a storm coming, thought the Doctor, and yet Dewfurth still did not seem to be suffering from the biting cold even though he was wearing the thinnest of clothing.

Dewfurth had finished digging, and drew the Doctor nearer. The Doctor peered into the freshly dug gap. He could see a skein of material, broad strands of vegetable matter crisscrossing like a rush mat. Where had he seen this before, he pondered. His recent recovery and the biting cold of the wind seemed to be numbing his brain. 'From the thickness of these,' he said, 'it could be quite big. What... five metres? That would be a big plant.'

Dewfurth was shaking his head. He pointed to the far end of the escarpment.

The Doctor seized at his own hair in a gesture of astonishment. 'That must be ten times... what, *fifty* metres?'

'Oddly, for a plant, it even had a kind of rudimentary brain stem,' said Dewfurth, as he moved further along the edge of the great mound of snow. It took him a full minute to reach the spot he wanted. 'That would be about here. I can remember when we removed it, all those years ago.'

The Doctor struggled over to join the scientist, aware that it had started snowing again, and that the storm was on its way.

'Years ago...?' he prompted.

'Decades,' said Dewfurth as the Doctor dug handfuls from the fresh snow bank in front of him. 'The whole thing is smaller than it was originally, of course. Over the summer periods, when this part of the mountain isn't covered with snow, the main flesh of the creature rotted away and just left the infrastructure, all the dead vascular tissue.'

'Yes, all this hard xylem,' said the Doctor, 'the elongated tracheids. These are huge and extensive. I think this can be only one thing, you know.'

'What's that?'

'It's a Raab,' said the Doctor. He dusted his hands off, and stuck them under his armpits to warm them up again. 'Believed to have originated billions of years ago in the Odonto Ceti region.'

'Well, of course,' said Dewfurth sarcastically. 'Billions of years ago, yes.'

The Doctor gazed at him, his face a mask of innocence. 'You were very lucky, Mr Dewfurth. This whole planet was lucky, in fact.'

Dewfurth didn't look at all convinced. 'Luck didn't come into it, Doctor.'

'I mean it. You may find it hard to comprehend a plant species like the Raab, which travels for hundreds or thousands of years through space. Each of these huge plants - this is a small one, by the way: they can grow as big as five hundred metres long - each of these plants absorbs minute amounts of energy as they travel between planets. They almost invariably make a heavy landing on barren asteroids or small moons, somewhere with small mass and relatively low gravity. The impact spreads their seeds all over the immediate area.' His hands sprang from the warmth of his coat, and he threw them wide, as though scattering rice at a wedding. Now he brought his hands together, clasping them tightly. 'A handful of the many billions of seeds will make it through the rest of the cycle. They grow with dramatic speed, absorbing huge amounts of sustenance in mere months, very much more than they did in space. They're like starving people let loose in a delicatessen: they consume everything and anything. When they're large enough, they explode their small new shoots off the asteroid, out of its low gravity.' His hands sprang apart in an explosion of fingers and thumbs. 'And so they continue to grow over the following hundreds of years in space as the cycle starts again. Searching for the next asteroid.'

'Sounds extraordinary,' said Dewfurth.

'But they're remarkably sensitive to even the weakest gravitational forces. There's no point in getting trapped on a large planet. So what could have brought it into the gravity well of *this* planet?'

'What do you mean, no point?'

The Doctor set his mouth in a grim line. Really, sometimes it was just like teaching the slowest boy in the class. 'Could you throw a rock hard enough from the surface of an asteroid so that it vanished into space?'

'Well, yes.'

'And could you throw it hard enough from one of Drebnar's moons so that it didn't fall back to the ground?'

'Maybe. On the smaller moon, probably.'

'And could you throw it hard enough from here so that it left Drebnar's atmosphere?'

'Of course not... Ah, I see what you mean,' said Dewfurth. 'If the Raab can't throw its seedlings back into space, they just fall on to the planet and die.'

'Worse,' said the Doctor. 'They fall back on to the ground, and start growing at a phenomenal rate. Within months the life cycle is enormously accelerated, and they consume all the resources on the entire planet. Then, unable to escape, they all die out at once.'

'But the planet is rendered barren,' said Dewfurth solemnly. 'I see what you mean about how lucky we've been.'

The Doctor nodded vigorously. 'So, I wonder what drew it here in the first place.'

'What could have brought either of them?' asked Dewfurth.

The Doctor wheeled around, seized Dewfurth by the torn lapels on his lab coat, and shouted at him: 'What?' The snow was beginning to whip around them, and the Doctor's dangerous tone was just audible above the low moan of the quickening wind. 'Raab are rare, unbelievably rare. You wouldn't expect to see more than one every couple of thousand years. Two landing together is unheard of.'

'It arrived at the end of last autumn,' said Dewfurth. 'Sempiter's very excited about this one, of course. Because it's freshly arrived.

'Oh no,' said the Doctor.

'Oh yes,' replied Dewfurth. 'We've got another one. Only this one's still alive.'

Chapter Nine
'The Second Time Around'

They made their way to the far side of the Lake of Ice, where Dewfurth showed the Doctor the second of the creatures.

The Doctor had never seen a live Raab before. He did remember showing an illustration of one to a former travelling companion, several lifetimes ago, and explaining about its unimaginable size. She had dismissively described the creature as 'the Jolly Green Giant's very own sweet corn'. Now he could see that even that underestimated its scale, but her description was still apt.

Recent snowfalls had covered the vast alien creature with a dusting of snow and ice, but there were still vast expanses of brown-green flesh visible. A thick outer layer of hard, grey vegetable matter encased an inner ear of vast pods, which seemed in the failing light of morning to be suffused with a yellow glow.

It covered an area the size of a football field, and was angled up the side of the mountain. He and Dewfurth had skirted around the lake to where the creature had crashed into the mountainside. It had struck the base of a col which linked one stretch of rock to the mountain on which the research station was perched. Here, far below that, Frontier Worlds staff were scurrying around the Raab. Green motorised sledges, the same type that the Doctor and Fitz had seen previously, ferried back and forth, creating a deep furrow in the snow which disappeared around the mountainside.

The edges of the snowstorm now swirled around them, and the Doctor struggled to see what the trailers were carrying. 'We need to get closer.'

Over the next twenty minutes, they scuttled down from their vantage point and approached the Raab crash site. A line of Frontier Worlds staff were co-ordinating the movement of ski trucks, and formed an informal barrier which prevented the

Doctor and Dewfurth from approaching the Raab. Beyond the eddying snowflakes they could hear the whine of power tools.

They reached one of the ski trucks. The Doctor lifted the heavy tarpaulin roped over the back of the trailer, and immediately his nostrils were assaulted by a pungent scent. It was an intense vegetable smell, like a compost heap, like the smell of a whole year's new-mown grass rotting down into fertiliser.

'Oh dear,' he said.

'It does stink, doesn't it?' agreed Dewfurth.

The Doctor scowled at him. They were practically nose to nose. 'Something stinks, Dewfurth. What are they doing?'

Dewfurth blinked innocently, obviously baffled by the Doctor's sudden anger. 'They're removing it from the mountainside.'

'What?'

'See, there.' Dewfurth pointed out two men in splattered green overalls, walking away from some kind of hut or shelter, possibly after a shift break. One was strolling nonchalantly back towards the huge Raab, and munching a piece of fruit. The other was wearing a shoulder harness and a large bag, almost as big as he was, on his back; in front of him, he carried a sputtering mechanical device, with a wide funnel pointing forward. The first man had obviously tired of his snack and tossed the piece of fruit towards his colleague, into the funnel opening. The sputtering device whined into action, and shredded the small piece of fruit.

'We're removing the Raab, piece by piece. We don't have trucks big enough to take it all at once –'

The Doctor could feel the blood suffusing his face. 'You idiots! The Raab must have been so confused when it was pulled to this planet that it wasn't prepared for impact. For that we should be thankful – its huge seed load is still inside that tough outer husk. If your men are slicing into it, they risk exposing the seed pouches. They could scatter them all over this area!' He could see that his outburst had shocked Dewfurth, who was standing silently now. With an effort, the Doctor brought his temper back under control.

The ski truck ground its gears and moved off down the rutted snowy track. This revealed a couple of Frontier Worlds security staff on the far side. The Doctor drew the scientist back and they made their way to the small hut on the periphery of the work zone.

The hut was merely a shell, a five-sided plastic construction dumped on the mountainside to offer some shelter for the workforce to have breaks in poor weather. There was no floor, just cold, hard earth and some hardy plants growing around the edges of the rough furniture and where the workmen's boots had not trampled them.

The sudden absence of the wind inside the hut made the Doctor's ears sing. He shouted louder to compensate, and Dewfurth looked suitably cowed. 'What you're doing here is terribly dangerous. If the Raab explodes its seeds, they could cover this whole area within minutes. Some of them will drift down the mountain, and the cycle will continue. But none of the new plants will be able to spray their seeds out of Drebnar's atmosphere.'

Dewfurth nodded. 'This is a very fertile planet, of course. That's why we came here in the first place.' He wasn't cowed after all, the Doctor saw now - he just wasn't concerned at all. Worryingly, it was as though he were somewhere else, detached from everything that was happening around him. 'We supply seventy per cent of this region's food, you know,' he concluded, as though it were a geography lesson.

'"Breadbasket for the array of nearby planets",' the Doctor said to himself. 'It could wipe out this whole system.' He seized the scientist's shoulders, and shook him until his teeth rattled. 'Come on, man, we have to stop this!'

'Why should I?' said Dewfurth, as cold as the snow outside. 'At least I'll die with the rest of them. You're the one who wants to save me. So save them instead, and leave me here to die.'

The Doctor glared at him, and stamped his feet in a little dance of fury and frustration.

Dewfurth sat down on one of the rough benches. 'Look at these plants growing here,' he said. 'What can you see?'

The Doctor blinked at them. They were scraggy specimens in the mud, with red-veined yellow flowers and seed pods resembling claws. '*Lotus corniculatus*,' he said, 'or very like. Pretty, aren't they? And rather unusual, particularly up here on the mountain, I'd have thought. Sometimes called bird's-claw, because of those unusually shaped pods. Or, because of their colour, bacon-and-eggs plants. Goodness, that reminds me how hungry I am. Aren't you? Perhaps we should try to find something to eat...'

Dewfurth wasn't to be distracted. 'Frontier Worlds Corporation would see them as something to be exploited, pure and simple. We wouldn't ask if they were pretty, or if they had an interesting name. We'd ask if they could become a profitable cash crop. And, since we found the Raab, we'd ask whether we could exploit their DNA. Bird's-claw, that's interesting. How could we use the genetic code for birds' claws in this plant? How can the plant be used to affect animal life?'

The Doctor stared at him, horrified. 'That doesn't make sense. Where's the moral view there? And where's the commercial sense, what's more?'

'We're beyond that,' Dewfurth said sadly. 'We've been beyond that for decades. Just as I'm beyond saving.'

'Rubbish!' snapped the Doctor, exasperated, trying to bite back his angry words. 'Listen –'

'No, you listen to me! I don't have to tell you any of this. I just *need* to. So shut up, and listen.' Dewfurth's sudden rage contrasted starkly with his previous calm. The Doctor studied him. He was right on the verge of cracking again.

'I conducted the first Raab analysis,' continued Dewfurth urgently. 'We were able to change the DNA of some fish. We were pleased when their entire reproductive cycle halved, and each generation lived longer. We couldn't wait to try it out on people. And the people we wanted it for were –'

'– yourselves,' said the Doctor quietly. 'You were desperate, weren't you?'

'We'd spent two decades setting up Frontier Worlds, and then

Reddenblak Corporation appeared. We faced another decade fighting off these new competitors, and we thought we wouldn't live long enough to see our dreams become a reality. It seemed such an obvious thing to do. Use our skills at genetic modification.'

The Doctor screwed up his eyes in puzzlement. 'You were able to survive that fall; your treatment works. I saw the evidence in the remains of your sloughed-off flesh out there in the snow. So why aren't you pleased?'

'Oh, that was fifty years ago,' said Dewfurth in an impatient tone. He looked at the Doctor and smiled as the other's jaw dropped open. 'Oh dear. You hadn't realised.'

'You look no older than forty.'

'Sempiter and I are the oldest. We were over fifty when we sold up and first came to Drebnar. We brought in the others afterwards, bright young things, brilliant researchers just leaving education. We hired them thirty years later to help us continue developing Frontier Worlds. We filled their pockets with gold, gave them a stake in the company - you know, all the usual corporate tricks.' He watched for a reaction. 'I'm a hundred and two, Doctor.'

'You wear it well,' said the Doctor. 'I speak as one who knows.' He indicated Dewfurth's youthful hands, his smooth skin. 'How often?'

Dewfurth turned his hands over, examining them as if he'd only just seen them. 'I've lost count. Many dozens of times.'

'And no one notices?'

'Who really cares? Even Mozarno's wife doesn't know about it. We treat him at HQ once a year when he needs it. She sees he isn't ageing, but doesn't know the whole truth. Besides, over the last thirty years the process has affected his mind. He has no short-term memory these days. His wife keeps herself and the house as it was when he can last remember it. Dyes her grey hair. Serves the same meals. They're both living a lie, though at least he doesn't know that. There's an odd kind of honesty in that, I suppose.'

The Doctor thought about his visit to the Mozarnos, and held back another angry outburst. Instead he said, 'What went wrong?'

'Well, it had worked, hadn't it? All those decades ago, it had worked, just as we knew it would.' Dewfurth's eyes had brightened again at the memory, but faded just as quickly. 'In the excitement of the moment, or the urgency of the threat from Reddenblak, or whatever... we lost our scientific rigour. We were so busy telling ourselves how we could use it that we didn't stop to ask ourselves whether we should. By the time we noticed, it was too late. We saw it first in the experimental fish. They'd mutated over many generations. But each generation happened faster, we'd increased their reproductive cycle - halved it, quartered it, then changed it by an order of magnitude. By the time we worked out what was happening, it was too late for us. We'd had the treatment, and there was no route back.'

'These fish...' said the Doctor.

'In the Lake of Ice,' Dewfurth explained. 'It's an enclosed environment, fortunately. There's nowhere for them to go. Their evolution has accentuated one of their characteristics, and now they're very dangerous little killing machines. Hah!' It was a bitter cough of laughter. 'Biological machines. I've turned us into biological machines, with a tiny flaw. And the tiny flaw gets bigger with each new generation.'

The Doctor softened his voice, talking calmly. 'What flaw?'

'You've seen how we can rejuvenate ourselves, be born again. It can happen every year, and now I've found that it happens if we are fatally injured. It's happened too often,' he shuddered. 'Too often to stay human, certainly.'

'What do you mean?

Dewfurth was shaking now, starting to sob again. 'I know what we had to surrender for our immortality. The Raab element grows stronger with every rebirth that we endure, and it's harmed some mental attributes, different for each person it seems. Self-worth, short-term memory, moral strength...'

'And you?'

'I told you I was the pessimist.' Dewfurth gave him a sad smile.

'From what you've told me about the Raab, Doctor, I've even more reason to be pessimistic. And, as I think I've mentioned, I feel I have no reason to go on.'

'But you've been unable to kill yourself,' said the Doctor calmly. 'You're just putting yourself through unnecessary pain.'

'I'll find a way.' Dewfurth stood up, and stretched as if he had just got out of bed. 'Sempiter's got no compunction about exploiting the Raab, and telling him about the seed pods isn't going to make any difference. It's the only thing making a difference in the corporate fight with Reddenblak, the only thing that gives him an edge with the Darkling crop. Don't look so innocent: you know that, Doctor. You're with Reddenblak – that was the only reason I agreed to talk with you in the first place.'

'Ah, well actually –'

The sounds of the door opening behind him made the Doctor whirl round. Two more Frontier Worlds workers had stepped into the small room, ready for their rest break. The first one tugged his ski mask off to reveal a pale, puckered face with a broken nose dumped untidily in the middle. 'What are you doing in here?' he demanded.

Dewfurth pushed past him, waving his identity card.

'Sorry, sir,' said the worker, and turned to the Doctor. 'What about you?'

The Doctor waved him away. 'Personal assistant to Mr Dewfurth. Excuse me.' He hurried outside, returning his identity card to his jacket pocket and hoping fervently that the worker hadn't read it too closely and seen the lettering at the top: TUFTY CLUB, 1968.

He carefully crossed the roadway cut out by the ski trucks, lowering his head against the wind and snow, which whipped through the air directly in his face. The storm had worsened. He caught up with Dewfurth after twenty metres.

'Come back,' he yelled at the scientist, tugging at his sleeve. Dewfurth's flimsy lab coat flapped wildly in the savagely cold wind.

'What's the point?' snarled Dewfurth. 'You're so worried about it, you deal with it. Leave me to die.'

'Help me stop them.'

'Do it yourself.'

The Doctor refused to admit defeat. He tried to keep his long, wild hair from blowing into his eyes, attempting to maintain eye contact through the blinding gale. He recognised the despair in the other man's eyes; he'd seen it before on the ledge of the research centre, just before Dewfurth had jumped. 'OK, I will do it myself. But I need you to tell me what's bringing the Raab here.'

'How should I know?' snapped Dewfurth, spitting out the snow that blew savagely into as his mouth as he spoke. 'Maybe they love this kind of weather.'

'What's this Darkling crop you mentioned, and where is it?' gabbled the Doctor, clutching at Dewfurth's sleeves again. 'Come on, we need to go somewhere safe to talk.'

Even in the icy wind, Dewfurth's eyes were filling with tears. 'There is nowhere safe for me any more. I won't go the same way as Mozarno. I can't.'

Nearby, two workers were trudging towards the Raab, dark shadows in the white snow. The man carrying the portable shredder had a silhouette like a giant tortoise. The engine of his shredder sputtered into life as he prepared to descend to the work site.

Dewfurth snatched his sleeve away from the Doctor's grasp. 'Good luck, Doctor. And goodbye.' He held out his arm to shake hands.

The Doctor paused to find the right words to change Dewfurth's mind, and then he noticed that Dewfurth had handed him his identity card while they shook hands.

Dewfurth was stumbling across the snow towards the two workers, yelling into the wind. They heard him, and turned. Dewfurth threw himself forward at the man with the shredder.

The Doctor couldn't reach him. Dewfurth had dived into the funnel. The shredder coughed into renewed life. The bag behind the worker pulsed as it started to fill.

The horrified worker belatedly realised what was happening, and killed the motor. It was clearly far too late, and only the ends of Dewfurth's legs fell back out on to the snow, still barefoot. The patch of red blood was soon covered with fresh snow.

The Frontier Worlds staff flew into a commotion. The Doctor almost froze to the spot, appalled at his inability to save Dewfurth. Then common sense prevailed and, still shaken, he hurried off in the opposite direction, away from the Raab work site.

During a brief lull in the storm, he could see the dark, oval shape of the weather-control balloon, its tethering lines wavering in the wind.

Maybe they love this kind of weather.

The Doctor looked at the identity card in his hand. The holographic image grinned at him in a way that Dewfurth never had, an old image of a happy man in middle age.

He slipped the card into his jacket pocket, and continued through the snow.

Chapter Ten
'High Hopes'

'Welcome, Mr Dewfurth,' said the display panel.

'Thank you,' the Doctor said to the text on the screen, and gave it a half-bow. 'I'm very pleased to be here, you stupid insecure system. Oh.' His insult tailed off as the screen displayed a second message.

'Please provide your fingerprint confirmation,' it said.

'It's at times like this,' said the Doctor, rummaging around in his capacious jacket pocket, 'that I thank my good fortune in recovering my sonic screwdriver.' Who'd have thought that the spare would have rolled under the TARDIS console and remained there through two entire lifetimes? Lucky that this incarnation was a little more house-proud than its predecessors, otherwise he'd be without this handy little device now throbbing between his fingers, this security door would not be opening in front of his eyes, and the console room would by now be an inch thick in dust. The TARDIS autocleaning systems missed the nuance of that precise balance that lay somewhere on the spectrum between scrupulous clinical hygiene and slobbish fungal growth, the point that allowed the genteel smell of old dust on leather volumes but didn't permit crumbs to be trodden into the carpet. There was only so much you could trust the time machine to do, and feather-dusting his knick-knacks wasn't one of them.

Just as well, otherwise the sonic screwdriver would now be consigned to the dustbin of history. Instead of which, here he was, stepping out of a freezing snowstorm and into a less freezing cable car.

The journey up proved to be somewhat unnerving. The hawser to which the car was attached rose at about forty-five degrees, but was also swaying violently from side to side in the battering it got from the snowstorm. Fortunately, the Doctor's sense of balance, plus an acknowledgement that there was little he could reasonably do if the car was flung from its mooring on the hawser, meant that he soon calmed down. He concentrated instead on what he was going to do when he got to the weather platform, high above him.

The first thing was to identify what on the weather platform was creating the Tuckson-Jacker interference and drawing the Raab to Drebnar. Secondly, he had to disable it. Thirdly, he had to contact Compassion or Fitz in Frontier Worlds HQ...

The list continued as the cable car maintained its slow and unsteady ascent. Soon he was above the snowstorm, looking out of the iced-up window at the fluffy grey mass of clouds.

Seventhly, he had to work out what the Darkling crop was, and, eighthly, *where* it was...

Outside, he saw the platform approaching and sensed the car slowing to a halt. Just before the platform obscured the view, the Doctor spotted the weather balloon itself looming ominously over the whole area like a smooth, dark thundercloud. The Frontier Worlds Corporation logo dominated the side of it, and a lightweight glider was slung beneath it, presumably for emergency escapes.

Eleventhly, he needed to know more about where the Raab were coming from, and if there may be more of them on the way.

The cable car clanged to a halt as magnetic clamps seized it in a rough embrace against the side of the platform.

Nineteenthly, he needed to get his list in some sort of priority order.

The doors hissed open.

The platform proved to be surprisingly cramped. It was the size of a double-decker bus, but separated into several different interlinked compartments. Racks of busy machinery stretched up above his head to the roof of the building, which could be reached using a set of steps like library ladders, which rolled along the wall on wheels.

There was a deep hum permeating the whole building. It was the sort of noise that humans don't notice until it stops, yet the Doctor could feel it in his bones. The room smelled of oil and static. The hairs on the backs of his hands tingled, and the long brown curls on his head snaked about as though he were in zero gravity. It must make him look like a younger Albert Einstein, he mused. Or possibly Ludwig van Beethoven.

The first section in the tall room contained the human-computer interface for the weather-control system. The various display screens were filled with complex diagrams and detailed textual descriptions. Fortunately, some previous user had patently struggled with the interface, and therefore provided explanations in large writing and crude but clear illustrations, and stuck them on sheets of paper above the display screens.

A smiley sun, a big asterisk-sized snowflake and a bucket of water tipping on its side were helpful indications of the weather conditions above one screen. Above another, a simple map of the area at the base of the mountain showed the positions of the city, the Frontier Worlds HQ, the nearby jungle. There was a black square marked beyond the jungle and next to a meandering line which must indicate a river but, unlike the other landmarks, this did not have any text annotations.

With deft flicks of his wrist, the Doctor switched everything off. There was a corresponding change in the note of the hum, which slowly died away. He pulled the dials off the end of their control sticks, and popped them into his pockets. That would prevent anyone from altering things in a rush, at least until he could find a more permanent way of switching things off.

He stepped through the door beside him into the next compartment. Ah, the communications room. He seized a nearby computer keyboard, flicking his fingers over the alien symbols like a world-class Subbuteo player.

First, he needed to make some adjustments to the Frontier Worlds security firewall. Next, he created a software agent to seek out references to Compassion or Fitz in the corporate computer system. And then a quick e-mail to a departmental secretary at Reddenblak.

Since he was now using the e-mail system, he decided he might as well send Fitz and Compassion a detailed message explaining what he was doing, and how they could help. So he rattled his fingers over the keyboard again, and started with the following text:

SEBZ WNZRF OBJZNA
BOGNVA VASB BA QNEXYVAT PEBC, ENNO, YRIRY GRA

But he didn't have time to complete the message. The door to the next section opened, and the Doctor looked up, startled. 'I'm so sorry,' he began, rising from his seat at the controls. At the same time, he dextrously sent the unfinished message and then disconnected himself from the system with a fleet series of keystrokes behind his back. 'I didn't realise this room was in use...' His words tailed off when he saw who was coming in.

What was coming in, rather. It was tall, it was shiny, it was making a hissing noise. 'You're a robot,' he observed.

'Well done,' said the robot. It had a blank metal head, but the features on its face were surprisingly mobile. Its little metal eyebrows were frowning over its narrow round metal eyes. 'Clever of you to spot I wasn't just a bloke in a suit.'

The Doctor gave the robot a big reassuring grin. 'Well, I get that all the time, of course,' he said. 'But I can see from your exquisite exoskeleton that you're plainly the genuine article, the real McCoy, absolutely it. Bit of a hiss from that servo in your leg, mind you. Shall I have a look at that for you?' He waggled the sonic screwdriver like a magic wand, and gave the metal man an ostentatiously broad wink.

The robot took a thudding step closer, and snatched at the device. The Doctor whisked it away, and then waved his hands at the robot like a bird's wings. The sonic screwdriver had vanished. He danced backwards across the narrow communications room, out of range of the robot, and reached for the handle of the door where he'd entered. It resisted his urgent twisting.

'You're locked in, of course,' said the robot.

The Doctor opened his eyes very wide, and slapped his

forehead. 'Am I? That would explain it.' He couldn't quite place the robot's voice, but it sounded strangely familiar.

'It is my duty to protect Frontier Worlds' assets from Reddenblak Corporation agents.'

The Doctor stood with his arms akimbo, protesting his innocence, and trying to look much more affronted than he had any right to be. The robot's leg continued to make a puttering hiss. It was tapping its foot impatiently on the floor. 'Of course!' said the Doctor suddenly. 'You're the robot that Mr Sempiter built all those years ago. How marvellous!'

The robot's metal eyes widened like two camera shutters. 'Am I?' it said. Then it slapped its hand to its forehead. There was a bit of a clang.

The Doctor grinned even wider, and noticed that the rubber lips around the robot's speech loudspeaker were doing the same. 'Fascinating. I suppose that's to reduce the common fear that people have of robots, the lack of empathy and expression. You're able to imitate people!'

The robot stood facing him, arms akimbo, its face a picture of mechanical amazement. 'Am I?' it said with a wide-eyed grin. It slapped its forehead again with a tinny clank.

'Yes,' said the Doctor. 'But don't overdo it.'

The robot was surprisingly strong, despite its apparently spindly arms and legs. The Doctor found that he was quite unable to break its grasp, and was soon being bundled backwards through the weather platform.

Before it had seized him, he had been unable to reach his sonic screwdriver. The advantage of ripping the lining of all your pockets, he acknowledged, was that it made it easier to load them way past capacity and thus amaze friend and enemy alike by the prodigious quantities of stuff that you could produce in an almost endless series. The disadvantage, of course, was that the vital item would usually drop through the gap and vanish around the back of your jacket.

There was a moment's panic when he thought that the robot was about to drop him off the edge of the platform, after which no doubt it would slap its tinny forehead in amazement and say 'oops'. But that moment passed, and he was soon thrust into the small featureless cabin that had first brought him to the station, and that still hung beside the floating building.

The robot stood, tapping its foot on the metal gangplank that led to the cable car. The Doctor hovered in the doorway, wondering how he could get back on to the platform. 'Mr Sempiter really made an impression on you, didn't he?'

The robot fluttered its metal hands briefly, and suddenly it was holding an identity card. It showed a picture of the robot, smiling, in 3-D. It slotted the card into a reader by the cable-car door, tapped at a control panel with a surprisingly delicate touch, and then stood back as the car door swished shut.

The Doctor pressed his nose against the little window in the door. The car was locked from the outside. The magnetic clamps at the side popped loose, and the car started its lurching descent. The robot gave him a wave, and a broad wink with one shuttered eye.

The car continued its journey down the hawser. The storm seemed to have abated while the Doctor was on the platform, perhaps because of his interference with the control system - he couldn't tell. Why had the robot sent him off the platform, ensuring his escape back to the surface? The Doctor mentally patted himself on the back. Obviously his own cheery demeanour and willingness to assist the robot had rubbed off on the creature in no small way. It was imitating him in more ways than the obvious. Hurrah for being nice, he decided.

As the journey continued, he began to have second thoughts. The cabin's steady descent took fifteen minutes, which gave him plenty of time for further reflection. As it approached its destination on the ground, he finally understood.

The magnetic clamps stuck to the outside of the car with a muffled thump.

The Frontier Worlds guards were waiting for him outside in the snow when the door swished open.

Chapter Eleven
'What's New'

Compassion was famished.

She'd been away from her terminal for nearly an hour, a break enforced by her supervisor, Nilloc Jascot. At this crucial stage, she didn't want to draw unnecessary attention to herself, and so she'd done what Jascot had requested. Not exactly what she'd requested, though. 'Get off to Level Three, Nancy. The rest of your shift are down there already, getting something to eat and drink.'

So Compassion had reluctantly snapped the connection, locked up her terminal, and gone to the canteen. She'd bought just a cup of coffee, and sat at a lonely table in the corner, on her own as usual. She'd sat for forty-five minutes, holding the cup between her hands, as usual. Watching the surface of the liquid film over. Not lifting it up, not inhaling its little cloud of rising steam, not drinking it. As usual.

Compassion was aware of Jascot's eyes following her down the length of the huge Data Hall as she arrived back at her desk before everyone else. But what could Jascot do? Nancy Sinatra was her most productive staff member: she did the work of two normal shift workers. Jascot trod the narrow line between allowing Nancy to work herself to death and missing her data quota - and missing her data quota wasn't going to earn Jascot her company bonus, was it? Besides, tireless Nancy, prettily plump Nancy, didn't look as if she were suffering from malnutrition.

Compassion knew that Jascot thought all this. She'd read her on-line personal journal - it had only medium encryption.

Pora Darg had arrived back now, and leaned across from his terminal at the next desk. 'Slow it down, can't you, Nancy?' he muttered. 'You're making the rest of us look bad.'

Compassion ignored him, and brought up the network connection immediately. The data washed around her, soothing her immediately. If Jascot had still been watching her, she'd have seen the tension in her shoulders melt away.

Compassion was famished. And the back of her mind was parched.

She closed her eyes, not looking at the screen, not watching where her fingers moved across the keyboard, what gestures and pressures she made on the touch-sensitive surface of her monitor.

She slipped straight into the deep end of the datastream, and allowed herself to be swept along by its steady insistence. Waiting for the invitation, as usual. Sometimes it seemed like only a minute, sometimes a millennium; the hands on her watch and the figures on her system clock were out of sight, out of mind, out of the flow of time.

Suddenly, or at last, there was the invitation. She was standing on the shore this time, holding her pale hand out towards Compassion. The sleeve of the woman's dark-blue ball gown fell back as she beckoned. Compassion struck out against the datastream and towards the beach, signalling to the woman. Not drowning, but waving. Safe and welcoming.

The woman pirouetted on the shore, her feet floating above the sandy surface, her tiara sparkling, her smile full of stars. Behind her, a wall of fire bloomed and flared. Compassion smiled at the conventional metaphor.

Then the colours came again. Blues, greens and greys eddied around her, splitting and coalescing and mixing and evolving. They swirled into a hollow tube, which penetrated the flaring brilliance of the flames, and at once she was through to the other side, beyond the corporate network security system.

She planted her feet firmly in the damp sand of the beach, feeling the grains squeeze between her bare toes, the wind tugging gently at her pale-blue dress, tousling her long strands of red hair behind her. She saw that she stood on a round peninsular of sand, small as a cartoon desert island and complete with a solitary looping palm tree. Ahead of her was the sea. In the middle distance, dolphins leapt from the azure water. Above them, clear as daylight, she could see stars circled by planets, planets circled by moons. Beyond were more planets than she could count. Uncharted knowledge, unread information, frontier worlds at the edge of her experience, waiting to be colonised.

She knew she could lift her feet from the sand and rise into the air, that she wouldn't stop until she was spinning around those planets like a new moon. Every instinct in her wanted her to make that first small leap, to loosen her bond with the sand, to fly free.

Instead, she pirouetted briefly on the beach, then stepped back through into the Frontier Worlds data landscape.

QUERY RESULTS
KEYWORDS: FRANK AND SINATRA
USER GRIZ ELLIS IS CURRENTLY ANALYSING WORK PATTERNS FOR USER FRANK SINATRA.
PERSONNEL FILE CONTAINS:
JOB APPLICATION (DATED)
INTERVIEW RESULTS (PASS)
POTENTIAL (LOW, BUT ACCEPTABLE)
DNA ANALYSIS (ON FILE)
CAREER HISTORY: (1) DATA-ENTRY CLERK; (2) APPOINTMENT BY GRIZ ELLIS (DIRECTOR) AS PERSONAL ASSISTANT IN GENE LABS.
WORK PATTERNS: UPDATE CURRENTLY IN PROGRESS, PLEASE WAIT.

QUERY RUNNING
NEW E-MAIL FOR USER NANCY SINATRA OR USER FRANK SINATRA (ENCRYPTED) FROM USER JAMES BOWMAN.
QUERY RUNNING
CROSS-REFERENCE TO USER NANCY SINATRA (SISTER)

Well, thought Compassion, I suppose that's what they mean by a relational database.

QUERY RUNNING

QUERY RESULTS
KEYWORDS: NANCY AND SINATRA
ON-LINE PERSONAL DIARY: NO UPDATES (MEDIUM ENCRYPTION).
USER NILLOC JASCOT IS CURRENTLY ANALYSING WORK PATTERNS FOR USER NANCY SINATRA.
QUERY RUNNING

Compassion dumped the data for 194 Gene Treatment Forms which she'd prepared last night, and immediately overtook her entire shift.

NEW E-MAIL FOR USER NANCY SINATRA AND USER FRANK SINATRA (ENCRYPTED) FROM USER JAMES BOWMAN.
QUERY RUNNING
DISPLAY E-MAIL
SEBZ WNZRF OBJZNA
BOGNVA VASB BA QNEXYVAT PEBC, ENNO, YRIRY GRA

ENDS

Compassion smiled. 'Very amusing, Doctor. A childishly simple Earth-based character encryption.' And thus not anything the Frontier Worlds systems or personnel would recognise.

QUERY RESULTS
KEYWORDS: JAMES AND BOWMAN
CROSS-REFERENCE TO REDDENBLAK PUBLIC DATABASE (PERSONNEL)
NO MATCH FOUND
CROSS-REFERENCE TO REDDENBLAK PUBLIC DATABASE (CUSTOMERS)
NO MATCH FOUND
CROSS-REFERENCE TO DREBNAR PLANETFALL IMMIGRATION RECORDS
NO MATCH FOUND

So what has he been up to? Compassion asked herself.

SAVED E-MAIL FOR USER NANCY SINATRA AND USER FRANK SINATRA (ENCRYPTED) FROM USER JAMES BOWMAN.

Erase, Compassion said.

ERASED
QUERY RUNNING

NEW QUERY
KEYWORDS: DARKLING OR RAAB OR LEVEL TEN
CLEARANCE: OMEGA
QUERY RUNNING

INTERRUPT: FRANK SINATRA
SECURITY VIOLATION. USER FRANK SINATRA (CLEARANCE SIX) IS ATTEMPTING TO LOG IN AS USER GRIZ ELLIS (CLEARANCE OMEGA).

Compassion told the security system not to be so pedantic. 'You need his data card, you sap,' she told Fitz. 'Watch your tail, he's sniffing you out.'

When Fitz came back on line later, she told the system to log him in as a separate session. No point in booting Ellis off his terminal, she thought. Fitz's terminal had no lock-up security, so she set that up while she was there, making the password ALURA and providing him with a suitable prompt. And the choice of lock-up images all looked very dull, so she decided to brighten Fitz's day, thinking of the woman in blue dancing freely on the beach.

QUERY RESULTS
KEYWORDS: DARKLING OR RAAB OR LEVEL TEN
CLEARANCE: OMEGA

Now these results looked more interesting. Compassion

considered the mass of unstructured data swilling in front of her. She stretched her mind wide, and the information coalesced into three shapes, each becoming a door.

QUERY RESULTS
KEYWORD: LEVEL TEN

The door opened at a push, and she entered the room. It was full of scattered papers, a whirlwind of documents which slowly settled on a table in the centre. The papers included building plans for Frontier Worlds HQ and schematics of Level 10. She picked a pencil out of midair, and scribbled 'Nancy Sinatra' and 'Frank Sinatra' on a security access list.

Next she flicked through a pile of documents which were categorised 'Clearance Level 10', decided they were all irrelevant, and dropped them into a waste bin.

The bin's round top squeezed together like a mouth: 'Erased,' it told her.

That was not what she intended: permanently deleting so much information was bound to draw attention. She reached into the bin again, hauled out the papers.

'Retrieved,' said the bin in a sulky tone.

QUERY RESULTS
KEYWORD: DARKLING

The second door was stiff, but a firm push opened it to reveal a small room. Apart from the entrance door, it had completely blank, bare walls. A solitary box in the centre held a folder of photographs showing a field of brilliant yellow corn, and a single sheet showed a list of internal mail points – HQ1 Reception, HQ3 Canteen, DK Darkling Zone, MR Mountain Research, and so on.

The remaining papers were single sheets, all with reference numbers and the legend 'See Raab file'. They included 'Reddenblak', 'Dewfurth' and 'Sempiter'.

She conjured up an image of Fitz's office, and threw a handful of papers at the printer.

Before she left the room, she noticed a picture window in the far wall. For a moment, she thought that she was being watched by a couple of figures, their cold eyes staring through the glass. But when she looked again the curtains were drawn.

QUERY RESULTS
KEYWORD: RAAB

She found that the third door was locked, and wouldn't yield to her shoulder. She took a few steps back, preparing to rush at it, but found her way blocked by an odd figure.

The newcomer had both hands jammed deep in the pockets of his long brown overcoat. The brim of a dark fedora was pulled down over his eyes. 'I wouldn't go in there.'

Compassion thought she recognised the voice. 'Who are you?'

'I'm an agent,' he said in a tart tone. He waved a stethoscope which had appeared around his neck. 'No more clues.'

'Hugely amusing,' sighed Compassion. 'Are you in the system at the moment -?'

He interrupted her before she could say his name, and the fedora moved from side to side. 'No. I'm just here to watch the watchers. Can't be too specific, their security scans are based on keyword identification. No names, no packdrill.'

He pulled one hand out of his pocket, and sprayed a pack of cards in her direction. Compassion surprised herself by catching them all. The cover was overprinted with words like 'longitude and latitude', 'profit and loss'.

'I can't get these physical files past the firewall,' he explained to her. 'You need to get them to the Evil Empire.'

She studied the pack of cards in her hand. Somehow, they were in a little package with a bow on top. 'How?'

'E-mail follows with full instructions,' he replied, sounding as though he were reading off a card. 'Please ensure tha-'

She frowned at him.

'Please ensure tha-' he repeated, stopping in exactly the same place. 'Hmm,' he concluded. 'Carrier lost.'

'You're a big help,' she grumbled. She decided that she was going to see what was behind the third door, the one marked 'Raab'. The one behind the agent. She motioned him aside with her hand. 'Get out of the way.'

'Don't say I didn't warn you,' he grumbled. He turned sideways and vanished, like a cardboard cutout rotated through ninety degrees. Compassion took a run at the door, and the jamb splintered. On the third blow the frame broke away. Then she pushed the door, which tumbled off into blackness, a dark pit with no discernible bottom.

Compassion grabbed desperately at the broken frame, the splinters biting into her palms as she struggled to stay away from the chasm. Obviously, the Raab data was all in a disconnected system, completely separated from the main Frontier Worlds systems. The pitch-blackness told her that even the backups had been erased. And this remaining reference wasn't even a stub: it was new, deliberately constructed as a security trap. Behind her, the gurgling growl of an angry dog could be heard. Compassion turned slowly, fighting the urge to run.

It was a brutal, long-nosed creature. Its mouth hung open, the nose wrinkled, saliva dripping in thick strings from its yellow teeth. The dog wasn't looking directly at her, but was sniffing the air. Scenting its prey.

It started to turn. Compassion faced away from it. Heard its guttural snarl again. Heard its claws skitter on the ground as it began its run. Pounding behind her. Too fast to outrun. Don't run. Nowhere to run.

Mustn't think of...

No! Must think, must think, must think, must think...

The dog's hot, rank breath was at her neck.

Must think, must think of...

Compassion picked out thirty-seven more Gene Treatment

Forms from those she'd prepared the previous night, and dumped them straight into the database.

Slow it down, can't you, Nancy? You're making the rest of us look bad.

A huge dark shape snarled past Compassion in a cloud of hair and spittle, and vanished into nowhere.

Then she felt a hand clamp on her shoulder.

'Nancy? Nancy?'

Jascot was shaking her shoulder. Compassion jolted upright.

'Oh, Nancy, I thought you were asleep for a moment,' said Jascot. She giggled. 'That would be most unlike you, I know. Then I noticed that you were still typing.'

Compassion looked at her but said nothing.

Jascot cleared her throat, nervously. 'You're well ahead on your data transcriptions,' she said, 'and I was going to suggest you have a break anyway. But as it happens there are a couple of visitors in reception who have asked for you to be their chaperone until their official meeting begins.'

Compassion didn't move. 'Why me?'

'Why not?' said Jascot. 'You know how the company likes to share privileges with our best employees. This is a chance for some face time with our clients. They're waiting for you in Reception Room Three.' She smiled encouragingly. 'It's an honour, Nancy, really.'

Compassion logged out, feeling the familiar sense of disconnection and loss. She stood, blinking her eyes to adjust to the levels of light in the long Data Hall. A drawer slid out of her computer terminal, revealing a data cartridge.

Beside her, Pora Darg was slapping the top of his computer screen with the flat of his broad hand. 'This damn thing's crashed,' he moaned.

Compassion reached the door at the far end of the hall just as the mail-delivery trolley arrived. It was pushed by Stinricz Lowfer.

'Hello, Stinricz.'

'Hello, er...' Lowfer scrunched up her face into a frightening shape as she struggled to remember.

'Nancy. Nancy Sinatra.'

'Sinatra, unusual name. Can't think of any mail I've delivered for you. Met a Frank Sinatra in the canteen a couple of times. Mail Point HQL.'

The two women talked for a few minutes until their conversation was interrupted by a commotion at the other end of the Data Hall. Pora Darg had been hauled out of his seat by two security guards, and security chief Kupteyn was staring straight into his face from close range.

'I don't know what you're talking about,' Darg was babbling, his voice high-pitched, incredulous. 'How could I be creating an access violation? My system's frozen.'

'Tell that to our systems security team,' barked Kupteyn.

Compassion slipped out into the corridor, heading for the lift.

They were waiting for her in Reception Room 3, as promised. It was one of several small but comfortable rooms on the HQ's lowest floor, near to the main entrance. Compassion knew they were used as waiting areas for visitors, and remembered sitting quietly there herself several months ago just before her job interview.

She hadn't expected to be a chaperone for visitors - she was, by her own arrangement, a lowly data-entry employee. Meeting two strangers, so shortly after her close escape from the database security trap, seemed too much of a coincidence. Both visitors stood when she entered the room.

'You kept us waiting long enough,' grumbled the man. The lines in his long, narrow face suggested that scowling was its natural expression, his default demeanour. He flexed his fingers, as though he expected to be doing something with them, but couldn't remember what.

The woman, in contrast, stood quietly by his side. 'Ms Sinatra has been kind enough to agree to look after us until our meeting begins.' She was short and plump, and she spoke in a surprisingly high-pitched voice. Like her colleague, she was wearing a grey linen suit. She had piled her dark hair high on her head in a vain attempt to look taller. Compassion's thoughts were interrupted by the man again. 'Half an hour we've been stuck here. If I'd known, we could have arrived thirty minutes later. Time is of the essence.' He raised a hand to his head in a self-conscious gesture. Compassion studied his hairline. Surely that wasn't a wig?

'Frontier Worlds is such a busy place,' said the woman. 'It's very kind of Ms Sinatra to see us at such short notice.'

The man snorted, flexed his hands again, looked around, and then sat down. He smoothed his dark hair, but the unruly strands continued to stick out at odd angles. 'Do you have the package, Ms Sinatra?'

Compassion fingered the data cartridge hidden in her pocket. 'Package?'

'Dr Bowman said we should contact you,' said the woman.

Compassion didn't react to the Doctor's alias.

'Oh come on,' said the woman, whispering so that her squeaky voice didn't carry too far. 'The "Darkling" crop. We were promised positional information and business projections.'

Compassion returned her cool gaze directly now, refusing to react. 'The company has to depend on the confidentiality of its staff. You people could be auditors, come to test me out. And I am only a data-entry clerk. Level Three clearance.' Now she leaned in, crowding the woman. 'Perhaps you could show me some identification.'

The woman passed her a business card.

'Thank you,' said Compassion. Satisfied with what she saw, she handed over the data cartridge. 'The company depends on all its staff to be vigilant.'

'Strangely inappropriate under the circumstances,' said the man. 'We can see ourselves out, Ms Sinatra.'

Compassion sat alone for a few minutes, allowing them time to exit the building. When she left the room, she saw Direk Merdock. He was at the security post, a gloomy cabin sited next to main reception. Compassion saw his face light up the depressing little place when she went past. 'Hi, Nancy!' he called. 'Are your visitors OK?'

'I think they just left,' she replied.

Merdock looked like a puppy to whom she'd offered a biscuit. 'Let's see.' His cheerful face clouded over as he scanned his computer screen. The only names I can see here are... What company were your visitors from?'

Compassion gave him a big, stupid smile. 'Oh, sorry, Direk. I can be so slow. If they're Frontier Worlds staff they don't need to get special access, do they?'

'That's right,' said Merdock.

'They were from the research station,' lied Compassion.

Merdock laughed, and tapped his computer screen. 'You had me worried for a second there. I mean, you'd hardly be meeting *these* guys, they're executives from Reddenblak. The Evil Empire,' he added conspiratorially. 'Our big rivals. Only Sempiter and the board are allowed to talk with them. They obviously think they can turn up any time they like.'

He kept her talking for a few more minutes, obviously unable to find the words or pluck up the courage to ask her to have lunch with him some time. In the end, Compassion made her excuses and walked off.

In the privacy of the lift, she removed the plump woman's business card from her pocket:

Jiulyan Larruge. Senior Vice President, Reddenblak Corporation. Compassion tore it up. It was strangely inappropriate to hang on to it, under the circumstances.

Chapter Twelve
'There Are Such Things'

The warning came as a bit of a shock. It flashed up on the computer screen, in so bright a red that it seemed to illuminate the whole of the small room. I thought about this for a few seconds, and decided it would look more suspicious if I was caught working in the dark, rather than red-handed (or rather red-screened) trying to read someone else's data files. I flicked on the desk lamp - that would be OK.

The warning was timing out, a little stopwatch shape in the corner counting down to zero. The warning said:

YOU NEED HIS DATA CARD, YOU SAP. WATCH YOUR TAIL, HE'S SNIFFING YOU OUT.

You'll recall that I've learned the rudiments of pickpocketing, on the strict understanding, of course, that it was entirely 'theoretical' and 'for information purposes only'. The easy part is to distract the mark with a touch or nudge somewhere else, while you're actually removing the item of value. The difficult part on this occasion was the prospect of touching or nudging Smelly Ellis; with no bargepoles to hand, I was going to have to steel myself to steal.

I went into his office holding my breath, and not through nerves. I'd whipped the item before you could say raspberry tart, though not before receiving a lecture on what a significant error it was to interrupt him for trivial reasons, and 'not to make the mistake of overfamiliarity, Frank'.

Back at my computer, I logged in as Ellis. The screen asked me:

LOG IN AS SEPARATE SESSION? YES NO CANCEL

I didn't get a chance to answer. The selection pointer thing scooted across the screen as I watched and indicated 'Yes'.

The next thing I noticed was his in-basket and calendar. Then, without my doing a thing, the printer sprang into noisy life in the corner of the office. I closed the office door, and squeezed past my desk to check what was coming off the printer.

There were nearly forty assorted sheets about a project called 'Darkling' and, to my further astonishment, a schematic diagram of Frontier Worlds HQ Level 10. It was like finding that a pile of ten-bob notes had been posted through my front door. I scooped them up, stuffed them in an envelope, and dropped it on the desk.

I was about to slip back around the desk and into my seat, to see whatever else was happening on Ellis's user ID, when I nearly slammed my face into the back of the door.

Ellis barged right in as if he owned the place. Well, I suppose he did, really. With one hand he was holding a box full of glass containers, obviously another pile of poo for me. With the other hand he was exploring the inside of his left nostril. Satisfied with the exercise, he briefly examined the results of his excavation, and saw that it was good; so he lovingly scraped it off his fat forefinger and on to the edge of the box, and set the box down on my desk.

When he looked up, he found me standing behind him, apparently trying to close the door with my nose. 'Ah, Mr Sinatra...'

I knew I was in trouble, because he only used my surname when he wanted to be sarcastic. I made a big deal out of tugging off my lab coat and hanging it on the hook behind the door. 'Hi boss. Just off...' Just off where? Damn, he was going to detain me, and I hadn't got a plausible excuse to escape.

And the phone bleeped. I stared around in panic for a moment, before I remembered I was wearing the headset.

'Hey Frank, you won't believe –'

'Hannawwww!' I yelled into the speaker. 'Suuuure, don't have a hissy fit, I'm on my way up with that report *right now*.' I could hear her little squawk of indignation just as I cut the line. I showed Ellis the unusual and possibly somewhat frightening sight of me smiling. 'They're gunning for me up on Eight. Gotta get this to the Chairman's office, or I'm toast.' I snatched up the envelope from beneath Ellis's nose, and turned to leave.

'Mr Sinatra!' bellowed Ellis. I could hear a spray of spittle pattering down on my desk like acid rain. 'Wait just a moment,' he added in his quieter, more studiedly menacing tone.

I turned reluctantly.

Ellis was investigating his other nostril now, perhaps in search of a personal best. With any luck, he'd pull out his digit and find his brain impaled on the end. 'I happen to know for certain that Mr Sempiter is extremely busy, and won't want to be disturbed just at the moment.' He was enjoying it, the crumb. 'But, I imagine that you'll want to see the delightful Ms Applin as soon as you can. So you can run along...'

I was almost through the door when he gobbed on my desk again.

'Wait just a moment, Mr Sinatra. You can run along after you've explained *this*.' He was pointing at my desk. At a glance I took in: my flask of coffee, freshly made that morning in the debris of the apartment kitchen; the box of glass-encased faeces; and - oh God, the computer screen. I wondered whether to pick up the desk lamp and plug him with it now. How could I explain the sight of his personal files displayed on my computer screen?

'You know about the company's clean-desk policy, Mr Sinatra,' he said, staring at me with a baleful eye. Well, *the* baleful eye to be exact. 'It's a thoughtless error - you should know better by now. Get this stuff tidied away before you leave. Nor can I approve of your screen-lock image.'

I staggered around the desk in disbelief. Ellis's pudgy finger was quivering with indignation at the screen. There, revolving slowly about its axis against a grid-pattern background of question marks, was a line drawing of the TARDIS.

'Nonstandard images are a virus risk - you should know that.

This is a careless lapse in security procedure – even junior staff know that. Get it changed to a company-approved image before you leave this room.' And, with that, he stalked out in a cloud of fetid air.

At this point, I picked up the heavy desk lamp from the lab table, chased after Ellis in his office and struck him three sharp blows to the back of his head in swift succession, until he lay dead on the floor in a pool of his own blood and brains.

Well, of course, I didn't. But I should have. Instead, I sucked air through my gritted teeth, tidied my desk, switched off the computer screen, and hurried through the door and out to the lift, pausing only briefly in the corridor to kick myself for my cowardice.

On the way out, I passed Kupteyn. I tried not to meet his eye, but I could feel his machine-gun glare raking my back as I called for the lift. I did chance a look at him when the lift door pinged open, and on second thoughts he did look as if he'd put on weight. I decided now was not the time to draw this to his attention.

My spirits lifted at the prospect of getting out of my tiny office, searching Level 10, trying to find out what had happened. After months of hunting down boring data, this was like a breath of fresh air.

I looked at the destination selectors. Levels 1 through 9 were simple press-buttons, but 10 required an identity card to be slotted in beside it. I was fumbling in my pocket for Ellis's card, when I saw Ellis himself half running, half waddling towards the lift, tugging the underpants from the crack in his backside with one hand. I turned away and looked through the glass back of the lift and up the broad well that ran the height of the headquarters.

Unfortunately, Ellis reached the transparent doors before they closed, and was able to squeeze his noxious bulk through. I thought about faecal smears under glass, and knew I couldn't hold my breath for more than three floors. So much for a breath of fresh air. I took my mind off the smell by concentrating on the lifts on the other three sides of the large well, making up stories for the occupants I could see in them.

We stopped only at Level 6, marketing. Brab Tonquis saw Ellis, and made some excuse about waiting for her colleagues to join her in the next lift along. So we carried on, we happy two, to Level 8.

'This is your stop,' said Ellis. I looked blank. 'The Chairman's office? The delightful Ms Applin?' I squeezed past carefully. 'My stop too,' he said after a moment, and followed me out.

Hannaw's office was an antechamber in front of Temm Sempiter's main office, like an airlock in which people were prepared for their meeting with the Chairman. With every step I took down the corridor, I worried more about what I was going to say to Hannaw when I saw her. Ellis was behind me, and he'd expect me to hand over the envelope. Hannaw would open it, find the Darkling documents and the floor plans for Level 10, and that'd cause an even bigger stink than Ellis.

We arrived. Hannaw didn't look pleased with me – I'd cut her dead on the phone, and there was no worse crime among gossips. I didn't get chance to speak the feeble excuse that was forming on my lips. Ellis had decided to pull rank and go first, the ponce.

'Hannaw, in my morning meeting with Temm, did I leave my security card here?'

Hannaw shook her head firmly from side to side. I was intrigued to see that her coiffure didn't move, as though she were wearing a helmet of blonde hair. I hadn't noticed that before. 'No, Mr Ellis.'

While they were talking, I lounged against the door jamb to Sempiter's office. The door was open, and I could see an expanse of thick, expensive floor covering, a curved desk as big as the Oval, panelled walls on which a handful of large photographs were grouped in frames. From the way they shimmered, I guessed they were 3-D images.

Hannaw seemed to be blowing her nose. 'Shall I advise security for you, Mr Ellis? They can cancel your old identity card and organise a new one.'

Ellis coughed up some phlegm, thought about her suggestion,

or perhaps what he was going to do with the phlegm, and then said through the mouthful, 'No, it's such a nuisance being disconnected while they authorise and master another one. I'll keep hunting for a while.' He wafted out. At least he didn't spit on the floor.

Hannaw spritzed herself with perfume. Then she sprayed her desk, too. The mechanical bird on her desk chirruped in its cage. 'Where's this report, then?' Hannaw asked me brusquely.

Along the corridor, I could see that the indicator showed a lift approaching this level. 'Sorry, babe,' I said, clutching the envelope to my chest. 'I've got a few more pages to ink first. I'll drop you a dime later.'

I reached the call button just in time to stop the lift passing Level 8 on the way up. I was pushing my way in when I found it was still occupied. The other person stood awkwardly in the corner, facing away from the glass back wall as though hiding. It was a shock when I saw it was Temm Sempiter.

I'd seen him at our Frontier Worlds All-Employee Meeting only a week before, rallying the crowd about our vision and mission and why we were unlikely to get any bonus pay this year. And I'd seen him on the mountain earlier this week, hunting for the Doctor. But close up, here in the harsh overhead light of the lift, he was almost unrecognisable. What identified him was the way he was tapping his foot imperiously on the floor, irritated by my interruption.

I don't know if I told you that I recently saw pictures of Marlon Brando at the end of his career. I couldn't believe it was the same guy from *On the Waterfront*, which I saw in 1961 from the back row of the Roxy, Hammersmith, with my main squeeze, Mary. Well, it was that kind of change in Temm Sempiter, but it was almost overnight, not over almost forty years. Sempiter was fatter, greyer, exhausted. His clothes looked too tight, and his skin looked too loose.

'What do you want?' he asked, and his voice was a croak.

I fumbled with an apology, saying the first thing that came to mind. 'I was delivering this printed report to your office, sir.' I tapped the envelope.

Sempiter held out a hand, on which the fingers looked like five grey slugs. I knew I couldn't hand him the envelope. Even in his condition, he could work out I shouldn't have a schematic of Level 10.

So I shook his hand firmly. 'Pleased to meet you at last, sir. I'm Frank Sinatra, PA to Griz Ellis.' The skin on his hand puckered in my grip. It was as if he were wearing cold grey gloves.

'Pleased to meet you,' he lied. 'This lift is going to Level Ten, so you'll need to take another.'

'I'll ensure this report's delivered to your office, sir,' I said.

Stupid, Fitz! You're obviously trying to leave Level 8, which is where his office is.

Nevertheless, I stepped back out on to the landing. Sempiter mumbled his thanks, and suggested that I could save time by e-mailing it to his secretary.

I met his bloodshot gaze as the doors started to close. 'Excellent idea, sir,' I crawled desperately. 'The e-mail of the species is more deadly than the mail. Ha-ha.'

The second that the lift doors shut, I legged it for the emergency stairs.

I reached Level 10, wheezing and blowing like some kind of beached sea mammal. Maybe I'd start using the TARDIS gymnasium again. After all, one day soon I'd be thirty and, face it, that's when the rot sets in.

I checked out the security door across the stairs. There was a number-code keypad and a slot for security cards. I tried the slot, and the door eased open.

I was confused for a moment by the lighting, which was unlike any other Level I'd been on, more diffuse, spilling softly from wall-mounted brackets. Ah, walls, that was the difference - all the other levels had open balconies which looked out into the well of the building, but this was closed off on all sides.

The lift further along chimed its arrival, and nobody got out. And then I saw Sempiter was leaning on the side, heaving great whoops of breath as though the effort were too much for him. Before he had a chance to see me, I crept across the corridor and through the first door. And did a double-take.

I slid the floor plan out of the envelope, and checked - the dimensions were right, though there was no other indication of purpose. It was Sempiter's office again.

Or at least, it was designed and laid out just like Sempiter's office on Level 8. The same huge desk, the jungle of carpet, the panelled walls. The framed 3-D photographs, a man and a woman posing awkwardly at some kind of outdoor event, seemed familiar too. They were spotlit, over a fancy table full of real flowers. Compared with the rest of the room, it looked like an altar. And then I twigged. They looked like Sempiter, so they were probably his parents.

In the opposite corner of the room were a toilet and shower room, each as big as my entire apartment. To either side was a tall, slatted wardrobe in rich dark wood, full of Sempiter's business clothes. No casual stuff - did the guy never rest? These suits, all grey, wouldn't fit him now, though - he should send them all to Oxfam.

It was while examining the clothes that I heard the main door opening. My gut lurched in panic and I looked wildly around the room. Like a bare-arsed lover in a French farce, I hopped into the wardrobe, pulled it shut from inside and peered out through the slats. My heart sank when I spotted the envelope of printouts on the corner of the desk where I'd dropped them in my haste.

Sempiter staggered into the room, looking anything other than an irate husband. He was awkwardly tugging his trousers off, and kicking his shoes away. He tapped his foot impatiently on the posh rug while he struggled with the buttons on his jacket, which stretched grotesquely across his flabby gut. I was uncomfortably aware that I was at a peepshow for uglies, but unable to make my excuses and leave.

Sempiter was naked now, apart from his shirt. He dropped on to the chair at the desk, dragged open a drawer, took out a bottle of ink. Odd time to write a memo, I thought. Odder still, he drank down the entire contents, some of which slopped down the sides of his face. Not ink, then. He slumped across the desk, arms outstretched.

As good a time as any to make my miraculous escape, I decided. That was before Sempiter tried to stand, and then fell awkwardly between the desk and my wardrobe. He raised his head, and started to moan.

It was a low keening sound, like the noise you hear at funerals when people are trying not to cry and embarrass themselves in front of friends and relatives they've not seen for years. It grew into an uncontrollable sob, then a howl, a kind of baying disbelief that shook Sempiter's ghastly grey jowls.

Now the sound became more guttural. His hunched form lolled to one side and fell across the rucked-up cotton rug, the grey arm falling into a spotlight glare, neon-bright now in the darkened room. I remembered, from that wet-fish handshake in the lift, the puckered folds of skin on his hand, but I hadn't noticed the veins standing out so much. In the harsh spotlight, I could see the thick veins... pulsing.

And then with a groan, as if he were stretching before reluctantly getting out of bed on a Monday morning, Sempiter tensed all his fat limbs and released them again. He knelt up, his whole body now looking like the skin of an abandoned milk drink. I couldn't suppress a tiny cry of shock: he was sitting, staring directly at me.

I fought down the urge to kick the slats out and scramble past him to the door. Had Sempiter locked it? Could I reach the handle before Sempiter reached me? The blood thudded in my head, and my chest ached with the hollow pounding. I couldn't breathe – until I realised that I just wasn't trying to. I took in a tiny gasp, and exhaled what I hoped would be a silent breath but which sounded to my sharpened senses like a rasp on metal.

He wasn't staring at me. He was facing me, but his eyes were fast closed. The moaning was subsiding, and the lips were sealed. He tugged at the front of his shirt. He didn't try to unfasten it, and the pearlescent buttons tore and spun off into the room, one pinging against the slatted wardrobe door and making me jump. In a slow movement, Sempiter shrugged his shoulders, and the shirt fell in an untidy heap behind him.

I could see the creased, grey-mottled skin of Sempiter's hairless chest. He moved his knobbly fingers across the flaccid pectorals, as though caressing them in a ritual gesture. The fingers met at the breastbone, and pressed. And pressed. With the sound of a plaster being stripped from flesh, the skin split open.

The fingers peeled back a deep layer of fleshy material, as though pulling back another, inner shirt. The arms drew back over the nipples and across the front of the shoulders, and then Sempiter arched his back and shucked off the folds.

I swallowed hard, tasting the blood where I'd bitten the inside of my cheek.

Sempiter had hunkered back now. I couldn't tear my eyes away from the sight, even though I could feel the bile rising, hot and sharp at the back of my throat. Beneath Sempiter's torn skin was an angry-looking red surface, puckered as though it had been in the bath too long. Or the skin under a blister if you can't resist the temptation to burst it. That was it. It was new, a second skin.

He wasn't making any sounds now. He shook off the right arm, and reached over with the newly uncovered limb to scrape the old skin from the left arm, as casual as though he were stripping wallpaper. Shreds of skin dropped to the expensive floor covering, where they curled and discoloured.

With both arms free, the new hands could reach up to touch the face. It was as though a young man had reached from behind Sempiter and placed his hands over the tired, old-man's eyes. And then pushed, hard.

This was the point where I was copiously sick in the back of the wardrobe. Before I could turn away, the hands had casually pushed back the face from beneath the chin, and it slipped over the top of Sempiter's head like a pantomime mask. There was a sticky squelching noise. Beneath was the raw red image of another person's face, the new eyelids still closed, but the stranger's fuller lips breaking into a smirk – a grimace? And now opening to reveal even white teeth where previously there had been stained yellow tombstones.

The headpiece rolled down the creature's back. Gravity took a hold of the weight and it dropped to the carpet with a wet smack. The new skull had a full head of short, wet, glistening hair. It even had the same side parting as before.

I was shaking, and biting the inside of my cheek to stop myself from yelling. I could literally feel the hairs on my own skin prickling. The first of Sempiter's new red flesh was turning a translucent white now, like it was healing before my widening eyes.

The arms returned to his haunches, which were still covered in Sempiter's old, baggy grey skin. The fleshy suit he was now discarding.

The creature slid forward until it lay palms down on the rug, and started to lever itself to an all-fours position. Within another few minutes, he had stripped off the legs like a ghastly pair of trousers, complete with socks.

Sempiter lay for a few minutes amid the cleaved remnants of his former body. Finally, and not a moment too soon for me, he got up, a piebald mass of wrinkled new red and white flesh.

I braced myself as he hesitated in front of the wardrobe. Instead of opening the doors and finding me cowering in there, however, he moved, surprisingly agile, to the bathroom. Shortly, I could hear the hiss of the shower starting.

I knew I had to get out and get away. I pushed open the slatted door, willing my leaden legs out from the cramped confines of the wardrobe. I made the mistake of looking too closely at the curled remnants of Sempiter's grey flesh as it dried on the carpet, and had to turn and throw up again into the wardrobe. I wiped my face on the sleeve of an expensive jacket, quietly apologised to

Oxfam, and staggered out through the main office door.

I was congratulating myself on this fearless escape when I walked straight into Ellis in the corridor. I almost knocked him down.

'Mr Sinatra.'

'Oh, er, hi.' He was waiting for me to say something else. So was I. Nothing came.

'I'm here looking for my missing authority card,' said Ellis. 'What are you doing here?'

I had one of those what-the-hell-am-I-doing panics, the sort that involve worst-case scenarios, like weighing up the girl who's chatting to you at the dance and concluding that she could be an axe murderer.

What did I know? I was in an unauthorised area; I'd just come out of a room where a man had peeled himself like a banana; I'd left an envelope on his desk full of sensitive printouts; I had Ellis's missing authority card in my pocket; I probably had bits of grey skin on the soles of my shoes; I smelled of vomit. Well, at least Ellis wouldn't notice the last one.

Wait a minute, I had his authority pass in my pocket.

I stooped down, and made a big thing about picking something off the floor. 'Is this your authority pass, Mr Ellis? I think it dropped out of one of your pockets when we collided just now.'

He considered the possibility, then pocketed the card. 'Thank you, Mr Sinatra, how serendipitous. This is a restricted-access area. I was able to key in a security code to get to Level Ten, but perhaps *you* are making a mega, mega mistake.' He breathed a rancid breath down his nose. 'How did you get here?'

'Came up with Mr Sempiter, sir.' Brilliant!

'And where is he now?' Oh bugger!

'He was having a bit of a turn in the lift when I met him by his office on Eight. I showed him into a room down the corridor and left him… er… to it.' What, and I didn't call for first aid? Didn't stay with him? Didn't even get him a glass of water? Worst-case scenario: kick Ellis in the goolies and have it away on my toes before he uncrossed his eyes.

'Thank you, Mr Sinatra.' Ellis allowed himself the pleasure of a hacking cough. 'Perhaps we can review what significant progress you've made with the faecal analysis later today.'

'I may need a little more time,' I mumbled. 'I'm a little behind.'

'That's what I meant,' said Ellis tartly. 'Carrot, carrot.'

I looked blank.

'You say carrot, and I say carrot,' said Ellis.

I peered at him through narrowed eyes. If you looked closely, you'd have seen a light bulb appear just above my head. 'You say potato, and I say potahto,' I corrected him.

'Same difference,' said Ellis, knowingly tapping the side of his pustular nose.

At this point, his phone communicator bleeped. I couldn't hear the other side of the conversation, but it seemed to agitate him. He shut off the connection, looked directly at me, and said, 'Where is Mr Sempiter now?'

'Shouldn't really be disturbed,' I croaked, with my back to Sempiter's office.

Unfortunately, at precisely this moment, the door swung open. I restrained my shriek of surprise. Sempiter stood in the doorway to his office in a bathrobe, barefoot and pale, looking just as if he'd stepped out of the shower. He towelled at his hair. 'I heard the phone, Griz,' he said to Ellis. 'You'd better come in.'

Ellis looked at me. 'I'll speak with you later, Frank.' I realised he expected me to go to the lift, which was waiting. I stepped in, and allowed the doors almost to close, and then thumbed the open button again.

I caught the end of their conversation as they went into Sempiter's office.

Ellis was saying, 'You look like you've benefited from your convalescence.'

'Our natural health treatments are a tremendous tonic to one's system,' replied Sempiter, his nasal voice clear and distinct.

'So, you're feeling better?'

Sempiter laughed heartily. 'Like a new man.'

Chapter Thirteen
'Softly, As I Leave You'

After the close encounter with Sempiter, I'd gone straight to Level 4 to see Compassion. To my surprise and dismay, she wasn't there – her phone headset was lying by her screen-locked computer. As I arrived, the guy at the desk next to hers was being manhandled from the room, semiconscious, by Kupteyn and two of his hounds. I stayed well clear so that they didn't break me as well as all the other things they overturned when they dragged the poor schmuck across the floor by his heels. Kupteyn was threatening to break his neck, of course.

I wanted to grab Compassion's shift supervisor by the neck too and give her a damn good shaking when she refused to tell me where Nancy had gone. I didn't because (a) the ugly woman had no neck inside the collar of her plain yellow top and (b) I wanted to leave a message. I told the supervisor that our father was dangerously ill, and needed to see the doctor right away. Then I hared off for the lift again, and raced back to the lab, to destroy any incriminating evidence. So long as I left only faecal-analysis reports, nothing could drop me in the shit.

My computer was still connected to Ellis's user ID, but the TARDIS image was twirling on my screen lock. I tried my usual password, but a message popped up on the screen immediately:

SHE'S NO MOLL:

Alura. I was back on line.

I did the drag-and-drop thing that Compassion had explained to me, ensuring that all my local files were scrubbed cleaner than a nun's knickers. That done, I had a quick gander at Ellis's user ID again. He'd got a private note in his calendar, which he must have added earlier that day, reminding himself that Sempiter had a meeting booked this afternoon with representatives of the

Reddenblak Corporation. Interesting stuff, since even I knew these guys were the opposition, definitely the Men in Black Hats as far as Frontier Worlds Corporation were concerned.

As I pondered the significance of this, I heard my phone bleeping. I picked the mobile headset off my desk where I'd abandoned it earlier, and said, 'Compassion.' I could have kicked myself. In fact, I may well have done.

'Love and sympathy yourself, you ignorant rat,' replied Hannaw. A pause. 'Did you just use a rude word?'

'Banged my buns on the chair, babe,' I winced. 'Is this a quickie? I'm snowed.'

This was not what Hannaw wanted to hear. Clearly she'd been expecting a grovelling apology for my terrible rudeness earlier in the day, the full Sorry Sundae, with whipped cream and a cherry on top.

'Well, hey, I only called to say Sempiter's dragging me away for a while,' said the ice queen in a dangerously brittle tone. 'I'd send you a message, if I thought it might filter to the top of your *busy* in-tray.'

'Sorry, hon – things to see and people to do. Y'know how it is.'

'Sure.' Businesslike voice. Boy, was I in trouble. 'I've been trying to catch Griz Ellis. If you see him, please ask him to contact me about deputising for the Chairman at a meeting this afternoon while he's away. Thank you *so* much, Mr Sinatra.'

'The Reddenblak meeting?' Damn. I considered biting my tongue off.

'Ye-es. How would you know about that, Frank?'

'Lucky guess.' Conversational gear change. 'So, you're going away for a while, huh?'

'Mm-hnn. I can tell you're not interested.'

I was closing down Ellis's user ID while she spoke, and I made a noise to suggest that her supposition was spot on and that perhaps she'd like to hang up and leave me in peace now. Well, that was the gist of the noise, anyway.

'Yes, I'm the bag carrier on the trip once again for that heartless git Sempiter. He's tracked down a guy he wants to talk to about some DNA work. Odd name, though: Dr James Bowman.'

I almost fell off my chair and really bruised my buns. 'Hey, Hannaw... er... that *does* sound interesting, can you tell me -'

Hannaw could tell at once that I had my undies round my ankles, and swiftly kicked me in the keister. 'Gotta go, hon. Things to see, et cetera, et cetera. Y'know how it is. Whoops, the Chairman's just coming down the corridor.'

The line went dead. The phone headset bleeped again immediately. It was Compassion, using her especially stern voice.

'What have you been doing hogging your phone line? We have to meet. Now.'

The canteen was nearly deserted as the working day wound down to a close. It was no great loss to be advised in solemn tones by the hatchet-faced harridan at the beverage bar that they were no longer serving light refreshments. I took this as a good omen, and Compassion and I grabbed a quiet table out of the four hundred quiet tables available.

I leaned across, so that no one could overhear me, and hissed, 'Why are we meeting here?'

Compassion craned her neck as she looked ostentatiously around the entire room from where she sat. The canteen was completely empty.

'OK,' I said more loudly, faintly irritated and not caring that I was showing it. 'Why *are* we meeting here? I thought we had to do this kind of thing at home. Walls have ears, and so on.'

'We don't have the time,' said Compassion. 'We need to make our move. Some weird stuff's been happening.'

'No kidding, Miss Marple,' I said, and told her about Sempiter's transformation on Level 10. Compassion listened patiently until I finished, rarely showing any surprise, until I told her I'd barfed in the wardrobe, and even more when I confessed I'd left the envelope up there. 'I'm not sure that Ellis knows about any of this,' I concluded.

'Unlikely that he doesn't know. He's one of the major shareholding directors. Perhaps Sempiter could be involved in this thing alone.'

'Sempiter's gone off on his own,' I pointed out, and explained about the call from Hannaw. 'He delegated his ordinary business meetings to Ellis, which must be a bit tricky for him. Imagine the other people's reaction when Smelly Ellis is in the chair - I bet someone hits the fire alarm just so they can escape. Meanwhile, Sempiter's off somewhere to a meeting with Dr James Bowman. That means the Doctor could be in trouble, Compassion.'

Compassion put her finger to her lips to indicate quiet, and a couple of canteen staff meandered past and away from us. When they were out of earshot, she said, 'The Doctor's supposed to be working for Reddenblak. He gave me some stuff to pass on to them, business data and some planetary coordinates. I didn't have time to check the data for myself.'

I was amazed and relieved. 'You've seen the Doctor?'

'No,' hissed Compassion, fingering her lips to tell me to put a sock between mine. 'He sent stuff through the system, though I think most of it went astray. Point is, the Doctor must have access to some Frontier Worlds databases. So maybe Dr Bowman has set up a business meeting with Sempiter.'

I shook my head, my anxiety returning. 'Sempiter had a different kind of business in mind when he was last hunting for him. Could the Doctor still be on the mountain?'

Compassion said, 'He has to be near a communications station. He sent us an encrypted e-mail. A really short one, not very helpful. I assume he did it in a rush. All it said was "Obtain info on Darkling crop, Raab, Level Ten". Well, you've got some idea what's happening on Level Ten now. I can't find anything on Raab - that's probably on an isolated system up on Ten as well. Not much to say about Darkling - most of what I found is in that printout...'

'...now on Level Ten...'

'...which you thoughtfully placed on a desk up on Level Ten. I did discover one other thing related to Darkling: there's a DZ internal mail address. DZ equals Darkling Zone. And where do you suppose it is?'

'On Level Ten?' I said at once.

'You're not even warm. It's the other side of the jungle, to the west of the city. Stinricz Lowfer from the mail-room told me that no internal mail goes there or comes back. She said it's a standing joke in the mail room that the box is always empty.'

'Those laugh-a-minute mail-room guys,' I said. 'Lowfer, told you, huh? So how's your shoulder?'

She smiled. 'I don't bruise easily. You've seen this Darkling Zone already, you know.'

'How? I haven't been west of the city since we arrived.'

Compassion's smile threatened to become a grin. 'It's on your kitsch calendar, Fitz. Except in that picture it's growing a conventional wheat crop. So the Doctor tells us to look for the Darkling crop, I find a DZ postal address that's never used, and you've got a 3-D photo of the Frontier Worlds site for genetically modified field trials.' She shook her head, as though she could hardly believe it. 'That's so typical of a big corporation. They're good at getting stuff organised from scratch - they've screwed down the security really tight on this new Darkling stuff, I can't hack in at all. But the lumbering conventional processes let them down - photographic evidence left from previous work, automatically assigning a mail point. They didn't spot that stuff because it was below their radar.'

There was movement from the other side of the room. I recognised members of Compassion's shift team making their way across from the vending machine, each carrying their individual choice of foul poison to a table in the middle of the canteen. Several of them were in an agitated discussion about someone called Pora Darg. Then the shift supervisor was standing by our table.

'You heard about Pora?' she said to Compassion. And added almost immediately, 'I'm sorry, have you heard from the doctor?'

I felt myself tense. It was like having cramp seizing every muscle in my body in an iron grip, except not as much fun.

Compassion seemed calm. 'He's with Father now,' she said. Her face slowly crumpled, and her grey eyes started to shine wet. Her mouth did that going-down-at-the-sides thing, and she burst into tears, trying to talk in half-choked words.

I sat stupidly there for a minute before jumping up to comfort her, grasping her hand and holding her to me. 'I'm sorry...' I said to the supervisor as I stared at the ID badge pinned to her plain yellow top. 'I'm sorry, Nilloc. Please excuse us, it's a difficult time. He's very old... er...'

A resurgence of weeping from Compassion, and the not-so-subtle pressure of her nails in my palm, stopped me digging myself in any deeper.

Supervisor Jascot nodded, mouthed an apology, and went back to her colleagues at the other table. She glanced back once, giving us a reassuring smile. It was a human gesture of solidarity, and I felt a bit ashamed that someone who knew so little about us could show such sympathy.

I sat down again opposite Compassion, nursing the indentation she'd made in my palm. Compassion had her back to her colleagues, and was able to glare at me. The tears had vanished abruptly, as if a tap had been turned off. 'You idiot. "Father is dangerously ill, he needs to see the doctor." Our personnel files show that we're orphans. Maybe I should have written that bit down for you.'

'When I worked at the garden centre, there was a guy whose granny died every time we got a new manager. He went through three grannies in the time I was there, and got compassionate leave every time. Hey, compassionate leave...'

The thought trailed off. Compassion was not looking pleased, and showed me a tiny gap between forefinger and thumb. 'We're this close to finding the real Doctor and -' the tiny gap narrowed - '*this* close to getting discovered for the frauds we are.'

She told me about her odd meeting in reception with the Reddenblak executives, and her close escape from the security system which had then got Pora Darg arrested.

'If our cover's not blown yet, Fitz, then it's about to be. We have to get in Level Ten, get the Raab information, get the Doctor, and get the hell out of here. And we have to do it tonight, after people have gone home - we won't even go back to the apartment.'

I looked at my watch. Its orange face smiled back at me

reassuringly. Or perhaps accusingly.

'I can't,' I said. Compassion did that wrinkly thing with her nose – you know the one: it shows she's either confused or exasperated. Probably both, on this occasion. 'I need to see Alura first.'

'Don't get involved, Fitz.'

'I am involved. She's staying at the apartment. She's... between jobs. I'll go home, right now. Tell her it's over, get my stuff and quit. I'll be back here by end of business.'

'We haven't got time, Fitz – that's where this conversation began.'

'I have to tell her I'm going, it's only fair. Not to do so is inhuman.'

Compassion's tone was emphatic. 'She's not human.'

'It's a translation convention, damn it. Human, Drebnaran, little green men, what the hell does it matter? This isn't about what race she is: it's about treating her like a person. Because she cares about me, Compassion. More than I care about her. More than I deserve.'

Compassion was lowering her voice carefully, to remind me we might be overheard. She seemed to be studying me closely with her cool grey eyes. The all-too human tears she'd faked for Jascot were long gone. 'So this is really about you, Fitz.'

'No, it's about showing...' I couldn't avoid it, really. 'It's about showing a little *compassion*, Compassion. And you know, that's the bloodiest thing about this. It's not that you don't care, is it? It's just that you don't know how to. Strange. I'd have thought you'd have some idea, that you might just understand.'

'I don't understand *you*,' she said.

I scraped back my chair, rising to leave at once. 'That's the thing, Compassion. That's entirely my point.'

'Man, are you hot,' said Alura. She spread her fingers across my chest.

'It's probably all these bedclothes and... y'know.'

'No,' she grinned. 'You're really good-looking.' And she laughed her little laugh.

I struggled up on to my elbows, squashing the pillow. She slid sideways to accommodate me.

'Do you remember?' she said. 'That's something you said the first night we slept together. I didn't understand it, then. But it seemed to make you happy.' She snuggled her head against me again. 'I love it when you're happy. It reminds me why I love you so much. That and the sweet things you say. "Take my lips, I want to lose them." Do you remember? "Get a piece of these arms, I'll never use them." You're so romantic, Frank.'

I still lay there in silence. Perhaps she thought I was reminiscing about our first meeting. Of course, I was twisting inside, unable to tell her this was our last.

I don't know if you can understand it, the way my guts were churning – it was a physical thing. On the transport back here I'd thought about every word, the neat phrases, the particular emphasis, the sincere gestures, as though I were rehearsing for a play, instead of preparing to ruin my girlfriend's life. As usual, the shift workers leaving with me on the bus had not wanted to meet my eye, so my mutterings on the back seat had drawn a few anxious looks. I was the nutter some of them had to sit next to.

My girlfriend. I'd anticipated her reaction in my performance, of course. There'd be tears, a little anger, an eventual reluctant acceptance. It was all so easy, but that was because I was writing it in my head, the way I wanted it to go, not the way it would go.

Not the way it did go.

'Thanks for coming home early,' Alura said. 'I've had a really tiring day.'

What had thrown my prepared speech to begin with was the way she'd welcomed me into the apartment. She'd let herself in that morning, with the key card I'd given her, and she'd tidied the place completely, as a surprise. I spotted a bread roll that she'd missed, still under the table where I'd kicked it during breakfast. I hated to think what horrors she'd faced in the toilet.

'Do you really have to go back to the lab this evening? I'll be so lonely…' She was kidding me, snaking one arm round my waist under the bedclothes to hold me tight. She gave a big yawn, and I felt myself wanting to yawn too.

Better make a move, I thought. I reached over to the phone by the bedside, and picked up its dead receiver. 'Room service? I'm going to be leaving in a hurry, so bring me a piranha-fish sandwich and make it snappy.'

Alura smiled and hugged me closer, putting her head on my chest. 'When we have a place of our own, we can afford to have a phone connection.' I could feel that water rising around me again. 'Who'd have thought we'd be together like this, Frank?' Her breath felt warm on my skin. 'I don't suppose you ever really see what's coming next. Even if you think you've got it all sorted out, that you know what you're looking for in life, there's always something that can jump out of nowhere and surprise you.' She angled her head, trying to look at me. She circled the little patch of hair around my nipple. 'You're quiet. Tell me, Frank, what are you looking for?'

The escape hatch, I thought.

'Frank?'

'Back on my... home planet,' I began. 'My father made an important decision about my life even before I was born. He decided he had to get away from his own country – he couldn't survive there any longer. So he ended up in a different country, one that went to war with his former homeland. And he suffered in his new home for who he *wasn't*, not who he was.'

Alura gazed at me, into me.

'I've never told anyone this,' I said. You'll know that's true, of course. 'My father would get melancholy sometimes. When he'd had a little too much to drink maybe. Or on his brother Jürgen's birthday, or his friend Franz-Joachim's, or any of the other people he'd left behind. He said that sometimes he almost wished that he'd never left. Almost. And he told me that I'd've had a different name in that former homeland. If I'd been born there, he'd've called me Franz-Joachim.'

'Are your parents on Drebnar? Or on Creal?'

I kissed her forehead. 'My parents died many years ago. I guess what I'm saying is that we may think we know what we're looking for, but events conspire against us. If my father had made a different choice, you'd be in bed now with Franz-Joachim

Kreiner. Except, of course, he'd never have met my mother. And you'n'me would never have met in a million years.'

'Oh, Frank.' Her beautiful khaki eyes were edged with tears.

'There's no point asking what could have been. You have to deal with what comes next. I can't spend my life looking for Franz-Joachim. Neither should you.'

'I know what I'm looking for. I'm looking at him right now. And I know exactly the person Alura Trebul is. Who she wants to be.'

After that, of course, I couldn't bear to tell her. That water had risen up into my eyes.

I held her in my arms, touching her hair softly with my lips. From where I lay, I could see my inoculation scar. It was itching, and it reminded me of my link to Frontier Worlds Corporation. It reminded me of a mark on my Uncle Jürgen's arm, a line of faded blue numbers that my father hadn't wanted to explain to me.

When Alura fell asleep next to me, I slid out from her warm embrace and left her in our bed. I got dressed, and the last thing I put on was the orange watch she'd given me.

Then, like the no-good fake I am in these circumstances, I wrote her a note. Not even a good note, just careless words written hurriedly on a scrap of paper, because she'd tidied things away and I couldn't find a decent sheet without opening drawers and disturbing her. I folded it, and propped it on the sideboard next to the pearl-handled scissors and the bits of wire which somehow she'd overlooked.

I dropped my front-door key card on the table. There were a few magazines and papers scattered on the carpet, but I left them where they lay.

I didn't kiss her before I went. I hunkered down by the bed and listened to her as she purred in her sleep like a contented cat. I was thinking: this is it, this is the last I'll ever see of her, I can handle this. My heart would break if she should wake and see me go.

So, I thought, softly as I left her there. No time like the present. No time, when you travel in time.

Hey, that's my job, right?

Chapter Fourteen
'All the Things You Are'

Temm Sempiter studied his nails thoughtfully. The cuticles were even and smooth above the perfect half-moons at the base, and then the pale-pink skin showed through each clear nail until it reached the tidy arc of white at the tip of his finger. They were polished, unblemished. Once again.

He reached out a perfect forefinger and pressed the intercom button. 'You can send him in now.' He didn't listen to Hannaw Applin's reply, just flicked the device off.

He took a moment to check the time on his wrist chronometer. It was in the same style as those that Frontier Worlds awarded to all its long-serving staff, those who endured the poor conditions and worse pay and didn't decide that their decision to move to Drebnar was a mistake all along. The rival Reddenblak Corporation offered nothing better, and so a surprising number of staff got to ten, even twenty years of service. It amused Sempiter to think that such long service continued to be rewarded with a timepiece, a reminder of how their lives had passed by, spent and never to be recovered, in the service of his Corporation.

The figures on the face of his timepiece glittered like tiny stars. His watch was made of more precious materials. But then, of course, so was he.

Sempiter rose from his chair, a swift and easy motion that belied his chronological age. How pleasing, he thought, to be able to walk around his personal space again without stumbling, with no need to halt for breath, with no fear that he would catch sight of himself in a reflective surface and be repulsed by what he saw: death before life.

The cover slipped from the mirror above the polished side desk as he tugged gently but firmly at the soft material. Now he would look at himself. The dark-brown hair, fashionably short. The trim eyebrows above clear green eyes. The aquiline nose that reminded him of his father's.

His father.

The picture on the wall beside the mirror showed his parents at the beach, on that last summer before they had been diagnosed. It was a perfect day: a clear sky and an empty beach, and just him and his mother and father there, together, watching the foam spill on to the sand. That was how he remembered it. Or that was how he chose to remember it, rather, because he had been two, and couldn't really recall it at all. It was simply what they'd told him in the final stages of the wasting disease, three years later. It was the memory he had rehearsed repeatedly. That made it true. He breathed in deeply, inhaling the fragrant bouquet in the vase that adorned the small table set in front of the photograph.

He moved to his desk and switched on the bird in its cage. It chirruped obediently at once.

His communicator chimed just as the two guards were bringing the man in. Sempiter gestured to them impatiently, indicating that they should dump the untidy newcomer on the broad chair by the far wall. He himself moved with a dancer's grace to the other side of the room where he could take the incoming call.

It was from Ellis. Even though the scientist was far away at the base of the mountain, the sight on the monitor display of his pockmarked face and shabby lab clothing brought the smell to Sempiter. And he no longer wanted to smell such things with his new nostrils, see such things with his clear new eyes. 'Yes? I am in a meeting, Griz.' He checked his watch. 'Time's pressing on.'

'You're right about the time,' Ellis replied smartly. None of the usual sycophantic pleasantries, Sempiter noticed. 'I've just come from a meeting of my own. You know who with.'

Sempiter exhaled loudly. 'As I said to you before I left, I have absolutely nothing more to say to Reddenblak.'

Ellis indulged himself in a glutinous sniff, leaning out of camera range briefly to do so. Sempiter could hardly bear to listen for much longer as Ellis continued to explain how representatives of the Reddenblak Corporation had asked to meet the Frontier Worlds board. They'd offered an agreed buyout of the company.

'It's the ideal time to sell,' concluded Ellis.

'I disagree. I disagreed two years ago, I disagreed last year, I disagreed last month...'

'You're a control freak, Temm.'

Sempiter sniggered. 'No use trying to sweet-talk me, Griz. I have my voting shares, and now...' He brandished an identity card at the screen. 'Now I have Klenton Dewfurth's as well.'

'Klenton?' said Ellis. 'Where is he? We've been trying to reach him for days. People down here are getting worried.'

'Bad news,' said Sempiter. 'He jumped ship.'

Ellis whistled through his uneven teeth. 'No wonder you've been keeping it quiet. But don't you think your board have a right to know, Temm? Did he go to Reddenblak?'

'Not important. Just don't count on seeing him again.'

'But if he's gone to Reddenblak... Don't you see, Temm, we can do the deal with them, and still carry on our research. Let Reddenblak take the strain of the day-to-day business.'

'Griz, listen to yourself,' sighed Sempiter. 'Do you even believe what you're saying? Reddenblak's sole objective is to increase their market share by their usual strategy. Their *only* strategy: diversify, embrace, extinguish.'

'Oh yeah?' coughed Ellis. 'Then why are they so interested in the Darkling crop?'

Sempiter felt his composure vanishing. If he couldn't stay calm, then he might burst little blood vessels all across his smooth new face. He tried a cold tone, though his voice still quivered with repressed rage: 'Just how do they know about Darkling? Now, Griz, you wouldn't have -'

'Of course not,' he retorted, spattering the camera with spittle. 'We ran a check on all outgoing e-mail, and it was sent from Klenton Dewfurth's account. But he resigned, why is his user ID still active?'

Sempiter turned his back on the communications screen, and

looked around for the scruffy man who had been brought into his office. 'I'm just starting a meeting with the person who saw Klenton leave the building. I'll deal with it, Griz. And Griz… there will be *no* deal with Reddenblak.'

Sempiter shut down the connection with a savage blow of his fist. He glared at the empty seat where the scruffy man should have been sitting.

'Interesting you should let me listen to your business calls,' said a calm and educated voice from a different part of the room.

'It can't help you,' replied Sempiter ominously.

He had located the man, over by the photograph table. Despite his dishevelled clothing, the newcomer was standing confidently, nonchalantly. He had taken the 3-D image from the wall, and was angling its frame in the sharp light of an overhead lamp. Sempiter stalked over, trying not to let his irritation show. He took the photo, and hung it back on its hook, adjusting it so that it was level once more.

The newcomer was definitely the same man who he had seen on the roof security cameras that day, trying to prevent Dewfurth from leaping to his death on the rocks below. Now the velvet of his long, green jacket was rather tattered, and one sleeve was tearing away from the shoulder. The wing-collar shirt was filthy and bloodied, the scarf a mass of matted fibres.

But the face… A fierce intelligence shone from the startling blue eyes, and the half-pursed lips seemed to suggest something between pensive thought and wry amusement. Sempiter refused to let him take control. He pointed to the picture. 'My parents,' he said. 'I remember that day well. It was one of the perfect moments of my childhood.'

Now those pursed lips were amused. 'I thought they died before you were old enough to know them.'

'And how could you know that?'

'Well,' began the man expansively, 'you're now - what? - one hundred and five?'

Sempiter scowled fiercely. He didn't like this turn in the

conversation, and was just as irritated with himself for letting it show.

'OK, OK,' said the man, raising his palms defensively. 'I didn't mean to be rude. Let's call it a round hundred. So... what did your father die of? I'd guess it was a fast-developing progressive chronic disorder of the central nervous system characterised by impaired muscular co-ordination. Early symptoms would be tremors in the hands and fingers. Maybe involuntary movements of the feet?'

Sempiter was aware that the man was staring at his feet now. Aware, with a flush of anger, that he himself was tapping his foot on the plush office carpet.

'You're mocking me,' he said, trying to make his tone dangerous.

'Not at all,' said the man, moving over to the nearest chair and dropping into it with a little bounce. 'So, a hereditary disease. Ankylocerebrosis? Paldanquinous aetuldeteriorosis, possibly? Javelwatter's disease? Ah, so it was the aetuldeteriorosis.'

Sempiter had flinched at the correct identification, the medical incantation that had haunted him throughout his life. This scruffy man's appearance belied his ability to control. It was ridiculous, implausible, as if a hobo had been revealed to be a neurosurgeon slumming it.

'I'd hazard that the disease killed him a few years after this was taken? You can see the blurring in the hologram.' The hobo gestured to the picture on the wall. 'Just there on your father's little finger, as though he couldn't stop the tremor while it was being taken. Crude, those early 3-D cameras, weren't they? That would make this photo more than a hundred years old. Which would make you a little older than that. I doubt you remember that time at all. That must be why the moment seems so perfect to you. Memory cheats.'

Sempiter paced around his desk, coming to a halt just in front of it. He leaned back on the edge, conscious of how he was now trying to control his foot tapping in front of this unnerving stranger. The artificial bird's sensors detected his proximity, and the creature chirruped brightly at him. He jabbed at the OFF switch in vexation. 'How do you know about aetuldeteriorosis? Most people couldn't even pronounce it.'

'I'm a doctor.'

'Well then, Doctor...?'

'Just Doctor.'

'Well then, just-Doctor, I think you concocted this pathetic farrago of guesswork and half-truth from the nonsense spouted by that pitiful wreck Dewfurth.' He waved the identity card again, so that this Doctor could see it. 'My security staff found it on your person, along with some strange confectionery. And these items...'

He held up two half-shells, joined together in the middle and with a string spooled around it. 'That's a yo-yo,' said the Doctor. 'It's a toy.' Sempiter held up a short metal cylinder with a bulbous end. 'That's a sonic back-massager. I'm plagued by herniated invertebral discs. You know how it is.' A stubby black cylinder with a screw top. 'That's a fountain pen, but be careful: it leaks a little at the... oh dear.'

Sempiter looked at the fountain pen. Ink was dripping from the screw join, and had stained his fingers. Two perfect cuticles and a neatly trimmed nail were now a dark blue. He gave a shout of anger, and flung the items on to the desk behind him.

He wheeled back on the Doctor, who was still looking up at him mildly from the seat, gazing into him with those astonishing blue eyes, not at all scared by Sempiter's rapid change of mood. 'You're sad about your parents, of course,' he was saying. 'Sometimes I can sense that sort of thing in people. You spent so long telling yourself that time was a great healer, that everything would be all right in time. And then, just when you thought that you had established yourself with your company, the disease caught up with you. In its own time.'

Sempiter snarled, 'No.'

'I imagine the symptoms started in your foot,' continued the infuriating voice. 'You realised you were running out of time.'

Sempiter lunged forward, looming over the Doctor, towering

above him where he sat. 'Time means nothing to me.' He thought his decades of research, the slow construction of the Frontier Worlds facilities, the growing threat of Reddenblak. He remembered the powerless feeling when the aetuldeteriorosis was diagnosed in him, and his frantic search for a cure. And finally, the alien creature, Dewfurth's successful initial research, and the annual renewal of his very being. A renewal that would now allow him to live for ever. 'I could teach you something about time.'

'Oh, really?' sneered the Doctor. He suddenly jumped up from his seat, seizing Sempiter by the arms. Sempiter was so surprised that he couldn't react to the assault, until he realised it wasn't an assault at all. The strange Doctor stood in front of him, holding his wrists firmly but doing nothing more. Sempiter could feel the warmth of the stranger's skin, though not as warm as he had expected, not as warm as normal people's hands. And he could feel the thump-thumpa-thump of a double pulse.

'Mr Sempiter, I'm a bit of an expert, if I do say so myself. So let me tell you now that, while Time is a fine teacher, she eventually kills all her pupils.'

'Not me,' retorted Sempiter, the syllables fired like bullets. He twisted his wrists, and reversed the grip on the Doctor's arms, seizing them in a powerful hold. He watched the Doctor's reaction to his cold flesh, and then the moment when the Doctor realised that he had no pulse. 'I have nothing to fear. I am dead already.'

'No,' whispered the Doctor. 'Your desperate experiment on yourself may soon seem like that, though. As the alien element within you, the Raab element that renews you, starts to renew itself. Starts to overtake you. How soon before you can't tell where Temm Sempiter ends and the Raab begins? So, to be pedantic, it's not death. It's just a different kind of life.'

Sempiter laughed aloud, the emotion shaking his whole frame. 'Yes, I suppose there is immortality in that. You know, Doctor, I've so wanted to meet you. You have something I need.'

The Doctor smiled politely, and nodded at the desk. 'Well, you've got Mr Dewfurth's identity card back. And you can keep the fountain pen.'

'No,' said Sempiter, watching the Doctor's smile disappear abruptly. 'I need your DNA.'

Sempiter bustled about in front of a bank of equipment on the other side of the laboratory. The machinery whined into life, an ascending and anticipatory note. He had slipped on fresh white overalls. They reminded the Doctor of Dewfurth's lab coat. Which helped take his mind off the array of shiny metal surgical instruments which Sempiter was adjusting on a bright white counter.

The Doctor flexed the muscles in his arm experimentally. The metallic straps that held them to the operating chair did not budge. What was it that Harry Houdini had taught him? Tense your muscles while you're being tied up before the escape, so that the ropes are only binding you loosely when you relax later on. He didn't think that was going to help much here. And the other one? Hiding skeleton keys in flaps of skin cut into the calluses on his hands. Yuk! The Doctor was able to twist his hands round in the restraints, and could see the pale white skin on his palms and long fingers. Smooth as a baby's bottom. Pianist's fingers, he thought. One day, I suppose I should learn to play the piano with them.

Sempiter was engrossed in laying the operating equipment out neatly, to the precise millimetre, making the tiniest adjustments. He was a little boy again, ensuring that everything was in its place, everything was exactly how it should be, just like the picture on the box. The Doctor shivered. He told himself it was because the room was so cold, even for him. It didn't matter to Sempiter, of course. He'd detected the absence of a pulse when he'd held Sempiter's wrists, and felt the cold, white skin. The room was icy-cold too, though the absence of external windows meant that there was no way of telling what the weather outside was like, or what time it was. The Doctor's inner clock told him it was late afternoon. It would still be bright outside.

'I'm glad you decided not to struggle,' said Sempiter. His voice echoed in the sterile environment, and made the Doctor jump in surprise. 'My security staff can be rather heavy-handed.'

'They made a real mess of my clothes,' said the Doctor. He nodded his head as much as the chair restraints would allow, indicating the torn pile of clothing tossed on the clean floor. 'I don't think my accident insurance covers that.'

Sempiter kicked the pile further into the corner. 'I don't see why you're so attached to them.'

'Non-iron shirts are so difficult to find in my line of business.'

Sempiter had stepped up to him in the chair. 'They were ruined, anyway.' He ran a smooth white finger across the Doctor's bare chest and pressed down on the soft flesh near the shoulder so that the Doctor winced. 'That's an angry-looking bruise.'

'Not half as angry as I feel,' growled the Doctor.

'You've made a remarkable recovery, wouldn't you agree? Your clothes are clear evidence that my men shot you yesterday morning. You certainly bled enough for us to obtain a useful sample from the snow where you fell. And yet, there's no entry or exit wound. Just this rather unpleasant contusion. How did you manage that?'

'It was just a flesh wound... aah!' The Doctor cried out as Sempiter's finger pushed and probed at the sensitive area on his shoulder. It was even more painful when Sempiter released the pressure suddenly.

'The blood sample proved very interesting,' said Sempiter. He was standing by the computer equipment again, studying a display screen. 'At first, I thought the system calibration was out of whack. And yet... there it is.' He gestured at the display screen with a flourish. The Doctor could see the familiar triple helix rotating on one of its axes. With this technology, of course, Sempiter couldn't display the fourth axis, and so wouldn't have spotted the temporal imprimatur. 'It's astonishing,' Sempiter went on, clearly unable to keep the awe out of his voice. 'Even from this small sample, I could identify sixty-nine chromosomes in what appear to be twenty-three uniform groupings.'

The Doctor smiled a thin smile. 'You must be so proud.'

Sempiter switched off the display, and the triple helix spun into nothingness. 'The ordered nature of your unusual DNA suggests to me that you could be extremely useful, Doctor. Far more useful than anything we've found on this planet so far.'

'Oh, I think you're just flattering me,' said the Doctor, subtly flexing within his constraints again. Still nothing gave. 'Don't misunderstand me, though. I could sit here all day and listen to you. In fact, I think I may have to.'

Sempiter stooped beside him, whispering in his ear. The Doctor could feel the cold breath wafting on his skin, moving the curls of hair. 'Are you so rare, Doctor? So very valuable... Are there more of your kind here on Drebnar, I wonder? Who were you trying to contact while you were up on the weather platform, hmm?'

'I was just fiddling with your weather database,' the Doctor said quickly.

Too quickly. Sempiter had stepped away again. He connected with his assistant on the intercom, instructing her to instigate a search of the records of all employees' DNA samples. He paused to check his wristwatch. 'I'm going to prepare the subject here in the lab, Hannaw,' he said into the intercom. 'Hold all my calls. No exceptions.'

Now he turned back to the Doctor, who ceased his futile struggle with his bonds. 'Well, they can look for your accomplice, Doctor. I don't want to be disturbed while I take another sample for study.'

'I'm touched by your interest.'

Sempiter had picked up one of the sharp metal implements. 'I'll need a fairly substantial sample. At this point, I usually tell the patient some reassuring untruth. You know the kind of thing: "This won't be painful", or "This will hurt me more than it hurts you". However, you know that I'd be lying. After all, you are a doctor.'

The metal instrument rasped as he twisted the cutting edge into position.

'I think we both understand that this is going to be very painful indeed.'

Chapter Fifteen
'All Or Nothing At All'

Sempiter placed the cutting edge of the metal implement over the Doctor's left heart, and prepared to push. The Doctor let out a piercingly shrill scream. He'd had a number of travelling companions who used to do much the same thing, and he was pleased with the effect it had now. For added effect, he fluttered his hands at the extremes of their restraints

'Lucky this room's soundproofed, we don't want to frighten the staff,' Sempiter said. He stood back and looked at the Doctor's chest. 'Besides, I haven't started yet. Don't be so feeble.'

The Doctor looked down too. There was a little round ring of teeth marks where the device had started to bite into the flesh. 'But that thing's so cold. Couldn't you breathe on the end of it for a bit. Oh, I suppose not,' he added. 'That would make it colder still, wouldn't it?'

Sempiter scowled. 'I think I may have to gag you.' He watched the Doctor's fingers continuing to flap about on the chair arms. 'And that won't do, it's too much of a distraction. Honestly, whoever designed these chairs wasn't thinking about how they were going to be used for real.' He swiftly undid one of the restraints, wrenched the Doctor's hand behind the chair and secured it with a strap. Then he did the same with the other.

The Doctor imagined that he must look more than ever like a chicken dressed for the oven. He eyed up the cutting device, and tried not to think too much about giblets. 'Whoever designed these chairs probably wasn't thinking about this kind of operation on conscious patients.'

'Well, there are many benefits in obtaining a live sample,' Sempiter explained, as though he were talking to a toddler.

'Did they explain the benefits of anaesthesia at your medical school?' asked the Doctor. He didn't want to be rendered unconscious, but was trying anything to delay the savage operation. He was having some success with relaxing his muscles behind the chair, although the prospect of the cutting device coming back towards him was making him tense up again involuntarily. His toes curled around the side of the footrest.

The cutting device made a zizzing noise as Sempiter tested it in midair, studying the end of it with a satisfied smile.

'The operation will kill me,' the Doctor said plaintively.

Zziiiizzzzz!

'And this is a problem in what way, precisely?'

'You're a cold character in more ways than one, Temm Sempiter. No pulse, low body temperature. You're obviously more at ease with machinery than with people. Like that robot of yours on the weather platform.'

'Right,' said Sempiter emphatically. He put down the cruel implement and looked around the room. 'I really am going to gag you.'

'And that mechanical budgerigar in your office,' the Doctor continued, gabbling as fast as he could. 'What's that called?'

Sempiter tore off the sleeve of the Doctor's discarded shirt, and tested it for strength. 'The canary doesn't have a name. It's a machine.'

'Of course,' said the Doctor, rolling his eyes theatrically. 'Giving it an identity would make it more real. And real things have feelings, real things can feel pain and loss. As you did when your parents died, Sempiter.' He watched Sempiter for a reaction. 'As I will when you cut into my flesh.'

'Your loss is my gain.' Sempiter advanced with the shirtsleeve.

The Doctor wriggled his head aside. 'No, you'll lose the chance to discover what Dewfurth told me... er, told us... about the alien vegetation on the mountainside. They're called Raab. Mmmph!'

The shirtsleeve was stuffed into his mouth. It tasted of sweat and blood. Oh well, he thought, I gave it my best shot.

Sempiter slowly pulled the strip of shirtsleeve out of the Doctor's mouth, like a conjuror producing flags of many nations.

'Yes, you mentioned that name before. What are the Raab?'

The shirtsleeve had soaked up the spit in his mouth. The Doctor smacked his lips together a few times, and licked them before he spoke. Then he briefly explained about the Raab, trying not to lose Sempiter's interest with too much detail, but all the time struggling behind the chair to release his wrists. 'Do you know how terribly risky it is to use the Raab? You thought you could splice that genetic code into your own, and prolong your lives. And now you've seen what it's done to your colleagues over the years: Mozarno has no mind, Dewfurth became suicidally depressed...'

'So what's *my* problem?' smiled Sempiter indulgently.

The Doctor stared up at him, wondering how to respond to this challenge. 'It was Shar Mozarno who saw the possibilities from our analysis of the alien tissue,' said Sempiter. 'He conducted all the early analyses, he was brilliant, definitely a good hiring decision. Even if he'd known what could happen to him, I think he would still have taken that personal risk. And why not? After all, we'd handcuffed him to the company by making him one of our prime shareholders, so he had to take that business gamble too. That's what I liked best about him.'

'He's still alive.'

'If you can call that living,' snorted Sempiter. 'Meanwhile, the... Raab did you call them? The Raab have new uses already. We've extended that research to natural foodstuffs. The Darkling wheat crop has developed nicely on Drebnar's fertile ground, but it's a hundred times more successful since we've been fertilising it with a mulch made from the Raab.'

The Doctor's mouth had suddenly gone dry again. 'You're not serious. You're deliberately introducing Raab tissue into the local flora? That's terribly dangerous.'

'That's business,' said Sempiter. 'The Darkling crop will see off Reddenblak, for sure. All the other frontier worlds in this solar system will be dependent on the output of Drebnar. Dependent on the output of Frontier Worlds Corporation. That's strangely appropriate, don't you think?'

The Doctor could feel his bonds starting to loosen behind the chair. 'I think it's insane, Sempiter. And so are you.'

Sempiter smiled, and the Doctor could see a wild look of triumph in his eyes. 'I could stand here all day while you flatter me, Doctor. But I don't intend to.' He reached again for the dreadful cutting implement. 'Now you, Doctor - your DNA looks like a much more promising avenue of investigation for my rejuvenation project.'

The words tumbled out of the Doctor like a waterfall. 'Listen to yourself, Sempiter. Listen to what you're saying. You asked me what effect the Raab experiment had, what your problem was. I can tell you what you've done to yourself.'

'I've made myself strong. I've made myself immortal.'

'No, the Raab DNA is continuing to change you utterly. Ask yourself how Mozarno's forgetfulness became a total loss of short-term memory. Ask yourself how Dewfurth's pessimism became suicidal tendencies. Ask yourself how you've lost any moral and ethical perspective in your business dealings.'

'If the Raab have removed any weakness in my business dealings,' said Sempiter, 'then it was a trade worth making.'

'Deals, trades, business,' shouted the Doctor, hearing his voice crack. 'We're talking about people's lives, not just the bottom line. You're going to cause the Raab to wipe out all life here, and jeopardise other lives across the whole system. That Raab's seed load will scatter right across this fertile planet, and there's no way for the new seedlings to escape from Drebnar's gravity.' He stared imploringly at the other man, trying to halt him by force of will alone. 'It's like Reddenblak's strategy, remember? The Raab will diversify, embrace and extinguish.'

The Doctor was alarmed and disheartened when Sempiter began to laugh, a loud barking that echoed its mocking sound around the stark laboratory. 'And these vegetables,' he guffawed. 'These Raab are that intelligent, are they?'

'No,' said the Doctor coldly. 'Their life cycle may be as complex as Drosni-Ptorak subquantum statistics, but actually they're as lacking in cunning and deceit as a bowl of *lollo rosso* salad. You're going to ask me what Drosni-Ptorak subquantum statistics are, I suppose.'

'No, I was going to ask you what *lollo rosso* salad is.'

'You're allowing the Raab to grow unchecked in an uncontrolled experiment in a fertile environment. Drebnar provides food for this whole system. You'll do untold damage not just to this world but to others too. You have no way of knowing what effect it will have on your Darkling crop, what genetic mutations you're introducing into the population. You don't even recognise the changes that have happened to *you* with each of your regenerations over the years. Years,' he spat indignantly. 'That's an insignificant fraction of time for the Raab, you can count their lifespan in millennia. How many more changes can you survive before you're no longer Temm Sempiter at all?'

Sempiter came up very close, emphasising the power and control he wielded over his captive. The Doctor could feel that icy breath across his face, and he closed his eyes involuntarily as the man spoke.

'I survive. I am stronger. I'm surprised at you, Doctor – I thought you'd recognise how alike we are. We both understand genetics. We both have tissue-deep regenerative abilities.' He brandished the cutting tool again. 'And until now we both expected to live long and comfortable lives.'

The Doctor lashed forward savagely with his upper body. He felt his arm squeeze against the back of the chair. An agonising shooting pain speared through his wounded shoulder. And his forehead connected with Sempiter's nose, with a sickening crunch.

The Doctor opened his eyes to see Sempiter fall backwards, howling and clutching at his nose. His white laboratory coat was spattered red with blood as he tried to staunch the bleeding from his face. The cutting device had spun out of his grasp, and lay buzzing around and around in a tight circle on the floor by the far wall.

The scientist had fallen down in a weeping, moaning heap by the bank of equipment on the other side of the laboratory. The Doctor saw how close the rest of the surgical equipment was to Sempiter, and wriggled desperately in his chair, wrestling to free his hands. They finally slipped from their bonds, and he reached down urgently to release his legs from the metal restraints.

Sempiter was looking in disbelief at his bloody hands. He stretched up to the surgical instruments behind him, tugging at the silver tray on which they were all neatly aligned. It fell to the hard lab floor with a splintering crash.

The Doctor was peripherally aware of Sempiter surveying the chaos of instruments around him, looking at his face reflected in the silver tray, giving a bellow of rage. And not without some justification, thought the Doctor as he continued to struggle with the foot restraints. The nose was squint, a bruised and broken mess in his smooth, pale face.

Just as Sempiter reached for one of the nearby cutting implements, the restraints snapped back. The Doctor took three long strides across the laboratory floor, raised his leg, and kicked Sempiter across the side of the head. Sempiter pitched across the room, the cutting implement spinning from his grasp.

The Doctor hopped around the room for a while, nursing the toe he'd stubbed on the side of Sempiter's head. When the pain had eased a bit, he kicked the rest of the wicked-looking medical instruments well out of reach across the floor. When he finally turned to look at Sempiter, he found him sprawled across the white floor, bleeding from the face.

'I think we both understand,' said the Doctor quietly, 'that was very painful indeed.'

His internal clock told him now that he must have been sitting in that chair for a couple of hours. He'd suffered longer enforced immobility, but nonetheless he felt somewhat unsteady on his legs, and his calves were beginning to cramp. He perched for a moment on the side of a table, massaging his muscles, stretching his limbs so that they would not betray him as he planned his escape.

The Doctor hurried over to the corner of the room, never letting Sempiter out of his sight. 'Stay where you are,' he told him, 'or I'll give you a cauliflower ear.'

Sempiter gave a little whimper of dismay, and lay still.

The Doctor could find only thin white lab coats in the tall cupboards at the edge of the room, so he went and retrieved his battered pile of clothes. Blood had stiffened the cravat, so he abandoned that. The shirt would just about do, minus one sleeve. The waistcoat was tattered but would suffice, and the green coat was just barely salvageable. His trousers were on their last legs, and the fly buttons were all missing, mute witness to the way the guards had wrenched them off him on his arrival. Only his Marks and Spencer underpants seemed undamaged, so he slipped them on first. He pondered whether he should wear them over the trousers to keep the flies closed, but decided that would be ostentatious.

Sempiter was making signs of sitting up, so he pushed him back down on the floor as he walked past on his way to the computer console. While he was there, he tore out the intercom. 'Don't want you phoning anyone while you're locked up in here,' he said to Sempiter over his shoulder. 'No point in shouting: this place is soundproof, remember?' While he was at it, he also tore out all the physical connections for the computers. The wall plugs sparked and fizzed in protest at this abuse. 'And no systems access, either,' he added. He smiled to himself at the memory of Fitz struggling with the communications system. 'The e-mail of the species is more deadly than the mail.'

From where he still lay on the floor, nursing his battered face, Sempiter glared venomously at him. The Doctor stepped towards the exit door, waving a handful of belongings at the bruised and abandoned scientist. He locked the door from the outside, flicked the DO NOT DISTURB sign into place, and ran like hell.

Sempiter didn't know exactly how long he waited for someone to come and discover him, because he had misplaced his wristwatch somewhere. He guessed it was at least ninety minutes. Ninety minutes of useless banging on the exit door until the heels of his hands were bruised, ninety minutes of fiddling with snapped connectors and loose wires in the smashed communications systems until his clean white nails were broken or thick with dirt and oil. Ninety minutes in which his temper peaked and then ebbed away, until he was more embarrassed than furious when Hannaw Applin finally opened the door.

Sempiter brushed away Applin's initial apologies about disturbing him despite the notice outside. She had been worried about disobeying his strict instructions about no interruptions, but also concerned that he hadn't contacted her for his traditional perusal of business communications and e-mail in the middle of the evening.

Sempiter had also had time, during that hour and a half, to reflect repeatedly on what the Doctor had said before he left. Applin's babbling regrets about missing the business communications brought it home with a jolt. 'He said "The e-mail of the species is more deadly than the mail". That's what Ellis's idiot assistant said to me in HQ yesterday.'

They were striding down the passageway that led from the isolated laboratory and back to the main office areas of the research station. Sempiter took the stairs three at a time. Hannaw stumbled after him, trying not to get her heels caught in the metal grille of the treads.

'Who?' said Applin.

Sempiter had stopped to consider the question. Applin looked away suddenly, embarrassed to be caught staring at the bruised mess of his face. He had refused to allow her to call a medic. 'Do you mean Frank Sinatra?'

'Yes. He said exactly the same thing to me. Has that DNA search thrown up anything yet?'

She stared away again. 'No, sir,' she said to her feet.

'Then forget it. Look out Frank Sinatra's DNA record – I think we'll find that it's the same as the Doctor's. They're in this together.'

'Frank?' asked Applin. 'That conniving sod. Oh, excuse me, sir, I didn't -'

'Forget the sentimental attachment,' snapped Sempiter as they rounded the corner and swept into his office. 'Get me the DNA record. Get me a cold compress. And get me a connection to security at HQ. Any time in the next twenty seconds will be fine for all three.'

It actually took her fifteen minutes, but Sempiter didn't care. He was whooping with delight when he saw the DNA record for Frank Sinatra.

'Look at that!' he yelled at her. 'It's a standard double-helix, but there are the same overformal structures in the plasmid. This has been organised and ordered, for sure. I'll bet my bonus that this is a developed splice between normal DNA and the Doctor's. It can be done! We need to get hold of this guy.' The excitement and emotion spilled out in his voice. He didn't care what he sounded like - this was confirmation of his theory. And, if they could get to the Sinatras, then he could even do without the Doctor. He studied another DNA record on his display screen. 'Whose is this one?'

'His sister,' explained Applin snappishly. 'Nancy Sinatra.'

'Whoa!' he said. He tried to let out a low whistle, but his bruised lips didn't make the right sound. 'This one's got even more of the structure. She must have the regenerative DNA elements too -'

'Mr Sempiter?' Applin was interrupting him again, he noted with a twinge of irritation. 'I've got that connection to security chief Kupteyn that you wanted.'

'Good. Do we have Sinatra's home address? Do we know where he'll be?'

Applin was switching through the Kupteyn connection, but also adjusting her own phone headset. 'I have Sinatra's personal number,' she said. 'I can connect to him and activate his phone headset. Then I'll keep him busy while security home in on his signal.'

'Excellent,' snapped Sempiter. 'The Doctor will try to make contact with his associates, and then we can recapture him too - Ah yes, Kupteyn, I have an urgent collection for you...'

He explained to the security chief what was happening. Finally, he explained that he would be travelling back to HQ himself to supervise the interrogation. 'I'll be with you by -'

Sempiter had looked at his wrist to check the time. It was a gesture born of habit, and he saw at once that there was no point.

He hadn't noticed that the Doctor had taken anything before he shut him in the laboratory. But now he realised what the Doctor had waved as he locked the door.

The timepiece in one hand. And the keys to Sempiter's personal flyer in the other.

Chapter Sixteen
'I Could Have Told You'

'What kept you, Fitz? I've been waiting for hours.'

'I'm surprised you waited.'

'I nearly didn't, but you've seen the layout of Level Ten.' Compassion wasn't smiling. She was scowling in the doorway of the lift, her arms folded savagely in front of her. All she needed was a rolling pin and hair curlers to complete my mental image. I decided not to mention this to her for a while. A couple of decades maybe.

The lift door pinged open, and I was surprised to find we were already on Level 10 of the HQ building. The corridor was in out-of-hours darkness, except for the occasional emergency light.

'While I was waiting, I used the time to do a bit more research while you fought your way here through heavy traffic, heaving crowds, and stampeding animals.'

'Sarcasm isn't your strong suit,' I said. 'Tell me what you did - that'll make you feel better. Better than me, I mean.'

I stepped out into the carpeted corridor of Level 10, and then hopped straight back in as the entire corridor was suddenly illuminated with overhead lights.

I stared at Compassion in a panic. She just gave me one of those looks down her freckled nose. 'I managed to do plenty of surfing round the systems,' she continued calmly. I've worked out from the security wiring diagrams which are the main rooms up here, since everything else is classified. And I've worked out how the automatic motion-detection lights work during the night shift.'

I squared my shoulders to suggest nonchalance, and to try to disguise the fact that I'd been hiding behind a large rubber plant in the lift. I stepped boldly back into the corridor, and fell over a round - and full - waste bin. I crashed down painfully on to the comfortable carpet, and the bin rolled away, scattering a trail of scrumpled paper.

'And', hissed Compassion and she hauled me roughly to my feet, 'I found out what the cleaners' schedules are. The bins are left outside the offices for supervised collection first thing in the morning. Watch your step. We're running late.'

'That sounds like a major bit of investigation. How did you manage all that?'

'It's a knack,' she said tartly.

I was making my way down the corridor to Sempiter's office, trying not to limp. 'I'm glad you didn't waste any time, then.'

Compassion pulled me round by the shoulder and stared me straight in the face. 'You're the one who was wasting time, ***Frank***. You're the one fraternising with the locals, instead of looking for the Doctor.' As if she cared, huh! But while she harangued me, she never blinked once. She just carried on relentlessly in her cold, threatening tone. I hadn't realised that her grey eyes could look so angry. 'This is not a game any more, Fitz. We have one chance at this. Just one. I got us computer authorisation to be here. But once the defence data-mining system works out that we only got that authorisation today, *and* that this is our first visit to Level Ten, *and* that we're here well after the working hours we're contracted to in our terms and conditions of employment, it'll shove forty thousand volts up the backside of every security guard on site, and they'll be up here and all over us like a rash. So put your arse in gear, and get a move on.'

Then the lights went out, and I could see only her face in the emergency lighting. We must have been standing close together and very still, and the motion detectors had decided there was no one there. It was suddenly so quiet that I could hear my heart beating. No, the sound was too slow and measured for that. Compassion's tirade had set my heart racing as if I'd just run up the stairs.

'Where's that noise coming from?' I whispered.

Compassion was already moving off past Sempiter's office, and the motion-detecting ceiling lights flickered alarmingly back to life. When I reached her at the end of the corridor, she had her head pressed against the door. Then she encouraged me to do the same. Now I could also feel the steady whumph-whumph noise of pumping machinery pulsing against my ear.

'What's in here?' asked Compassion. I shook my head. I hadn't got this far on my previous visit.

Compassion swiped her identity card through the reader, and the door clicked open with a distinct hiss of air. She stepped inside, and the lights nearest to us started to spark on erratically.

The steady pumping noise was the air conditioning, which made the room uncomfortably chilly in comparison with the corridor. I shivered, and not just because of the cold, I think.

The lights overhead continued to come on in a chain reaction along the ceiling, like the Oxford Street Christmas lights flickering into life. They slowly revealed a cavernous room, and I was reminded of the first time I had stepped into the TARDIS and been astounded by the sheer scale of what was behind the small outer door. In this room now, rows of low cabinets branched off in a maze of narrow corridors, stretching for hundreds of yards in three directions. I pointed into the middle distance. 'This room must take up one entire side of this whole building.'

Compassion squinted into the light. 'What am I looking at?'

'Seven years,' I muttered. 'Five for good behaviour.'

'It must be a research laboratory,' Compassion said.

I studied a panel of controls on the wall just inside the door. 'So what's this?'

Compassion gave it a cursory glance. 'Air conditioning, heating, life support. This is a sealed area.' She pointed at a cluster of cylinders attached to the wall, which I had assumed were fire extinguishers. 'Those are fire extinguishers,' she said helpfully.

'Thanks.'

'But those', said Compassion, indicating two further cylinders, 'appear to be filled with herbicide. The chemical composition suggests it's something like ethylene dibromide.'

I looked blank, obviously, so she asked, 'Why would you keep a spray device full of herbicide with your emergency equipment?' She didn't answer her own question, but instead took five steps into the room. There she began studying the nearest of what must have been ten scrubbed white tables stretching across a clear space in the room. Each of the low cabinets I'd first noticed had holes in the top, and the sides were shuttered.

I prised the lid off a nearby box. It was one of about twenty, each the size of a teachest, and all stacked neatly against the wall. As soon as the lid came off, my nostrils were assaulted by a horrible smell. It reminded me of the well-rotted manure we used to sell at the garden centre. I had a quick shufti in the box, and saw that it was half-filled with a sort of moist green-black earth.

I pressed the lid down before the pong overwhelmed me, and then opened one of the low shutters on a nearby cabinet instead.

I found myself looking into a cage about a yard high and two yards square. 'Er… Compassion, come and see this.'

She was swiftly at my side. 'It looks like a snake has shed its skin.'

'That's not a snake,' I said, and pointed into the corner of the cage where a pallid shape was nuzzling in a bed of filthy, matted straw. It looked like a shaved cat, but, as we watched, it started to lick at its back, and strands of dark hair began to separate. I pointed to the collection of shucked grey skin that Compassion had first noted. 'You can see the fur there. And there, you can make out the ears… the eyes… It's shed its entire outer layer. Just like Sempiter did.'

We unshuttered the next five cages. Inside each was another creature, every one in different stages of some kind of change. Some larger animals had shed their skins in several pieces. Another cage contained mouselike creatures with insect legs growing out of them, and they stumbled around in the new, bright light as though unsure how to use these unexpected additional limbs. In the last of the cages on the row, three squat plants had sprouted thick flower stems, which closer examination revealed to be wavering, vestigial animal heads.

'These are the creatures Sempiter experimented on first,' I said, feeling sick. 'Before he did it to himself.'

I kicked out angrily, thoughtlessly, at the next row of low cabinets, and the shutters fell down with a clatter. At once there was a frenzy of movement from inside, almost an explosion of feathers, and a canary flitted from the back of the cage and peered out coyly at us through the bars.

'Oh, you poor thing,' I said, abashed. The canary looked like Joey, my Aunt Beryl's bird, which we used to look after when she went for her annual pilgrimage to Skegness. 'I'm sorry, I didn't mean to frighten you.' I hunkered down beside the cage, and made kissing noises at the bird. I looked around to see if there was something I could poke into the cage as a peace offering, settling in the end for just pointing my finger encouragingly towards the bars. At which point, the sweet little creature chirruped a series of high notes, spat a gobbet of something, and pecked swiftly and viciously at my hand.

I pulled my finger away just in time, and fell back heavily against the next row of cabinets. Joey pecked repeatedly against the bars of his cage, with a savagery that belied his size. I could see now that the canary's beak was edged with razor-sharp teeth. The bars were pitted and scored from previous attacks, and I suddenly felt rather less like offering the bird a bit of cuttlefish. 'Who's an ugly boy then?'

'There must be hundreds more of these experiments here,' said Compassion, who seemed neither alarmed nor amused by my undignified near miss. 'I wonder if the Doctor is one of them?'

I was about to suggest we call out and see if we got any response, when there was a chirruping sound by my right ear. I let out a great shout of alarm and dismay, which frightened Compassion more than anything so far. As I scrabbled fearfully at the side of my face, my hands tangled in something. I tugged at it, wrenched it from my head, feeling in the same instant a sharp pain in my other ear. I was ready to fling the creature to the floor and stamp it to death. Which was the point at which I realised that it was my phone headset, signalling an incoming call.

I paused for a second to regain my composure and check that my Y-fronts were still dry. Then I thumbed the receive button.

'Hey, Frank,' said Hannaw's voice. 'What's happening?'

I was silent for a good ten seconds while I got my head around this sudden turn of events. Meanwhile, the budgie from hell spat at me again. I staggered to my feet. 'It's Sempiter's PA,' I mouthed at Compassion, who was glaring at me.

'Hello?' said Hannaw's voice from the earpiece. 'Frank? Are you there?'

'Er... yeah, hon. No sweat,' I lied. 'Got a knot in my cable.'

'Sounds kinky,' she said. 'I thought I'd give you a call to see where you were at –' She broke off abruptly for a fraction of a second, and then continued. 'So, how are you?'

My sense of unease returned at once. What Hannaw was *not* doing was telling me how *she* was, the dreadful mess that she was facing, and what a big bad bitch life in general was being to her personally at that very instant. I had distinctly heard her asking about me. What I *couldn't* hear, in the background, was the distinctive tap of a keyboard or the sound of her having a sneaky drag on a ciggie, both the traditional cues on all her previous phone conversations that told me her attention was in neutral and she wasn't really listening. In fact, she was obviously hanging on my every word. That worried me.

This all flashed through my mind in an instant, of course. 'I'm up to no good as usual,' I said.

'Where are you?' Her voice was sweet and innocent. Definitely not like her: *...to see where you're at*, she'd said earlier.

'Just hanging round the apartment, y'know. Got a few pallies round, having a few brewskies...' Compassion was making cutthroat signals. 'Where are you, babe? It's late.'

A pause. 'Yeah. Mr Sempiter's asked me to work on awhile this evening.'

Mr Sempiter? Asked me? Not 'that git-faced tosser's working me ragged'? I could practically see him hovering over her shoulder.

Compassion looked as if she wanted to wrench the headset off me.

'Hannaw, honey, can I call you back? I need to siphon the python.'

'No need,' she said, too quickly. 'I'll stay on the line.'

'Uh-huh,' I said. I took the headset off, and jammed it in the mad canary's cage, then ushered Compassion towards the exit. 'We've been rumbled,' I said. 'We need to get out of here. I think they can track me through the headset. That's why I left it with Tweetie Pie. With luck, he'll be gobbing on them just as we're vanishing over the horizon.'

'We need to find the Doctor,' said Compassion, hurrying past me on the way to the lift doors. 'If we can't find him, we need to find where he parked the TARDIS.'

We could see that the lift wasn't on our level any more. Someone had called it to another floor, and it was going down.

I chased behind Compassion as she ran round the corridor to the next lift. I shouted after her, 'I can't just vanish like that.'

Compassion was giving me another 'you what?' look.

'I can't,' I said again, my calm voice belying the fact that my stomach was churning, my heart racing. 'I told Hannaw that I was at home, so they might go there. Alura's still at the apartment.'

'What?' said Compassion coldly. She jabbed at the lift-call button with her thumb, probably pretending it was my eye.

'Yeah, all right,' I admitted. 'I didn't dump her. I... it wasn't the right time... oh Christ, Compassion, I just couldn't. I left her a note,' I concluded lamely.

'You left her a note.'

'Even if she's read it, she could still be there. Maybe even waiting for me to come back and change my mind.'

Compassion let out a huge sigh, and squeezed her eyes shut tight in a gesture of utter exasperation. 'Fitz, that's exactly what you are doing, changing your mind. Or at least, what passes for your mind. Why not *use* it instead? Get your headset back and warn her.'

'No phone at the apartment.'

'I won't let you go back there, Fitz.'

I said, 'You can't stop me. Come on, Compassion. It's... well, it's the *right* thing to do.'

She was about to say something, but the lift doors snapped open and I jumped inside. I couldn't bear to look her in those angry grey eyes, so I pressed my nose against the glass wall and stared down into the well of the building as the lift descended.

Suddenly, on one of the lower floors, a strip of lights sprang into life. Some of the cleaning staff, I thought. So why were they running? In fact, why were they all wearing security uniforms?

I darted quick glances at the three other lifts, one in the centre of each of the other walls. All three were moving up from the lower floors. And they all had security staff in them.

I whirled to the lift controls and thumped every button with the heel of my hand, almost knocking over the rubber plant beside me in my panic. 'They're on to us.'

The lift stopped on Level 7, and we hurried out. Immediately, of course, the movement sensors switched on the corridor's ceiling lights, and I froze. We couldn't have made it more obvious if we'd waved a big placard saying 'Level 7! Come and get us!'

Compassion shoved me in the back to get me moving. We tried the handle of each office we passed. They were all locked, so we picked our way quickly between the sentinel waste bins full of rubbish until we reached the corner of the landing.

Compassion peered quickly over the balcony and into the well of the building, checking where the guards were. When the lift further along the next corridor pinged open, Compassion immediately bundled us into the emergency stairs. We huddled together behind the door, trying not to breathe too loudly. I was sure that my heart was hammering loud enough for them to hear it from as far away as the ground floor.

It pounded louder still when I heard the security chief's snarling voice. It was Kupteyn himself, coming along the corridor from the lift. 'I want him found,' he bellowed. 'This was where his lift stopped. I want to get my fingers around Sinatra's scrawny neck and snap it like a twig. So keep him alive – I don't care how badly damaged he is, just make sure he's still conscious.'

I tried not to whimper too loudly behind the door. Compassion was holding tight to the handle on our side. It sounded like Kupteyn and two, maybe three, others were standing the other side of the door.

'No one here, Chief.'

'Team Six, get up to Level Ten and check that phone trace. You, check the stairs.'

The handle rattled. I was about to fling myself down the emergency stairs behind us, when I realised that Compassion was holding the door closed. Maybe she had really strong wrists. More likely, they weren't trying very hard on the other side.

'Can't have gone this way, sir, it's locked.'

'A fire exit, locked?' Kupteyn snapped. He was obviously talking into his communicator again: 'Team Four, check access stairway three up to Level Seven.'

'Sir!' An excited tone in another guard's voice. 'Lights just came on in that office across the way!' There was the sound of boots pounding off down the corridor.

We slipped out into the corridor again. Across the divide of the building's stairwell, opposite us on the same level, I could see Kupteyn and his team breaking into an office, which was the only one on the corridor with its lights blazing. Some poor overworked idiot must have woken up in his office and activated the light sensors, and was about to get an even ruder awakening from the security team.

Compassion, meanwhile, was grappling with the potted plant from the lift. She hefted it over the balcony. Compost and leaves scattered into the well of the building and on to the balconies below us. Almost immediately, movement sensors on several of the other floors snapped on their ceiling lights. Then the big pot slammed on to the ground floor far below with a shattering crash.

'Oops,' I murmured to Compassion. 'There goes another rubber-tree plant.' We crouched behind our balcony.

The sudden illumination of lights on other levels, and the noisy crash of the falling pot, distracted the guards. Kupteyn was already shouting demands, his harsh tones reverberating around the huge well of the building. It was a wonder that he bothered with the communicator at all: they could probably hear him throughout the whole HQ. 'They're on their way out,' he bellowed. 'I want a team out to his apartment immediately. Get on to weather control and clear us. Do it now!' He ran to the nearest lift, and the last thing I could hear before the doors closed was, 'Where's Ellis? We need him, too.'

I watched the glass lift descending, Kupteyn still silently gesticulating with wild movements of his thick arms.

'Compassion!' I realised I was clutching at her arm. 'We're stuck here, and they're on their way to the apartment.'

She merely pointed at the lower levels. It took a moment for me to grasp what she was showing me. 'They're all going back down. We can follow them wherever the lights have already come on. They will be able to see us if we use the lifts, so we must use the stairs.'

We threaded our way down the stairwells, avoiding other people by cutting across each landing where necessary. I hadn't realised there were so many security guards in the building. Maybe I should've got out more.

Then we got a bit too casual about things, because on Level 3 Compassion literally walked into a security guard as he came out of an office. He raised his percussion rifle, and she spun him round in an easy movement so that he had his back to me.

'Direk!' she said in a breathy tone. She stared at his rifle as if he were exposing himself. 'You gave me such a fright! What's happening?'

'Nancy,' said Direk Merdock. The rifle wavered uncertainly. 'What are you doing here?'

Compassion rolled her eyes theatrically. 'Oh, working late again, you know.' She gestured to the long data-entry office behind her, where a handful of the hundreds of desks were still occupied by after-hours staff. 'Direk, I was supposed to meet Frank in the lobby. Have you seen him? I called him earlier, but he cut me dead. I hope he's all right.' Her eyes were filled with anxiety. God, she was good at this, I thought sourly.

Direk lowered the rifle, and I could see he was giving a sad little shake of his fetchingly brain-free head. 'Oh dear. I'm afraid I may have some bad news about Frank,' he began, holding her gently by the elbow. 'Let me explain as we take the lift down. My shift's just starting...'

Oh damn, he was going to turn around and see me where I stood opposite the lift in the middle of an otherwise clear corridor. No open doors behind me. Direk too far forward to clobber, and still armed. The stairwell too far back for me to reach in time.

So I didn't hesitate. Which is just as well, because if I'd have thought it through more carefully I certainly wouldn't have attempted anything quite so bloody stupid. What I did was this: I jumped over the balcony, and clung on to the rail on the other side. As I slapped into the other side of the railing, I lost my grip and dropped about a yard until I was just able to clutch desperately at the bottom of the balcony.

My feet were dangling in midair, four floors above the hard surface on which I knew the pot plant had previously shattered into hundreds of tiny pieces. I tried not to look down. In doing so, I found I was looking in through the glass window of the lift right beside me. Compassion was holding Merdock by the forearms, a casual and affectionate gesture designed to prevent him looking round and seeing me.

As the lift started to go down, I knew what I had to do. I swung my legs across and slumped over the flat metal roof of the lift car, hoping the noise would be masked by the clank of the machinery.

When the lift reached the ground floor, I watched from above as Compassion and Merdock stepped out of the lift. She had linked arms with him, and they walked carefully across the deserted lobby area, stepping around the remains of the rubber plant and its splintered container. At one point, Compassion twisted her foot on a loose piece of pot, and fell against Merdock for support, laughing. He clung on to her to stop her falling, and she whispered a thank-you in his ear. At the same time, she was making a frantic little head movement and rolling her eyes at me.

Of course, that was when I twigged that I was supposed to be getting the hell out of there while she distracted him. I slid down the side of the lift. As my feet hit the floor, Compassion took Merdock's spotty cheeks in her hands, caressing the hair around his ears with her fingers, her head close to his, and - Bloody hell, she was snogging him! Tongues as well. Eurgh! Over his shoulder, her eyes were open, watching me. She turned him and waved me on with one free hand, while I slunk past and tried not to stare.

I was going out through the main doors when I heard them talking again.

'What was that for?' Merdock was saying.

'I wanted to see what it was like.'

'And what was it like?'

'Well, you were there too, Direk.' Compassion gave a girly little laugh I'd never heard before. 'So, when does your shift end?'

He groaned like the grumpy teenager he almost certainly still was. 'Aww, it's just starting...'

I saw her edging towards the exit, reluctant to leave him. 'See you tomorrow. For coffee, eh?'

As Compassion walked out of the building towards me and into the cold damp night, I saw her radiant smile snap off like an electric light.

We were fortunate to be able to catch a public-transportation bus quickly. Compassion sat, saying nothing, just staring intently through the front windscreen. A solitary drunk meandered up to her and looked at her from close range. She just put up her hand and calmly but firmly pushed him in the face until he stumbled over backwards.

I chattered away throughout the whole journey, saying

something, anything, to keep me from thinking about Alura waiting in the apartment. Would she be safe? What would I be able to say to her even if she was?

We got to our stop, only to see our connecting bus vanishing into the dark night. Compassion started to run, and for one surreal moment I thought she was going to chase the vehicle, try to catch it, like a dog that doesn't know it's beaten. I stumbled half-heartedly after her, wondering where she got her strength from after three nights without sleep at Frontier Worlds HQ.

We ran for thirty minutes, with frequent brief stops. Compassion continued running on the spot whenever I needed to catch my breath, as though she were an athlete on a training run. On one of these occasions, she also slotted her receiver back on to her ear.

Just before our apartment building came into view, I finally noticed that it wasn't raining. Yet it always rained at night, didn't it? That was what I remembered most about this godforsaken city - the long evening trips through sodden streets, not caring that the rain was pouring off the brim of my trilby because I was walking with Alura on my arm.

Alura.

I wanted to rush past Compassion and into the apartment, but she made me wait while she scanned the streets around our building, obviously trying to hear things with her receiver. When she was satisfied there was no danger, she released her surprisingly firm grip on my upper arm, and followed me into the building.

We hurried across the hallway, past the mangled remains of the chandelier. There was no sign of our concierge.

I fumbled for my key card, feeling that familiar where-did-I-leave-it panic before remembering that I'd left it behind for Alura. I'd planned never to come back. Now it was the only place I wanted to be.

I didn't need the key card. The front door was ajar. Compassion wanted to hold me back, but I managed to shake her off and barge in, stupidly telling myself that I'd fight my way past anyone in there.

Compassion was staring around with disdain. 'This place is less of a mess than I remember.'

I stared around at the too-tidy room. The apartment was much as I'd left it. The key card was on the table, the magazines were scattered on the floor.

A vase had fallen over on the sideboard, and water was dripping slowly and splashing into a damp patch on the carpet. My too-hasty note was still on the polished surface, unfolded, sodden.

I slammed open the door to our bedroom. Alura was lying on my side of the bed, staring across the room at me. The dead phone was off its hook, cast aside on the bed.

Alura didn't move. She didn't say anything.

The bloom had gone from her beautiful dark skin. The blood was a stark patch of red across my pillow. The pearl-handled scissors stuck out of her, brutal evidence in the side of her neck.

I should have warned her, I wanted to say to Compassion. I should have told her how I felt.

'They're coming. We have to go, now!' Compassion was dragging me away, back into the main room, and I didn't resist. All I could think of over and over and over was that I should have told Alura, I should have told her, I should have told her. But now I knew I couldn't even tell Compassion.

Chapter Seventeen
'It's Nice To Go Travelling'

Compassion was dragging me back towards the apartment's front door, and I was letting her. Not caring where I went, what I did. The room stumbled around me, leached of colour, a grey mass. The sideboard seemed to slide past, and I tried to reach out for the soaked note I'd left there. She'd read it, I was telling myself stupidly. She'd read it, and that was why.

Compassion yanked hard at my reaching arm. 'Concentrate, Fitz.' She slapped me in the face - hard. I stared at her stupidly, fighting the little-boy urge to cry. She slapped me again, and I began to get angry instead. 'They broke radio silence, and now they're coming up the stairs,' she snapped at me. 'We'll use the window, and drop off the balcony.'

'Yeah, right. I've had plenty of practice recently.'

'Humour,' Compassion said bleakly, and I felt her grip slacken. 'That's a good sign.'

She was ahead of me through the window, and over the edge of the balcony. I hesitated on the far side of the windows, pushing them back into place and peering through a crack. In the apartment, three broad dark figures burst through the main door and fanned out like FBI agents in a cop show. I actually felt my chest lurch when Kupteyn stepped in after them. How had we got here before them? Did they get lost, or had they taken the tourist route?

I didn't wait to hear what Kupteyn said. I struggled over the balcony, let myself down until I was holding on by just my fingertips. On my wrist, the bright orange face on my watch leered at me. Then I let go, dropped the rest of the way, and landed fairly comfortably in the grassy border by the roadside. Immediately, I looked around for Compassion. She was already making away from the apartment block, hurrying over the damp ground.

I caught up with her sooner than I'd expected, beneath a flickering street lamp. Then I spotted why. There was a crumpled, dishevelled figure shambling in our direction, dragging one foot slightly in the wet road. For a heartbeat I thought it was the drunk from the bus. I was even pulling back my arm to punch him smack in his dirty face, when I placed him. It was Griz Ellis.

'Frank...' he croaked. He stumbled towards us and, much to my disgust, seized me by the shoulders. Beneath the street lamp I could see his one good eye glittering with an odd light. 'I had to find you.'

I disengaged his arms gently and looked around as though searching for people following us. More importantly, that way I didn't have to inhale his halitosis. I held my breath and had another look at him.

His mad hair was flat against his head, damply matted there, as though he'd run through a rainstorm. This was no longer the smug, unbearable, overweening Griz Ellis I'd left in the office earlier that day, though. If it was possible, his clothes were even more like leftovers from a church bazaar, and flecked with blood. His face was covered with spots of red, his hands too. I didn't think I could face any more blood.

'I trusted them, Frank,' he said, his eyes flicking to Compassion and back, uncertain who to trust. 'Mega mistake.' He gave me what seemed like a very long look. And then he scrunched up his already very ugly face, buried it in his podgy hands, and started to weep copiously in the middle of the street. If I hadn't been so terrified about escaping, I might have broken down and cried alongside him.

'We need to go,' said Compassion with no trace of sympathy. She set off briskly down the road, jerking her head for me to follow. 'Come on, we have to get back up the mountain and find the Doctor, or the TARDIS.'

'They want to kill me,' wailed Ellis, trailing after me, hanging on my arm like a beggar. 'Kill *us*,' he added.

I started to think about Kupteyn breaking into the apartment. Wondered how long it would take him and his cronies to get back down the stairs. Compassion was at the next corner. I tried to pull my arm away from Ellis. 'How did you get here?'

'They were coming for me, Frank,' blustered Ellis, his eye rolling like a marble. 'I found out that Sempiter's got a team working on weird stuff on Level Ten. Dreadful, dreadful stuff, Frank, I can't tell you.'

'I might surprise you.'

'A perversion of our work, Frank,' he persisted, laying it on a bit thick I thought. At the same time he was squeezing my arm hard. 'Sempiter's been keeping things from me. When I found out, he authorised his guards to seize me, all my research materials, and any of my staff!'

'In descending order of importance,' I sneered.

'I had to come and warn you, Frank!'

'How did you get here?'

'They tracked me down to my apartment...' started Ellis.

Compassion barked a bitter laugh over her shoulder. 'What sort of idiot goes back to his apartment when he knows he's being pursued?'

I ignored the jibe. 'How did you get here, Ellis?'

'I had to break out of my own window!'

'Yeah, tell me about it,' I agreed.

'Well, my apartment's on the second floor...'

'No, I mean -' I glared at him. 'Do you have transport? How did you travel here?'

'My company flyer, of course.'

Compassion spun on her heel and faced him. 'Obviously,' she said, suddenly attentive. 'You know, your pursuers are ransacking our apartment now, looking for you. We can get you away from them, if you take us to your vehicle.'

It was parked neatly at the next corner, a smart four-seater flying machine with stylish rear fins that made it look like a Ford Zephyr designed for Flash Gordon. The undercarriage was less sleek, with large heavy wheels and most of its storage in thick metal cages.

And, since it belonged to Ellis, I wasn't too surprised to note that it was painted in a dynamic beige with taupe highlights. Teetering stacks of paperwork were piled on all the seats, and even the driver's position had a folder squashed on to it in the shape of Ellis's ample backside.

Ellis fumbled in his pockets, retrieved his identity card, and used it to scrape dead flies off the windscreen.

Compassion plucked the card from his bloodied fingers, and used it to open the door, which yawned widely apart at the front. Ellis shuffled forward, reversing into position in the driving seat with the easy grace of a rhinoceros.

I got into the back section. The familiar and dreadful stink of Griz Ellis permeated every fibre of the interior. Ellis might look and sound like a shadow of his former self, I thought, but his traumatic flight from Frontier Worlds had in no way damaged his food-to-fart converter. I couldn't work out how to open the flyer's window, so I wafted the open door on its hinge for a bit to no avail, gave up, and decided to breathe just through my mouth.

Compassion stood outside the car, staring in at Ellis. 'I'll drive,' she said.

'This is my flyer,' he said. It was that old imperious tone.

She stared him down.

'This is my flyer,' he repeated.

She was pointing down the street now. Ellis and I both followed her gesture. Outside our apartment, a squat, dark-green Frontier Worlds security vehicle was pulling up with a squeal of brakes. Three security guards started to get out to meet Kupteyn, who was just leaving our building.

He stared down the street and saw us, and did an impeccable double-take. He had obviously seen Compassion, probably because she was waving at him with her fingers.

'What are you doing?' I shrieked.

She held the identity card just out of Ellis's reach. 'Getting in to drive this heap,' she said, and her lips smiled in a thin line. 'Get out, Ellis.'

Ellis was having none of it. He shuffled his bulk across to the passenger side, spilling paperwork around him as he plopped his fat bum firmly in the seat in front of me.

Compassion slid into the vacated driving position. I could see from her look that she was half considering how to push Ellis out through the opposite door of the flyer. But we could all hear a lot of shouting from further down the street. Kupteyn was bellowing, and, though we couldn't quite make out what, he was clearly making angry hand signals to get the guards back into the security vehicle. Its doors hadn't yet slammed closed before it started to barrel down the roadway towards us, flying at us with unbelievable, frightening speed.

No, we were speeding towards them. I clutched grimly on to the seat in front as the acceleration pressed me back in my own. The security van itself had barely begun to move. Even from where I sat in the back, I thought I could see its front-seat passengers widen their eyes, or throw their hands up in front of their faces, and I knew we were going to hit, going to hit hard, going to smack straight into them at sickening, killing speed.

Compassion wrenched at the steering column, and I left my stomach behind on the ground as Ellis's flyer... well... it flew, of course. It corkscrewed up into the air and then steadied before making two huge, surging loops. We plunged onward into the sky, with only dark and threatening clouds visible above us to provide any orientation.

'Oh, God,' I groaned at Compassion as we levelled out at last. 'Did you see what I had for breakfast?'

'Of course not.'

I studied the scattered paperwork on the seat next to me. 'Do you want to?'

Within minutes we had shot high up above the city. When I felt a bit braver, I opened my eyes and peered cautiously out of the window. We were travelling over the spaceport dock, and the loading cranes far below reminded me of my old Meccano set.

Ellis seemed to have regained some of his composure now, and was fussing at Compassion. 'You're pulling too hard on the power lever, my dear. Much too hard. It's a mistake to waste too much of the fuel capacity early in the flight.'

Compassion seemed to be growling. Or was that the engine?

'And you're overrevving on the banking movements, not keeping a steady speed as you turn in midair. Any flying instructor will tell you that is enough to fail you on your basic test - it's an obvious mistake. Big mistake.'

Compassion took both hand off the controls, and looked sideways directly at Ellis. The flyer immediately started to veer off to one side and down. She sounded strangely calm as she said, 'Would you like to instruct me? To demonstrate?' More calm than me, certainly. I tried to think where the vehicle might keep parachutes. Then I started to worry about how I didn't know how to put on a parachute. So I tried to console myself by deciding that they were probably very securely and unreachably stowed in the heavy storage section slung below the flyer.

'Go on, show me,' Compassion repeated to Ellis.

Ellis's good eye stood out on a stalk. 'Er... perhaps I'll leave it to you.'

Compassion smoothly took control again. 'And that's the correct answer,' she said. 'You survive into the next round.'

'Survive is right,' said Ellis bitterly. 'That's all I can hope to do, now. Sempiter will try to pin the blame on me and my team for those experiments on Level Ten. Can you imagine what he was doing up there?'

'No,' said Compassion. Her brusque answer cut off my comment about our earlier visit.

'So,' I said after a pause, 'what will you do now that you've... er... resigned?'

Ellis settled himself more comfortably in the seat, and started to pick wax out of his ear with his little finger. 'Perhaps I'll go home,' he said. 'Back to the land, just like I've always wanted to.'

'Put down some roots?' I prompted.

'Yes,' said Ellis, oblivious to my sarcastic heard-it-before tone.

Putting down some roots. The steady thrum of the flyer's engine was hypnotic, conducive to reflection. Alura wanted to settle down. She'd been more ready for that than I had realised. Or than I'd been prepared to admit. More ready, or more desperate. I squeezed my eyes shut tight, feeling the pressure build behind them, the noise rising in my head, filling my mind. What had I done to her? What had I made her do?

The engine note changed as the flyer's angle flattened again. I opened my eyes to watch the ground far below us for a few minutes. We had got beyond the level of low cloud now, and the milky light of a pale moon lit up a stretched canopy of treetops as far as I could see. 'I thought you said we were going up the mountain,' I noted. 'And that's way off in the other direction.'

Compassion cocked her head on one side. 'All the signal traffic says we're blocked off from there at the moment. Local law enforcement aren't pleased with our flight path, and Frontier Worlds security are between us and the Research Centre.'

Ellis poked his fat fingers towards the controls. 'You can't know that. You haven't got the communication net activated. It's dangerous to travel out this far without it. Stupid, even. Big mistake. Mega mistake.'

Compassion favoured him with a cold sideways glance. As she turned her head, I could see the receiver slotted into her earlobe. There was no obvious join between metal and skin, it was simply part of her once more. 'I don't need your communication net,' she told Ellis.

Ellis was unconvinced. 'Besides, they'll know this is an executive vehicle. So they'll know I can monitor all their security communications. If I was them -'

He got no further. We all snapped our attention to the front of the vehicle as another flyer veered out of nowhere and across our path from somewhere beneath us. Its navigation lights blazed in the night sky, leaving smeared trails across my retinas.

'If you were them,' said Compassion grimly, 'you'd pursue us while running silent.' She wrenched at the controls, and our flyer accelerated to the side and away. I slammed into the side window, and my head buzzed with pain. 'Where did they come from?'

'The Darkling Zone complex?' I said. 'On the far side of the jungle?'

Ellis stared over his shoulder at me. I could make out his amazed expression. He seemed about to say something, but was interrupted when Compassion hurled our vehicle into another evasive manoeuvre.

'Overrevving,' Ellis admonished.

'Shut up,' she snarled. 'We need to shake them.'

Ellis shook his head so fiercely that his flattened greasy hair finally started to peel away from his head. 'That's one of our new transport shuttles,' he said. 'We can't outrun them. And we've nowhere to hide.' He lurched forward in his seat. 'Let me talk to them...'

Compassion slapped his hand away from the dashboard. 'Just watch me,' she said, and wrenched again at the controls. There was a horrible free-fall moment as we spun in the air, and then we were suddenly facing the other shuttle. The engine note seemed to gutter briefly, strained to its limit, and then hiccoughed back to roaring life.

The pale moon lay behind the other shuttle, so I could make out its bulky shape as we started moving towards it. At least I knew the routine now, I thought, the chicken run. I braced myself between the seat and the side wall, preparing for the last-minute movement when we would veer past our pursuers.

But then what? Ellis had already said we couldn't outrun the shuttle. And where were we going to hide out here, way above the jungle?

We gathered speed. The treetops below whizzed past faster and faster.

I figured it out at that point. We weren't going to outrun them. We were going to run into them.

My mouth was full of cotton wool. I could hear myself

mumbling nonsense words of futile protest as Compassion loosed us at the other vehicle.

She did make a small adjustment at the very, very last second. Our heavy undercarriage must have sliced into the entire top half of the other shuttle, and we spun wildly away from the crash as the other vehicle literally disintegrated beneath us.

Our flyer's engine whined up the scale, gave a sudden spluttering pause, and then cut out.

'Don't even think about mentioning overrevving,' said Compassion in the sudden quiet. 'Brace yourselves.'

All around us the metal of our flyer groaned or shrieked in protest, trying to hold together as it began to drop. There was a growing crack in the floor beneath my seat, and the hissing, whistling noise of air rushing past.

Outside, the jungle canopy raced up to meet us.

Chapter Eighteen
'I'm Walking Behind You'

I must have blacked out when we hit. I don't remember much about the crash, except the noises - the rending, tearing sound of branches on the outside, and my screaming as we plunged below the tree line.

I don't know how long I was out. Maybe it was only a few seconds; certainly the flyer was still sparking and smouldering around us when I did come around. There was a huge pain across my chest where the safety belt had squeezed it, and a dull ache in the back of my skull where my head must have whiplashed back against the headrest. I could feel a sore patch on my arm, where I'd bruised it around my inoculation scar.

Ellis was slumped forward in the front seat, like a puppet with snapped strings. Under other circumstances, I'd have assumed his noisy breathing was a sign of a heavy night, or catarrh, or both. I popped my seat-belt buckle, and leaned into the front passenger section to check. Ellis was deeply unconscious, and I didn't know whether to shake him to try to rouse him. I didn't much want to touch him, to be honest with you. More importantly, where was Compassion?

A steady cool breeze, icy-fresh compared with the muggy flyer interior, was my first clue. Fragments of glass over the controls was the next. The front windscreen was smashed, punched outward over the front of the vehicle.

My heart hammered faster still. Compassion had been thrown through the glass. A long smear of blood stretched across the beige front of the vehicle.

I wondered briefly about throwing up again. Instead I gave a shrill shout when a face appeared at the window beside me. I could hardly believe that it was Compassion. She had a gash over her right eye, a lifted flap of dead white skin that oozed blood down her face. The blood matted her copper-red hair, and had soaked a vivid patch on her white shirt. 'Get out,' she said. 'We have to get moving.' She stepped away to the rear of the vehicle.

I popped the door, and half fell out into a patch of jungly undergrowth. Behind the flyer was a strip of churned ground where we had slid to a halt. A stretch of broken trees beyond revealed a luminous patch of night sky, but all around us the jungle pressed around us, silent and dark.

Compassion was recovering things from below the rear of the flyer, where the only undamaged storage was. I remembered how we had collided with the Frontier Worlds shuttle, and hearing it stripping away all the other heavy containers. I imagined Ellis's research scattering with the remains of the other shuttle, a shower of burning fragments in the night, unnatural rain over the jungle.

Ellis. I stuck my head back into the flyer, which now smelled of smoke and blood. Compassion pulled me back out. 'Leave him.'

'He's still alive, Compassion.'

'Leave him,' she repeated. She handed me an axe that she'd recovered from the back. Its handle was embossed with the words FOR EMERGENCY USE ONLY. There was the sound of more rummaging from behind me, and Compassion lifted out a number of other items - torches, blankets, some odd-shaped equipment which I assumed were spares for the vehicle. There was even a small and dented trunk full of odd tools I didn't recognise at first, until I unfurled a section of badly stained, olive-green waterproof cloth and worked out they were the components of a sort of tent. A small, oval medical kit completed the collection.

Compassion emerged from her final examination of the flyer's storage container, and was offering a squarish metal box to me with one hand. She held her other arm awkwardly against herself, as though she'd hurt it.

'Are you all right?' I indicated her arm.

She blinked blood away from her eye, as though it were a mere irritation. 'I'll be OK.'

'Yeah, right,' I said. I looked inside the metal box. It was surprisingly heavy, and seemed to be full of cakes, forty or fifty of them packed in different colours of foil. The words on the wrappers told me they contained various high-protein, high-energy, high-fibre food concentrates. They were manufactured and packaged by Frontier Worlds Corporation, of course, and each had the implausible title Nutrition Bar. 'Looks like he had time to pack dinner.'

'Emergency rations,' Compassion replied. 'He won't be needing them. Come on.' I tried one of the cake bars, and it tasted revolting - sour and cloying.

Compassion recovered the axe from me, took a couple of halting steps away from the wreckage of our flyer, and then stood with her head cocked to one side as though she were listening, or scenting the air. Who did she think she was, Minnie Ha-Ha? 'The signal traffic is very faint,' she said at last.

'You didn't damage your earpiece in the crash, then?'

'Obviously.' She pointed into the jungle. 'We should go this way.'

'What about Ellis? We can't just leave him.'

She didn't even look into the flyer. 'You carry him, then,' she said. 'But he'll just slow you down.' Then she limped off into the jungle.

I stepped away from the flyer, astonished when I looked back at it now to see how buckled and twisted the exterior was. I could hear Ellis's heavy breathing. The prospect of lugging his malodorous body was not appealing.

Apart from the pain in my chest and head, I was remarkably unscathed. I didn't know how Compassion was going to manage, but she was already swinging the axe at the worst of the lower-hanging vines and branches, hacking a path through and disappearing into the dark.

The raucous sound of Ellis's breathing reminded me he was still there. It wasn't like when I left Alura, I told myself. We weren't close; in fact he'd made my work life pretty miserable. Even if he was fleeing from the same people as Compassion and I were, he was going to be a burden; he was going to slow us down. And Compassion was already vanishing into the jungle.

Thus rationalising my decision, I reluctantly concluded I should abandon Ellis to fend for himself. Not *very* reluctantly, though.

I scampered after Compassion, clutching as many of the emergency provisions to my throbbing chest as I could. The metal box of food weighed a ton.

'I'm glad I changed my underwear this morning,' I chattered as I struggled through the snagging brambles and hanging vines. 'My mum always said that they should be clean, in case I was involved in an accident, so that I wouldn't embarrass myself in front of the ambulance driver. Hospital clothing is one-size-fits-all and no-size-fits-Fitz, she told me.'

'You're babbling,' said Compassion without turning round. 'But talking is good. Try to stay awake. You're in shock.'

I watched her limp ahead. I resented her analysis of me. 'I'm OK. You're the one who needs help. I may end up having to carry you. I'm sure you'd rather have Direk Merdock sweep you off your feet. Though actually, I can't imagine anyone sweeping you off your feet.' I thought about how she'd kissed Merdock, and her reaction afterwards. 'Not without them using some kind of road-cleaning vehicle, anyway.'

If anything, she increased her pace, keeping one arm stiff beside her. The axe in her other hand sliced through the undergrowth. Forging ahead. But going where?

I'd been lost in a forest before, of course. I'd boasted at school about it, how I'd used an instinctive sense of direction and native cunning to rescue my entire family from a crisis of Rider Haggard proportions at the start of our biannual holiday. For some reason, my father had insisted on taking the Hythe link to the Isle of Wight that year, which meant an extended journey through the New Forest in our exhausted Hillman Imp. My mum, no navigator, had taken us on the road towards Fordingbridge by mistake, and there had been a minute or two when we'd worried a bit about missing our ferry. I had (a) spotted the road signs we should have been following, (b) got out of the car for a toilet break in the rain, and (c) patted a New Forest pony which was dozing on the road's warm tarmac directly in front of our car. You can imagine how this became an epic adventure of piloting a vessel under extremes of physical endurance, fierce weather and untamed wildlife. As a story told while playing marbles in the playground at St Edward's Primary, it had convinced my solitary friend George Cullen. Eventually, I think I'd even convinced myself.

So, as Compassion and I now fought our way through a midnight jungle, I was silently reminding myself that I should walk with the nonchalant step that comes from knowing that I had proof already that I was expert at identifying north from the position of moss on trees, adept at catching, skinning and cooking a rabbit using only string and dry twigs, and capable of having a quick poo behind a tree without getting it down the back of my legs.

Reality swiftly intervened. After what seemed like an age, I sat down with a thump on the damp surface of a toppled tree trunk, and called after Compassion. I saw her torch beam bouncing around as she returned to where I had collapsed. She stared at me with an ill-disguised contempt.

'Oh, God,' I moaned. 'My legs ache, my back aches, I'm parched and famished and I want to go home. How long have we been walking?'

Compassion didn't even think about it. 'A little over twelve minutes.'

I angled my torch, and checked my watch. She was right, of course. I wanted to cry, not sure whether from the tiredness or the sight of the orange smiley face on my wrist. So I looked at Compassion instead. She didn't have a smiley face. The gash over her eye was still seeping blood, but she'd made no effort to clean it up. 'You should do something about that cut,' I told her, rummaging about in the medical kit. 'I'm no expert, but I did see something similar on an episode of *Dr Kildare*.'

'Dr who?' said Compassion. She put her fingers up to her forehead, and looked surprised when they came away stained with blood.

When I motioned to help her treat the wound, she waved me away. 'If you're hungry, then have something to eat.'

Perhaps she'd seen my reaction earlier, because she also waved away my offer of a delicious Nutrition Bar. When had she last eaten? She had more stamina than I had, that was for sure. I tore open another of the foil-wrapped cake bars, and chewed off half of it in one big bite. It tasted absolutely foul, of course. I tried one with a different wrapper, and that was worse. Several dozen more peered up unappealingly at me from the box.

Compassion's torch bounced off again. In the light of my own torch beam, illuminating her vanishing back, she seemed to be limping less.

The many and varied contents of the survival kit were scattered all around my feet. I looked at the cake bars, the complicated tent components, the blankets, the tools, the whole panoply of redundant items that I'd brought from the wrecked flyer. I scooped up as many of them as I could in my arms, leaving behind the heavy metal box. It was still hot in the night jungle, that sticky kind of heat that gums your clothes to your clammy body, so I reluctantly dropped the tent. I also decided to abandon the more disgusting of the Nutrition Bar cakes, which is to say all of them, and stumbled after the vanishing flashes of Compassion's torch.

Compassion continued to slash a passage for us through the worst of the undergrowth, alternating the axe between hands. After about two hours she explained, with no sign of exhaustion in her voice, that we still faced a long trek to the nearest edge of the jungle. By her calculations, whatever and however she was doing them, she reckoned that we'd find the Darkling facility within a day, and from there we could get back to the mountain and find the Doctor or the TARDIS. Her tone suggested she didn't care which.

I resigned myself to following after her like a trained poodle –

or perhaps an unthinking mule, I thought sourly as I considered the declining bundle of provisions in my arms. Every time I tripped on a root, or slipped in a slimy patch of jungle muck, I lost something more from the pile, along with the last shreds of my dignity. After I'd fallen down for the millionth time, I reluctantly had to concede I didn't want to get up again. 'Can we stop? I need a rest.'

'There's a clearing just ahead. You can sleep there.'

I slowly dragged myself forward, and dropped my pitiful collection of belongings to the ground. They made a muffled clatter on the mossy covering of the clearing. It was an almost circular break in the tree line, no bigger than my room in the TARDIS, really. Compassion thought it was safer for us to rest here, because it would give us some advance warning of any approaching wildlife.

'Approaching wildlife?' I croaked.

Compassion was starting to build a small fire. 'There are two thousand four hundred and seventeen different species on this planet, according to Frontier Worlds Corp records, and they have only surveyed twenty-six per cent of the surface.' The fire crackled, lit up her face in orange and yellow. It reminded me of the orange face of Alura's watch. I looked at it now, and noticed that the strap was damaged. I must have caught it on something in the crash.

'How many of these different species are near us? How many are dangerous?' I could hear my own voice quavering a bit.

Compassion cocked her head on one side. Either she was studying me for a reaction, or she was tipping all the relevant facts into a big pile on one side of her brain. 'One thousand and twelve in these kinds of forest. Only six are thought to be dangerous to people.'

The circle of trees around us remained eerily quiet, but it was late in the night. I flinched as a pair of small moths flicked across my line of vision and to their crispy fate in the growing flames.

'The fire will deter animals,' said Compassion. 'And I will stay on watch while you sleep.'

'Sure,' I said. 'Like I could sleep now?' I was lying of course: I could have dropped down on the spot and fallen into a profound and dream-filled sleep. That was entirely my problem. 'Compassion?'

'Yes.'

'What do you dream about?' She didn't answer. 'Compassion, do you ever wonder if your dreams are your own?' Still silence, apart from the sound of her calm and steady breathing, and the occasional snap and hiss from the fire.

I was thinking about the remembrance tanks on Anathema. Remembering them, dreaming about them. It's like a snake eating its own tail: the whole thing just goes around and around and around. As well as I can understand it - and since no one seems to want to talk with me about it that's all I've got to go on - I survived that previous adventure thanks to the remembrance tanks.

The tanks were created and used by Compassion's people, the Remote. Before I met the Remote, I'd thought that living for ever was impossible, unless I counted the experience of sitting through *Gone with the Wind* with my parents. Correct me if I'm wrong, of course, but the Remote don't really die on Anathema: they are reborn into new bodies. They grow each new body in these tanks, a blank slate on which friends and relations and acquaintances can inscribe their memories of the deceased. Reincarnation, aided and abetted by anyone who knows you. Assisted resurrection. Regeneration, I suppose.

That kind of remembering happened to me, over many regenerations, as far as I can recall. But I suppose that's my point, really. When I think of my mum, for instance, I remember her last and best in the home, not in *her* home. I'm not sure I can remember the colour of her hair, her favourite food, her dress size. What if my friends remembered me wrongly? Remembered what they wanted me to be, or what they assumed about me, or what I'd wanted them to think of me - not what I was? How would I even know? Let's face it, I'm lucky if I can remember my own shoe size, or decide on my favourite colour.

And then there's the problem with trying to be other people. If I'm pretending to be Frank Sinatra, are my eyes still grey? Or would I remember them as blue?

All my teenage years I dreaded becoming like my dad. He wouldn't argue with the Bennetts down the road who mocked his accent. He never commented when the Krapper family refused to acknowledge him in the street, as though they held him personally responsible for every Allied death in the war. He was shocked when I mocked their crappy surname and their crappy attitude in front of him, mortified when I did it to their faces. Dad wanted me to be more like him, more deferential, more cautious, though I knew I wasn't going to be frightened and cowed that way. Thank God my father hadn't been the one of those on Anathema remembering me back to life.

But who had?

These thoughts have swirled round in my mind like water vanishing down a plughole. Do you know when you sometimes go into a room and can't remember why you went there in the first place? I'm left with that kind of feeling. What did I forget? Who did I forget?

'Get some sleep,' said Compassion, still staring into the fire.

I shuffled uncomfortably on the mossy floor. 'I daren't. I don't know what I'll dream. Compassion, I can't know what I used to be before I was recreated by the remembrance tanks. Each time I was an imperfect copy. And I was copied over and over and over again across all those years.'

'The TARDIS put that right. It remembered you as you were, before Anathema.'

'And what if its memory's no more reliable than my friends'?'

'It's reliable.'

'How can you know?'

'It is.' She wrenched her eyes away from staring at the fire. I could see it flickering in her hot gaze.

I pointed to the axe beside her. 'What if I'm like the farmer's old axe? You know. He's had it for twenty years. Oh yes, he's replaced six handles, and changed the head three times, but he says it's still his old axe.'

Compassion didn't respond.

'I've been frightened to fall asleep. Not just tonight, but in the TARDIS too, because it's all around me. I'm supposed to feel safe there, it's my home. And the TARDIS was supposed to bring me back to my previous self. But what if it changed me? What if it's still changing me? That's what I dream about.' Still silent. 'Compassion, what do you dream about? Tell me.'

There was a long pause before she said, 'You should have some of the food. You need some.'

I confessed that I'd abandoned all the horrible food bars. 'I'm sorry. Did you want one?'

'No, I don't feel the need to eat just now.'

'You don't seem to need much.' The ground was cool and soft under my clammy back. My body was telling me to sleep, and my mind was fighting to stay conscious. I let my eyes close. 'You don't really need me,' I whined. 'Why are you waiting for me?'

The fire popped briefly as she stirred it. 'It's the right thing to do.'

'You're starting to sound like the Doctor,' I said.

'You make that sound like an insult.'

I mumbled a half-apology. Then I must have dozed off. I don't remember what I dreamed.

Compassion was shaking me awake with one hand, and covering my mouth with the other. I struggled briefly until I worked out what was happening.

She was making shush noises, and pointing across the clearing in the direction from which we'd arrived. I could still make out the end of the last stretch of hacked undergrowth.

Something was coming our way. From the noise it was making, it was big, and it didn't care that it could be heard snapping branches and crunching twigs and bracken underfoot. Or under paw. Or claw. It was probably ugly and dangerous, too.

Compassion gripped the axe. I stood beside her, and we kept the fire between us and whatever it was charging unseen towards us through the jungle. Barely able to look away, I managed to spot a couple of rocks the size of house bricks, and picked them up.

Me with two house bricks. Compassion with an axe. What were we like?

The thing broke cover.

It was huge and dark green with darker patches, like camouflage. I couldn't make out a head, just a mass of waxy skin which dully reflected the flames from our little fire.

Compassion seemed to shrug in resignation as the branches parted to let it through. I pulled my right arm back and flung one of the rocks at the creature, but it didn't reach. I hefted the other rock into my right hand, and threw that one harder. It struck the lower edge of the creature, sinking into its dirty olive-green surface.

The skin seemed to ripple and fall forward in a horrid torrent of flesh. And the creature said 'ouch!'

The rest of the tent covering slipped to the ground in the clearing to reveal Griz Ellis, nursing his left foot. 'That was a stupid thing to do,' he snapped.

At this point, I observed that Compassion had already sat down again beside our cosy camp fire. Ellis hobbled over to the fire. He dropped down on to the ground like a sack of King Edwards, and started to pick one hairy nostril.

Big, ugly, and dangerous. Well, two out of three ain't bad.

'You left me back in the flyer,' Ellis said to me indignantly.

Compassion said to him, 'You would just have slowed us down.'

He was so outraged at this that he had to stop picking his nose. I said quickly, 'We thought you were dead.' I wondered why I still felt so deferential to him in the middle of nowhere, with him sitting in a heap next to me and smelling like a latrine.

'Major error,' growled Ellis. 'Though I would soon have been dead if I hadn't worked out where you went. You've left a trail wide enough for the even the biggest and most stupid charax to walk after you…'

'Charax?' I said.

'Don't ask,' said Compassion. She lay down on the ground, and pretended to go to sleep.

Ellis, meanwhile, was in full spate. 'You left behind vital pieces of survival equipment, like the thermal tent –'

'Not much use in this weather.'

'You dropped vital food concentrates…' I was dismayed to see him produce the box of disgusting cake bars. 'And worst of all you were travelling upwind, you pair of cretins. Stupidity is clearly the dominant gene in your family. Don't you know that travelling upwind is the best way to get tracked, caught and eaten by wild animals? Big mistake. Fortunate for me then that you're a pair of imbeciles, and I was able to reach you so quickly. I could practically sniff you out myself.'

'Wait a minute,' I spat at him, my anger boiling over suddenly like a pan of milk. 'It's your company that's run us out of town, and it's your security team who caused us to crash in the back of beyond. And as for sniffing us out, I want to tell you that you're the smelliest thing I've ever encountered. And bear in mind that I have been to Whipsnade Zoo.'

He looked at me quizzically, then obviously thought better than to ask. Instead, his expression changed to one of smug satisfaction. He may not be in charge at the office any more, but I could see he considered he was still ahead on points in this conversation. 'That's right, Frank, waste your energy on pointless arguments, and bring all the local wildlife here, why don't you?' He had started to put up the survival tent. 'Big mistake.'

Chapter Nineteen
'I've Got You Under My Skin'

We waited until Ellis was sound asleep before we abandoned him. He lay sprawled in the recovered tent. His mouth was wide open, and from it rose a bizarre gargling snore. The tent was naturally full of gas. Natural gas, I suppose. I hoped there were no sparks from the fire: he could be roasted alive in seconds.

'He's out cold,' I whispered to Compassion. 'Let's go before he wakes up and tries to follow us.'

'It will be light again soon.' Compassion peered in at him through the flap. 'We should kill him.'

I tugged her away from the tent by her arm. She was holding the axe in the other hand. 'Kill him?' I asked. 'Kill him? Are you insane?'

She pulled her arm free, turning away from me with a little shrug. 'Haven't you wanted to kill Ellis?'

'Metaphorically,' I hissed. 'All right, so I don't like him at all. He's a filthy, loathsome, foul-smelling bully-boy with no social graces who made my work life a total misery and who I would cross the city to avoid on even my loneliest evenings. But if I killed everyone who fell into that category I'd have slaughtered my school's entire First Eleven by the end of first term.'

'When you put it like that,' said Compassion, 'you start to wonder what Nadaly Allder ever saw in him. She's escaped him now, at least. But he'll find us again soon enough.' She didn't stay to argue further, she simply vanished ahead of me out of the clearing and into the undergrowth.

I trudged after her angrily for another half-hour. At one point, I suggested that we should make it impossible for Ellis to find us by cutting a clear path, then doubling back on ourselves and taking a less obvious route at a tangent to the original. Compassion was unconvinced: 'I think he will find us again.'

She stopped suddenly. To my bemusement, she was standing unnaturally erect, her head held high, as though she were sniffing the air, sensing something. The early-morning sun was starting to filter through the gaps between the tallest trees, slanting shafts of grey light spilling around her. I recognised the expression on Compassion's face. It was the last thing I had expected out here in the back of beyond.

'You're getting signals, aren't you?'

She slumped her shoulders. When she faced me, she had closed her eyes, concentrating. She swayed her body to and fro for a while, for all the world like a radar dish. She was obviously taking the piss, and I told her so.

She smiled her biggest grin. It was so unexpected, as I'm sure you can imagine: she'd hardly been a barrel of laughs these past months. When she opened her eyes, they were eager, alive. 'It's you, Fitz. I don't know why I didn't notice earlier.'

'It's me *what*?'

Compassion flipped the axe with a twist of her wrist, and it thudded into the bark of a fallen tree stump behind her. Then she stretched out her palms towards me, stepping through a shaft of morning light. 'You were so worried about bugs in the apartment,' she said.

I took her hands, feeling a bit stupid. She released my right hand, and proceeded to roll up the sleeve on my right arm.

'Ow, careful, I've got a big bruise there,' I said.

'No,' said Compassion, as though she were talking to a stupid child. 'You've got a bug there. It must have been activated since yesterday, and I didn't notice in the middle of all the other signal traffic.'

I stared at my inoculation scar, my Frontier Worlds Corp mark of ownership. I still couldn't see anything apart from the bruise.

Compassion pinched the centre of the bruise. When she pulled her forefinger away, it had a small silver disc stuck to it, smeared with blood.

'They didn't just inoculate you when you joined the medical

research team. They bugged you.'

I stared at the tiny device, which she'd just placed on my palm. 'How did you get that out?'

She pointed at a nick in the centre of the bruise. 'It wasn't far below the surface, and it has a sharp edge - that's how it was inserted in the first place.'

I was just about to crush the nasty little thing between a couple of stones when I was interrupted by the sound of a disturbance in the nearby undergrowth.

Griz Ellis stumbled across some low logs and confronted me, his face about a foot from mine, his good eye glittering with malice. From this distance, I could see a scratch where he must have snagged his forehead on a low branch. If it had been an inch lower, he might still be tangled in the jungle behind us by his straggly eyebrows. 'So,' he snapped. 'What's your excuse this time, Mr Sinatra?'

He stepped back a little when I interposed my hand between our faces. 'So, Mr Ellis,' I said sweetly. 'What's *your* excuse?'

He at least had the decency to look abashed.

'What's bugging you, Ellis?' I said. 'I know what's bugging me.'

Ellis plucked the bloodied little tracker device off the end of my extended forefinger. He studied it incuriously, as though I'd returned something he'd previously lost and decided wasn't worth searching for. 'Ah,' he said after a while.

This plainly wouldn't do as an answer, so Compassion and I stood looking at him in silence while he thought of something to say. Eventually, he said, 'Yes, well, how else did you think I could keep up with you?' He flicked it away into the jungle. 'I put it there when you were inoculated, all right? I thought you were one of Sempiter's stooges, and I wanted to know where you were. Sempiter's cronies are after me too, remember?'

We obviously didn't look terribly convinced. I was pleased to hear a note of desperation entering the fat old fraud's plummy voice. 'Let me come with you,' he appealed. In fact, as he stood there in his grimy office clothes and battered sandals, it was the only appealing thing about him.

Ellis fumbled in his pocket, and I sensed rather than saw Compassion brace herself next to me. We were unarmed. I could see the axe, embedded in the tree stump behind him. But Ellis had simply produced his Frontier Worlds identity card, and waved it at us. For some reason, I thought of Chairman Mao's little red book. This was all he had left to appeal to, as if the company were his politics, his religion. His whole life, the poor, sad, smelly bastard. 'Please let me come with you,' he repeated. 'I can get us into the Darkling Zone facility. And you can find us a way there.'

He looked as if he were about to cry again. God, I hated that. Compassion had lost interest, and was looking around, as though planning to leave.

'You know, I really don't trust Sempiter. Nor his brutish security thugs, especially that dangerous oaf Kupteyn. Truth is, Frank, I want to cut a deal with the Reddenblak Corporation.' He paused, raising his tatty eyebrows for maximum effect. When there obviously wasn't any, he plunged on. 'Sempiter won't work with them, but I want to offer them my own research. Sempiter found out, and that's why he wants me dead. It's why he wants you dead, too.'

What about the odd menagerie up on Level 10? How could he *not* know about that? And yet nothing I'd seen of his work tied him to it. He hadn't actually witnessed Sempiter's whole bizarre transformation. I pondered the possibilities in silence.

My silence must have really been getting to him, because he bustled a bit closer, and held me by my elbows in a pathetic gesture of appeal. His dreadful breath washed over me, and I turned my head aside with a little moan, which Ellis obviously took to be disagreement, rejection. He gripped my elbows together, and his voice became more desperate, pleading. 'I can help you, Frank. I can. I know they're getting close to you, getting close to you and your sister and your friend.'

Despite the stench, I looked directly back in his eyes at this. 'What friend?'

There was a fresh spark in his eye. He'd made a connection.

'Sempiter's people are closing in on him. I can help you prevent that. You can save your friend, you can save Franz-Joachim Kreiner.'

He was grinning at me, showing all his yellow-brown teeth at once. He'd played his trump card, the information that would give him power and control over me.

But he could only have heard that name from Alura. And he could only have heard it at the apartment this morning. Before she was killed.

I could feel a wail growing in me, a slow surge from the pit of my stomach, filling my chest, forcing it way up my throat until it became a bellow, a howl, an inhuman sound of uncontrolled rage. It can't have taken more than a few seconds, but it felt at the time like a storm building and building and finally bursting with a terrible ferocity. My head throbbed with the sound, and I squeezed my eyes tight for a moment. Then I opened them wide, and lunged for him, snarling like a wild animal.

Ellis was completely unprepared, and fell beneath me as I pummelled at him, seeking out his spotty, pudgy, ugly face with my balled fists. He rolled away into a foetal position, protecting his head. I was preparing to kick into his huddled body when I heard Compassion's voice, oddly clear under the circumstances: 'You see, you do want to kill him.' That's what stopped me for a second.

'No,' I said. 'But I really want to hurt him. Did you kill her, you son of a bitch?'

Ellis peered up at me cautiously. The cut across his forehead was bigger now. 'No,' he said. He flicked a glance behind him, following my gaze. Three yards behind him, well beyond his reach, the axe was sticking out of the tree stump.

Now he was fumbling in his pocket again, panicking, jabbering at me in a desperate voice. 'I didn't kill her. I just talked to her. I just talked to her. Oh God, you have to believe me...' He was having trouble getting his ID card out of his pocket again, and I half expected him to suddenly brandish it at me and pull rank.

Instead, he pulled a gun and brandished that at me instead.

I took a step backwards, and bumped into Compassion. She was standing very still.

In front of us, Ellis's handgun covered us, unwavering. Ellis sounded a bit winded, but his voice was calm, a complete contrast to his previous babbling. 'I really didn't kill her, you know.' Pause. 'Kupteyn did that.'

I motioned as though to spring at him. The handgun cracked, astonishingly loud in this part of the jungle, and I heard a bullet whistle through the air past our heads and smack noisily into a tree behind us. Ellis made a tutting noise and, never for a moment losing focus on us, rose awkwardly to his feet.

He was grinning his yellow smile again. 'I had hoped that you would lead me to your accomplice, or that your accomplice would come to you. Was it the name that gave me away?'

I glared, unwilling to help him. He continued regardless, unmoved by my insolent silence. 'I'm afraid she was most unco-operative, tried to hold us back with those cheap scissors. Tried to raise the alarm on the phone. When he went to stop her, Kupteyn was rather too forceful.'

I bit back every foul obscenity that rose like bile in my throat.

'Before she died, the only thing she said was that name. "Franz-Joachim Kreiner". I rather assumed that was your friend, the one on the mountain. The one I so much wanted to meet. My error, I realise now.'

Compassion spoke, and from the way her voice sounded, and how Ellis's baleful eye tracked sideways, I could tell she was moving away from me. I felt shocked that she could sound so calm, so composed, so uncaring. 'Why did you leave the apartment if you knew we were going there?' Oh, and so rational, of course.

Ellis was pointing the gun at a point midway between us. 'I really *don't* trust Kupteyn or Sempiter, you know. I'd persuaded Kupteyn to take his doltish security team beyond the next apartment block, to maintain radio silence, and to wait for my signal to move in. I said they'd scare you away if you saw them waiting. I didn't tell them about the tracking device, of course.'

'Obviously,' said Compassion in her cool tone.

The gun flicked at her briefly. 'Don't move any further,' said Ellis. 'I can afford to lose you.'

'Afford?' I said. I wondered how good his aim was. Isn't it harder to judge distances with only one eye? Mind you, I didn't want to test this theory out for myself.

'Ah, Frank,' said Ellis. He was obviously feeling more in control of the situation, because he was able now to adopt his familiar condescending tone and pick at his face with his free hand. 'I've been aware of the unique properties of your DNA ever since you joined the company. Come on, how else would a complete newcomer get a job as my personal assistant? You've implausible qualifications, a dubious career history, and you're as ugly as sin. But the health biosample I took when you joined was absolutely fascinating.'

'Keep flattering me,' I said stiffly. 'You know how I love that.'

'You probably don't even know it,' Ellis continued. 'Everything about your biological make-up is too organised, too regimented. It sounds poetic, and damned unscientific, but I'd say it's like a symphony that's been over-rehearsed. There're none of the little idiosyncrasies that you get naturally, the irrationalities of usual evolution. It's like you've been... manufactured. You're perfect material. And your charming sister is too. You're what I'm going to offer to Reddenblak. But I can make do with just one of you.' He made a grandiose gesture at the jungle pressing in around us. 'Under the circumstances, that is.'

'You knew about those disgusting Level Ten experiments.'

'That's right, Frank. And I was conducting a little observation of my own, down in the basement.' He smiled, pure evil. 'You, Frank.'

In the corner of my eye, I saw Compassion stiffen. The handgun motioned abruptly in her direction again. 'I *will* kill you,' said Ellis.

'You killed Alura,' replied Compassion, as though she were agreeing with him.

Ellis shook his head. 'Not at all. I offered to call medical assistance for her if she gave me the information I was looking for. At the end, I thought she had. That was just too late. Alas.'

He straightened his arm, steadying the gun in her direction. ***I will kill you***, he'd said. It wasn't a threat, it was a statement of intent.

I bellowed at him now. I stood in that jungle and I just hollered and yelled straight at him, as though I could knock him down with the power of my words alone. 'You killed her, all right. You killed her. You let her die, you did ***nothing*** to save her. You just watched her bleed to death on that bed and you stood by. You ***killed*** her. You haven't an ounce of human compassion. No compassion at all. No compassion. No compassion. Now, Compassion! Now! Get away! Run for it!' The tears were pouring down my face. '***Get away, for Christ's sake! Just run!***'

And, bloody hell, if that's not exactly what she did. Without another word, she buggered off into the jungle.

Ellis's attention, as I'd planned, was on me. So his shot at her went wide before he got a chance to focus.

With a speed belying his bulk, he took half a dozen rapid steps towards me, spun me round, and gripped me around the throat. I felt him jam the barrel of the gun into my temple.

I stood stock still. I was suddenly cold, scared stiff. The tears were prickling in my eyes again. I'm not sure if I was more frightened that he would pull the trigger or that he wouldn't. Ellis yelled into the jungle after Compassion: 'Get back here. I'll track you down anyway, but I'll kill your brother first. I'll do it now.'

'Forget it,' I choked. 'She's not coming back. We were never that close…'

'Shut up!'

A moment later, we must both have heard the rustle of undergrowth behind us. Ellis wrenched me around bodily, and I felt my neck give a little noise like when you crack your fingers together. I wasn't sure whether I was more worried about a broken spine or being devoured by whatever animal had sneaked up behind us. It was bound to eat me first: Ellis would be too disgusting.

Compassion was staring at us from ten yards away. How the hell had she got round the back of us so quickly? She was standing on the tree stump, and she had the axe in her hand, hanging down beside her.

'Yeah, right,' said Ellis. He was holding me close now, we were practically cheek to cheek, and his arm was choking off my air supply.

He pointed the gun at Compassion.

Compassion's hand came up in a rapid underarm action. The axe flipped end over end towards us, and Compassion fell to one side. I heard the report of the handgun, and thought she was hit. Then Ellis gave a bizarre little shriek, his grip slackened, and he dropped away from me.

As Ellis fell, he dragged me back with him. I disentangled myself as fast as I could, scrabbling desperately for the handgun. It was a moment before I registered properly what had happened.

The morning light through the trees cast Compassion's shadow over me. I sat up on my haunches. This was just in time to see Compassion stoop down over Ellis. She was studying the axe, which protruded from a deep wound smack in the middle of his forehead.

I felt I was making goldfish mouth movements at her. The words wouldn't come out.

Compassion pulled the axe out of Ellis's head, and wiped the gore off on to his crumpled business suit.

'Big mistake,' she said to the corpse. 'Mega mistake.'

Chapter Twenty
'The Tender Trap'

Sorrel Linoir sipped at his coffee. He curled his finger politely around the handle of the china cup, an indulgence he allowed himself only in the boardroom. Like the coffee, in fact. This was not the ersatz company beverage that you would find in any of the machines which were ergonomically positioned all around the Reddenblak HQ. Linoir knew what was in that. He knew better than to drink it. He knew better than to offer it to his distinguished visitors.

Linoir dabbed the coffee foam from his jet-black moustache with a printed silk handkerchief. The moustache was a recent addition, of which he was very proud. He'd bought it at the same time as his smart new wig.

'Are you sure you won't take a cup with us?' he asked, gesturing across the polished boardroom table at the exquisite coffee set. The set he'd brought with him from Creal originally. His gesture was an flat-palmed signal, an indication of openness, trustworthiness. He remembered that from the *Introduction to Body Language* book he'd read the previous week.

His guest smiled, and shook his head. 'No. Thank you.'

Linoir settled back momentarily in his plush chair and then, remembering from the book that this suggested discourtesy by being overcasual, leaned forward again. He folded his hands on the desk. Then he put the handkerchief back in his top pocket. Then he folded his hands again. Then he placed them palms down on the table, hoping that they wouldn't leave sweaty marks on the polished surface. He wondered whether he was looking indecisive.

'Mr Dewfurth,' he said. 'I should have said when you arrived – it's a pleasure to meet you at last. Isn't it, Jiulyan?'

Next to him, his business partner Jiulyan Larruge nodded

solemnly. The pile of hair on her head waggled precariously. Larruge was a woman of few words and a majority shareholding. She could afford to be taciturn. Besides, thought Linoir, Larruge's squeaky voice didn't command respect in these kinds of situation.

Larruge seemed to be examining her fingernails with great fascination. 'You're not what I expected, Mr Dewfurth,' said Linoir.

'Am I not?' said Dewfurth, his face solemn. Linoir studied him across the expanse of the desk. They'd purchased this to create an impression when they'd first decorated the room. On reflection, it was a nuisance. You either had to sit right next to your visitors, thus unable to keep helpful paperwork beside you or display key information on a nearby screen; or you had to sit at the other side of the table, separated by two metres of wood and leather. 'What were you expecting?' continued Dewfurth. The question was politely expressed, but still sounded like a challenge.

I was expecting you to be able to afford a suit that fits you, thought Linoir to himself. Perhaps Dewfurth sensed this, because he tugged briefly at the cuffs of his jacket, which did not quite reach his wrist, his shirt sleeves unbuttoned and flapping out of the ends.

Linoir shuffled his hands again, looking down at the sleeves of his own smart, pale, linen suit, safe in the knowledge that he was ahead on points in the sartorial stakes. Creating the right impression with business dress was important too, the book had told him. 'I'm not sure what I was expecting,' said Linoir at last. 'It's always difficult when one has dealt previously through intermediaries, don't you feel?'

Dewfurth inclined his head politely again. 'You feel we can come to an arrangement, Mr Linoir?'

'Mr Sempiter and Mr Ellis rejected our previous offer. And that was only this week. The terms of our tender have not changed.'

'But the business intelligence has,' smiled Dewfurth. 'Has it not?'

Larruge leaned back expansively in her seat, allowing her jacket to fall open and reveal her creased white shirt and tasteless tie. Her suit was lined and rumpled. And now she was stretching her hands behind her head, and doing that odd thing with her fingers, tapping on her head and making a sound like a galloping horse. Linoir smiled at their guest, and kicked his partner under the table. Larruge gave a bit of a startled cough, and stopped fingering her hair.

'What business intelligence are you thinking of, Mr Dewfurth?'

'Doctor.'

'What business intelligence are you thinking of, *Doctor* Dewfurth?'

Dewfurth stood up, and put his hands flat on the table. Controlling Behaviour, noted Linoir to himself. Chapter 18, if he remembered correctly. 'Come on,' said Dewfurth testily. 'I've travelled all this way to help you arrange an agreed merger with Frontier Worlds Corporation. Don't pretend you're not aware of the Darkling Project or you wouldn't have approached us in the first place.' When Dewfurth leaned forward, Linoir could see the gap between his shirt and his stretched brown belt. The top of his trousers didn't fasten properly.

'What's this about a Darkling Project?' asked Linoir. He tried to keep his tone light, and not to get caught scanning his notes on the visual display beside him.

'What's this about an agreed merger?' coughed Larruge.

Dewfurth raked them with his piercing blue gaze. The early-morning light from the window behind him made his wild hair look like copper flames. 'Merger, takeover, what does the terminology matter? You'll purchase the majority shares of Frontier Worlds and have control of the Corporation. How difficult can this be?'

'Forgive me if I sound obtuse,' said Linoir. 'What has changed since Reddenblak's previous offer, on the same terms, which was so categorically rejected by the Frontier Worlds board?'

'Darkling,' snapped Dewfurth. He had obviously seen Linoir's incautious glance at his display screen, for he suddenly leapt up on the boardroom table and slid across its polished surface. He swung his legs over the edge of the table (why wasn't Linoir surprised that his guest had discarded his shoes?), and dropped to his feet on the deep-pile carpet. Dewfurth's quivering finger was already pointing at details on the display screen. 'Darkling Zone, Darkling Crop, latitude and longitude, business projections, NEBT, threat to your core business, eight out of ten owners say their cats prefer it... What more do you need? Don't try to haggle us down, or Sempiter may work it out for himself and try a reverse takeover.'

Larruge had been startled by Dewfurth's slide across the table, but this latest suggestion made her choke on her top-quality beverage. She mopped indecisively at the spillage down her trousers with a Reddenblak napkin, muttering about poison pills and golden shares.

'How can you tell what we know about Darkling?'

'Who do you think put the intelligence into your business-intelligence unit?'

Linoir remembered the woman at Frontier Worlds who had given them the data cartridge. Nevertheless, he affected to look shocked. 'That's unethical.'

Dewfurth laughed at him. 'That's business. Meanwhile, what's to stop you making this offer? You've seen my terms.' He walked slowly back around the room and resumed his seat, propping his unshod feet up on the table. 'Have you ever heard of the Brilliant Corporation?'

Linoir exchanged glances with Larruge. 'No.'

'They were a light-bulb manufacturer. Light bulbs were their core business. They didn't diversify. They didn't need to: they had the monopoly on cheap, efficient, widely available, industry-standard light bulbs. They were delighted when their light-bulb research division came up with an innovation. Not a brighter light bulb, or a whiter light bulb, or a slighter light bulb. An everlasting light bulb.'

They looked at him blankly.

'They weren't so Brilliant after all,' prompted Dewfurth. 'Not by a long way.'

Then the bulb went on over their heads.

'The Darkling Crop?' said Linoir. He stroked his moustache pensively.

'Your industry's everlasting light bulb,' said Dewfurth. 'Shall we see you in the Frontier Worlds HQ later today?' He jumped to his feet, shuffled them into his shoes, and strode to the boardroom door. He pulled his drooping trousers up around his waist.

Linoir rose to see him out. 'Thank you, Dr Dewfurth,' he said.

'Don't mention it,' said Dewfurth. 'And, please, just call me Doctor.'

Chapter Twenty-One
'In the Wee Small Hours of the Morning'

I'd insisted that we stop and rest. Or, at least, that *I* stop and rest. A combination of the exhausting journey so far, lack of food, and the nasty shock of nearly being axed to death meant that I was literally shaking where I stood. Compassion stared at me closely for a few moments before agreeing.

She obviously had no idea why I was so furious with her when I should have been so grateful. Not that she'd actually want gratitude, of course.

The image of Ellis's face was etched in my mind - the dreadful axe wound that hacked deep into his forehead, cutting across his scraggy hairline and into the top of his skull, lumpy rivulets coagulating down the cheek and below the chin into his shirt. Then I couldn't stop myself from seeing Alura, the scissors in her neck, and her blood on my pillow.

Her watch was still on my wrist, the stupid buckle flapping loose again. I lay awake and thought about the girl, and never ever thought of counting sheep.

So maybe it was strange that it was only some time afterwards that I thought about Compassion's face. The scar over her eye had faded quickly; it was just a thin pink line in the freckled flesh. She was checking Ellis's handgun, evidently disgusted to find it was out of ammo.

She stood next to me while I lay on the softest bit of jungle clearing that I could find. A growing twitter of birds was welcoming the growing light. I looked up and around, remembering the ghastly canary on Level 10 and anxious to find normal birds flying around the jungle. Way up above us, past the tree line, I could still see the needle points of the unfamiliar stars in an alien sky - an unknowable alien sky at that, and one that was brightening with every second.

Who was I kidding - unknowable alien sky? Back home on Earth I wouldn't have known the Big Dipper from the Plough. But, whereas there I could struggle through the crowds from Archway to King's Cross every day without having to take the tube, here I couldn't walk more than twenty yards without getting hopelessly, dangerously lost in the jungle.

I lay on the ground in silence like this for maybe thirty minutes. There was a sick feeling in my chest, a lump of black dread that told me I was utterly alone, even with Compassion beside me. Why was she waiting here for me? She'd dispensed with Ellis without a qualm. She didn't need me any more than she needed him, she could just have run, just have gone, left Ellis rotting in the jungle and me as good as dead.

'Should we bury him?' I said at last. As an attempt to break from my morbid thoughts, I admit it was an unlikely topic.

'No point,' said Compassion. She still hadn't sat down, she just stood over me like a Buck House guardsman. 'Ellis will never be tracked down. The animals will find him before anyone.'

Tough meat, I thought to myself. 'Some epitaph,' I said. ' "Here lies the famous bioengineer Griz Ellis. He brought cheap and nutritious food to the jungle." '

Compassion said nothing. We stayed like this, in uncompanionable silence, for some while, until Compassion stated abruptly, 'We should go, now.'

I thought she was going to leave me where I lay. It was as if a huge weight held me to the jungle floor. The morning heat felt oppressive - already my grubby shirt was soaked through with sweat. It was that being-in-bed-on-Sunday feeling. So I just lay there, closed my eyes and thought about being in bed at home in London. Being in my tired flat in Archway, with Alura next to me.

Compassion poked me in the ribs with the toe of her boot. 'Are you OK, Fitz?' I'm not sure what surprised me more, the kick or the question. When I snapped my eyes open, she was standing over me. She looked worried. I'm not sure if you can picture that.

'What's the bloody point?' I said, and turned over away from her as though I were rolling myself more tightly in the bed sheets and dragging all the blankets with me. 'You can knock it off with the concerned-friend routine, too. You don't need me. You can find the Doctor without me. Leave me here to rot with Ellis. I can find out if he smells better once he's been dead for a while.'

'Of course we need you, Fitz.' She sounded so sincere that I had to look back and convince myself it was actually her talking. 'You don't think the Doctor would let me leave you here anyway, do you?' She jerked her face into a tight little smile of embarrassment. 'The Doctor trusts you, he doesn't trust me.'

'I don't see why. You've got all the moves. You're tuned into his way of thinking. Literally, most of the time, with that bloody earpiece.'

She stroked absently at her earpiece. 'I can pick up the details, I suppose.'

'You're a mine of information,' I went on gloomily. I propped myself up awkwardly on my elbows. 'He doesn't need me. The Doctor never wanted me with him anyway. He tolerated my company as someone to keep Sam busy. And as soon as she left the TARDIS he swapped you in. I'm there on sufferance, that much must be obvious. Especially to you.' I was laying it on a bit thick, I must admit. But that big lump of fear and helplessness was still squatting on my chest. I thought about flopping back to the ground again, letting it pin me there like a butterfly on a display board.

Instead, Compassion sat down beside me, and actually put her arm around my shoulders. 'He likes you, and he needs you. We both do. You can... see the big picture. The Doctor's off at so many tangents. And I think he gets lost in the detail.' She pointed up at the sky, at the fading points of light way above us. 'I look up there and I can tell you from the Frontier Worlds database about the star names, and the position of the nearer planets like Creal and Dofor, and when the weather system was programmed in to create this cloud system. There's a vapour trail just over there that comes from the weekly shuttle run across to Anmart. Those clouds are thunderheads, cumulonimbus, they look like anvils or hammerhead sharks. I learned that from the Doctor. He seems strangely fascinated by clouds, don't you think? Maybe they're like him - they're ever-changing. And the more you look at them the more you think you can see things, even stuff that's not really there.'

I shrugged off her arm. 'So, you're telling me that there's loads of stuff I wouldn't know. Thanks, Compassion, I feel *lots* better for that.'

'No, you'd see the obvious, the most important thing first. I'd see clouds and stars and vapour trails. The Doctor would see scientific classifications and animal shapes. You'd probably point out that the only reason we could see those things while we were staring up at the sky was because someone else had stolen our tent during the night.' I didn't look her in the eyes, but her soft voice persisted. 'I know you miss Alura terribly, and I'm sorry. And that's the important difference between us: I can tell you about love and companionship and belonging, because I can quote you philosophers and psychiatrists and neurologists and poets. But that's just words, Fitz. That's just the theory, related second-hand. You've experienced it. You can tell me what it feels like, what you thought, what you did.'

My eyes prickled. That lump had made its way up to my throat now. 'Being in the TARDIS,' I said. 'It's changed me, I suppose. It can change you too, if you'll let it.'

There was a sort of odd light in her cool eyes, as though she were going to tell me something more. But, before she could speak, there was a sharp rustling from across the clearing. From where Ellis's body lay.

The torpor fled from my body like a rat up a pipe. Some sort of animal must have found the corpse. We should clear off, I thought, before it decided it wanted a *warm* main course.

Compassion had seized the axe, and was striding swiftly over the clearing. For a fleeting, unworthy moment, I thought about scarpering and leaving her to fight off whatever it was. But, after hearing the closest thing to a personal confession from Compassion, even I couldn't chicken out on her. She'd revealed she was more like me than she'd ever really be prepared to admit, and stupidly I felt I had to prove I could be like her, too. So I edged across to where she stood beside the corpse.

Compassion was looking at it calmly. I couldn't stop myself from drawing in a sharp, shocked breath.

Ellis wasn't dead.

Yet he couldn't possibly be alive, either.

His head had sundered, and hung in two peeled sections like a split fruit, still attached to the neck. The hair looked just as wiry and wild as ever, but the skin of the cheeks and forehead were brown-grey, and looked dried, puckered. With a moan of horror and disgust, I could see why, and I could tell what was causing the noise we'd first heard.

A new head was pushing out of the bloody chasm in the old one, fresh growth from the dead carcass. We must have watched it for a minute, maybe more, as it emerged, rocking from side to side as it worked its way into the air, pushing the dried remnants wider to either side.

It was another few moments before I registered that Compassion was asking me a question. 'I said, is this how Sempiter was?'

I could only nod. I looked at Ellis's body. Black tendrils of hair had surged from every opening - his cuffs, his open-neck shirt, even his nostrils and ears. The tendrils wormed their way into the ground around Ellis, burrowing into the jungle floor. 'His hair's grown,' I croaked. 'That's supposed to happen to dead people, isn't it?'

'No,' said Compassion. 'People once thought it did, because the skin shrinks back after death. There's way too much growth here for that.' Was she mocking me?

Suddenly, Ellis's dead fingers spasmed, clutching desperate handfuls of soil and squeezing them hard, pulling down into the damp earth.

Back to the soil, I thought. 'Oh God,' I said faintly. 'I say potato... and he *is* potato.'

Compassion nodded, evidently pleased with my observation. 'Of course. It's a root system.' With anyone other than Compassion, I'd have suspected deadpan humour.

The creature's chest raised up as its back formed a shallow arch, and then dropped back to the ground again. Compassion and I both stepped away warily.

The ragged remnants of the old head had now been shrugged aside, and the pale, moist flesh of the emerging head glistened in the early light.

Both of the new eyes snapped open. They rolled around in the new head experimentally, and locked on to mine. The thin grey lips stretched into a ghastly grin of recognition.

At which point, Compassion's arm came down in a sharp arc, and the axe sliced into the dead-white flesh of the freakish creature's neck. Its mouth opened wide, issuing a ghoulish, inhuman shriek of pain and rage and disbelief.

Compassion struck another blow into its face, then another. I had to turn away.

The shrill screams cut off abruptly. When I braved it enough to turn and look, she was getting slowly and calmly to her feet. The cleaved remains of Ellis lay in large pieces in front of her. There was a distinctive, muddy smell, like the vegetable tray when you've forgotten to empty it for a few weeks.

I turned away, feeling nauseous again, and sat down heavily on one of the toppled tree trunks. Eventually I turned and looked at Compassion. I couldn't believe it: she was rifling through the corpse's jacket pocket. After a moment, she produced his ID card from the bloody remains. 'This will be useful when we reach the Darkling Zone facility.'

She was so calm. I just stared at her, speechless.

'*You* wanted to kill him, earlier,' she said at length, as if having read my thoughts.

'But I couldn't do it, could I?'

'He was responsible for Alura's death.'

That brought the blood to my face in a scalding rush. 'That's a cheap shot, Compassion. This isn't a game, and it's not a revenge tragedy. It's real and horrible and frightening and I want to be anywhere but here right now. Anywhere. You can be as logical and dispassionate and amoral as you like, just don't drag me in.'

Compassion stared at me. It was as close as she was going to get to anger, a cold note in her voice and her demeanour. 'I did what was necessary to survive.' She put the axe beside me on the tree trunk. 'You would do the same. If you had to.'

She walked away from me and out of the clearing. A bird skittered up from the ground, chittering in anxiety as Compassion passed by.

I turned over the axe in my right hand. Through the mess of blood, the letters stencilled on the handle read, FOR EMERGENCY USE ONLY.

Before getting up and following Compassion, I pulled back my arm and threw the axe away from me into the jungle as hard as I could.

Chapter Twenty-Two
'Fools Rush In'

The jungle ended abruptly. We stepped through a clump of overhanging vines and were suddenly on a stretch of dry brown earth. It led down via a bear-slide scramble to a river, maybe twenty yards of green-brown water separating us from a tall, soily embankment on the far side. Behind us now, the jungle tree line curved away, a sharp contour beside the river as it meandered off into the distance.

Compassion indicated the river. 'What do you think?'

I thought about a warm bath, a cup of cocoa and a pair of carpet slippers warming by the fire that burned so incongruously in the corner of my room in the TARDIS. What I said was, 'I think it's worth a try.'

The morning sun was low in the sky, but I could still feel it hot on the back of my neck as we scrambled down the bank to the water's edge. The air was muggy, and I knew it would soon become oppressively hot.

Compassion dived straight into the river, and set off across it in a powerful crawl. I stared after her. Then I thought of the Lido back home, and dived in, ignoring a fleeting impression that the river looked deep and cold and smelly.

After a few feeble strokes, I realised that it *was* deep and cold and smelly - and fast-moving. The tug of the undercurrent had seized me, and was dragging me away from the bank at worrying speed. I didn't even have time to splutter a cry for help before Compassion was holding my head above the surface and pulling us through the murky water. Within a few minutes, we were squelching the last few steps through a becalmed stretch of water beside the opposite bank.

I was covered in pond scum, yucky green algae that frankly did nothing for my poise and temper. Maybe that was why I didn't thank Compassion. Maybe it was because she was already scampering up the embankment.

I followed her, grumbling to myself.

The embankment was too regular, the piled mud too tidy, for it to be entirely natural. As I breasted the rise at the top, gasping for breath after the climb, it reminded me of my boyhood explorations of the railway depot near home. But at the top of this embankment there were no crude barbed-wire barriers, and nor was there a view of grimy shunting yards and dark, mysterious, enticing engine sheds.

Instead, I saw a huge, square field. I thought I'd seen fields back home on Earth, furrowed stretches of soil like the contours of a brown candlewick bedspread thrown over sheets and pillows. Later in the year, they'd turn slowly into pale zones of green and yellow on the same rolling hillsides, more like a quilted blanket stitched in contrasting colours. But I'd never stood before a field this size, all planted with the same crop. And the colour was astonishing – a vivid canary yellow stretching to the brow of the next hill.

I did recognise it, mind you. 'That picture on the kitsch calendar doesn't do it justice,' I said to Compassion once I'd got my breath back. 'How did you know it was here?'

'My unerring sense of direction,' she said with no apparent irony. 'Yes, it's the Darkling crop.'

Several hundred yards into the field was a squared-off area containing several flat-roofed buildings. To one side of these was a strip of grey tarmac, obviously a landing area for delivery flyers. To the other side were a number of enormous storage cylinders, each as big as a petroleum tanker stood on edge. Bizarre vehicles, with long protruding metal arms and odd barrel arrangements, stood in front of them. Or was it behind them?

'What are they?'

Compassion pointed further across the field. I could now make out another of the machines cutting a swathe through the crop, leaving a pale wake behind it. 'Combine harvester.'

'What?'

'Town boy,' she smiled at me. 'They cut, thresh, and clean the crop where it stands and throws the baled-up straw out on to the field. How did you think they did it?'

I nodded. 'Naturally. That explains the complete absence of straw-chewing yokels leaning on their scythes.'

'This is Frontier Worlds Corp's best-kept industrial secret,' said Compassion as she started down the bare soil of the hill and towards the bright yellow field. 'Yokels with scythes are unlikely to be a feature of their security system.'

The thick shafts of the darkling crop rose tall and straight around us, the ears of wheat two or three feet above our heads so that we couldn't see what was around us as we made our way through the field. We were able to walk between the sown rows, which were not straight but rather curved around the contours of the field. Compassion explained that this was to make more efficient use of the land and the harvesting equipment, or so she'd learned from the Frontier Worlds computer system.

Way off to our right I could hear the machinery - a combine harvester, had she called it? I had worried that we would get swept up in its jaws, cut and threshed and cleaned. But Compassion seemed to know where she was headed, as usual, and I tagged along behind.

We were walking along corridors of turned earth which stretched between the tall lines of corn. The soil was different down here, no longer the powdery brown of the embankment around the river, nor even the more loamy black of the jungle. I kicked at the clods of earth, revealing a greenish-brown mixture. It was a compost or perhaps a mulch. When I'd worked in the garden centre at West Wycombe, I'd learned the difference, but this stuff had a heavy old-vegetable smell. It reminded me of the stuff in the tea chest on Level 10. And, unfortunately, it revived memories of the dead Ellis back in the jungle. I trudged on, trying not to think about it too much.

The sun was higher in the sky now, growing hotter, and spilling in golden cascades through the bright yellow ears above us. A light, warm wind blew into our faces, rustling the foliage and drying us out. When I scratched at my stubble, flakes of dried green pond scum peeled away or stuck under my dirty fingernails. My skin and hair may have been drying off, but my clothes still felt soaked through. I made an excuse about needing to pee, and stopped to unknot my soggy Y-fronts.

As I was doing this, I noticed something on the ground. Or, rather, I didn't see what I expected to see – there was no other plant life than the Darkling crop. Each stalk stood tall and strong, with no little offshoots around it, no undergrowth, and not a single weed. I caught up with Compassion and mentioned this.

'The Darkling crop's been designed that way,' explained Compassion, not breaking her step for a moment. 'Frontier Worlds has a proprietary weedkiller which eliminates all other plants, but Darkling has been genetically modified – it's bred for resistance to the weedkiller's hormones and toxins.'

'And another thing,' I said. 'There are no animals. No birds, no fieldmice, not a sound or a sniff. In fact,' I went on, cautiously aware that I may be revealing one of my more irrational phobias, 'there haven't even been any spiders' webs strung out between the stalks.'

'Same thing,' said Compassion, her tone of voice unchanged. 'There isn't enough variety in the flora to support insects or field animals, and those that might eat the Darkling crop are also killed by the weedkiller toxins.'

'And no insects means no birds, nothing for them to feed on. Not so clever after all. You're saying that to create these new food stocks Frontier Worlds is destroying the food chain.'

'Yes.'

I looked up between the rising ears of corn and into the empty sky. 'No birds, no birdsong,' I said. 'It's going to be a silent spring around here. Unless you like the sound of machinery, I suppose.'

The combine harvester was still buzzing in the distance as we stepped out from the field. A patch of cracked grey tarmac led to the low, flat-roofed buildings we'd seen from the top of the embankment about an hour earlier.

We skirted around the perimeter cautiously. There was no greeting party of straw-sucking farm hands waiting for us, nor were the buildings ringed with burly bruisers bristling with small-arms weaponry. We needed to get a vehicle to escape back to the mountain, and the only way to reach the flyers and large transports seemed to be from the loading areas inside the buildings.

From our journey around the perimeter, we could see that there were doors in the side of each building, around which a security camera would sway from side to side in a desultory fashion.

We tried for a while to find a way through a less obvious access point. The huge cylinders I'd seen earlier turned out to be fuel-storage tanks for the farm equipment, and the area was cordoned off with high, sharp-wire fencing and signs which warned that the transport fuel was highly flammable. Oddly, this was the first time since leaving the apartment that I suddenly craved a Woodbine.

Further round the building again, two huge combine harvesters were being repaired by Frontier Worlds staff in grimy green overalls. We didn't get too close, but I imagined they were sucking air through their teeth and doubling the repair estimate. 'Genetically modified crops, that's yer problem guv: plays 'avoc wiv yer cuttin' blades.'

'Shut up, Fitz.'

'Sorry.'

Compassion decided we should go back round the side of the building, race up to one of the access doors on a camera's blind side, and use Ellis's ID card to let ourselves in. This would have been a brilliant plan had she not, in her haste, overlooked the sign informing people that this was an emergency fire exit.

At once, an alarm klaxon sounded from a speaker above the door. We hopped into the building and slammed the door shut again, in the hope this would silence the alarm. The klaxon wailed on, unaffected. I swivelled around, looking for an obvious escape route. 'Yeah, very smooth, Compassion. So, what's your next brilliant suggestion?'

Compassion strode calmly down the corridor, went straight up to a wall-mounted alarm device, and struck it hard with the flat of her hand. Another klaxon started up, echoing through the whole building. 'OK,' she said. 'The fire door is open. The fire alarm has been sounded. I think we should start a fire, don't you?'

We scurried down the corridor, trying each door that we passed the hope of finding something combustible. Further along, several offices opened up and people stepped out, moving quickly and calmly away down the corridor. One woman moved towards us, struggling to carry a loud-hailer in one hand while pulling on an armband which said FIRE WARDEN. When we reached her, Compassion said, 'Here, let me help,' and took the loud-hailer from her.

The woman was just thanking her for this timely assistance when Compassion whacked her over the head with the instrument, and she dropped to the floor. Compassion gave me the loud-hailer, stripped the armband off the unconscious woman, and we continued down the corridor.

By the third door, we found an office with a desk full of paperwork, and two men shuffling stuff from pile to pile. They seemed strangely unmoved by the commotion outside, even when we burst in.

The guy nearer to us had long greasy hair and a supercilious look. He was lighting a cigarette. 'Not another test,' he said wearily through a little cloud of smoke.

I snatched the ciggie out of his mouth. 'This is no drill, mister. No smoking on company premises. Get your bum out of this seat and get off to... er...'

'Get off to your fire assembly point,' intervened Compassion smoothly.

'Yeah, right,' said the second guy, settling back into his seat and taking a little swig from his plastic cup.

I flicked on the loud hailer, leaned across the desk, and shouted,

'Hello? Can you hear me? This is not a drill.'

The guy slopped coffee down his trousers. It was probably my imagination, but his hair seemed to slipstream away behind his head. He and his pal scarpered out of the office, holding their ears and muttering oaths.

I took a long drag on the guy's cigarette, swallowing the smoke and letting it back out through my nose in a long, luxurious stream. 'You're never alone with a Strand,' I murmured.

Then I grabbed the lighter that he'd left on the desk and set fire to several sheets of paper. We locked the door as we left, and took the key with us.

'That should keep them occupied,' said Compassion. 'Now let's go with the flow. They're hardly going to check IDs while everyone's heading for the escape transports.'

We almost made it, too. Just at the last corner, before we reached the loading bays, there were two security guards. One vanished through a nearby door, chaperoning anxious personnel towards a waiting delivery transport. The other guard turned and spotted us. I was preparing to bustle forward, brandishing my loud hailer officiously, when I saw that the guard was Direk Merdock.

Compassion sashayed towards Merdock. 'Why, Direk. Where were you at coffee time?'

Merdock raised his handgun. 'Er...' he said. 'No, Nancy. I know what you've done.'

'Done?' said Compassion sweetly.

Merdock's aim wavered between me and Compassion. 'You and Frank. You're Reddenblak spies. And I thought you were my friends...'

Fortunately, this almost lachrymose accusation was cut short when Compassion punched him squarely on the nose, and he fell back into the transport bay with a wail of pain and surprise.

'Oh dear,' said a voice beside us. 'So much for giving you a second chance, Merdock.'

I dropped the loud-hailer with shock. Standing before us was security chief Kupteyn.

'The Sinatras,' he said. His face couldn't decide whether to grin or snarl, so it tried to do a horrid combination of both. 'I had hoped Merdock would make up for his earlier stupidity. I was sure we'd be seeing you again. Where's Mr Ellis?'

'Gone to ground,' said Compassion, eyeing Kupteyn's handgun.

Kupteyn made a tutting sound, and waggled the gun. 'Then you can help me unearth him. Mr Sempiter is anxious to talk to all of you, and I'm not supposed to kill you.' There was an uncomfortable emphasis in what he said, I thought.

'Did you say that to Alura?' I snapped. 'Were you *supposed* to kill her, Kupteyn?' I clamped my teeth together, biting down hard, trying to keep control.

Kupteyn looked momentarily confused. Then a light switch went on at the back of the empty room that passed for his brain. 'The girl at the apartment,' he leered. 'She had a name after all.'

I nearly did something very stupid. I nearly threw myself at him and got myself killed. Perhaps Compassion sensed this, because she gripped my arm.

There was a feeble groan from the transport area.

'Direk, no!' yelled Compassion. 'Don't shoot!'

I flashed a look at the slumped figure of Merdock. He wasn't pointing his gun: he was holding his smashed nose tentatively between his fingers. Kupteyn had jerked a glance at the young guard too, which is what Compassion wanted. She kicked at the fallen loud-hailer, which clattered into Kupteyn's legs.

While Kupteyn was still yelling in pain and surprise and anger, Compassion pulled me back down the corridor and around the bend. We pushed through a gaggle of Frontier Worlds staff who were walking briskly towards the transport area.

Kupteyn was right behind us. Unable to get a clear shot, he lunged at me, seizing the damp collar of my shirt with one hand and tugging me back. Compassion was ahead of me, and didn't notice. 'I'm going to snap your scrawny little neck, Sinatra,' he grunted. 'Or maybe I'll put a bullet through it instead. Or a pair of scissors.'

I head-butted backwards, connecting with his forehead. The

gun fell from Kupteyn's grasp and he released his grip on my collar. One of the passing staff caught the fallen gun with her foot as she hurried by, and the weapon skittered away down the corridor. Kupteyn hesitated about whether to go after it and risk losing us.

Compassion and I seized our chance, and rushed for the emergency exit door where we'd first come in. Its alarm klaxon was still honking its futile warning as we raced through it and into the crop once more.

I glanced back to see Kupteyn crashing through the emergency door. He saw us vanish into the tall corridor of corn, and then chased off around the side of the building. For a moment, I had the crazy notion he may have given up, or maybe gone for reinforcements.

Then I heard the rattling noise of a huge engine starting up, and knew that Kupteyn had gone for one of the combine harvesters.

Compassion was haring off down the greenish-black corridor of soil between the curving walls of wheat. I hastened after her. Behind us, the combine harvester's huge wheels squealed in painful protest on the tarmac, and then I could hear the whirring sound of the cutting blades. It was a rising note as the blades got faster. There was a chugging sound, followed by a shrieking, tearing noise as the enormous machine started to bite its way into the crop behind us.

I almost ran into Compassion, who had stopped to force her way through the line of wheat and into the next corridor. I moved along a bit, and did the same, wondering what she was doing. The combine harvester roared closer. When I looked back, panicking, I could actually see Kupteyn in the small driver's cabin, way up above the ears of wheat. And he saw us. He leaned forward in his seat, as though he could urge the machine on faster still.

Compassion had burst through the wheat now, and we fled back in the opposite direction, just out of range of the combine harvester's cutting width. Kupteyn saw us, and I saw him curse as he struggled to turn the whole massive vehicle.

We burst out behind the combine, stepping out into its wake, ten rows wide. Compassion was picking her way cautiously though the sharp stubble and over the curved contours of furrowed earth. All around us, particles of straw scattered down like confetti. The acrid tang of the combine's exhaust choked me, and I stopped for a second to hawk and spit.

Just in time.

A huge bound bale of straw was tumbling from the rear of the combine. It missed me by a yard or two. But it hit Compassion full on, and she was thrown heavily across the bare expanse of shorn stalks. The bale looked like it was pinning her down, or she was unconscious. Even from where I looked, I could see the cuts across her arms and face.

The grinding sound of the combine behind me changed key, and the whole thing started to turn on its axis. If it came back this way, it would slice Compassion to shreds.

I turned, yelling fit to burst and waving my arms, and then dived back into the tall corn again.

I'd realised what Compassion had been doing. The Darkling crop had been sown along the contours of the field so that the giant combine harvesters could traverse it for long stretches on the same level. By cutting across the lines of wheat, she had been making the combine struggle in different directions and angles. It was slower than running the length of the corridors of corn, but it was slower still for the combine.

Kupteyn had seen me. The combine protested violently, then lurched forward towards me. The ground churned, and the massive whirling cutters whined in the air above the yellow crop heads before dipping back into it with a buzzing crash as the vehicle's wheels bit into the earth again.

It was too close. I tried running back across its wide embrace, down the corridor of wheat, but my foot was caught between two closely planted stalks.

The furious sound of the straining engines roared everywhere, and the green-black earth flew up in chunks around me. The blades were getting too close. I wrenched my foot free, feeling my shin scrape raw. I flung myself aside as the combine heaved past in a shattering blast of exhaust and noise and particles. The huge tractor wheels, each as tall as a man, mashed the ground beside me.

For a moment, the combine faltered, struggling to mount the next contour, and I was able to clamber up the nearest wheel. The vehicle was rocking, trying to get a grip. Before it started moving again, I scaled the dusty metal sides of the monster machine. Ahead of me I could see the cabin, and Kupteyn struggling with the controls inside.

He couldn't hear me approach over the top of the vehicle. I could feel my heart hammering away, as though it wanted to outdo the tumult of the combine itself. I paused for a moment, ensured that I was properly balanced, and took three very deep, calming breaths.

Then I tugged at the cabin door. Kupteyn didn't know what was happening until I had grabbed him by the lapels on his uniform, and wrenched him from the driving seat. He recovered enough to twist aside, and we fell together on to the flat horizontal surface of the combine, beside the driver's cabin.

The vehicle was still rocking back and forth, its wheels struggling on the muddy incline. Within seconds, Kupteyn was on top of me, straddling me, and his hands were at my neck. Above the din of the straining engine, Kupteyn was bellowing at me, his face contorted with rage: 'I will snap you like a twig, Sinatra. Like a piece of straw.'

He was squeezing the air out of me. I dug my nails into the back of his hands, but the pressure of his fingers just increased. I flung out my hand, grasping for something, anything, with which to hit him. I was just able to reach into the driver's cabin. Touch the gear lever with my outstretched fingers.

My vision was blurring at the edges, becoming a long tunnel, and at the end I could see only Kupteyn.

My fingers wrapped around the gear lever. Could I pull it loose?

Instead, I pulled it into a different gear. The combine harvester gave a tremendous lurch as it changed direction, and started to reverse. Disorientated and surprised, Kupteyn was thrown over my head. He clutched desperately at my right hand, which I'd been using to pry his hands loose from my neck. I was being dragged with him as he slithered towards the front of the combine, towards the churning blades.

I tried to cling on to the top of the vehicle with my free hand and my legs, but Kupteyn's weight pulled me aside. He dangled over the very edge, his eyes wild with fear. I was able to hook my legs around the driver's cabin, so that I lay stretched painfully against it.

The combine continued its bumpy journey in reverse, lumbering awkwardly over the ridges of the field. Kupteyn was only just holding on, his fingers clenched around the face and strap of my watch. The broken buckle bit into my wrist.

I could see the combine's savage blades whirling below us. I looked into Kupteyn's desperate eyes.

I braced my legs. Reached out with my left hand.

Unfastened the buckle on my watch strap.

His eyes wide in horror, Kupteyn fell shrieking into the blades. There was a clunking noise, and the threshing sound slowed briefly before resuming its usual note.

I struggled up and into the driver's cab. To the left-hand side of the combine harvester, the uncut stalks and ears of the Darkling crop were showered with red.

A dreadful realisation dawned in me. Compassion was lying unconscious on the ground, and I was reversing towards her. I hauled savagely on the steering column to twist the massive vehicle in a different direction. The engine protested as the mighty bulk of the combine swivelled.

I sighted along the rear of the combine, as though looking down a rifle barrel. When the vehicle was angled just right, I hauled on the steering column again.

The combine harvester was churning its way across the field in a straight line, heading directly for the fuel storage tanks.

Then the entire frame of the vehicle shuddered as the wheels struck a new ridge of earth. I was flung sideways across the top of the combine, slid helplessly over the edge, and dropped into the Darkling crop.

I was briefly surrounded by the bright yellow tops of the crop, and then I was tumbling through the foliage, sharp leaves and stalk snatching at my hair and clothes and skin. It broke my fall just enough that I didn't break my neck. The combine thundered away from me.

I struggled over to Compassion. She was bruised, and her face was striped with straw cuts like bizarre dot-to-dot lines between her freckles. I was amazed to find she was coming round. I'll be honest, I was amazed she was alive.

I was in the process of telling her this, in fact, when the combine harvester reached the fuel tanks. It made a grinding, crashing noise, soon followed by one, then two dull explosions. An enormous gout of flame leapt into the sky, and it began to shower burning particles.

We fled down the nearest corridor of wheat stalks, away from the Frontier Worlds facility as fast as we could. Behind us, the Darkling crop was soon a rolling wall of scorching fire, consuming everything in its path.

We didn't stop until we had reached the embankment by the river. From our vantage point, we could see the flames spreading swiftly over the whole of this side of the field. In the centre of all this, the transports and flyers of Frontier Worlds Corporation fled into the mid-morning sky, like animals and birds fleeing a forest fire.

A small explosion bloomed in the central building, lifting off a section of the flat roof and scattering it across the opposite half of the field and starting a new series of fires. A dark pall of smoke curled up after the disappearing flyers, and particles of wheat flickered up into the air, some catching fire as they rose.

'As plans to steal transport and flee the scene go,' I said to Compassion, 'I'm afraid I can only award us two out of ten.'

'We do seem to have hampered the Frontier Worlds genetics

programme, though,' she replied.

'I don't think so,' said a new voice. 'As plans to hamper the programme goes, I'd award it less than one out of ten. In fact, I wouldn't even use vulgar fractions, and believe me I'm in the mood for saying something extremely vulgar at the moment.'

That was the point, of course, when you finally showed up. But I'll grant you one thing: you can certainly choose your moment to make an entrance, Doctor.

Chapter Twenty-Three
'Come Fly With Me'

The moment before, Fitz had been staring at the pall of black smoke rising from the Darkling crop, and wondering how to feel. Should he be happy that the foul experiment was being razed to ground before his eyes? Or miserably worried that he and Compassion were stranded between an inferno and a jungle with no transport, no directions, and bugger all to eat for miles around?

When he saw the Doctor, he made his mind up in an instant. 'Doctor! I've never been so glad to see anyone in my entire life. And that includes several naked women.'

The Doctor, it had to be said, was obviously rather less enthusiastic. 'You pair of young idiots! This could ruin everything...'

'Well,' said Fitz, shuffling his feet a bit, 'that's the pleasantries over with.'

'Look at that,' the Doctor continued. 'Go on, look. Look!' He grabbed them both roughly by the shoulders and spun them around to look at the Darkling crop. 'What can you see?'

'I can see collateral damage to Frontier Worlds Corporation,' said Compassion in the quietly sarcastic tone that she usually reserved for Fitz. 'I can see all the staff escaping safely in company vehicles, so you can't be objecting about loss of life.'

'The field itself doesn't have any wildlife,' Fitz interjected. He thought about making some crack about Kupteyn at this point. Instead, it seemed like a good point to offer a few salient facts from the home side, the Doctor's team in the field so to speak: 'You see, the Frontier Worlds Corporation is just disrupting the food chain. They need to grow corn not weeds, so they've genetically engineered Darkling to survive their weedkiller. The weedkiller kills all other plants in the field except their corn - weeds, wild flowers, the lot. No wild flowers, no insects. No insects, no animals and birds. No birds, no birdsong. No birdsong makes Drebnar a dull place.' Fitz was warming to his theme. He folded his arms and leaned back, very pleased with his bravura summary. 'In short, by setting light to their disgusting crop we've brightened the planet, and sent the Corporation's secret cash crop up in smoke.'

'Up in smoke.' There was that tone in the Doctor's voice, the one that said 'Exactly!' His long, thin, grey-sleeved arm poked over Fitz's shoulder, and described a curling gesture up into the sky, indicating the expanding black plume of smoke pouring off the fuel-storage areas and the adjacent wispy grey columns spiralling off every part of the huge field.

Wait a minute, thought Fitz, his grey-sleeved arm? What was this bizarre business suit the Doctor was wearing? And why were its cuffs somewhere near his elbows?

'Up in smoke,' the Doctor repeated, oblivious to any puzzled looks about his sudden loss of dress sense. 'You clumsy, heavy-handed couple of overenthusiastic amateurs! You think you've sabotaged their plan to expand the Darkling crop across this planet...'

'Er, not exactly...'

'...but what you've actually done is to scatter the delicate seeds all over this extremely fertile planet!'

'Oh...' Fitz felt the need to sit down heavily on the embankment and put his head in his hands. From this more comforting position, he could watch glumly as the flames throughout the field licked swiftly out of control. The hot air rose from the growing inferno, carrying seeds up into the afternoon sky. 'Oh sod,' he concluded. 'We didn't think of that.'

'Didn't think –' At this point, the Doctor did that thing he did when he was really frustrated and couldn't quite find the words to express it, swapping the weight from one leg to the other. His version of hopping mad. 'Didn't think?' he raged. 'What else have you had time to do since I got you into Frontier Worlds? Was it too much to expect that you'd act on my instructions? That you'd pay attention to the clues in my e-mails? That you'd realise that an isolated experimental crop site was placed this far away from the rest of their corporate facilities precisely *because* there was a risk of cross-contamination?' With an apparently supreme effort, the Doctor presumably restrained himself from slapping them both across the face. The tension seemed to ease out of him like a deflating tyre. 'I don't think I should say any more at this point.'

'When's that ever stopped you in the past?' asked Compassion.

She had no tact, thought Fitz, and stepped in with, 'So. Crazy threads. What's the special occasion?'

The Doctor had the decency to look a bit embarrassed at this point. But then he did look like he'd been last in the queue at a charity-shop suit sale. The trouser legs were halfway up his shins, way above the very tight pair of narrow black shoes (no socks), and with the waist band stretched beyond endurance.

'I was trying to talk some business sense into the Reddenblak Corporation,' the Doctor said, and tugged hopelessly at the suit sleeves. They merely sprang back up his forearms again, revealing that the cuff buttons on the shirt were also unfastened. Fitz thought he recognised the pale-grey material, though. He was also struggling not to laugh out loud.

My own clothes weren't very business-like,' continued the Doctor. 'So I borrowed some of Temm Sempiter's from his office.'

Fitz jumped to his feet. 'You've seen Sempiter? Where is he now? How did you get away from the mountain? I suppose you brought transport? Have you got any food? Or ciggies?'

The Doctor allowed this torrent of questions wash over him while he looked them both up and down. Compassion must have seemed a right mess, her face freckled with small cuts and her red hair full of yellow straw. Fitz tried to look suitably forlorn at this point, he felt he deserved a bit of sympathy too. Eventually the Doctor said, 'You look like you've had a rough time.'

Fitz nodded. 'Well, I won't go into details, but we've had a busy day.'

Then he explained briefly about the stuff they'd seen on Level 10, and the way that Sempiter had transformed himself before his eyes. The Doctor indulged him with his I'm-listening-to-you-politely smile, which made Fitz wonder how much of this he already knew.

Compassion nudged Fitz in the ribs. 'Are you going to stay here gassing until the security guards come and find us?'

'No,' said Fitz in his aggrieved voice.

'And have you forgotten what the Doctor said about those seeds scattering over the whole area?'

'No, of course not,' he snapped. 'Do you think I'm an idiot?'

She narrowed her eyes as if appraising him. 'The jury's still out, Fitz. So what do you propose?'

It was a moment before Fitz realised she'd switched her cool, grey, appraising gaze on the Doctor, and had turned the whole thing into a challenge. Which the Doctor rose to, of course. Fitz could usually tell when the Doctor was getting one of his ideas, because he started talking nineteen to the dozen and shuffling backwards and forwards as if he were using his feet to measure for carpet. He sucked his forefinger and held it in the air.

'The current conditions will confine much of the cloud of dust and particles to this immediate area for the time being, but that local weather system's not going to last more than an hour. Plus I know there's some hope that a lot of the seeds thrown up by the explosions and the hot updraft will already have been toasted by the fire.'

'How so?'

'Because, Compassion, I was able to get some information about the Darkling crop from my study of the database while I was on the weather-control platform, and I gave you enough pointers in my e-mail for you to find out for yourself, not that you seem to have followed up any of my helpful hints. So I can say with some confidence that the crop may be very resistant to their weedkillers, but it's quite fragile when it comes to extremes of heat or irrigation.' The Doctor seemed oblivious to the filthy scowl that was developing on Compassion's face. His own was lighting up as the idea crystallised in his mind. 'Oh, well of course - the *solution* is as plain as the freckles on your nose! Or as easy to spot as the receiver in your ear. I really am disappointed that you brought that out of the TARDIS after what we agreed.'

Compassion said nothing, just stared at him. The Doctor had stopped prancing about and his mood had changed again. He was gazing at her, grinning wildly. 'Yes?' she asked testily. 'The solution?'

He gave her a reassuring wink, which seemed to make her angrier still. Fitz filed this reaction away in the back of his mind, so that he could use it himself in the future to provoke maximum annoyance.

'Local weather system, weather-control platform, extremes of irrigation,' the Doctor said excitedly. 'Solution, literally - it's obvious! Cause a torrential downpour, wash any viable seeds out of the sky, and drown the lot on the ground.' More pacing up and down. 'I'll get back up the weather-control platform and switch on the taps. Meanwhile, you must get back to the Frontier Worlds HQ, close down those experiments on Level Ten, and then keep my new friends from Reddenblak occupied until I can get there. Oh, no!'

His sudden enthusiasm seemed to have drained away. 'What's the problem?' asked Fitz

'These shoes,' the Doctor said, as though it were the end of the world. 'They're an absolutely dreadful fit. I shall get the most terrible bunions. Right, off we go.' And the little cloud of gloom had already passed. He had his arms around their necks, and he was bustling them off to where he said he'd parked Sempiter's stolen flyer. 'Here we go. Fitz, while we're travelling, you must tell me exactly what's been happening since I've been away, right from the beginning. Don't spare the details, and I won't spare the horses.'

So Fitz told him, right from the beginning. And they were soon racing through the afternoon light towards the city, towards...

Well, towards *what*? Fitz pondered. How did the Doctor think they'd get out of this one?

Chapter Twenty-Four
'Stormy Weather'

Thank goodness for the sonic screwdriver, thought the Doctor. Suitably adjusted, it could cut through a steel bulkhead, alert all the dogs within a nine-kilometre radius or remove a speck of dirt from someone's eye. It was light, compact, balanced, stylish, and required no documentation. What's more, it came with batteries included, albeit Evergreen-brand, kinetically self-regenerating diuturnix batteries manufactured by the now-defunct Brilliant Corporation. And here it was, now, fusing an electronic lock in a cable-car door.

On the other side of the door, a robot was hammering fiercely against the heavy-duty glass of the window. The Doctor smiled his most dazzling smile back through the glass, switched off the screwdriver with a flourish, twirled it around his finger and dropped it into the top pocket of his ill-fitting grey business suit. He'd transferred the other contents from his own jacket earlier, though had given up on most of the stuff in the pockets after the first ten minutes.

He pressed the DOWN button on the door controls, and the magnetic clamps disengaged from the side of the weather-control platform. In fifteen minutes the cable car would reach the snowy ground far below, where the Doctor had parked Sempiter's stolen flyer earlier before beginning his own ascent. 'Toodle-oo,' he mouthed, and waved his fingers at the robot. The car began its journey back down the swinging hawser.

As it vanished, the robot gave a little wave back, recovered itself when it realised what it was doing, and resumed banging on the door.

The Doctor mentally patted himself on the back for his little ruse. He'd known that the robot would recognise Dewfurth's ID card being used, and that it would be waiting for him at the top of the hawser. It had been a simple subterfuge to tempt it into the cable car, hop out and seal the door. Now he would have at least half an hour before the robot could return, since the car would travel all the way to the bottom before coming back up again. He may even get another half-hour just by pressing the DOWN button again after that.

In the tall and narrow room full of computers, monitors and information displays, the Doctor looked around with interest. The robot had been able to reset the weather controls again, despite the Doctor's theft on his previous visit of the control knobs. It was a matter of moments before the Doctor threaded the knobs back on their spindles, and started work in earnest. With much clucking of his tongue and saying 'aha!' and scratching of his wild curls, he was able in the first few minutes to decipher the systems that controlled the weather patterns for each area in the vicinity.

There was a small but real risk that by reactivating the weather-control system he was sending further random Tuckson-Jacker signals into local space and the closer reaches of the space-time vortex. If that drew further space-time vehicles to the planet, or in extremely rare circumstances brought a third Raab crashing to the surface, he'd have to... well, he'd have to *duck*, he supposed.

To prevent the Frontier Worlds staff continuing their dangerous harvesting of the second surviving Raab on the mountain, he arranged for a blizzard of snow to wipe out the entire area around the mountain research centre and the Lake of Ice. To force the delicate Darkling seeds out of the atmosphere, drench them and destroy them, he set up a fierce and localised typhoon over the Frontier Worlds facility beside the jungle. And, while he was at it, he remembered how Fitz and Compassion had been so sour and unappreciative when he'd dropped them off at Frontier Worlds HQ, so he decided to bathe the city in glorious sunshine. What a bizarre combination of weather in such a small area and such a short space of time, he reflected happily. It reminded him of the time he'd lived in the South of England.

Rain and wind lashed the side of the weather-control platform, making a sound like dried peas bouncing off a biscuit tin. The blizzard over the mountain had started.

It wasn't obvious how to switch the system off remotely. The Doctor dithered for a while about whether to hang around for a couple of hours and press the OFF switch, or to hack into the software and get it to stop automatically. He convinced himself that he couldn't just wait around, and was about to leave when the first lightning bolt struck the weather platform.

The entire structure rocked from side to side like a ship in a storm. The Doctor had just picked himself off the lurching floor when a second strike bounced the platform around once more, and he was thrown into the wall with a nasty crunch. He looked around at the bank of monitors, which could only be linked to the external cameras. Quickly he ran over to them and began to press ON switches.

The image on the first screen fizzed into life. It showed a dizzying view directly down on to the boiling clouds below the platform. They looked like the skin on an enormous bubbling rice pudding, and they were brilliantly illuminated from beneath with flashing sheets of light. In addition, a series of sparkling points crackled and cavorted above the cloud layer like wicked, gleeful sprites. These dancing sparks of energy licked up occasionally at the platform. The Doctor realised that they were earthing themselves through the platform and down the hawser wires that tethered the station and the balloon to the mountainside. Oh dear, he reflected, he hadn't quite got the storm he wanted over the mountainside research station. As he watched, a vicious spike of raw electrical energy sprang up out of the cloud, snowing the picture on the monitor again.

He looked at another. This fresh view showed the adjacent hawser, the nearest route to the ground. He could see the cable car rocking dangerously along and down it. There was an odd shape flapping at the side of it. He zoomed the camera image, and could see that it was the door, hanging open, smouldering.

The platform rocked again as another bolt hammered into it.

The hawser wire seemed to glow as the energy channelled down it, and the cable car burst into flames.

'Oh dear,' said the Doctor, dusting down his terrible grey suit as he lay sprawled on the floor. He drummed his fingers irritably against the nearest computer console. 'That wasn't supposed to happen.'

'I should hope not,' said the robot. 'That would make me extremely cross.'

The Doctor jerked his head towards the exit. The robot was leaning casually against the door jamb, as though nonchalantly surveying the scene in the control room. Its foot tapped a staccato rhythm on the metal floor, so it certainly seemed to be somewhat peeved. It even had steam coming out of its ears.

After he'd recovered his composure and looked more carefully, the Doctor saw that the robot had little wisps of smoke coming out of several joints, and that its right arm hung uselessly by its side. 'You were struck by lightning,' the Doctor said, tilting his head to one side as he assessed the damage.

'The cable car was struck by lightning,' said the robot. Its nasal tone had lost some of its inflection. Its previously expressive eyes seemed to be jammed open, so that it looked permanently surprised, as well it might under the circumstances. 'I've had a devil of a job crawling up that hawser.'

'I'm sorry,' said the Doctor, and he meant it. 'I just wanted to keep you out of the way while I put things right. Protect my colleagues. Save the planet. That sort of thing.'

'I understand. I suppose you see that as your role.' The robot tilted its head on one side to consider the Doctor, who was still on the floor. 'You appreciate, of course, that my role is to protect Frontier Worlds' assets. Ensure that corporate equipment is used for management-approved business purposes only. Save energy. That sort of thing.'

The Doctor got to his feet. 'Can't we come to some arrangement?'

'I have to restrain you now,' said the robot. 'Please don't resist, and I won't have to harm you.'

'No need for that,' said the Doctor hastily. He waved his hands in a frantic little gesture of conciliation. 'I'll come quietly if you can explain why I should. Let's be reasonable about this. Logical, even.' He showed the robot his biggest, most genuine, most endearing smile. 'I'm the Doctor, by the way. What should I call you?' He reached out as though to shake hands.

The robot studied the outstretched hand with a pop-eyed expression of puzzlement. 'I don't have a name. I'm a robot, you know.'

'Oh, get off with you,' the Doctor snapped in exasperation. 'You're sentient. You have opinions, not just programs. You're an individual.'

'I'm an employee. My terms and conditions are hardwired.'

'You're more than that. You're capable of learning. You can adapt your behaviour for whoever you're with, to make them feel more comfortable with a machine. That makes you more than the sum of your components.'

The platform lurched as two more bolts struck it in fast succession. The robot slumped down on the floor beside the Doctor in a tangle of metal limbs. It propped itself up on its good arm, and surveyed him with its baleful artificial gaze.

The Doctor leaned towards it, lowering his voice conspiratorially, so that he was barely audible against the background rattle of the storm outside. 'Don't you worry that your Corporation is endangering this whole planet? Maybe this whole system?' He explained briefly about the Raab and the Darkling crop. 'Is that going to help your company survive? Zero population means zero per cent market share. Things are starting to look a bit bearish, wouldn't you say? If you don't help me, you'll be responsible for wiping out Frontier Worlds Corporation.'

'My primary responsibility', insisted the robot, 'is to protect Frontier Worlds' assets from Reddenblak agents. You're a Reddenblak agent. Is that logical enough for you, Doctor?'

'Ah,' said the Doctor excitedly, getting up on his haunches. The horrid suit was so tight that it pinched him all over. 'Well now,' he continued, 'your boss Sempiter is allowing the Raab to do what Reddenblak want to do. The Raab will unwittingly grow, devour, and destroy all life on Drebnar. They will take over by natural means. They'll diversify, embrace and extinguish - just like Reddenblak threaten to do to your company.'

The robot considered this in silence for a while. The Doctor smiled appealingly at it, saying 'well?' and 'hmm?' occasionally to encourage it to make a decision.

Eventually, it said, 'This needs a bit more consideration.'

'Hurrah!'

'Meanwhile, Doctor, I'm placing you under arrest.'

The robot's good arm shot out as it attempted to seize the Doctor by the scruff of his neck. It had obviously forgotten that its other arm was no longer capable of supporting its weight, and toppled over with a clang.

The Doctor sprang to his feet, looking around hurriedly for an exit. 'What would you say', he gabbled, 'if I told you this: "The next thing I say is true; the last thing I said was a lie"?'

'Get off with you,' snapped the robot, finally managing to stand up again on the rolling sea of the platform's floor. 'You'll be asking me to calculate pi next.'

It dived at him. The Doctor threw himself aside, but the robot swiftly closed in.

At this point, the weather station took another huge lurch. Throughout the cabin there was a reverberating twang, like a giant elastic band being plucked, and everything lurched over at forty-five degrees. The robot toppled sideways, and its head connected with the wall with a clanking sound. The Doctor winced at the noise, but then saw that the robot was neither harmed nor bothered by the blow. The room straightened a little, but remained at a sharp angle. The Doctor seized hold of the nearest set of library steps and scuttled up to the top rung.

'Come down,' shouted the robot. 'There's nothing up there but the emergency exit hatch.'

The Doctor stared up at it. 'Fancy that.' He flipped the lever and the round metal lid in the ceiling sprang open. The wind outside howled, and air was sucked out from the cabin into the atmosphere. The Doctor poked his head through the gap, and felt the rain lash his face. His light-grey suit soon soaked dark as he struggled out on to the ridged roof of the weather station.

The wind whipped hailstones at him, icy talons scratching at his hands and face and eyes. After the subdued surroundings of the weather-control centre, the brilliant afternoon light shone painfully through the whirling white storm about him. Lightning strikes continued to batter the platform.

And now the Doctor could see why the platform continued to lurch at its odd angle. The hawser holding the cable car had sheared clean through, and a ragged end lashed around beneath the enormous balloon. It swung dangerously in his direction. The Doctor threw himself flat, and it whipped overhead through the hailstorm.

From where he lay, clutching at the roof of the building, the Doctor could see a short ladder poking up towards the balloon. It ended at an elevated scaffold of metal and plastic, where a small two-person glider was tethered. It was the emergency escape vehicle, a snub-nosed thermoplastic tube with stubby wings either side, and it was shuddering in its cradle as the vicious winds buffeted it. He could reach this, he knew, and abandon the weather platform. But when he tried to head towards it, he found that his foot was held tight.

The robot had levered itself out of the hatchway and grabbed hold of the Doctor's left ankle. However, its useless right arm flopped about in the gap, unable to propel it all the way on to the roof. The Doctor pulled his right foot back, and kicked at the robot's good arm. He was rewarded with a grinding noise as the robot's gears protested, and its grip loosened enough for him to wrench his leg free. Behind him, the robot drummed its fingers irritably on the roof.

Another huge blast of lightning battered the platform, and it wobbled alarmingly in the grip of its remaining cables beneath the balloon. The entire building groaned in pain, and the hawsers shrieked in protest. There was a sudden bang, followed by a whiplash crack, and a second hawser snapped. One end fell away beneath the platform, lightning flashes pecking at it immediately as it vanished. The other end of the hawser thrashed around wildly, banging against the platform, slapping the side of the scaffolding supporting the glider.

The Doctor half crawled and half slid over the bucking surface of the roof, and managed to grasp the lower part of the ladder. He hurried up the cold, icy rungs, popped the emergency access button beside the glider, and started to struggle inside. Once he had cleared the scaffold, he kicked away the ladder, which tumbled free from the platform.

The robot had struggled across the roof, and now glared up at him with its wide disbelieving stare. The snapped hawser swung around again, whipping sharply towards the robot. But the robot had anticipated this and, stepping smartly aside as the hawser approached, seized hold of the cable with its good hand and was carried away into the hailstorm.

The Doctor slammed shut the glider's cockpit lid, and scanned the controls in front of him. There were only two: one was a release mechanism, and the other was the joystick. The release mechanism must be iced solid, the Doctor thought, because it was absolutely refusing to budge.

Through the cockpit window, the Doctor could see the robot moving towards the glider as the pendulum swing of the hawser brought it back. It had somehow managed to clamber further up the wire towards the balloon, using its good arm and its feet for purchase.

More lightning battered the building. Another huge twang signalled that one of the two remaining hawsers had snapped. The sharp edge of this cable flicked upward, and embedded itself deep into the huge balloon above. The skin of the balloon was stretched, punctured and finally ripped into a huge gash.

Supported only by one cable, the weather platform started to topple into a vertical position, pulling the balloon out of shape and tearing the gash wider. The glider's nose pointed down alarmingly.

The robot swung past the glider window, clutching desperately at its cable.

The Doctor kicked at the release control in front of him. The mechanism was still stuck fast. Then he spotted a small, handwritten sticky label attached to the instrument-free dashboard in front of him: PULL AND THEN PUSH, it said helpfully.

He pulled and then pushed. There was a satisfying clunk, the lever snapped into position, and the glider detached itself from the scaffold.

Just in time. An enormous electrical charge had been building around the weather-control platform. The Doctor could feel it coming, could sense it building. So it wasn't entirely a surprise when it broke like a tidal wave over the platform, though its effects were shocking and dramatic. The final hawser sundered with a percussive snap, and the whole weather-control station dropped away from beneath the balloon and the glider, plunging into the broiling clouds below.

The balloon rose sharply, but then the tear suddenly widened and the whole deflating structure started to descend. The robot swung helplessly from the cable below it.

The Doctor hardly had time to take all this in. Freed from its moorings, the glider had started to fall. It had nose-dived into the bank of snow clouds before the Doctor had taken hold of the joystick.

Sprites of lightning sparkled around the thermoplastic hull, dazzling him, disorientating him. He could sense that he was dropping like a stone, though the brilliant whiteness of the clouds around him made it impossible to tell how the craft was orientated, where he should steer.

The glider started to spiral down through the clouds, powerless, directionless, out of control.

Chapter Twenty-Five
'Call Me Irresponsible'

Over the mountains in the distance, just visible from the Frontier Worlds HQ building, clouds gathered, gloomy, threatening. Fitz wondered what they might portend for the Doctor, who had steered off into them in Sempiter's stolen flyer with little more than a cheeky grin and a cheery wave. Gloom seemed more appropriate, Fitz told himself.

'I didn't think we'd ever see inside this place again,' he told Compassion as they walked across Level 2 towards the lift.

Compassion had said nothing since the Doctor had left them in the executive parking area which linked to Level 2. She showed no feelings, expressed no thoughts about what the Doctor had asked them to do. It was as though she were going with the flow, just doing what the Doctor had asked. Fitz thought of the playground taunts he'd faced at St Edward's, when they'd teased him into smoking behind the music room: 'Can't do it, won't do it, headmaster won't allow it. And krauts just have to obey orders, ain't that right, Kreiner?' He was dying for a fag now.

Compassion had produced Ellis's identity card and used it to get them into the lift. There were no alarm bells, no suddenly closing doors, no crowds of guards surrounding them. Fitz allowed himself to relax a little, even to peer into the well of the HQ building through the glass wall of the lift. The reception area, far below, was bustling with new arrivals. Escapees from the burning wreckage of the Darkling facility had been returning for some time, and this had made it easier for the Doctor to steer the stolen flyer unnoticed into the headquarters docking bay in the middle of all the other craft arriving. 'One more fish in the shoal,' he'd said, grinning like a shark.

Fitz's reflective equanimity lasted just up to the point when he and Compassion stood outside the Level 10 laboratories again.

'I don't know that I want to go back in there,' Fitz admitted. He hovered awkwardly by the door, hardly daring to meet Compassion's scathing gaze.

'You know what the Doctor asked us to do, Fitz. Close down the experiments, and keep the Reddenblak people in the building when they arrive. The experiments are all in here.'

Fitz didn't have time to make a feeble excuse before Compassion had popped open the door and stepped inside. She handed him Ellis's security card for safekeeping. Fitz studied it. The card showed a 3-D image of Ellis, looking surprisingly tidy. Quite unlike the man Fitz had worked with, not how he remembered him. And nothing at all like that final image of him in the jungle.

Fitz nervously followed Compassion into the room. He was surprised and even more apprehensive to find the place still bathed with brilliant light. The operating tables were the same set of scrubbed white surfaces, and the expanse of the whole area and its serried rows of covered cabinets once again took his breath away.

Compassion was busying herself at a control panel on the wall beside the door, next to the odd collection of cylindrical fire extinguishers. After she pressed a sequence of keys, a background hum suddenly cut out. Compassion had switched off the air conditioning. Fitz hadn't noticed the noise until it stopped. 'What's the plan?' he asked. 'Are you trying to find a way of opening all the cages and letting the creatures out? Hey, how are we going to get them out of the building? There must be hundreds of them. The lifts are going to be busy for a while. Do you suppose there's a freight lift?'

He tailed off when he saw her expression. 'Letting the creatures out?' she repeated. 'How can we let them out into the environment? They're part of the problem.'

'I don't understand.'

She stopped tapping at the control panel for a moment. 'Do you want to take that friendly canary with you? The one you met on your last visit.'

'Blimey, no thanks.' Fitz considered his reaction, and peered at the nearest storage cabinets nervously as though the violent little bird might be close at hand. 'What if we just let it out of the window, though?'

'Yeah,' sneered Compassion. 'Pass the problem to someone else. Let it bite them in the ear. Or let it interbreed with those birds in the jungle, maybe?'

Fitz stared at his fingernails. 'OK.'

'Good,' said Compassion, and resumed work at the controls.

'So what are we doing?'

'Just what the Doctor ordered.' She had finished her adjustments to the air conditioning, and was now lifting across one of the odd extinguishers. It was one of the two that they had seen on their earlier visit to the room. 'I'm shutting down these genetic experiments for good. They're in an evolutionary cul-de-sac.'

'Er... Compassion,' said Fitz. 'You're fitting that hose into the air conditioning.'

'The chemical indicators on this cylinder suggest it contains a kind of ethylene-dibromide compound. That's weedkiller to you and me, Fitz. From this panel here, we can pump gas throughout this whole room.'

Fitz was appalled. 'You'll slaughter thousands.'

'This room's air conditioning is isolated from the rest of the building,' Compassion continued calmly. 'But you're right: it's toxic enough to harm people too, so we shouldn't stay long.'

'No, hang about, that's not my point. There must be...' Fitz surveyed the room swiftly. 'There must be four hundred cages in this room. And each has at least one animal in it.'

Compassion seemed engrossed in her handiwork. She started to attach the second cylinder of weedkiller. 'Rescue your canary, if it makes you feel better.'

He pulled her away from the panel. She faced him, a surly look on her face. She was still holding the second cylinder, as though it were a weapon. He half expected her to spray him with the hose. 'Compassion, these animals in here can't help what they are.

It's not their fault that they're in an evolutionary cul-de-sac.'

Compassion shrugged dismissively. 'So, we're just putting the dead into dead end.'

'Isn't that a bit... well, irresponsible? Unethical?' said Fitz uneasily.

'So, who paid your subscription to the Animal Liberation Front?' Compassion threw the switch on the control panel, and the air conditioning whooped into renewed life.

Life, thought Fitz, defeatedly. 'What gives us the right?'

The rising hum of the air conditioning faltered and died. For a second, Fitz wondered if Compassion had switched it back off again.

'Indeed,' said a nasal voice from behind them. 'What gives either of you the right to destroy my work?'

Fitz nearly jumped out of his skin. When he wheeled round to stare at the main door, he saw Temm Sempiter. Someone he had already seen jumping out of his skin. Sempiter was tapping his foot in that familiar, imperious manner.

Four security guards stood beside him. They all looked as if their brawny bodies were bursting out of their bright green uniforms, so there was no chance of making a fight of it. One of the guards, Fitz noticed, had a sticking plaster over his nose, and at this point he recognised him as Direk Merdock. Merdock wasn't his usual, smiling, accommodating self. The way he was aiming his gun at Fitz's chest rather underlined this observation.

Fitz fumbled in his pocket, frightened at every moment that they might think he was pulling a gun. Instead, he produced the identity card. 'We're here on the authority of Mr Ellis.'

Sempiter snorted with laughter. 'Most amusing. I can well imagine you were in cahoots with Griz. So where is he?'

Fitz looked at the 3-D image, and thought of the jungle again. 'He had an accident.' A pause. 'But he vested his authority in us, and gave us his identity card.'

Sempiter's foot tapped away. 'The excuse of any common thief. Besides, Griz Ellis's estate goes to Nadaly Allder. They had... an understanding, you know. One that is still legally enforceable.'

Compassion had calmly continued to press more switches on the control panel, but it was soon obvious that nothing was happening.

'We've isolated the power,' rasped Merdock. 'Come out or we'll shoot you.'

Sempiter waved this brutish comment aside with an effete gesture of his hand. 'No need to get all excited. And I'd rather they weren't damaged.' He pointed into the room, to the control panel beside Fitz and Compassion. 'Disconnect the other cylinder.'

Compassion didn't move.

Merdock snatched the cylinder of weedkiller from Compassion's grasp. With his other hand, he aimed his handgun at the side of her head. 'Do it, Nancy.' He didn't look like a boy playing soldiers now. Even his face looked older, thought Fitz.

Compassion turned, so that the barrel of the gun now pointed at her forehead. Her eyes were fixed on Merdock. 'I'd hate to get damaged,' she said coldly, and started to detach the cylinder hose from the panel.

Fitz watched Merdock step back out of the room and set his cylinder against the wall.

Sempiter moved away, watching through the door as Compassion worked. His skin looked tighter, older than when Fitz had last seen him this close. It also seemed greener, as though the colour of the guards' uniforms were reflected. His face looked bruised.

A sudden hissing noise made Fitz wrench his gaze away and look back into the laboratory. Compassion had torn the cylinder hose away from the wall, and a steady stream of watery vapour was whooshing out of the end and spraying about the room. With a final heave, Compassion hefted the cylinder far into the room. It handed with a clonking sound on the hard white floor, and rolled off under one of the tables, still spewing its contents.

While people were still standing there in shock, Compassion hopped out of the laboratory to rejoin them and shut the doors behind her. The hissing sound of the weedkiller cylinder cut off suddenly as the airtight doors sealed.

Compassion rubbed her finger on her smock, leaving an ugly stain. The weedkiller cylinder must have sprayed across her right hand and lower arm as she disconnected the hose.

Merdock had his hand on the door control, ready to go in and remove the cylinder, when Sempiter screeched, 'No!'

Everyone stared at him.

Merdock stepped in front of Compassion. She was smiling at him rather smugly. Merdock pulled back his hand and whacked her across the face. Her head snapped to one side with the force of the blow, and when she straightened it again Fitz could see a red weal already forming on her cheek.

Sempiter ignored all this. He was staring at the sealed door. After a moment, he seemed to snap out of this reverie, and looked at Compassion as if she were a laboratory specimen. 'Never mind. I shall just have to make do with you, Ms Sinatra.'

Compassion just put up her hand and calmly but firmly pushed him in the face. Sempiter fell backwards with a squawk of alarm, throwing his hands up to cover his face. 'Get her away from me,' he snarled.

Two guards seized Compassion by her arms and held her back. She showed no signs of wanting to struggle free. A third guard grabbed Fitz for good measure. Only one guard for me, thought Fitz, unreasonably offended by the implication.

Sempiter uncovered his face tentatively. A lot of his smug confidence had gone, replaced with a badly suppressed rage. 'Get the decontamination team, and get that room cleaned,' he snapped at Merdock.

The lift bell sounded, and Sempiter straightened. Fitz's stomach flip-flopped when he saw that it was Hannaw Applin, walking down the corridor in the way he'd once found so exciting.

'Mr Sempiter,' she said breathlessly, as though she'd run all the way up the stairs instead of just sashaying ten yards from the lift. 'We just received a message that some people are coming to see you. They're in transit, due any minute.'

Sempiter raised his eyebrows at her, as though to suggest she had gone bonkers. 'Then tell them to come back when there's a window in my calendar,' he said through gritted teeth. 'Some time next week.'

'They're from Reddenblak,' Hannaw persisted.

'Then I've a window for them some time next year.'

Hannaw took him gently by the elbow, moving close so that she could whisper to him confidentially. Fitz noticed how Sempiter shrank from the gesture.

After a few more seconds, Hannaw released his arm, and Sempiter straightened. His voice once again had its familiar, imperious tone. 'Hurry,' he told Merdock. 'We need to get these two out of the building and away immediately.'

Fitz felt the guard's grip on him tighten, and he was hustled forward. He managed to stop in front of Hannaw though, and gazed at her beseechingly. Not saying anything, just appealing for help, begging her with his eyes.

Hannaw squared up to him, and delivered a powerful open-palmed slap.

Fitz felt his face stinging from the blow. He looked to Compassion for sympathy. 'I'm hoping', he said eventually, 'that's a traditional local greeting we weren't told about.'

The guards hustled him and Compassion towards the lift. Sempiter continued to chivvy them along: 'Come on, get these two specimens down to the ground floor. They're coming with me to the mountain.'

'A skiing holiday,' said Fitz. 'Oh, you shouldn't spoil us.'

Sempiter's voice was low and dangerous when he leaned in close to speak in Fitz's ear. 'I don't think I can promise you a holiday, exactly.'

From this close, Fitz could see the skin on Sempiter's face and neck. There was a definite green tinge to it. More striking were the areas where his skin had blistered and split. There were distinct, long stripes of darker green flesh, where Compassion's fingers had touched him.

Sempiter was still smirking as the lift doors closed on them all. 'But don't worry, Mr Sinatra. I can promise that I will *spoil* you a little.'

Chapter Twenty-Six
'A Man Alone'

The vast Frontier Worlds HQ's reception area had calmed down a bit when they reached the ground floor. Glorious golden sunshine spilled through the huge glass display window to one side, so that the elegant sculptures and tall exotic plants cast long, late-afternoon shadows across the polished atrium. The cleaning staff had done a rotten job, Fitz noted as his guard hustled him out of the lift, because there were still small areas of earth or compost from the dropped rubber plant.

He glanced over his shoulder. Compassion's two guards were pushing her next, with Merdock bringing up the rear, still carrying the cylinder of weedkiller and still scowling at the back of Compassion's neck.

Sempiter hurried across towards the exit doors, gesturing impatiently to the guards behind him. 'Come on, I haven't got all day,' he shouted. He looked at his wrist, as though checking the time and seeing that the watch was no longer there. So he scratched absently at his face and neck instead.

He had just reached the main doors when they opened in front of him and a small group of people stepped into the atrium. The new arrivals were looking around themselves appraisingly, like house hunters at a new property. Their clipboards and computers bristled in their hands.

Two of the group stepped out ahead of the pack, distinguished from their colleagues by their pale linen suits. The linen suit with the dark bushy moustache held out his hand to Sempiter.

'Looks like we're just in time,' he said pleasantly. 'Nice of you to come down and meet us in person, Temm.'

Sempiter tried to brush past him. 'Arrange an appointment, Mr Linoir. I have a pressing engagement of my own elsewhere.'

Linoir's voice echoed around the vast reception area. 'I'm not sure that really matters any more, Mr Sempiter. Your board has accepted the Reddenblak tender. That is why Ms Larruge and I are here to complete the formalities.' He indicated the dumpy woman standing next to him. Both were wearing linen suits. A uniform or a fashion statement? Fitz couldn't decide. He found himself fascinated by her dark hair, which was piled up on her head like an ice cream cornet.

'We decided it would be more courteous,' squeaked Larruge. 'We're aware that you're still opposed, but the rest of your board agree with us.'

Sempiter rounded on them, furious. 'Get out of my building. All of you. There's no place here for Reddenblak. How many times do I need to tell you that Frontier Worlds Corporation is not for sale?' His face had gone dark, bilious even, with the effort. Fitz thought the man was going to be sick. 'There's no seat on my board for you, Linoir.'

Linoir smiled politely, and beckoned to one of his group. A yellow-faced pumpkin of a man waddled forward with an embarrassed smile of greeting. 'You recognise Mr Regot?'

Sempiter narrowed his eyes. 'Employing my company lawyer won't help you either. If you haven't resigned already, Regot, you're fired.'

Linoir chuckled, looked at the now pop-eyed Regot, and shook his head slowly. 'You can't fire him, Mr Sempiter. He works for me. And that seat on the board you were talking about – I think I'll take the big one in the middle of that nice conference room you have on Level Eight.' He motioned towards the lift on the far side of the atrium. 'Shall we continue our conversation there? It's so much more private.'

Sempiter wheeled around. He must have suddenly noticed, thought Fitz, that small groups were gathering at the edges of the atrium, even peering down from the balconies on the lower floors, to see what all the commotion was about.

Fitz hissed to Compassion, 'These Reddenblak guys are the people you saw yesterday?'

'Yes,' she replied. 'But he's had a haircut since then.'

Sempiter was scratching his face in a frantic gesture, leaving striped nail marks in the skin below his jaw and down his neck. He beckoned to the guards holding Fitz and Compassion. 'Security, remove these people from the building.'

Fitz felt his guard release him.

Larruge was holding up her hands to the guards in a placating gesture. Fitz thought that the woman's high-pitched voice belied her bulky appearance. 'Before you do anything too hasty,' Larruge squeaked, 'we should tell you that, as of thirty minutes ago, Mr Sempiter is no longer the Chair and Chief Executive Officer of Frontier Worlds Corporation.' She studied her fingernails modestly. 'I am.'

Sempiter was about to explode into another burst of invective, but Larruge silenced him with a look. 'The guards will do what I tell them to, Mr Sempiter. Now, shall we continue this conversation upstairs?'

Sempiter beckoned to the guards again, but they stood back, uncertainly.

'Well, we can have the meeting here instead,' continued Larruge.

Sempiter stood in front of her, arms akimbo, his foot tapping its familiar rhythm on the reception floor. 'I am the largest shareholder in this company.'

'You were,' said Linoir. He smoothed down his moustache with his fingers. 'Ms Larruge is the majority shareholder now. She bought up all the public shares for bargain prices.'

'Our shares are not a bargain. We're worth ten times Reddenblak's market capitalisation.'

'You *were*,' repeated Linoir patiently. 'But after this morning's disaster in your Darkling operation your share price plummeted. Well, what would you expect? You have a secret project that is obviously a complete change in direction for your business, and it becomes public knowledge only when it is razed to the ground. Your company has as good as admitted that its core business is in terminal decline, and then saw its only alternative wiped out in the space of three hours.'

Sempiter still looked defiant. 'Public shares? Hah!' he yelled. 'You'd need those and every other board member's holding to outvote me.'

Linoir grinned his widest grin yet. Or was he baring his teeth, Fitz wondered. 'Funny you should say that,' said Linoir. Suddenly, Nadaly Allder was standing beside him, smiling sheepishly. 'Ms Allder was advised this morning of the sad death of Mr Ellis. His holding passes to her, and she has already agreed to sell to Reddenblak, as the late Mr Ellis had wanted. Mr Mozarno, on the other hand, gave control of his shares to his friend Dewfurth, who agreed the sale of those shares and his own.'

'I don't believe you,' snarled Sempiter. He looked to Fitz as though he were going a ghastly green-grey colour. Sempiter seized hold of Regot, and hissed into his face, 'Dewfurth's dead, and Mozarno's as good as dead. This is all lies.'

'I'm... I'm... I'm afraid not,' the petrified lawyer blurted out. 'It's all supported by the correct legal documentation.' He broke free from Sempiter's grasp, and shuffled back into the safety of his crowd of new colleagues. 'Ms Larruge is now in control of Frontier Worlds Corporation. The others have completed their transactions. You're outvoted. You're on your own now. Sir.' He added lamely.

A buzz of murmuring ran around reception as the little groups of people took in this revelation.

With a tremendous howl of protest, Sempiter threw his hands into the air and spun round, as though trying to take in the whole building with his cry of rage and disbelief. 'No!' he bellowed. 'It can't be true.' He span back to confront his Reddenblak enemies once more. 'So where is Dewfurth now?'

Linoir looked puzzled, uncertainty creeping into his manner for the first time since he'd marched into the building. He smoothed his moustache reassuringly. 'We were rather expecting to meet Dr Dewfurth here.'

'Dr Dewfurth?' said Sempiter. Something dawned in his angry

eyes. 'The Doctor?'

'Yes, it was the Doctor who first contacted us about this takeover plan. Where is he?'

Fitz was about to ask exactly the same question when someone threw themselves into him, and they both went down with a thump on the reception floor. He hardly had time to register that it was Compassion who had seized him when the world exploded into noise all around them.

Aged fourteen, he had kicked a football into George Cullen's dad's greenhouse, and he still remembered the distinctive sound that the breaking pane had made. The sound in the Frontier Worlds reception was a thousand times longer and louder than that. Chunks of thick glass scattered like marbles over the polished floor. There was a shrill shrieking noise as something large slid the length of the reception area, followed by a grinding crash.

Fitz disentangled himself from Compassion, and sat up in the debris. There was a jagged hole around the frame where the huge glass window had been. People cowered in the shelter beneath the balconies, or in offices into which they'd thrown themselves before the impact. Unable to get out of the way, statues and plants had been casually flicked aside, and lay in large fragments against the far wall. The cleaners were really going to have to earn their money tonight, Fitz decided.

A tinkling cascade of glass continued to spill from the security office on the opposite side of the large atrium. Fitz rubbed his eyes in disbelief. There was a glider sticking out of it, or at least the body of a glider, with its wings shorn off in ragged edges either side.

People started to recover from their shock at this sudden intrusion, and were picking their way across the debris and towards the glider. There was another sudden crash, and they all shrank back again. The pilot's cover had slapped open on top of the glider's broken back, and Fitz saw a familiar figure struggle out.

It was the Doctor, still wearing that terrible grey suit, shaking his head vigorously and towelling at his hair with his fingers. Dust and plaster and drops of water flew out from his tangled curls and bounced off the glider. He stared around at the gathering crowd worriedly.

'I'm so sorry,' he said. 'I am rather out of practice. Was anyone hurt?' He surveyed the crash scene from his vantage point at the top of the glider. Satisfied at last that no one was physically injured, he slid down the side of the glider and landed on his feet in a lithe movement, like a cat. He scooted over to one side of the atrium to comfort a man who was sobbing noisily. Maybe the poor guy was in shock, thought Fitz. Or maybe he was one of the cleaners.

With a final reassuring squeeze of his shoulders, the Doctor passed the sobbing man to the care of one of his work colleagues, and then trotted with a crunching noise over the broken glass and back to the main reception entrance, which was miraculously unscathed.

'My dear Mr Linoir. And Ms Larruge, delighted to see you again.' The Doctor pumped their hands fiercely as if he were trying to draw water from a dry well. He flashed his identity card at them. 'I believe this is all you need to confirm the transaction. You'll find that I've authorised the sale of my own and Mr Mozarno's shares, as we agreed.'

Sempiter lay in a heap on the ground where he had fallen. He scowled up at the Doctor, rubbing at the raw skin on his face and neck.

Larruge took the identity card. 'I'm happy to confirm your new appointment, Dr Dewfurth,' she said in her odd, Mickey Mouse voice.

'You got a job with Frontier Worlds after all, Doctor,' laughed Fitz.

'Well,' smiled the Doctor, sticking his thumbs behind his soaked grey lapels, 'the job's really with Reddenblak, of course. I'm their new scientific adviser.' His voice became more serious as he added, *sotto voce*: 'My first job will be to take you two up the mountain so that we can dispose of those Raab plants.'

'No!' shouted Sempiter, oblivious to the amazed and horrified looks he was getting from Frontier Worlds staff all around the room. He had struggled to his feet, and was pointing wildly at the Doctor. But he was shouting at Larruge and Linoir. 'He's not Dewfurth!'

'Yes I am,' protested the Doctor. He sounded so hurt that even Fitz thought he could believe him. 'I'm feeling much recovered since my nasty tumble down the mountain.'

Sempiter sneered. 'You look nothing like him.'

'I'm a changed man,' smiled the Doctor. 'And anyway, *you* can talk! Have you taken a look at yourself recently?'

Improbably, the Doctor had produced a little vanity mirror from his crumpled jacket pocket. Sempiter took the mirror from him suspiciously, and stared at the image as though it were a trick of some kind.

'You've gone too far,' said the Doctor in a quiet, sad voice. 'He was standing close to Sempiter, Fitz noticed. It was as though he didn't want to be overheard by the Reddenblak people, didn't want to embarrass Sempiter in front of them. 'I did warn you. The Raab tissue is starting to control you now. Soon you'll be less like Temm Sempiter than I am like Klenton Dewfurth. The new owners of Frontier Worlds won't allow you to continue these experiments, so I'm very much afraid it's the end for you.'

Their eyes locked for what seemed to Fitz like an age. He imagined the wheels going round in Sempiter's mind. He could see the veins in the man's torn neck sticking out, pulsing green.

And then, with a flurry of movement, Sempiter threw himself sideways, and seized a machine pistol from a startled guard. It was the youngster who had been holding Fitz earlier. Sempiter waved the pistol wildly around himself, and the curious circle which had gathered nearby suddenly widened, like a drop of oil on water, as people hurried out of range.

'I won't let you destroy me,' said Sempiter to the Doctor. 'I won't let you destroy the Raab.'

The Doctor was still shaking his head sadly. 'You are becoming the Raab, with every regeneration, and now with every passing moment.' He indicated the marks on Sempiter's neck. 'It's affecting your reason. Try to remember who you really are, Temm.' His pointing finger had become an open hand now. 'Give me the gun.'

'If the Raab is my future,' said Sempiter quietly, 'I'd better ensure that the Raab survives. There's nothing here for me now.'

He turned the gun towards Linoir, and then at Larruge. Finally, he seemed to make a decision, and the barrel levelled on the Doctor.

Fitz jumped in shock as the gunshot came from behind him. Merdock had fired on Sempiter.

The shot took Sempiter in the head, and he was thrown back, the machine pistol spinning off across the foyer. The body slumped down on the floor in a heap.

Fitz startled again. Sempiter had stood up. There was a neat hole slap bang in the middle of his forehead where the bullet had entered. Green ichor was starting to dribble out of it. Sempiter opened his mouth in a ghastly grimace, and his teeth were flecked with green too.

Merdock fired again. The bullet struck Sempiter squarely in the chest. Fitz saw the material of the expensive jacket explode outward. Sempiter staggered, but stayed upright. The grin widened, as though he couldn't believe it either.

Now Merdock was moving swiftly towards Sempiter. Fitz saw he was brandishing the long metal cylinder of ethylene dibromide, or whatever. Sempiter knew what it was, though. His smile disappeared at once, and he gave a howl of disbelief as Merdock hit the trigger and the stuff hosed out.

A stream of the liquid spurted over Sempiter. The howl of rage and pain grew louder, and he turned towards the exit and fled screaming into the afternoon sun.

Merdock gave a short, embarrassed laugh. Some people around him joined in, nervously at first. Others were standing in astonishment, surrounded by the wreckage from the crash and obviously still surprised and worried about their boss's bizarre departure.

Larruge pulled up an overtoppled chair, stood on its seat, and tried to calm the crowd around her with a prepared speech about synergised company structures and leveraging the combined assets of two pan-planetary organisations. Fitz noticed that the watching Reddenblak people lapped it all up, thought the shocked groups of Frontier Worlds staff looked at each other as though Larruge were talking a foreign language. In fact, a couple of them were ignoring her impromptu speech altogether, and were instead mimicking Sempiter's final cries as he had fled the scene: 'Waah! Waah!'

'Listen to those two idiots,' sneered Compassion. 'You'd think they'd be more worried about having a job tomorrow.'

'In stressful situations,' replied the Doctor softly, 'people can behave in unexpected ways.'

'And that pair *are* from the personnel department,' observed Fitz. He rubbed his hands together briskly. 'Well now,' said Fitz, 'that's seen off Sempiter. And he'll never get greenfly.' He studied the Doctor's fierce expression. 'Oh dear.'

The Doctor's quiet voice cut through the hubbub of noise around them, and he drew Fitz and Compassion close to him. 'Those gunshot wounds and the dousing in weedkiller will just accelerate the change in his metabolism.' He listened to a few more people as the story went around the room.

A security flyer screeched off into the air from in front of the building. A small group of bystanders rushed across to peer out through the remains of the main window. The Doctor pushed his way through them to see what had caused this fresh commotion. He hurried back to Compassion and Fitz..

'Sempiter wasn't just crying out,' said the Doctor, his eyes hooded. 'He was shouting the word "Raab". And earlier he said he would ensure that the Raab survives. We must get to the mountain and stop him.'

'You can't be serious,' said Compassion, but the Doctor had begun to run towards the exit.

'He is fast becoming a Raab himself,' he shouted back. 'You saw that bullet wound.'

Compassion and Fitz followed the Doctor, but Compassion remained unconvinced. 'He won't get further than the end of the street before he collapses, let alone clamber up that mountain.'

'He won't have to clamber,' said the Doctor. 'Look.' Fitz and Compassion followed the Doctor's pointing finger with their eyes. 'The security flyer,' said the Doctor. 'Obviously waiting for him outside the reception area. Come on, we must hurry! Sempiter will be on the mountain within minutes. We must stop him reaching that surviving Raab, or he could still destroy this planet.'

Chapter Twenty-Seven
'We'll Be Together'

'Still no response from the mountain,' said Compassion. 'I think this storm is preventing signals from getting through. I can't detect anything. It might help if you'd let me use my receiver.'

'Keep trying with that equipment,' said the Doctor. 'There must be someone still at the research station. They could get to Sempiter before us.' He yanked the steering controls hard right, and everyone fell sideways. Outside, the slush and sleet that had been lashing the transport's windscreen transformed into an ice-white wall. The hailstorm chattered and crackled on the hull like the sound of popcorn exploding in a cooking pot.

Fitz belatedly decided to buckle up, and struggled to fasten the straps securely while the Doctor swerved the vehicle through the air and towards the mountain. 'So,' he shouted, trying to sound conversational while actually yelling to be heard. 'Nice crate you've got here, Doctor. Is this your new company vehicle? Now that you're a scientific adviser, and all?'

The Doctor wrestled the controls again. 'No, the paperwork will take months. This belongs to Linoir. Or is it Larruge? I can never remember. Call it an advance on my first month's salary. Is that call getting through to the mountain?'

Compassion merely shook her head. She was sitting behind the Doctor and Fitz, halfway down the vehicle beside the communications equipment

'I'm rather afraid', said the Doctor morosely, 'that all the staff will have abandoned things after the storm first broke. Battened down the hatches, and returned to their homes or offices at the foot of the mountain until it all blows over. Perhaps I was too successful whipping things up on the weather platform.'

Fitz peered ahead of them, wondering how the Doctor could possibly make out where they were going. The hail had eased, but the white curtain looked just as impenetrable as ever. 'If the Frontier Worlds guys have abandoned things up there, what can we hope to achieve? Assuming we can even find Sempiter.'

'No need to find him,' said the Doctor, swerving abruptly once more. 'We just need to find the Raab, and prevent Sempiter from messing about with it until Compassion's friend brings the cavalry.'

Compassion leaned forward and said loudly: 'He's not my friend. And they are not the cavalry.'

'Get with the lingo, Compassion,' Fitz replied. 'Merdock's rounding up what security teams he can, and when they come charging to our rescue I don't care if General Custer isn't on the lead horse.'

Fitz saw the Doctor was looking sideways at him: 'Call them what you like, so long as they remember to bring all the weedkiller they can lay their hands on.' He grinned at Fitz. 'General Custer wouldn't be my first choice, though. Did I ever tell you what I once said to old Geronimoooooaahh!'

Fitz joined in the Doctor's wail of surprise as a huge grey shape loomed in front of them. The Doctor had banked the transport savagely up and right, and Fitz felt his back forced into the flight seat and his stomach abandoned hundreds of yards below them.

'Good grief!' exclaimed the Doctor. 'What was –' He clutched his head in both hands as he remembered. Then he clutched the steering controls again as the vehicle wobbled dangerously. 'Yes of course, it's the remains of the weather balloon. I'd forgotten, it must be flapping around in the wind like some kind of huge ground sheet.'

His fingers flickered over the nearby flight controls. 'And with the weather platform out of operation, the local meteorological conditions will slowly be returning to normal for this region. Which means...' (A few more calculations on the control panel.) 'We should fly in low and avoid the worst of the storm.'

The transport swooped down low. Fitz could feel the roller coaster sensation begin in his stomach just before the Doctor whooped again: 'Geronimooooo!'

They soon levelled out, and Fitz opened his eyes. He was astonished to find he could now see through the front window, though still alarmed by the speed at which the Doctor was urging the vehicle across the frozen landscape. Occasionally the transport would lurch into the air, as though taking an invisible humpbacked bridge, to avoid smouldering piles of debris. 'Weather station,' the Doctor mumbled apologetically to Fitz's unspoken question.

'Something else for Merdock's people to tidy up after you, Doctor?' said Compassion from behind them. She was watching the snowy surface whisk by at speed, though her face reflected none of Fitz's concern. 'How do you want to handle this when we arrive?'

The Doctor glanced back briefly at her. 'Fitz and I will get across to the Raab crash site. You get up to the research station and see if there are any staff there. Maybe your signals were getting through to them, and they'll recognise your voice.'

'Maybe they'll shoot you before asking questions,' said Fitz lugubriously.

Compassion set her thin lips in a straight line. 'My "friend", Merdock, seemed all concerned about me again. So he gave me his machine pistol.'

'So he did,' said the Doctor, and over his shoulder he waved a snub-nosed handgun at her. 'Ah-ah!' He tucked the pistol into his inside jacket pocket before she could snatch it back. 'I really don't approve of these things, you know.'

Fitz laughed. He'd seen the Doctor palm things before, but this trick had the added value of causing Compassion's face to crumple into a furious scowl. In fact, reflected Fitz, the Doctor was full of tricks and surprises and puzzles. It was only when he started to tell himself that the Doctor didn't seem quite human that he remembered that, oh yeah, he wasn't. Sometimes it was small things, like the way he didn't seem to sweat when it was scorching hot. Maybe that was the perspiratory bypass system he'd overheard him tell Compassion about one time. Other things seemed bigger, like when he knew odd trivia about folk he'd only just met. Like when he seemed to tell their future. Or read their minds.

Fitz was a bit rattled when the Doctor seemed to be reading his mind now. He leaned across from the steering controls and murmured, quietly enough for Compassion not to hear, 'Fitz, you suggested that the experience of these past few weeks hasn't humanised Compassion? Not even a little?'

Fitz had to confess that he'd failed to involve Compassion much in human matters. She'd seemed more engrossed in the Frontier Worlds computer network than in their network of colleagues at the site, he reminded the Doctor. In fact, he'd been more involved with Alura, despite the way the TARDIS had screwed up the translations.

The Doctor studied Fitz's reaction as he retold this part of his story, his head cocked to one side as usual, as though he were listening especially hard.

'You know Doctor, Compassion may have understood the words I was using better than Alura did. But Alura understood a whole lot more about what I *meant*. What I felt. More than Compassion ever could.'

Fitz could feel the water lapping around him again. He didn't know whether he wanted to sink below its warm surface and stay there, to let its liquid warmth fill his mouth and ears and nostrils. Or whether to emerge, burst through the surface and take a deep breath of fresh air.

'Alura understood me more than Compassion would ever *want* to.'

The Doctor was looking into him, somehow. The transport seemed to be flying itself for the moment.

'I miss her, Doctor. I'm sorry if that sounds banal.'

The Doctor squeezed his arm briefly. 'It doesn't make it any less true, Fitz.'

'If ever anyone had the wrong name, it's Compassion.'

'You may be surprised by what she's learned from you,' said the Doctor. 'I hope so, anyway.'

Fitz broke the Doctor's gaze, not sure if he could bear it any longer, and stared into the rear of the transport. Compassion looked back at him from the gloom, her face a blank mask.

Ten minutes later, the Doctor skidded the transport to a halt in a deep bank of snow. They found thick warm overalls and boots at the rear of the vehicle, all in the brash colours of Frontier Worlds Corporation.

Compassion helped the Doctor to clamber into one set, and Fitz wasn't sure whether it was an improvement on his disgusting second-hand grey suit. Compassion didn't offer to help Fitz into his coat and trousers, though. Maybe she *had* overheard, and was sulking.

'Now remember,' the Doctor said to Compassion as he adjusted the tie-strings on his hood, 'get whoever you find in the research centre down to the Raab crash site at once. The more people we have, the more easily we can restrain Sempiter if we have to.'

'And if he's already there?'

Fitz's dejected tone did not deter the Doctor at all. 'When we flew round the Raab, there was no sign of Sempiter's flyer. Either he hasn't arrived yet, in which case we wait. Or he's not going to arrive, in which case we don't have to worry.'

Compassion popped the side hatch on the transport, and the chill air from outside whistled in through the hole. 'All set.'

The Doctor said, 'Be careful, Compassion. If there are people in the station, they'll be suspicious. And they'll be armed.'

Compassion nodded, silhouetted in the doorway. She was brandishing the machine pistol in her hand.

The Doctor patted at his jacket pocket through the bulky Frontier Worlds uniform. He snorted an infuriated sigh when he found the gun missing.

Compassion said, 'You seem surprised by what I've learned from you, Doctor.' Then she turned and jumped out into the snow.

* * *

They trudged up the hill through the thickening snow until the white curve of the half-buried Raab appeared. Fitz noticed that the Doctor had turned to look back down at the frozen lake below them.

'Isn't that beautiful?' said the Doctor. His breath gusted in grey clouds around his head in the biting cold of the afternoon air.

'Beautiful?' Fitz said, wondering if the Doctor remembered their previous close encounter on the ice. 'Yeah, sure. I bet it's a real draw for tourists who enjoy ice and snow in volume. D'you reckon Eskimo Nell comes here for her holidays? She'd need to wrap up warm.'

The Doctor seemed to have lost interest already, and was making his way further up the hill. 'Where are we going?' Fitz wailed after him. 'Sempiter could arrive at any point around this... Raab thing.'

'True,' shouted back the cloud of steam ahead of him. 'But he'll want to get to the excavation site, where they were cutting into its flesh. And that's on the other side.' He was fast disappearing. Fitz stumbled after him.

Actually, Fitz stumbled after him for the next forty minutes. He could still feel the icy air stinging his cheeks, but the effort of keeping pace with the Doctor had made him break out into a sweat in his heavy winter clothing. Somehow, he'd also got the job of lugging around the weedkiller canister. It clattered against his side or dragged in the snow as he struggled onward.

Only when the Doctor paused was Fitz able to catch up.

'We're going the wrong way,' said the Doctor.

Fitz glared at him, his special Superman heat-vision look, but it seemed ineffective behind the snow goggles. He seemed to have been trudging around this huge frozen marrow for most of his adult life.

'Yes, I'm afraid we should have gone clockwise around the Raab,' continued the Doctor. 'We started at nine o'clock and now we're at three o'clock.'

Fitz thought this was a strangely appropriate mistake for a Time

Lord to make. Instead he said, 'We may as well keep going then. Only three hours to go.'

'That's the spirit!' said the Doctor with the kind of cheery smile that made Fitz want to kick him up the backside.

After another twenty minutes, they started to pass abandoned equipment. All the heavy stuff and the large covered vehicles must have been driven off, and would certainly have provided the best protection against an unexpected snow blizzard.

Eventually, Fitz spotted an abandoned snow bike. The Doctor got it to cough into reluctant life, and then steered it while Fitz clung precariously behind him.

By peering into the middle distance, they could see where a huge chunk had been sliced out of the Raab's side. The gap was visible in the crisp clear air ahead of them, now that the snow had stopped falling. Overhead, grey-white clouds were scudding swiftly away down the mountain. The snow bike buzzed as it sped over the snow towards the excavation.

'Why couldn't *we* use the snow bike in the transport?' grumbled Fitz into the hood of the Doctor's coat.

'Compassion had more need of it,' yelled the Doctor in the slipstream. 'To get her to the research station. I wonder how she's getting on. She must have reached it ages ago.'

Don't remind me, thought Fitz. He was about to expand further on his revised opinion about which party he should have joined when the snow bike suddenly jerked to one side, and he and the Doctor went sprawling in the snow.

The high-pitched note of a protesting engine whined past Fitz's ear. His first thought was that the Doctor had tried one of his less elegant manoeuvres and thrown them both off, and that the snow bike was now threatening to reverse over them. When he looked up, though, he saw a four-seat motorised sledge racing away from them. The front seats were uncovered, and he could see a dark shape at the controls. The driver threw the vehicle about, and it started back towards them.

It had come out of nowhere and knocked them off the snow

bike. Now it was returning to run them down.

The Doctor dragged Fitz behind an overtoppled transporter truck. Even in this cold, Fitz could recognise the characteristic odour of rotting vegetables that he'd smelled in the Darkling crop.

The engine note dropped, and the oncoming sledge slid to a halt fifteen yards in front of the truck. The driver stood up, and they could see it was Sempiter.

More accurately, it had once been Sempiter.

The apparition in the sled's driving seat was a mass of suppurating green flesh. The macabre transformation that had begun back at the headquarters had accelerated, and the eruptions from his flesh now covered the right side of Sempiter's face and neck, with further outbreaks of dark-green flesh over his chest and torso. One eye was partly covered by a bushy overgrowth.

Sempiter hadn't bothered to put on winter clothes. The shreds of his expensive suit hung from his haggard frame. Fitz hardly expected the monstrosity to speak, but when it did he could still recognise the familiar imperious nasal tones.

'Come out of there, Doctor. You too, Mr Sinatra.'

'No, thank you,' shouted back the Doctor. 'We're happy where we are.'

'Very well,' shouted Sempiter, brandishing a briefcase-sized box by its handle. 'Stay there and die, for all I care.'

'Personal effects?' Fitz muttered to the Doctor. 'Overnight bag?'

'Large explosive device,' said the Doctor quietly. 'Do you know where that canister went?'

Fitz looked hurriedly about them. There! The canister of weedkiller was half buried in the snow to the right of their truck. He pointed it out to the Doctor, who nodded at him.

The Doctor stood up, and started to move to the left of the truck. Fitz would have followed, but the Doctor shoved him back. Fitz got the message, and started to crawl through the snow towards the canister while the Doctor shouted at Sempiter, 'Do you think your aim is that good, Mr Sempiter? Can you reach us with that bomb? Perhaps if I stand a little closer...?'

Fitz seized the canister, and looked across the short expanse of snow towards the sledge. Sempiter was laughing at the Doctor, and waving the suitcase again. 'You flatter yourself, Doctor. This isn't for you. I'm going to detonate this in the remains of the Raab, and scatter its seeds to the winds.'

'What?' exclaimed the Doctor.

Sempiter used his free hand to point straight up at the clouds, which were hurrying along above them. 'Nice weather for it, don't you think?'

'No, we don't,' said Fitz quietly from beside the sledge. He had scurried across the snow, and was now crouching beside the passenger seat, angling the canister's hose directly at Sempiter. From this close, he could see the weeping sores in Sempiter's grey-green flesh. Sempiter looked down at him calmly, looked at him with eyes that had no white, just a mass of dark jelly. The ragged mouth flapped open in a horrible laugh. 'I'm dying already. This way, I'll live on in the Raab.'

'The Raab is affecting your mind at an instinctive level.' The Doctor's voice now came from the opposite direction as he emerged from the shadow of the truck and moved towards the sledge. 'Remember who you really are. You're a businessman. You're a scientist. You're a *person*, Temm.'

'What do I care?' snapped Sempiter, the fragile good humour vanishing like sun behind a cloud. 'There's no place in Frontier Worlds for me now. Frontier Worlds!' he sneered. 'You know, we chose that name because it captured our feelings and ambitions. Our dreams when we came to Drebnar five decades ago. We arrived here when this planet *was* a frontier world, one where we could build our own future.'

Sempiter stared at Fitz again with those impossible dark eyes. 'Well, I know what my future holds now that I'm not part of my own Corporation. So I'll explore a completely different world instead. The Raab's world. A whole new frontier. Go ahead, that stuff can't harm me. It can only help me.'

'In that case...' said Fitz, who turned the canister on its end, and thrust it violently upwards towards Sempiter's midriff. He felt faintly ashamed; what would Compassion say if she could see him behaving like this?

Sempiter doubled over with a dreadful wheezing cough, spitting green bile over the windscreen in front of him. 'Stop!' he croaked, lurching up again.

Fitz was on his feet, ready to retrieve the canister and if necessary deliver a further disabling blow. The Doctor was ploughing his way through the snow towards the sledge.

'Stop!' repeated Sempiter. 'Or we'll kill your sister.'

We? thought Fitz. Oh.

The cover over the back seat was sliding back. This revealed Compassion, which should have been good news. However, it also revealed that her neck was in the vicelike clamped hand of a dishevelled-looking robot. It had scorch-marks all over it. Fitz thought it looked like a reject from *Metropolis*. He also thought it looked as if it could snap Compassion's neck like a twig.

'They were already at the research station,' said Compassion simply, but her eyes suggested she was not so composed.

'Shut up,' hissed Sempiter. The metal hand tightened around her neck.

'You are a resourceful robot,' said the Doctor casually. Fitz saw that he too had stopped moving closer to the sledge, and was standing with his head cocked to one side, appraising the scene.

The robot hummed a noncommittal noise, and shuffled a bit in its seat to keep both the Doctor and Fitz in view. Compassion winced as the hand tightened further. Fitz could see that its other arm was completely missing. The robot cocked its head on one side as it watched him, its eyes wide and round.

The Doctor was still speaking. 'I suppose I should really congratulate you, Temm, since you devised the robot. I wonder how it feels about the way you're endangering this whole planet.'

Sempiter slumped back into the driving seat, and kicked the weedkiller canister into the foot well. 'You're wasting your breath,

Doctor. It's not human.'

'Not quite how you planned things? You wanted it to be human. You wanted it to be *you*. But are *you* still human, Temm? Just like your robot, your original aspirations went a bit astray. Think what you've done to the insects and birds in the Darkling Zone. And what you did to those piranha fish in the lake.'

A snort of derision from Sempiter. He looked back at the robot where it held Compassion. She hadn't moved during this entire exchange, hadn't tried to speak again. Fitz could see the skin stretched taut in her neck where the robot gripped her.

The Doctor took a tentative further step towards the sledge, placing the palms of his gloves on the bonnet. 'Do you understand the value of life any longer, Temm? Or are plants and animals and people just machines to create and control? Like your robot? Like the mechanical canary in your office? Even that's still caged.'

Sempiter chuckled. 'You put too much faith in this thing having a conscience, Doctor. It isn't remotely human. It's logical to a fault.' He turned his baleful gaze on the Doctor. 'And it is designed to protect me.'

Fitz looked at the Doctor too. He was exhaling in exasperation, the cloud of grey mist puffing out in front of him. Then Fitz saw his expression change utterly.

'No, Temm. You're wrong.' The Doctor had that look in his eyes again. Fitz felt his own spirits lift. 'The robot's designed to protect Frontier Worlds' assets. Your behaviour threatens those assets. And you no longer work for Frontier Worlds - there's no place in the Corporation for you now; you've said as much yourself.'

Fitz watched the Doctor's eyes, and saw that he had actually addressed all this directly to the robot.

The Doctor lifted his hands from the sledge bonnet, and held them palms upward in an entreating gesture. 'That's logical, isn't it?'

A sudden creaking metallic noise made Fitz dart a look at the rear of the sledge. The robot had released its clawlike grip on Compassion's neck, and was holding its one hand palm upward.

'That is logical,' it said. Fitz thought he recognised the voice.

The robot gave Compassion a brutal shove in her shoulder, and she spilled sideways out of the sledge and into the snow, where she lay in an undignified heap. Fitz had barely time to start bending to help her before he observed the robot launching itself into the front passenger seat.

Sempiter was taken by surprise, and struggled with the robot as it tried to seize him. It was hampered by the fact that its one arm was on the wrong side of its body to grab him. Spotting his opportunity, Sempiter threw the sledge into gear, and the vehicle shot off violently, throwing the Doctor aside and toppling the robot over into the rear seats.

Fitz watched the vehicle swerve in a half-circle as Sempiter tried to shake off the robot and steer towards the gaping wound in the side of the Raab.

'Come on! We have to stop him!' Fitz felt the Doctor hauling him back to his feet and dragging him towards their battered snow bike. The engine caught on the third attempt, and the two of them whizzed off in pursuit.

Sempiter's sledge was veering from side to side as the driver tried to maintain control. Fitz could see the robot trying to pluck Sempiter out of the driving seat and seize the steering, but its one arm made it difficult.

As the sledge passed the raw wound in the side of the dying Raab, Sempiter threw the briefcase bomb. It spun in an untidy arc and vanished into the maw.

'Keep going!' yelled the Doctor, and dived off the snow bike.

Fitz gaped in astonishment, but stopped trying to look back as the snow bike wavered, driverless, and the handlebars waggled dangerously. He leaned forward and seized them. Snow spurted as the front ski bit into the icy surface, and then the bike's nose came back up and he was shooting forwards again, plunging after the sledge as it charged downhill towards the Lake of Ice.

Typical Doctor, thought Fitz. He'll risk blowing himself to pieces, but not me.

Ahead, the robot lunged into the front seat again. But this time it seized the steering wheel and wrenched it hard to the side. Unable to cope with this exacting change in orientation, the sledge stuttered and then rose up on one side. The robot was thrown clear. The sledge continued on, slewing through the powdery white snow until it bumped to a halt on a bank beside the lake.

Sempiter struggled free from the overtoppled sledge. He made one futile attempt to push it back on to its ski tracks again, but the robot was getting back to its metal feet fifteen yards behind him.

Fitz swerved the snow bike to a halt at the top of the bank, just in time to see Sempiter scramble down and on to the ice. The half-man half-Raab creature slid over the snow-dusted ice, a dark green blot on its pure white surface, until he was twenty yards out.

The robot pounded through the snow. It stumbled past Fitz, gouging out deep chunks as its weight took it careering down the bank and on to the ice.

Sempiter stopped and stared back at it, tapping his foot as though waiting impatiently, watching the robot's slow progress towards him.

The robot got ten yards out before its left foot sank into the ice. It was far too heavy, Fitz realised. It was faltering as it tried to pull its leg free. Now it teetered on the edge of the broken area of ice.

It stared at Sempiter, its head cocked to one side in a way that Fitz recognised. He also remembered where he'd heard its voice before. It was like the Doctor.

The robot sank suddenly through the surface of the ice and vanished.

The Sempiter creature shouted with laughter. He eventually looked up and saw Fitz, who was standing on the precipice that dropped down to the lake. 'Come on in, Mr Sinatra,' he leered. 'The water's lovely.'

Sempiter folded his arms and leaned back smugly, daring Fitz to pursue him.

Fitz stared at the slide in the bank that led to the lake. He imagined picking his way across to where Sempiter stood, still tapping his foot in that familiar and infuriating way, waiting for Fitz to make the same mistake as the robot.

The ice around the foot seemed to sag, soften. Sempiter felt it move under him. The crack in the surface widened, and Sempiter dropped into the icy water. His hands scrabbled at the snow around the newly melted hole, and the ragged lips in his blurred green face opened in a shrieking howl of agony and despair.

The water by his chest and shoulders bubbled and boiled as the piranhas seethed around him.

Sempiter's screams cut off abruptly as his head vanished beneath the surface. The water splashed over the torn edge of the ice, spattering it with green froth, until the churning ebbed away.

Fitz returned to the snow bike, and drove slowly back up the hill towards the Raab.

The Doctor was shaking hands with several newly arrived Frontier Worlds staff, and introducing them to Compassion. When he saw Fitz, he gave him a huge grin, and waved the briefcase at him as though it were budget day.

Chapter Twenty-Eight
'Why Try to Change Me Now?'

The tanker vehicles throbbed in the early evening, and the liquid sprayed in flat arcs, dashing down on to the sides of the Raab. Fitz watched a dozen Frontier Worlds staff as they struggled to control the thick hoses, and to discharge the lethal cargo. More security guards were steering ploughs away from the decaying remains, digging grooves through the snow and into the mountainside. The runoff gurgled down the channels, flowing in pale-green streams downhill. Half a dozen fresh holes had been cut into the ice to allow the runoff to drain into the lake.

The team continued their gruesome task of dispersing the Raab remains. Further round the mountain, more tanker sledges in green and yellow Frontier Worlds livery were heaving their way uphill, their powerful headlights cutting through the gathering gloom.

'How's it going, Fitz?'

Compassion had sought him out, for some reason. She was staring past him, watching the work progress. Fitz didn't answer straight away, wondering why she was asking. He worked it out quickly enough: Merdock had been chaperoning her around the site, and she had found the first excuse she could to abandon him. Now, she stood next to Fitz in silence, trying to look interested in what was happening, like someone at a party who's been introduced to the bore in the corner, and has nothing to say to him. Nothing in common, apart from being in the same place at the same time.

Fitz eventually nodded towards the Frontier Worlds staff. 'Do you think they've learned their lesson?'

'Why are you asking me?' Compassion said. She looked down her freckled nose at him. 'Trying to convince me, maybe? Am I supposed to have learned something, is that it?'

Fitz bit his lip.

Compassion seemed to have found something to say after all. 'The Doctor's quite the social engineer, don't you think? Put us together on a project, and see what we *learn* from each other.' There was unequivocal scorn in her emphasis. 'Didn't work.'

'Why are you telling me?' replied Fitz. 'Trying to convince yourself, maybe?' He watched her reaction, such as it was. 'For what it's worth, Compassion, you helped me when we were in the jungle. After I thought we'd abandoned Ellis to die. I was ready to die there as well.'

She was studying his reaction, too.

'All that stuff you said about needing me,' Fitz continued. 'About how I've experienced things, not just heard about them. You said you'd learned from me. And it was just what I needed to hear at that point.'

She nodded. 'It was just what you needed to hear.'

Fitz felt his mouth hanging open. He felt the heat rising in his face. He felt stupid all of a sudden.

'Don't take it so personally,' said Compassion. 'In fact, you could learn something yourself. Remember that the Doctor isn't perfect, either.'

'I know that.' He sounded to himself like a grumpy kid.

Compassion said, 'You dote on the Doctor, Fitz. You haven't worked it out yet, how he *tolerates* us. Humans are just the Time Lords' embarrassing relations. Isn't it how you'd feel if you had to travel round with only inferior species for company?'

Fitz wouldn't accept this, and snorted back at her: 'You make us sound like pets. Is that your big idea, Compassion? We're the Doctor's pets?'

'Yes,' she said simply. 'But it's like the difference between cats and dogs. A dog thinks, My owner loves me and feeds me and takes care of me, so he must be god. A cat thinks, My owner loves me and feeds me and takes care of me so *I* must be god.' Her smile made Fitz angrier still. 'He's got you to sit up and beg, like a well-trained dog. Well, he won't change me.'

'Change?' said the Doctor, appearing beside them.

How much had he overheard? thought Fitz. He tried to rewind the conversation in his head, feeling flustered.

'I suppose you can describe it as change,' continued the Doctor. 'We do what we can.'

Had he misheard, or was he just affecting to misunderstand?

Compassion seemed unembarrassed by the Doctor's arrival. 'Was putting Reddenblak in charge a good change or a bad change?'

'Can't be sure yet,' said the Doctor. He was gazing at the salvage operation, craning forward as though this would help him see better in the fading light. 'Reddenblak aren't better than Frontier Worlds, they're just not as dangerous. Did you know that Reddenblak's crop seed is genetically engineered for one season only? The growing crop is sterile, so the farmers to whom they sell it can't reuse their own seed and have to buy from Reddenblak again the following year.'

Fitz gave a weary sigh. 'They're every bit as bad as Sempiter.'

The Doctor looked at him with sad eyes. 'They're the lesser of two evils. You can't usually put a society to rights with a snap of your fingers, or wipe out the bad guys by joining two wires together.'

'That's our job,' said Fitz. 'That's what we do.' The words sounded unconvincing even as he said them. 'You sound so defeatist, Doctor. That's not like you.'

'Things can't always be perfect,' he replied. 'We do what we can, Fitz. Look at that weedkiller pouring off the dead Raab. It's not completely biodegradable, and it's leaking on the ground and into the lake. But it's a compromise, a trade-off: destroy the Raab plant and maybe a lot of local flora and fauna; or risk the Raab exploding its seed load and wiping out everything on the planet.'

'Some scientific adviser you're turning out to be.'

'It's the choice I made. The change that was necessary.' The Doctor didn't seem be addressing this comment to Fitz any more. 'Do you recognise that, Compassion?'

'It's just more information. More data.' She rubbed the hole in her earlobe between finger and thumb while she considered his point. The Doctor had persuaded her to remove the receiver again, though Fitz knew this would be temporary, and that she'd done it just to avoid a pointless argument with the Doctor.

As if to confirm Fitz's thoughts, Compassion said, 'You won't change me, Doctor.'

The Doctor cocked his head on one side. 'Would that be so terrible?'

'You can't house-train a cat,' Fitz said sourly. 'You'll just get scratched.'

The Doctor laughed lightly at this. 'Please use the litter tray. Don't scratch at the console when you want to be let out.' He reached into the pocket of his green and yellow overalls. Fitz thought that he'd found a dead bird, but then he flicked a switch in its side and the robot canary hopped into life. 'Look what I rescued from Sempiter's office just now.'

He lifted his hand, and the bird fluttered away into the gloom.

'I was going to keep it as a pet. But perhaps it's better to let it make up its own mind. To work out what it wants for itself.'

'I know what I want,' Compassion said quietly. 'I want facts and opinions, not cuts and bruises.'

Fitz wanted to shake her until her teeth rattled, to upset her composure. 'You are changing, Compassion. You're getting cold and hard. I worried at first that the Faction had misremembered me, but at least the TARDIS changed me back to my crappy old human self eventually. You wouldn't know about that. How could you?'

'We're all evolving, Fitz. Maybe I have changed. It doesn't mean I have to let you and the Doctor decide what that change is. And it doesn't mean I have to like it.'

Fitz stalked off through the snow, before he tried to land a punch on her. He stopped beside the security staff, who for some reason were brushing snow off the TARDIS. He waved them away, and leaned his head on the cool surface of one blue door, feeling its familiar hum seeping into his head.

He felt the Doctor's hand on his shoulder. 'Regrets?'

Fitz returned him a weak smile. 'I've had a few. But then again -'

The Doctor wouldn't let him finish, wouldn't let him hide behind words. 'Don't stop caring, Fitz. Alura will still be there in your dreams. Remember her for what you had, not how you want to change it.'

The Doctor unlocked the TARDIS door. Fitz caught the familiar scents of sandalwood, of candles, of home.

'I'm not worried about my dreams any more, Doctor.' He tried to laugh it off with false bravado. 'Besides, I'm more likely to have nightmares instead!' He turned around again. 'What do you dream of, Compassion?'

His question seemed to catch her off guard. She narrowed her grey eyes at him. 'I dream of the time vortex,' she said.

'That sounds like a cue for us to leave,' said the Doctor, shooing Compassion through the open doors.

A small creature flitted down and landed on his shoulder, where it chittered a few cheerful notes. It was the robot canary. After another merry trill, it hopped into the air again and disappeared through the TARDIS doors. The Doctor laughed.

'What do you dream of, Doctor?'

'A nice cup of Earl Grey tea.'

Fitz had a last look into the failing light, still able to make out activity around the vast hump of the decaying Raab on the mountain behind them. 'Can we go somewhere a long way from here?'

'I have a local visit to make first.'

'You sound like...' Fitz's thought trailed off.

'...a doctor?'

He smiled a wan smile before he ushered Fitz through the TARDIS doors.

Chapter Twenty-Nine
'Who'

'Who did you say you were?' Shar Mozarno peered at the tall man in the bottle-green velvet jacket. He was drinking tea from one of Marog's best cups, which seemed like a bit of a cheek. Which reminded him, when had he last eaten?

'This is the Doctor, my love,' said Marog.

He looked from his wife to the stranger. This was more cheering news. 'Have you come to make me better? I don't remember being ill.' He chuckled, a sound from the back of his throat.

'I was going to be a doctor, you know,' continued Mozarno, smiling affectionately at his wife. 'I met Marog when she was a nurse. I'd always wanted to be a doctor, because I wanted to make things better, make *people* better. In the end, I decided there were more opportunities with the Frontier Worlds Corporation.'

The man was looking at him with a look of profound sadness in his pale-blue eyes. Mozarno said, 'I decided there was more money in biotechnology than in human biology.'

He stared through the big picture window. His garden was still visible in the light that spilled out from the room. Tomorrow, he told himself, he would start tending the flower borders again, getting them ready for spring.

The strange doctor was rummaging in his large jacket pockets. Mozarno watched him remove something, and turn it over thoughtfully in his hands. The big clock on the far wall chimed the hour.

'Who did you say you were?' asked Mozarno.

His wife sat down in the seat beside him and took hold of his hand, smoothing it over with a soft, circular motion. 'It's the Doctor, my love. He brought us good news about the Corporation. Your work was worth a great deal. Isn't that right, Doctor? You were able to help.'

The tall man with long hair was still looking at Mozarno with that sad smile. 'I did my best. Your work is finished now, Mr Mozarno. And I brought you this.'

He passed over a small watch. Mozarno felt its bright, cool metal in his hands, before slipping it over his wrist. The figures on the face of the watch glittered and sparkled in the room's poor light. Mozarno couldn't remember how long he spent staring, seeing patterns merge and coalesce. In the polished surface of the watch, he could see his father's face looking back at him.

When he looked around the room again, he was alone. He was sure that there had been someone there a second ago. Why else would there be two teacups on the side table?

Suddenly, the door behind him opened, and Marog Mozarno walked through it and back into his world.

He struggled to his feet and stumbled to her, almost falling into her arms. He clutched her close to him as though for the very first time, as his life began again.

The Eighth Doctor's adventures continue in PARALLEL 59 by Stephen Cole and Natalie Dallaire, ISBN 0 563 55590 4, available January 2000.

Acknowledgements

Invaluable assistants: Francis Albert, John Barfield, Steve Cole, Clare Jackson, Jac Rayner, Justin Richards, Eric and June Summerfield, Martin Tucker, Jon Tuttle.

Original title : Peter Lovelady and Tony Murray.

Project manager: Anne Summerfield.❤

DOCTOR WHO: THE NOVEL OF THE FILM by Gary Russell
ISBN 0 563 38000 4
THE EIGHT DOCTORS by Terrance Dicks ISBN 0 563 40563 5
VAMPIRE SCIENCE by Jonathan Blum and Kate Orman
ISBN 0 563 40566 X
THE BODYSNATCHERS by Mark Morris ISBN 0 563 40568 6
GENOCIDE by Paul Leonard ISBN 0 563 40572 4
WAR OF THE DALEKS by John Peel ISBN 0 563 40573 2
ALIEN BODIES by Lawrence Miles ISBN 0 563 40577 5
KURSAAL by Peter Anghelides ISBN 0 563 40578 3
OPTION LOCK by Justin Richards ISBN 0 563 40583 X
LONGEST DAY by Michael Collier ISBN 0 563 40581 3
LEGACY OF THE DALEKS by John Peel ISBN 0 563 40574 0
DREAMSTONE MOON by Paul Leonard ISBN 0 563 40585 6
SEEING I by Jonathan Blum and Kate Orman ISBN 0 563 40586 4
PLACEBO EFFECT by Gary Russell ISBN 0 563 40587 2
VANDERDEKEN'S CHILDREN by Christopher Bulis
ISBN 0 563 40590 2
THE SCARLET EMPRESS by Paul Magrs ISBN 0 563 40595 3
THE JANUS CONJUNCTION by Trevor Baxendale
ISBN 0 563 40599 6
BELTEMPEST by Jim Mortimore ISBN 0 563 40593 7
THE FACE EATER by Simon Messingham ISBN 0 563 55569 6
THE TAINT by Michael Collier ISBN 0 563 55568 8
DEMONTAGE by Justin Richards ISBN 0 563 55572 6
REVOLUTION MAN by Paul Leonard ISBN 0 563 55570 X
DOMINION by Nick Walters ISBN 0 563 55574 2
UNNATURAL HISTORY by Jonathan Blum and Kate Orman
ISBN 0 563 55576 9
AUTUMN MIST by David A. McIntee ISBN 0 563 55583 1
INTERFERENCE: BOOK ONE by Lawrence Miles ISBN 0 563 55580 7
INTERFERENCE: BOOK TWO by Lawrence Miles ISBN 0 563 55582 3
THE BLUE ANGEL by Paul Magrs and Jeremy Hoad
ISBN 0 563 55581 5
THE TAKING OF PLANET 5 by Simon Bucher-Jones and Mark Clapham
ISBN 0 563 55585 8

THE DEVIL GOBLINS FROM NEPTUNE by Keith Topping and Martin Day ISBN 0 563 40564 3
THE MURDER GAME by Steve Lyons ISBN 0 563 40565 1
THE ULTIMATE TREASURE by Christopher Bulis ISBN 0 563 40571 6
BUSINESS UNUSUAL by Gary Russell ISBN 0 563 40575 9
ILLEGAL ALIEN by Mike Tucker and Robert Perry ISBN 0 563 40570 8
THE ROUNDHEADS by Mark Gatiss ISBN 0 563 40576 7
THE FACE OF THE ENEMY by David A. McIntee ISBN 0 563 40580 5
EYE OF HEAVEN by Jim Mortimore ISBN 0 563 40567 8
THE WITCH HUNTERS by Steve Lyons ISBN 0 563 40579 1
THE HOLLOW MEN by Keith Topping and Martin Day ISBN 0 563 40582 1
CATASTROPHEA by Terrance Dicks ISBN 0 563 40584 8
MISSION: IMPRACTICAL by David A. McIntee ISBN 0 563 40592 9
ZETA MAJOR by Simon Messingham ISBN 0 563 40597 X
DREAMS OF EMPIRE by Justin Richards ISBN 0 563 40598 8
LAST MAN RUNNING by Chris Boucher ISBN 0 563 40594 5
MATRIX by Robert Perry and Mike Tucker ISBN 0 563 40596 1
THE INFINITY DOCTORS by Lance Parkin ISBN 0 563 40591 0
SALVATION by Steve Lyons ISBN 0 563 55566 1
THE WAGES OF SIN by David A. McIntee ISBN 0 563 55567 X
DEEP BLUE by Mark Morris ISBN 0 563 55571 8
PLAYERS by Terrance Dicks ISBN 0 563 55573 4
MILLENNIUM SHOCK by Justin Richards ISBN 0 563 55586 6
STORM HARVEST by Robert Perry and Mike Tucker ISBN 0 563 55577 7
THE FINAL SANCTION by Steve Lyons ISBN 0 563 55584 X
CITY AT WORLD'S END by Christopher Bulis ISBN 0 563 55579 3
DIVIDED LOYALTIES by Gary Russell ISBN 0 563 55578 5
CORPSE MARKER by Chris Boucher ISBN 55575 0

SHORT TRIPS ed. Stephen Cole ISBN 0 563 40560 0
MORE SHORT TRIPS ed. Stephen Cole ISBN 0 563 55565 3

THE BOOK OF LISTS by Justin Richards and Andrew Martin
ISBN 0 563 40569 4
A BOOK OF MONSTERS by David J. Howe ISBN 0 563 40562 7
THE TELEVISION COMPANION by David J. Howe and
Stephen James Walker ISBN 0 563 40588 0
FROM A TO Z by Gary Gillatt ISBN 0 563 40589 9